Whispers,
Books 1-3

Sophie's Secret
Don't Tell Mother
Krysta's Curse

Tara West

Cover Art by Tamra Westberry
Interior formatting by Heather Adkins | CyberWitch Press, LLC
cyberwitchpress.com

www.tarawest.com

Table of Contents

Sophie's Secret

Book One

For my yearbook and newspaper students who encouraged me to write. I hope you are pursuing your own dreams. And for Mary, my number one cheerleader, a young woman now, who is making a difference in the world. I am so proud that I was a part of your lives. I miss you all.

Finally, for baby Sophia. Your smile is my inspiration.

Chapter One

"Do you remember your first time?" My best friend, AJ Dawson, checked under the door to make sure her mother's feet weren't nearby.

I sighed, leaning against the cushioned, and surprisingly feminine, satin headboard of AJ's twin bed. For the past six years, I'd been trying to erase that awful experience from my mind. "Yeah."

"Who was it with?" Krysta Richards, my other best friend, scooted closer.

I shuddered as an icy chill swept up my spine. "My mom." I focused on one of the millions of Clay Matthews posters on the bedroom wall, trying to shut out that painful memory.

AJ's eyes widened. She pushed herself off of her beanbag chair and sat directly beneath me on her plush white carpet. "What was she thinking?"

I shifted my gaze to AJ's petite, white cosmetic table, which looked ready to crumble under the weight of her athletic gear. "She was depressed about my grandma," I breathed.

Next to the time my chubby butt split my too- tight leotards in ballet class, this was one Childhood memory I wanted to forget—my first telepathic experience. Though I heard my mother's voice in my head clearly, she wasn't speaking. She was on the phone, just listening, eyes downcast and shoulders slumped. I thought I was going crazy.

Then the voice was louder, echoing in my skull. *How can I live without her?* But Mom's lips didn't move. After she hung up, she began to weep, and then fell to the floor in a motionless heap. My grandmother had just been diagnosed with terminal cancer and given three months to live.

Although I was just a child, I knew I had been listening to my mom's thoughts.

At about that time, I met AJ and Krysta on the playground. We made unusual friends—AJ was the jock, Krysta was the princess, and until my recent transformation, I was the fat dork.

So how did we wind up as best friends? Our "gifts" drew us together. My friends were my safety net, AJ had visions and Krysta received visits from the dead. Around them, I didn't feel like a freak and we pledged to keep our gifts secret.

Luckily for us, we didn't have these supernatural experiences too often, or we'd have been labeled freaks at school. We just wanted to be teens, trying to survive the pressures of school, parents and fitting in.

Since this was the weekend, we could sit around in AJ's room, listening to The Band Perry, while forgetting about the outside world. Unless we were interrupted by AJ's mom.

"Whatcha doin'?" Mrs. Dawson, peered through a crack in the door.

"Go away," AJ's two favorite words for her mother.

AJ used this expression on her mom every ten minutes. Like clockwork, we could depend on Mrs. Dawson's unannounced interruption into our privacy. She didn't bother me so much but I didn't have to live with it.

"Such a little snot," Mrs. Dawson sweetly intoned and slammed the door behind her. That was that, until this exact dialogue would repeat itself ten minutes later.

Unless...every so often Mrs. Dawson added a twist to the routine, throwing me smack in the middle. Thank God she didn't do it this time or I would be forced to answer the question, "Sophie, do you talk to your mother like this?"

I would look from mother to daughter, hoping one would give me an out. When neither spoke, they left me with no choice but to answer honestly, "No, Mrs. Dawson."

AJ would roll her crystal blue eyes and say, "Her mother doesn't interrupt us every ten minutes."

AJ's way of saying the word "mother" like it was some venomous, foul stench, always fascinated me. I suppose this wasn't Mrs. Dawson's fault. If AJ and Krysta hadn't been wild children the summer before eighth grade, Mrs. Dawson wouldn't have become such a pest.

That was the summer Krysta's mom ran off with a bail bondsman. Krysta's dad worked nights, leaving no adult supervision at her apartment. Krysta begged us not to tell anyone about her mom. We kept our promise and AJ spent almost every night at Krysta's.

They ran around all night, hanging out with the wrong crowd. I didn't want to be caught up in their trouble, so I stopped answering their calls. They figured it out.

At the end of the summer, they were busted by the cops when AJ asked a guy at the gas station to buy her beer. I thought it was pretty ironic AJ didn't see that coming.

When my mom found out, she put me in private school for a year. I wasn't too surprised by my mom's reaction. She never had much faith in me, not when she could compare me to my two perfect sisters. I guess my mom was afraid I'd be influenced by my friends' bad decisions. What she failed to notice was I had already made the choice *not* to be influenced by them.

After Krysta's dad took up drinking, she found shelter at AJ's house on the weekends. Mrs. Dawson let Krysta stay because she felt sorry for her but she still didn't trust either one of them.

AJ put her head in her hands. "God, why can't she leave me alone?"

Ignoring her question, a question we'd heard a thousand times, Krysta painted her toes and I reached for Krysta's *Cosmo*.

"I wish my mom would buy me *Cosmo*." I couldn't believe I was reading a magazine with sex advice. Like girls did it all the time. I felt a twinge of jealousy that Krysta could read whatever she wanted, and then I remembered all the other crap she had to deal with at home.

"My dad's new girlfriend is only 23. She bought it. Does this pink match my skin type?" Krysta pointed her skinny toes at us; a concerned expression crossed her brow, as if all hope for life's happiness hinged on the color of her nails.

"Pink is everybody's skin type."

AJ didn't bother to look at Krysta's nails. She was too busy fuming over her mom's latest interruption. Besides, AJ wasn't the type to be interested in fashion. She'd worn her straight blonde hair in the same ponytail since I could remember. AJ was one of the few girls I knew who could still look good without makeup, which she only wore on special occasions. In fact, if she wasn't such a jock, with her bright blue eyes, perfect little nose, and high cheekbones, she'd probably be the prettiest girl in school. As far as clothes, much to her mother's disappointment, AJ picked comfort over style, preferring to wear old jeans and her softball jerseys.

AJ stretched out on her stomach and grabbed a rubber chicken off the floor. "Do you like his newest girlfriend?"

"I don't know. I guess." Krysta reached toward me and grabbed the magazine, flipping to the table of contents. "Does *Cosmo* say anything about nail color?"

Although her dad couldn't afford many nice clothes, Krysta followed the latest fashion trends by wearing her hair and makeup like Miranda Kerr or Gisele. She even dyed and straightened her dark curly hair in an attempt to look like blonde Taylor Swift. Quite a contrast to her large dark eyes and olive complexion. AJ and I didn't have the heart to tell her she looked stupid.

AJ flicked the chicken's head with her forefinger. "I bet it's cool not having your mother around bugging you all the time."

That was a totally insensitive thing to say. I felt it in my bones. I felt it in Krysta's bones, as I watched her hand clench the corner of the magazine, her face expressionless.

We both waited for Krysta's outburst. She said nothing as she set down the magazine and quietly walked out of the room.

"That was a stupid thing to say, AJ." I didn't criticize my best friend often, but this time she needed it.

"Go talk to her." AJ rolled her eyes and buried her face in her pillow.

"No, you go talk to her. You said it."

Okay, one of AJ's flaws—she didn't handle feelings well. Raised under the shadow of her jock big brother, she wanted to be like him in every way and that meant having no 'girl' emotions whatsoever.

AJ lifted her head and looked directly at me with widened eyes. "I don't know what to say. You're good at this stuff."

"Try saying 'I'm sorry'. Try asking her if she wants to talk about it."

"No!" AJ twisted her lips in that disgusted scowl, as if I'd just asked her to French kiss Cody Miller. Grody Cody Miller, the kid who was tricked into eating an Ex-Lax bar and crapped his pants on the bus.

Someone had to comfort Krysta. When I realized I had to be that person, anger fueled my movements as I stormed off. I hadn't even taken one step before knocking Krysta's shimmery pink nail polish all over AJ's white carpet. "Crap! Krysta didn't put the lid on this polish."

AJ jumped off her bed and rushed to the spill. "We've got to clean this up before my mother finds out."

"Whatcha doin'?"

Too late.

AJ's mom was surprisingly understanding about the nail polish. She only made us promise that in the future, we'd paint our nails in the kitchen.

Krysta came back from the bathroom, looked around, and grabbed some nail polish remover. She cleaned the spill like nothing was wrong. I was a little stunned by her reaction, but relieved I wouldn't have to prevent a confrontation.

The stain came up quickly, but the remover left a horrible smell. AJ and Krysta suggested we move to the living room, but I didn't want to go in there. The Mikes could show up. AJ's brother, Mike #1, and his best friend, Mike #2, were two grades ahead of us and very popular. I couldn't risk telling AJ and Krysta my secret with them around. Even though they went to a different school, gossip knew no limits in my world. I would never be able to show my face again if my secret was revealed.

"Let's just open the window and stay in your bedroom, AJ," I suggested while I climbed onto the bed and slid open AJ's window.

"Why? It smells in here." Krysta fanned her nose, acting like she'd pass out.

"Come on, Krysta, you paint your nails all the time. You're used to the smell. Besides," I hesitated, looking out the window to see if anyone was in the front yard, behind the bushes, or within one hundred yards of hearing distance. "I think I like a guy at school."

Smell forgotten, Krysta and AJ perked up like AJ's Shitzu, Patches, whenever we fried bacon. I feared they'd make too much of a big deal about this. After all, what if they didn't like him, or worse, what if they thought he was out of my league?

"Who's the guy?" Krysta cooed and smiled, recognizing the significance of this momentous event.

Sophie had a crush.

Innocent, awkward Sophie who couldn't even look a member of the opposite sex in the eyes. Crazed dreamer Sophie, who said she'd never ever consider a boyfriend, unless that boy was Taylor Lautner. Self-conscious, self-doubting Sophie, who'd just lost thirty pounds of baby fat last year and was still adjusting to new braces. That Sophie had a crush.

I read the looks in their faces—their widened, amused eyes.

Impossible.

I'd spoken the truth. I didn't know when it began, or how I started liking him, but I was in love with the guy who sat in front of me in English class, Jacob Flushman.

"Jacob Flushman!" They screamed in unison. Oops. I said that last thought out loud. The cat was out of the bag now; there was no turning back. "Yeah, him." I looked out of the window once more. One could never be too careful about these delicate secrets. If the Mikes found out, they'd tease me for sure. "Please don't tell anyone."

"Jake Toilet Flush?" AJ laughed and landed on a beanbag chair in the corner of her room.

"His name is Jacob. We're freshmen now; AJ, it's time to ditch little middle school names." Actually, we were still in the middle school because the high school was overcrowded. So last year, they turned our middle school into a junior high, keeping us in that juvenile prison against our will.

"Jake has big thighs."

Leave it to Krysta to point out any physical flaws. In her

world, everyone should look like they just stepped out of *Cosmo* or *YM*.

I pulled back my shoulders, ready to defend him. "He plays football. Football players are supposed to have big thighs."

"My brother plays football," AJ jabbed, "Jake sits the bench."

"Your brother also has a zit juice collection on his bathroom mirror. People still think *he's* cool." I thought in confessing my crush, my two best friends would have been a little more supportive, but all they did was make fun of him. Their rude remarks cut hard. I liked Jacob and slamming him was like slamming me, too. "I don't see either of you with hot boyfriends, or *any* boyfriends."

"Chill." AJ glared. "You don't have to get so sensitive. I get enough of that from my mother."

"Let's look at his yearbook picture."

I feared Krysta would mention the yearbook. Although I couldn't sense it at the moment, I knew what she was thinking. *Let's look at his huge thighs on the football page, so we can make fun of him.*

Krysta grabbed a yearbook off AJ's bookshelf.

Before she could turn the pages, I snatched it from her.

"Give it back!" She tried to grab it out of my hands.

At only five foot, two inches, she was no match for me. Last time I checked, I was five foot seven and still growing.

"Only if you promise not to make fun of him." In truth, I hadn't seen Jacob's eighth grade yearbook picture and I was very curious. Jacob had a crew cut, big brown eyes and the cutest little ears. I wondered if he was just as cute last year.

"I promise." She smiled wryly.

Knowing I couldn't trust her, I grabbed her *Cosmo* off the floor.

"Swear on Gisele." I handed her the magazine. Gisele seduced the camera lens with pursed lips.

Krysta placed her hand on the model's face. "I swear."

I handed Krysta the book. She could find his mug shot quickly. The way she liked to look at pictures, I knew she probably had the yearbook memorized.

Krysta could have done it in her sleep. She flipped open to

page twenty-three and pointed directly at Jacob. He had a lopsided grin and the pudgiest cheeks ever.

"Oh-mi-god!" I screamed, setting off a chain reaction with Krysta and AJ, who'd joined me on the bed.

"Now I see why you like him." AJ laughed and flipped her ponytail. "He lost a bunch of weight like you did."

"He did?" Until now, I hadn't known that. Jacob was new to Greenwood Junior High last year, when I was stuck in Covenant Christian Academy. Knowing this little fact made me like him even more. I was sure he *knew* what it was like to be teased about weight. He knew. Jake and I were made for each other. Now all I had to do was convince him.

But how? Although my friends insisted I wasn't that chubby little dork anymore, I had trouble seeing myself as anything but Sophie "So Fat" Sinora. Although Jacob sat in front of me, he had never turned around to talk or even smile. I doubted he knew my name.

"Hey." Krysta said. "Maybe you can go to Freshmen Formal together."

The dance was only four weeks away. It was supposed to be some kind of a junior high homecoming. Sounded lame, but I still wanted to go. Some of the other girls in school were brave enough to find dates for the dance. I thought about asking Jacob, but I shook at the thought of rejection.

"Yeah, maybe." My voice faltered.

I turned and stared at my reflection in the full length mirror hanging on AJ's closet door. I had been exercising all summer, so any remnants of fat had been replaced by toned skin. My hair looked perfect today, but that's because Krysta did it. Any other day, it just wouldn't do what I wanted. I could never get the makeup thing down. My mom said my green eyes and thick lashes were my best asset, although Krysta had them drowning in so much eyeshadow, I could barely see them. This, she said, would make my eyes look like a model's, but I didn't think so.

I tried to smile at my reflection, and then quickly sealed my lips. I hated my braces. Food was always getting stuck in them and they made my lips look fat. Krysta said it was fashionable to have fat lips, but I didn't see anything fashionable in looking like you were punched in the mouth.

I sighed, my shoulders slumping, when I realized I had a lot of work to do. Even though I had lost weight, I still felt awkward in my skin which didn't help my self-esteem one bit.

I had to make Jacob notice me before I asked him to the dance. I knew he wouldn't say 'yes' to a dork. I needed to prove to him and the rest of the school that I was cool. But kids were cruel, and they didn't let old nicknames die easily. So how could a girl get a new reputation?

Chapter Two

Why did the day have to begin with pre-algebra? I should have been in Algebra One, but the counselors didn't have faith in my education at the Christian Academy, so they made me repeat my math class with the bonehead freshmen.

And her. The meanest girl in school—Lady Gaga wannabe, Summer Powers.

I hated the clink and clank of her stiletto heels as she sauntered to her seat behind mine. I hated the tons of mascara she wore and the bright red lipstick she also used as rouge for her cheeks. I watched her rub it into her face once while I waited or her to finish admiring herself in her locker mirror. I was waiting because Summer insisted on keeping her locker door wide open, so I couldn't get nto my locker, which unfortunately, just like my desk, was right near hers.

She gave her heels one last click for good measure and plopped her butt in the seat behind mine. I waited for it. I knew it was coming. Summer had this annoying habit of resting her feet on the book basket underneath my desk.

No big deal. Most kids liked to be comfortable. I would have done it, too, if Mr. Steinberg hadn't placed me in the front row. That wasn't the problem. Her habit of shaking her feet throughout the entire 48-minute class period was the problem.

I had just completed two weeks of my freshman year, only forty more weeks to go. *Forty weeks of this!* I'd go insane. On the first day of school, it was just a light jitter, like an annoying little fly buzz. I turned around and asked her nicely to stop. She smiled and stopped.

The next day, she started the shaking again. I turned around and reminded her about her annoying habit, but in a nice way, or so I'd thought. She scowled at me and shook my desk harder.

When I was six years old, my biker uncle took me for a ride on his Harley Davidson. My brain jiggled for a week afterwards. This is how sitting in front of Summer Powers felt every morning in pre-algebra. I felt powerless to stop her.

Krysta told me Summer had been in five fights last year; she won every one. I was only in one fight in my life. In sixth grade, Patty Ledbetter called me a brat, so I fought her and I got my butt kicked. If any kid could have been dorkier than me, it was Patty. Her parents worked at K-Mart so getting beat by her was really hard to take. I was the laughing stock of the school.

Trying to concentrate on Mr. Steinberg while my head rattled was difficult, but I didn't need to pay attention. I knew this stuff. I was wasting my time in pre-algebra. Fractions. *Duh.* He had to keep stopping the class because Summer was confused, along with the ten other special eds who kept raising their hands. "What's a denominator again?" Were people really this stupid?

I couldn't stand it any longer. I had to see my counselor. Without wasting another aggravating minute, I raised my hand.

"What is it, Sophie? I thought you understood fractions." Mr. Steinberg pointed his giant arrow at me. What kind of a weirdo taught class with an enormous foam arrow on his hand? It was like a big yellow, pointy hand puppet. Sometimes, he even pretended the arrow would speak by answering questions for the class when they were too stupid to figure out the answers.

"May I go see my counselor?" I tried to keep my voice as low as possible. I didn't need the entire class knowing my business.

"Why? Is there a problem?" Great! The stupid arrow was talking.

For a second, I almost answered his arrow back, and then I realized I would look even more idiotic than Mr. Steinberg.

"I just really need to see her, Mr. Steinberg." "Do you have an appointment?" The arrow pointed directly between my eyes, as if it had the power to see into my mind.

"Yes." One little white lie. I had been raised to be honest, and so far, my parents had been pretty good at ingraining that principle into my mind. *But* they never said I couldn't lie to a puppet. "Okay."

Okay? It was that easy? If it wasn't for the psycho hall monitors on our campus, a kid could have easily gotten away with skipping class.

I reached under my desk for my binder. Summer's heels were resting on it, and I could tell by the way she held them firmly in place, she had no intention of helping me out. I yanked on my binder until I heard the banging of her heels against the metal bars. She didn't say anything, but she did give my desk one last shove before I departed.

Mrs. Ramirez greeted me with her pasted on smile. It wasn't like her smile was fake; she just always smiled. In my short time at Greenwood Junior High, I didn't remember Mrs. Ramirez ever having a bad day.

"How may I help you, Sophie?"

That was another incredible talent of hers; she knew every kid's name in the school. How did she do it? I couldn't even keep the names of my seven teachers straight.

"Pre-algebra is a waste of my time. I'm learning nothing." I tried to keep the whine out of my voice as I fidgeted with the creases on my binder.

"But we've just started our third week of school. If I move you to algebra, you'll be lost." Mrs. Ramirez offered a sympathetic smile.

"I can handle it. If I need to, I'll stay after school for tutoring. Please, Mrs. Ramirez, I can't suffer like this for a whole year." Somehow, despite my efforts, that high-pitched little whine slipped into my voice. I just couldn't help it. If I was going to change my reputation, I had to get out of bonehead math and far away from Summer Powers.

"Well, let me look at your classes." She pulled up a screen on her computer. "We might need to change your schedule."

What? Change my schedule! No, no, she couldn't take

away English. It was the only class I had with Jacob. Mrs. Ramirez was one of the few reasonable adults at this school. Surely, she wouldn't do that to me.

I tried to keep my voice calm, but I felt the shakiness in my throat. "Why? Can't I just switch first periods?"

"No." She answered quickly, without even looking from her computer. "All of the first period algebra classes are full. Let's see. Fifth period looks like the best bet."

"Fifth period?" How did I know she was going to say that? "Fifth period won't work."

Mrs. Ramirez looked up from her computer and studied me. "Why not?"

I tried not to let her see the panic in my eyes. Whatever happened, I *have* to keep my class with Jacob. "Because we are in the middle of a novel unit. I know the other English classes aren't reading Huck Finn and I'll have to catch up in English *and* in math."

"Well, I could put you in algebra if you are willing to drop your third period elective."

Third period was band, my second least favorite class. Mr. Martinelli was the kind of teacher who took pleasure in his students' misery.

Whenever he smugly smiled, folded his arms across his chest, and asked me to play, I couldn't even hold my flute steady. As I tried to control my nervousness, I inhaled sporadic puffs of air that sounded more like a dog panting than music. Mr. Martinelli told me he could lock a cat in a trash can, throw it down a flight of stairs and make better music.

"Ok. I'll drop band." I was ready to jump out of my seat. No more Summer, no more yellow arrow, and no more musical melodrama.

"So I'll have to give you a new elective first period." Mrs. Ramirez turned back to her computer and made several clicks with her mouse. "How about yearbook?"

"Yearbook?" This summer, when I reviewed my choice of electives, I hadn't even given that class a second glance. Ever since I erased that fat, ugly picture of me in my sixth grade book and replaced it with a Sponge Bob sticker, my mom told me she would never buy me a yearbook.

"I hear if you join the staff you get a free book."

"Really?" Wow! My day couldn't get much better. I'd get my own yearbook with Jacob's picture.

"Here." Mrs. Ramirez printed out a new schedule and handed it to me. "Go see Mrs. Carr. She's in room 200. She is short staffed this year. I wouldn't be surprised if she had you taking football pictures this weekend."

I had to be dreaming. Standing on the sidelines, watching Jacob Flushman and his masculine thighs as he raced toward me with the pigskin tucked under his arm. He scored a touchdown and I caught the moment with my lens. He grabbed me in excitement and planted a big kiss on my cheek. No. This was my dream. He planted a big kiss on my lips.

This schedule change was just the boost I needed. I was on my way to a fun freshman year. My confidence would grow. My life would change. So long to "So Fat" Sinora.

"Just what I need. Another new kid I have to train." Mrs. Carr looked down at me through thick glasses. "Do you have any photography experience?"

"No." I had wondered why this class was short staffed when students could get free yearbooks. Now I knew.

"Great." Mrs. Carr threw her hands in the air. "Do you know anything about PhotoShop?"

"No." I suddenly felt much smaller, much less significant than I had before walking through the yearbook room door.

"Terrific. There goes my first deadline." Mrs. Carr stormed off and threw herself behind her desk that was positioned in the center of the classroom. She was instantly engulfed by a huge flat-screen computer monitor on the desktop. Surrounding her desk were other computer stations, facing inward like a fortress, as if whatever was on them was top secret information.

"I can train her, Mrs. Carr." Lara "Spread 'em" Sketchum popped her head from behind one of the dozen large computer monitors.

"You're going to have to," Mrs. Carr groaned.

"I'm up to my eyeballs in paperwork. This administration doesn't think I have enough on my hands."

Lara smiled and I hesitantly smiled back. Although I'd never had Lara in a class and we hung out in entirely different circles, I knew all about her. She was the school slut. If I became friends with her, I could be labeled a slut, too. This year was my chance to prove Sophie "So Fat" was cool and making friends with Lara didn't fit in with my plan. What would Jacob think of me?

"Come sit over here, Sophie." Lara waved toward an empty seat next to hers. "I was just uploading freshmen mugshot pictures. I'll teach you how to do it, along with some of the basics of PhotoShop."

"How did you know my name?" I slipped in between a crack in the computer fortress and sat beside her.

"This is my third year on staff. I know everybody's face. Your picture has changed since seventh grade." Lara hesitantly smiled, then lowered her lashes and bit her bottom lip. *I'm not a slut. I hope you don't believe the rumors.*

Wow. I hadn't heard someone else's thoughts since before school started. Hearing her voice echo in my skull was suddenly shocking, and humbling. Lara wasn't the only student at this school who'd been branded by a label.

I almost goofed and answered her thoughts. That would have been a bad thing. People would've been afraid to come near me if they knew about my gift. "Thanks, I hope my picture looks better now."

"Yeah. You lost weight; you're actually pretty." "Thanks." Coming from Lara, that was a huge compliment. I guess whoever labeled her the school slut was jealous. With her long black hair, big blue eyes and perfect body, Lara got lots of attention from the guys.

"I'm just placing pictures of the freshmen on their pages. I'm already on the Fs." Lara must have seen my eyes widen, because she grinned after she spoke. "Do you like Jacob Flushman?"

Those traitors. Krysta and AJ blabbed their big mouths. But wait...they didn't talk to Lara, which meant it must have gotten around the whole school. I wanted to die. "How did you know?"

"My lens catches everything." Lara clicked her mouse and

pulled up a picture of students eating lunch.

I instantly recognized Jacob with his football buddies. They were laughing and throwing fries at each other. Then my eyes did a double take; I was sitting at the table behind Jacob and I was staring...no...drooling in his direction. Oh, how embarrassing. My mom had always told me I had an expressive face but did I have to make my crush so obvious? I felt a tinge of guilt for accusing my best friends of betraying me when my own stupid face was the culprit.

"Don't worry, your secret's safe with me." Lara gave me a reassuring smile and closed the picture.

Still stunned, I had trouble finding my voice. "Is...is that picture going in the yearbook?"

"Not if you don't want it to."

"God, no!" I accidentally screamed my answer. Mrs. Carr looked up from her computer long enough to scowl.

Lara nudged my shoulder. "Consider it deleted."

"No, wait." No matter how embarrassing I looked, I just couldn't stand the thought of deleting Jacob.

"I'll save you a copy first," Lara teased. "Jake does look cute in that picture."

Bad reputation or not, I knew Lara and I would become buds. A minor setback in my plan to prove to Greenwood I was cool. If Lara helped me in yearbook, the least I could do was help her uncover the myth behind the rumors. After all, if she wasn't a slut, someone was lying.

Chapter Three

Summer had to check her text messages and then put on her makeup while I waited to get my flute out of my locker. My annoyance was overshadowed by relief; I'd never need to carry around that rusted out hunk of metal again. I was so relieved after I turned it in to Mr. Martinelli, leaving his classroom for the last time.

Between waiting for Summer and turning in my flute, I was now late to my new class. Why was I so directionally challenged? Mrs. Stein's room should have been easy to find. Two hundred. Even number. Simple. Not hardly. I was going in circles. I knew I'd seen that 'Don't be a dope' sign by the bathroom entrance at least ten times. Some idiot was smoking pot and driving into oncoming traffic. The first time, the sign made me laugh. Now I wanted to tear it down and rip it to shreds, except that wouldn't look good on my school records. They'd probably think *I* was on drugs.

"Where's your pass?" Busted. The burly voice stopped me dead in my tracks.

I turned to face my captor, a school rent-a-cop. Man—maybe. Woman—I didn't know. Big, scary mammoth beast with spiked hair—definitely.

"I...I don't have one."

"Did you think I wouldn't catch you? The bell rang five minutes ago."

How could I answer without sounding like a complete idiot? "I'm lost."

"Lost? Are you one of Mrs. Frances' kids?" The beast

smiled smugly and folded its arms across its chest, obviously waiting for me to challenge the insult. Mrs. Frances' kids rode the little bus.

The list of people who liked to put me down was growing larger. I needed to stand up for myself, starting with the beast. "Mrs. Ramirez changed my schedule this morning so I am still learning my new classes. I don't know where Mrs. Stein's room is."

"Let me see your schedule." The cop grabbed the twisted paper from my hands and carefully eyed the document, as if looking for a watermark or something to prove the schedule's authenticity.

Because evil teenagers forge school schedules all the time. "I'm going that way now. Follow me."

I walked behind the beast, trying hard to decipher its gender. Dark roots, dyed frosted blonde at the tips, spiked with something, probably gel. Would a guy go through that much trouble to make each follicle stand up in a straight line?

Yes.

Jacob's best friend, Frankie Salas, would, but then again Frankie was perfect. From his angular jaw to flawless, tanned skin and large, dark eyes, Frankie could have been ripped from the pages of *GQ*, at least that's what Krysta always said.

The beast in front of me had no butt, a large stomach, and breasts that were either big man- boobs or small girl-boobs. By the time we arrived at room two hundred, which was located in hallway three hundred—go figure—I still hadn't figured out the cop's gender. When the beast turned around, I had the chance to check the name on its badge. Tyler. No help there.

The door to Mrs. Stein's room had one window, which was covered up with butcher paper. Tyler opened the door without knocking and I noticed a teacher was writing equations on her dry-erase board.

"You have a new student."

Her arm jerked. She dropped her algebra book and her dry-erase marker at the sound of Tyler's booming voice. She turned, hand on chest and momentarily glared at Tyler before focusing her gaze on me. Her entire face softened as she beckoned me toward the front of the room. "Welcome to

Algebra, dear. I'm Mrs. Stein. What's your name?"

"Sophie." I handed her my crumpled schedule.

"Sophie, how lovely." She looked at the paper before giving me a warm smile that reached her eyes. *Caryn's hair. Dark and smooth.*

How did I have two telepathic experiences in one day? And who was Caryn? I must have reminded Mrs. Stein of this person by the way she smiled.

Mrs. Stein retrieved her algebra book and clutched it to her chest. "Have a seat wherever you want. There are no assigned seats here."

I scanned the room for an empty seat. That's when I noticed the waving hand. I instantly recognized AJ, with her sporty blonde ponytail and the beat-up binder plastered with Clay Matthews pictures. I remembered her mentioning she had Mrs. Stein for algebra. "The nicest teacher in the school." Those were her exact words.

AJ had been real excited when she called me after registration this summer. Although her mom wanted her to take all honors classes, she allowed AJ the one exception with Mrs. Stein. The Mikes had Mrs. Stein. All the kids loved her.

"Hey." I sat down in an empty desk next to AJ, relieved to have a friend in class. I normally only saw her and Krysta during lunch.

"So, you finally ditched those losers in pre-algebra?" AJ smiled before we turned to the commotion at the back of the room. Tyler was trying to get to Grody Cody Miller.

Mrs. Stein was standing in front of Cody's desk, hands on hips, blocking the cop's path. "You're not taking him out of my class. If he misses one lesson, he'll be behind."

"Mr. Sparks' orders."

"I don't give a damn what Mr. Sparks said, Cody's not leaving!"

Usually students oohed and aahed when teachers swore, but not this time. They stared at her, eyes wide with something like awe. Some kids smiled. I could hear them whispering, "Go, Mrs. Stein."

I didn't get it. Grody Cody Miller was every teacher's worst nightmare. Cody had a bad attitude. He was always telling teachers off and disrupting class. Why wouldn't she have wanted him to leave?

"He left Mr. Benson's class without permission Friday. The principal wants to see him...*now.*"

Tyler peered around Mrs. Stein's shoulder and narrowed its eyes at Cody.

"So that makes a whole lot of sense. Take him out of one class for leaving another. He's not going. If Sparks has a problem with it, tell him to come see me during my planning period."

"But..."

"But nothing, Tyler. I've got to teach my kids. Please leave my classroom...*now.*" *You're not laying a finger on any of my babies.*

Mrs. Stein was passionate about her kids. She made that perfectly clear with her internal thoughts. When a person was extremely upset or angry, their thoughts were more likely to jump into my head. So, she thought of us as her babies? That was kind of cool, especially after coming from Mrs. Carr's class.

Tyler finally left the room, slamming the door. Mrs. Stein faced the door, back and shoulders rigidly frozen for what seemed an eternity. She inhaled a large breath and let it out before turning to the class.

AJ started the first clap and we all followed by rising to give Mrs. Stein a standing ovation. She deserved it for the way she stood up to that scary beast. That's when I decided when I grow up, I want to be just like Mrs. Stein.

Fourth period was a blur. I didn't focus on science Nazi because I was too busy thinking about Jacob and his masculine thighs. Besides, I was better off ignoring a teacher like Mr. Benson. If students asked too many questions, he had panic attacks and made us stand outside the classroom, as if we were deliberately slowing down his perfectly laid out lesson plans.

I remembered the incident Friday when Grody Cody raised his hand in the middle of a lesson and asked Mr. Benson to explain how a cell divided. "Does it have a brain? How does it divide if no one tells it to? If I was a cell, I'd just sit there."

I could see the veins popping out of Mr. Benson's neck.

His response—he made Cody wait outside the door. I guess Cody was tired of waiting to be invited back in, so he left.

After the bell rang to release us from our torture, I couldn't get to my fifth period class fast enough.

Crap. I left Huck Finn in my locker.

Not Huck the boy, Huck the book. We were assigned fifty pages to read over the weekend. Normally, Mrs. Warren didn't assign weekend homework, but Frankie Salas was late to class, resulting in a homework assignment for all of us. That was her policy. If one kid screwed up, we all suffered. It was usually a pretty good deterrent for tardies.

Not this time.

Although everybody was mad at Frankie for flirting too long in the hallway, we mostly kept our opinions to ourselves. As the most popular boy in school, Frankie could get away with ruining our weekend.

Passing time was only six minutes long. I rushed to my locker on the other end of the world, intending to grab the book and make the trek back to English on the other side of campus.

Not happening. Summer was at her locker, admiring her cheap Lady Gaga imitation Hairdo and texting at the same time. As usual, her locker door was open flat against mine, so she could get the best view of her face in the locker mirror.

Step one to a new image. Learn to speak up for yourself.

"Excuse me."

Summer didn't pause in her makeup ritual to look in my direction. Apparently, I wasn't even as worthy as a Maybelline smudge stick.

Maybe I wasn't loud enough. "Excuse me!" Summer closed her flip phone and stared thoughtfully into her lipliner, as if she and the cosmetic were the only two things on Earth. "Hmmm. Too pink for fall. I need something darker."

"I *need* to get into my locker." I tapped my foot to make her aware of my impatience. Although, I knew she really didn't care.

"Did you hear something, Lady?" Summer spoke to her Lady Gaga poster, which was taped just below her mirror. "I didn't think so."

"Hey, what are you doing on this side of the world? Isn't your next class in the one hundred hall?"

I turned to see AJ. "I'm waiting to get into my locker." I pointed at Summer, who was still consumed with wasting my time.

"That's easy to fix." AJ moved me aside and yanked Summer's lipliner out of her hands. She threw it in her locker and slammed it shut. "All clear." AJ faced Summer, narrowing her eyes in a challenging gesture.

Summer moaned, rolled her eyes and walked away.

AJ had the courage to stand up to anybody. How did she do it? Wasn't she afraid of getting her butt kicked? Sure, AJ was tough—a lot tougher than me. All her life, AJ had dealt with bullying from the Mikes, so she was used to fending for herself.

But AJ had a secret, other than her visions, that could be devastating if the wrong kids found out. After a horse riding accident, AJ tore the retina in her left eye. AJ's doctor said, one wrong punch, and she would lose sight in that eye forever. Even so, AJ wasn't afraid of a confrontation.

I couldn't risk my best friend's eyesight because I was too chicken to handle a bullying brat. "Hey, this is my problem, not yours."

"You're welcome." AJ looked at me with a smirk.

"I don't want you getting hurt over me."

AJ shook her head and snickered. "When are you going to learn to stand up for yourself? Summer wouldn't do anything to risk smudging her lipstick. For someone who can read people, you really can't *read* people."

"I mean it, AJ." Before I could finish my lame argument, I was interrupted by the sound of the tardy bell. "Oh, God!"

I ran to my fifth period class. Although, what was the use? I was tardy now. What kind of punishment had I brought down on my English class? Pop quiz? Essay?

Jacob was going to hate me.

Opening the door to room five-o-five, Freshman English, I slid in quietly and scurried to my seat at the far side of the room. Although I didn't see Mrs. Warren, I could hear her movement from behind a big pile of books that sat atop her desk. Maybe she hadn't taken roll yet. I received only a few evil glares as my fellow classmates caught me sneaking in late, but they didn't tell on me. They didn't want extra homework, either.

"You're late, Sophie!" Frankie Salas, who sat directly across from me, announced this to the entire class.

I felt every muscle in my body tense. Frankie turned to me with a grin.

I couldn't speak, couldn't move, couldn't unstiffen my frozen face if I tried. All I could do was stare at my tormentor and think, "Why?"

"Wh...what was that? Someone came in late?" The teacher's balding head popped up from behind a pile of books in the corner of the room. It took a moment to register it wasn't Mrs. Warren talking.

Substitute teacher, Mr. Dallin, or as we so fondly called him, Mr. Pick-N-Flick, had been teaching since the beginning of time and he hadn't earned his booger picking reputation for no reason. He was my oldest sister's math teacher. She told me he left crusties on her papers at least once a week. He was our sub for three weeks in my seventh grade geography class. On two occasions, I'd caught him digging for buried treasure. He was one reason I carried antibacterial hand lotion in my backpack.

Another one of Dallin's shortcomings, he had blessedly horrible hearing and eyesight.

My lucky day.

"No, no, Mr. Dallin. I said you look great, Sophie." Frankie winked. "Doesn't she look great, Mr. Dallin?"

I felt the heat rise from my chest into my cheeks.

"I can't tell. Let me get a closer look." Mr. Dallin heaved his huge frame upward, knocking over several books in the process. He waddled his way toward me. "Sophie? Sophie Sinora, is that you?"

"Yes, Mr. Dallin."

Mr. Dallin pushed the rim of his glasses higher on his rounded nose. "You've lost some weight."

"Yes, sir." I sank lower into my seat. Every eye in the classroom was on me. I didn't need them staring at my big lips or my messed up hair. I just wanted to disappear.

"You know." He folded his arms across his chest and dazed into space. Not uncommon for Mr. Dallin. "I taught your sisters in high school."

"They told me." Great. Please go back to your books, Mr. Dallin.

"Very popular and pretty. Wasn't your oldest sister Homecoming Queen?"

"Yes." Actually, they both were but I wasn't about to remind him. I had hoped that after a year's absence, my family legacy would be forgotten. Being the only fat dork in a line of beauty queens wasn't easy.

"That's right. Very popular and pretty."

"You just said that, sir." He was probably wondering if I was the mailman's daughter. I couldn't sink any lower, otherwise, I'd have been under the desk, so I tried to imagine I was invisible. I wasn't used to being the center of attention and having this drooling walrus hovering over me made me sick to my stomach.

"Well, Frankie, Sophie is turning into quite a beauty herself. In a couple years time, she could be the next Homecoming queen. I'd keep my eyes on this girl if I were you."

"Maybe I will," Frankie said evenly.

As expected, students snickered at this last comment while Frankie had the nerve to smile.

What a jerk. Pretending to like me. I glared at him out of the corners of my eyes.

Why would the most gorgeous guy in school play these games? What was in it for him? Did he want me to do his homework or was he just trying to add me to his long list of pathetic groupies?

Not wanting to know the answer, I fought not letting a sigh escape and faced forward, pretending to ignore Frankie. Besides, Frankie was way out of my league. I'd never expect to go out with someone as gorgeous as him, so why dream about it? Jacob was in my league, but he was the only one who didn't turn around when Mr. Dallin had the rest of the class staring at me. He didn't even laugh when Frankie was flirting.

I wondered why.

This could have been a good sign, but it could also have

been very bad. I wished I could have popped into his head. All my intuition failed me, and, as usual, my gift was stubborn. I had to satisfy my curiosity by simply staring at his perfectly small ears, buzz cut dark hair and thick neck.

Suddenly, Jacob jerked hard in his seat. "Come on. Come on. Yes!" The excitement in his voice held back in a whisper.

I peered over his shoulder and saw the screen he held in his hand as he cut down demons with his sword. I couldn't believe it. Jacob could have cared less about me. He was too busy playing with his little video game. Frankie and I could have made out on top of his desk and I don't think he would have noticed.

Mr. Dallin began speaking above the din of the noisy classroom. "Ok, everyone, your teacher will be out for the next six weeks."

As was always the case when we had a substitute teacher, there were no rules for classroom behavior. The class stopped talking long enough to exchange high fives and cheers. Nobody asked what happened to Mrs. Warren. Nobody cared.

"Her daughter is having a baby."

Mr. Dallin could have been speaking to empty desks. After the gone-for-six-weeks part, the students didn't want to listen to anything else he had to say.

And neither did I. I had more important things to worry about. Why didn't Jacob notice me? Even blind Mr. Dallin thought I was getting pretty.

Wham!

The classroom stilled as our attention was riveted on Mr. Dallin at the front of the room. He held the yardstick he'd just slammed across Grody Cody's desk. Cody looked ready to piss his pants. "Now, do I have your attention?"

Some of us silently nodded, but mostly we just stared.

"Have I finished collecting all copies of Huck Finn or are there any still missing?" He scanned the room.

I swallowed hard. Huck was still in my backpack. I tentatively raised my hand.

"Pass it up, Sophie."

I unzipped my bag with shaky fingers, accidentally dumping the contents on the floor. Why was I so nervous? This was Pick-N-Flick. He'd never beat his students before, at least not that I'd heard.

I tried to hand my book to Jacob, but he didn't turn around. He was so busy getting his butt kicked by a video game, he wasn't paying attention to what was going on in the real world.

"Jacob." I leaned forwarded and whispered, inhaling a mixed scent of hair gel and a strong, rich musk. But there was something else. Could it have been ketchup? I decided hair gel, musk and ketchup were the perfect odors for a guy.

"Jacob." I whispered louder. For days I'd been dreaming of the moment I'd get so close to Jacob I could almost kiss him. Here I was, asking him to take my book, and the moron wasn't even listening. "Jacob, Mr. Dallin is watching us. Take the book."

Nothing.

"Jacob!" Mr. Dallin's yardstick slammed down across Jacob's desk, causing him to drop his game.

"What the hell!" Jacob puffed up his chest and looked ready to jump out of his desk and punch Dallin.

Jacob was going to get himself in trouble and my Huck Finn was the cause of it.

"Jake, chill." Frankie leaned out of his desk and picked up Jacob's game. He placed it in Dallin's outstretched hand.

"That's mine." Jacob shot an angry glance at Frankie and then at Dallin.

"Not anymore." Dallin took both the video game and my Huck Finn and walked to the front of the room. He slid the little console in a drawer of Mrs. Warren's desk and put my book on top of the already large stack of books on the desktop. "Now that I have all the books collected, get out a pencil for a pop quiz on chapter six."

"This sucks!"

Jacob really needed to shut up. It was just a toy. If he kept it up, he could get suspended and miss a *real* game, his football game on Friday.

Jacob slammed his fists on his desk. "I don't want Pick-N-Flick getting crusties on my Nintendo."

Mr. Dallin narrowed his eyes at Jacob, his fat cheeks

swelled, looking like balloons ready to burst. He pointed toward the door and screamed at Jacob. "Get out!"

Jacob stormed out and slammed the door.

Mr. Dallin would probably send a referral to the office. Jacob would miss his next football game, maybe even be suspended from the team. This was all my fault. If I hadn't forgotten Huck. If I had stood up to Summer. If I hadn't been late.

"Sophie, can you take this to the office for me?" Dallin handed me a large, brown office envelope and an orange hall pass.

Why me?

I knew what was in the envelope—Jacob's referral. I felt as if all eyes in the class were upon me. I had two choices—throw it away and pray Dallin's ancient memory would forget the incident or seal Jacob's doom by delivering the referral. Either way I was screwed. Could my life get any worse?

Five minutes. That's all I needed to drop off a referral at the office and return to class. Ten minutes if I stretched it out some, walked slowly, took a potty break. Dallin wouldn't have missed me. He'd forgotten to write a time on my hall pass. This gave me some time to decide what to do.

I had always considered myself a good kid. Besides, I valued my weekends too much to get in trouble. I was thinking how easy it would have been to find the nearest bathroom and stuff the referral in the garbage. I had to wonder, though, was Jacob worth the risk? Would Jacob do something like this for me? Jacob didn't even know I existed. He proved that when he ignored me over his game.

"Sophie!" Caught up in my worries, I didn't even notice Jacob standing by the boys' bathroom.

"Hey." I was such an idiot. The boy of my dreams finally acknowledged my existence, he even knew my name, and all I could manage was 'hey'. I put my right hand behind my back, hiding Jacob's referral.

"Did you get kicked out, too?" His dark grey eyes simmered with anger, his lips drawn in a tight line. Suddenly, I realized his pissed off expression was kind of hot.

Stay focused.

"No." How did I tell him I was about to make his day worse?

His eyes narrowed. "Where are you going?"

I tried to recall one of the many pieces of wisdom my parents crammed down my throat. Honesty is always best. "To the office."

Jacob closed the distance until we were frightfully only a few feet apart. His nearness set off unfamiliar sparks of energy. My stomach began to twist in knots and I felt my entire body quaking inside.

He peered around my shoulder. "What's in the envelope?"

"I...I don't know." And honestly I didn't; although I suspected, as Jake probably did, that it was his referral.

Jacob moved closer. "You don't know?" His eyebrows rose.

His question felt more like an accusation. I was sure Jacob could hear my heart pounding. His nearness was about to shatter my nerves into a million pieces. I tried my best to regain composure. "Probably your referral."

"Yeah. I guess I lost my cool." He cast his eyes downward, his long, black lashes fluttered across his squeezable cheeks. "My dad's going to kick my ass when he finds out."

"Maybe he won't find out." I should have kept my mouth shut. That sounded like a promise and I was still unsure of what to do.

"He's friends with Sparks. He'll find out and I'll be grounded for a month." Jacob put his hands in his pockets and kept his gaze down before turning his large puppy dog eyes back to me.

How could I resist Jacob? He was so cute and sweet. "Well, what do you want me to do?" The pounding in my chest rose to my throat.

The corners of his mouth turned up slightly. "Maybe you could give that referral to me."

I couldn't still my shaking limbs. "And then what?"

"Dallin probably forgot about it already." Jacob reached around my back and grabbed my hand. I jerked, surprised by the tingling sensation of his skin touching my overly sensitive fingers. His nearness and the scent of musky ketchup was almost my undoing.

Oh, God, I could have died happy.

"Yeah. You're right." I gulped as I felt him gently pry the envelope from my hand. "But what if he doesn't?"

Jacob raised one edge of his mouth and flashed a lopsided grin. "Come on?" He already had the envelope opened and was scanning the document.

He fisted the paper into a ball and tossed it in a nearby trashcan. "Thanks. You know, Dallin is right. You have changed."

I jerked my head, trying to digest what he'd just said. He *was* paying attention when Dallin and Frankie were talking about me. Could this mean he was interested in me?

Before I could stop him, as if I would want to stop him, Jacob planted a kiss on my cheek. Although it was just a quick peck, that kiss lingered on my skin for an eternity. If it wasn't for personal hygiene, I would have never washed my face.

"See you later, Sophie."

I loved the way Jacob said my name, like chocolate pudding rolling off his tongue.

Jacob walked down the hall, leaving me standing there, stroking my cheek and contemplating his words, his kiss.

You have changed. What did that mean? Did he think I was cool? Pretty? His statement had endless possibilities. AJ and Krysta had to help me decipher his meaning on the bus ride home.

I sighed as I dreamily watched the cars pass by my window. He kissed me. He said I changed. "I wonder if it's time?" I said to no one in particular as I wondered aloud. A girl in love was allowed to wonder.

"Time for what?" Krysta asked in a disinterested voice while her nose was buried in a *Cosmo* article.

"Time to ask him to Freshmen Formal." I twisted my fingers and swished my feet. Nothing could burst this bubble.

"I think it's time for you to get a life." AJ's smug expression taunted me from behind her seat.

Stunned, I looked at her. "What's that supposed to mean?"

"Sits the bench." AJ held up her fingers and began a countdown. "Video games in class, referral, what's next?"

I rolled my eyes. "He had a bad day."

"No, he *created* a bad day." AJ leaned forward. "I think it's time for a new crush, Sophie."

"I'm not in the mood for this, AJ." Crossing my arms, I turned sideways.

AJ leaned closer. "Not in the mood for the truth?"

I turned back, coming within inches of her face. "Drop it, AJ."

"Fine." She slouched back in her seat and covered her face with her hands.

AJ wasn't the type to give up so easily. Something wasn't right.

"What's wrong, AJ?" I asked.

She peered at me through a slit in her fingers. "I fell asleep in Spanish."

Krysta flipped the page of her *Cosmo* before looking up. "Mess up your makeup?"

"No," AJ sneered. "I had a bad dream."

"What was it about?" I could feel my goose bumps rise. Whenever AJ had a dream, something bad happened.

AJ's voice faltered. "I'm afraid to talk about it."

"Why?" I already knew the answer. The tiny hairs on my skin stood on end, as I tried to rub the chill out of my arms.

AJ shrugged before looking out the window. "It might come true."

Krysta quirked a brow and set down her magazine, trying to keep her voice to a whisper. "Was this a dream or a vision?"

Recognizing the seriousness of the situation, I moved closer and Krysta followed.

AJ turned back toward us, her eyes glossed over with moisture. "Someone is going to die," AJ whispered. "I didn't see who it was, but I think it's someone close to us."

Krysta's eyes bulged, her jaw stiffened. "Are you sure?"

"Yeah." A single tear slipped down AJ's cheek. This wasn't happening. My entire body tingled with numbness. Fear took hold of me so tightly, I felt as if I would shatter into a million pieces. Was it me, was it my mom? "You didn't get a look?"

"It's someone old. I saw white hair."

I sighed, slightly relieved. "All my grandparents are dead."

"My grandpa is dead, but not my grandma." AJ gripped the back of her seat so tightly, her knuckles turned white.

Krysta squeezed her hand. "Maybe it was just a dream."

"Yeah." AJ's voice turned to stone. "Maybe."

Someone turn down that music. I'm trying to sleep here. Wait a minute. Is that my phone?

I rolled out of bed and fumbled through my dirty clothes strewn on the floor. Somewhere among the rubble was my cell phone. I had to turn off that stupid song before the noise woke my parents. AJ changed my settings again and downloaded Michael Jackson. Not funny. Her mom wouldn't buy her a cell, so she was always messing with mine.

I finally found my little lime green phone and flipped it open. Incoming call, Krysta, 1:30 am. Something was wrong.

I hit talk. "Krysta, what is it?"

I could hear muffled sobs in the background.

"She's dead."

"Who's dead?"

After a long pause, Krysta whispered her answer. "Grammy."

I felt the tightness in my throat, tears threatening to escape my eyes. "Oh, no...not Grammy."

Although Grammy wasn't related to Krysta, she'd been her neighbor for most of Krysta's life, up until Krysta's mom left and her dad lost the mortgage on house. But even after that, Grammy visited Krysta's apartment at least once a week, bringing her cookies and home-cooked meals. She was the closest thing to a grandma Krysta ever had.

Krysta hiccupped and continued crying.

I sat there for a few moments, letting her get some tears out before asking another question. "How, Krysta?"

"I...I don't know how."

Then I knew. Krysta had a supernatural visit.

Spooky.

Chills of fear swept over my neck and down my spine.

"When did she come see you?"

"Tonight."

"What did she say?" Although I was terrified, I still wanted to know the answer.

"She's not saying anything."

I dropped the phone, hastily picking it back up and accidentally pressing a few buttons while I tried to control my shaky fingers. "She's...she's still there?"

Krysta sniffed once before answering. "Uh- huh."

My mom had always told me it was impolite to talk on the phone when you had visitors. I wondered what she would have said in this situation. Even though Grammy was nice, I'd still freak if a dead person came for a visit. Krysta needed me so I tried to think of the right thing to say, but my brain was numb from terror. Clearing my throat, words finally found their way out of my mouth. "Do you think she likes you talking on the phone?"

"I don't know. She won't speak to me."

Creepy. Krysta must have been so weirded out. "What's she doing?"

"Sitting at the foot of my bed." "Where are you?"

I felt the fear in Krysta's voice. "In bed." Oh, God.

On bad days, when I felt cursed with my gift, all I had to do was remember poor Krysta. How did she manage to stay sane? Krysta needed my help, but I wasn't familiar with handling spirits. "So what do you want me to do?"

"Just talk to me until she goes away."

I felt Krysta's pain as if I was living inside Krysta's body. The agony of losing Grammy clenched my chest and then a spasm of guilt washed over me. *I'm sorry, Grammy.* I knew from her thoughts, Krysta didn't want to hurt Grammy's feelings, but she was also terrified.

"This is your last chance to talk to her before she's gone forever, Krysta."

"But she's been sitting here for over three hours."

I closed my eyes and tried to sense Grammy's thoughts, but I couldn't feel the turmoil I sensed in Krysta. Then the warmth washed over me; I heard Grammy's voice. *Peace.*

"I think she wants peace."

"Peace," Krysta sniffled, "how do you know?"

"I just listened to her thoughts." Completely amazed at what I just said, it was as if someone else was talking for me. Then it hit me; good, God, how did I just hear the thoughts of a dead person?

"Are you sure?" The tone in Krysta's voice changed to disbelief. "I didn't think you could control your mind reading."

"I can't, normally. I can't explain why I can do it now, but trust me, Krysta, she wants peace."

"How do I give her that?"

I closed my eyes and tried again to channel Grammy's thoughts through the phone. *Krysta at peace.*

Before I could hear anything more from Grammy, Krysta interrupted my thoughts.

"Sophie." Krysta let out a sob, the feeling of her guilt surged through me again. "This isn't how I want to remember Grammy."

"Try going back to sleep," I suggested. "Are you crazy?"

I knew Krysta wouldn't like that idea. Then again, I couldn't blame her. Just imagining a dead person staring at me while I slept, my entire body numbed with terror.

"She just wants to see you at peace before she departs. I think she wants to know you'll be okay without her."

"So you want me to go to sleep?" I heard the uncertainty in Krysta's quivering voice.

"Yeah." I reassured her. "But first maybe you should say goodbye."

"Bye, Gram. I love you," Krysta choked. Knowing this would be the last time Krysta would see her Grammy, tears stung my eyes as I swallowed a lump in my throat. "Okay, now lay down. Keep the phone on. I won't hang up, I promise."

Krysta hesitated before consenting. "Okay."

I heard Krysta snoring about a half hour later.

By this time there was no way I could sleep. I was sitting straight up in bed, lights on, trying to get over the shock. How was I able to control my gift? Would I be able to control mind reading from now on? Or was this just a fluke? Why was I able to use it on a dead person? A dead person! The fright from that encounter was still setting in. Until tonight, never, ever, had I read the thoughts of a ghost.

Chapter Four

Although AJ and I shared the same bus stop, Krysta's stop was two miles before ours. The next morning, I had barely enough time to explain Grammy's visit to AJ before we got on the bus.

Krysta looked at us through swollen lids. "They found Grammy this morning."

"Where was she?" I grabbed Krysta's hand and squeezed it for comfort.

"My old neighbor saw her in the backyard, lying in her flower garden, and called my dad." Krysta put her head down, letting a few tears slip.

AJ faced us from her front perch. "What happened?"

Krysta kept her eyes focused on her lap. "They think it was a heart attack."

"I'm so sorry, Krysta." I reached for a tissue out of my backpack and handed it to her.

"Thanks." Krysta dabbed her eyes with the tissue. "At least I was able to cry this morning without my dad asking questions."

I watched as Krysta quickly soaked the tissue, and I handed her another. "Will there be a funeral?"

"I don't know. Grammy doesn't have any family." Krysta nearly choked on her last words as she turned from us, staring out the bus window.

I put my arm around Krysta's shoulders. She fell into my arms and cried the rest of the way to school.

As soon as we got off the bus, Krysta reached into her

purse for her mirror. She gasped when she noticed her reflection. "I need to go to the bathroom. I can't go around looking like this."

"I'll go with you. Do you need to get to your locker before Summer gets there, Sophie?" AJ smiled accusingly.

"Yeah." I was ashamed my best friend knew I was chicken. I was tired from last night and I just wasn't in the mood to deal with Summer's crap today. I didn't like leaving Krysta, but AJ would be with her.

Just as I had hoped, Summer wasn't there yet and I was able to grab all the books I needed for my first through fifth period classes. Sure, backpacking fifty pounds of books was a pain, but not having to risk bumping into Summer was worth the extra tonnage. At least, that's what I kept telling myself.

Now I had fifteen minutes until the first bell rang and I couldn't walk the campus for that long lugging algebra, history and science books. I'd look like one of those brainy dorks. I opted for getting to my first period early. Maybe I could take a ten minute power nap at my desk. My limbs were numbing and my eyelids felt like dead weights. Obviously a side effect of last night's ghostly encounter.

I used my elbow on the door handle of the yearbook room to pry it open. The room was quiet and I didn't see anyone stirring. I could slip in and out in seconds. Out of the corner of my eye, I saw a feminine figure rush past me. I turned to see a slim hand grasping a circular door. The door rotated, engulfing the shadowy figure until she disappeared. The door turned loudly until it made a full circle. The space in the center where the girl had stood was empty.

Had Lara not told me about the darkroom yesterday, I would have been mystified by the girl's disappearance. The darkroom, Lara said, was only used for fun now, as digital equipment replaced developing pictures. Still, she told me when we were finished with our deadlines she would teach me how to develop film. I couldn't wait to hang pictures up to dry like they did in the old movies. For right now, though, I wanted to see what was behind that circular door.

Walking up to the entrance, I couldn't miss the sign. "No entrance without permission." Well, I kind of had permission.

Lara said she'd teach me. I was on staff, but Mrs. Carr had never given me permission. I thought about asking her. I would have hated to be on her bad side any more than I already was.

Come on, Sophie, make up your mind. Ok, leave, and ask Lara to show you later.

Decision made, I was about to turn when I heard the faint sounds of a girl crying.

Damn. I can't leave now. She might need me. Besides, helping someone in distress would give me a good excuse to see what's behind the door.

I stepped inside, not knowing exactly what to do. I'd been in department stores with circular doors before, but with those doors I could always see what was on the other side.

How hard could it be? Just grab the handle and turn. Within seconds, everything was dark. Pure dark, except for a faint light at the end of a pitch black tunnel. I hesitantly stepped out of the doorway, tripping over the bottom runner of the door. I reached into pure blackness, hoping to steady myself, and screamed when I found nothing to hold onto.

"Who's there?" The voice echoed at the end of the room.

I managed to grab onto the smooth surface of a wall without falling. "Me."

"Okay. *Me* doesn't help me at all."

Although we hadn't been friends long, I was pretty sure the voice belonged to Lara. "It's Sophie." Slowly, I inched my way toward her voice. I wasn't sure, but I thought I heard the sound of running water.

"Sophie, what are you doing in here?" By her agitated tone, she didn't sound too happy that I had interrupted her privacy.

I tried to make out her form in the blackness, but I realized the faint light I had seen earlier was just a thin strip at the bottom of my feet. There had to be a door separating us.

"I heard someone crying."

"I wasn't crying." Although I hadn't identified that 'someone' as Lara, she was quick to deny she had been sobbing. A sure sign of guilt.

I was closer to the door now and I had my proof when I heard her sniffle. "Yes, you were, Lara. I can still hear it in your voice."

"It's nothing," she breathed out. "I'm fine."

"No, you're not. Open the door, Lara." I moved my hands across the smooth surface, trying to locate the handle.

"I don't want to talk about it," she insisted.

But she did. She needed to talk to someone. I *knew* it. Maybe I could just listen to her thoughts. I closed my eyes, trying to summon my gift as I had done last night. *You can't help me. No one can help me.*

"Maybe I can." Before I realized it, I was answering her thoughts aloud.

"What?"

"I...I said maybe you can talk about it." Good save, Sophie. I gave myself a mental pat on the back for catching my 'oops' in time. I closed my eyes, willing my mind to hear what Lara was thinking.

Everyone at this school thinks I'm a slut thanks to Summer Powers, and if you knew what Jacob just said to me, I don't think you'd like him very much.

I could feel a knot forming in the pit of my stomach. "What?" She couldn't have just thought anything bad about Jacob.

"I didn't say anything," Lara blurted. "You shouldn't be in here. You haven't been trained yet."

"I'm not leaving. Tell me what's wrong." If Jacob was a creep, I had a right to know. But did I want to know?

"I already told you *nothing's* wrong!"

Lara wasn't ready to talk about her problem with me. That was understandable. We'd just become friends. I needed to get Lara to trust me. This sucked, because I knew once she told me, I might not like what I heard. Then again, maybe she was wrong about Jacob or maybe she misunderstood what he said.

"Look, I'm sorry for getting mad at you." The tone in Lara's voice softened. "Some guy on the bus called me a slut. You know, the usual."

"But you're not a slut."

Jacob couldn't have been 'some guy'. I wouldn't believe it. She wasn't hearing correctly. Or maybe it was someone who sounded like Jacob.

I heard the door open a crack and Lara's hand found mine.

"Thanks for not believing the rumors."

She pulled me into a small room with red lights on the ceiling. I noticed a large sink. Inside the sink was a faucet that was connected to a tube that ran water into a large basin. Beside the basin were three trays with a different color liquid in each.

Just like the movies.

"Whoa. This is cool."

Lara grabbed something that looked like my mom's salad tongs and used them to lift a picture of a puppy out of the water. She shook off the picture and hung it on what looked like a clothesline. "Do you want to see some pictures I developed?"

"Yeah." The darkroom made me forget about Lara's problem. The water, the lights, it was so...peaceful. "But wait, is there something else you want to tell me?"

"No. That's it. It's over. Do you want to see these pictures or not?"

"Yeah, I want to see them." I sighed in relief. I really didn't want to hear what else Lara had to say. Jacob was a sweetie. Wasn't he? An uncomfortable, sinking feeling, grabbed hold of my chest. Was it guilt? Lara was so thankful I didn't believe in the rumors, but I refused to believe her when it came to Jacob. Maybe Jacob did call her a slut. Maybe he was just having a bad day. Jacob was too cute and perfect to be a jerk all the time.

Chapter Five

Eeww. I shouldn't have asked for cheese on my burger. I shouldn't have asked for *burger* on my burger. I tried to digest the processed cardboard the lunch ladies thought to pass off as meat, but I just wasn't in the mood to eat. Not with the weight of the world on my shoulders.

"Do I need to kick her ass for you?"

"What?" I looked up to see AJ. I hadn't even noticed she was sitting across from me, trying to chew through a piece of leathery burger.

AJ's face twisted with disgust as she swallowed what she had chewed. "You look upset. Is Summer bothering you again or are you still freaked out about the ghost?"

"Neither." I turned my attention toward my soda. At least that was digestible, even if it was 150 calories and loaded with caffeine.

"Oh, I get it." AJ leaned back and smiled in the direction of the jock table.

Until that very moment, I hadn't even noticed them. Jacob and a couple other jocks were smashing ketchup packets, making a mess all over the white cafeteria walls.

I sighed. "He's part of it, but not all of it."

AJ arched her brow in disbelief. "Well, what's the rest?"

"I'm getting better at it." I focused on my drink again, trying to keep my voice low while speaking around my straw.

"At what?"

I hesitated, and looked around to see if anyone at the nearby tables was paying attention. "At controlling *it*."

"Oh, really," AJ smiled. "What am I thinking?" "Don't be a dork. First Grammy, and then..." Lara had not asked me to keep it a secret; then again, she didn't know I knew.

AJ leaned closer. "Finish."

I covered my mouth while I whispered my top secret information to AJ. Just because kids weren't in hearing distance, didn't mean none of them were good lip readers. "A girl in one of my classes is having problems."

AJ's eyes widened. "What kind of problems?"

"I don't want to talk about it. She probably doesn't want anyone to know." "What did she say?"

AJ wasn't going to let this one drop easily.

"She wouldn't tell me anything. I heard her crying, so I listened to her thoughts."

"Great." AJ backed away and narrowed her icy blue eyes. "So now you're using *it* to be nosey."

I tried to keep my voice low. I didn't want to cause a scene. "No, I'm not."

"Sounds like it to me." AJ threw the remnants of her burger into the wrapper and fisted it into a ball.

I looked over my shoulder, quickly scanning the room for any eavesdroppers. "What's your problem, AJ?"

"I don't know." AJ raised her voice. "Why don't you pop into my head and find out?"

I could feel my body shudder in fear that I would be found out. When we revealed our gifts to each other six years ago, we made a promise to secrecy and AJ was about to blow it with her big mouth. "Don't be a jerk, AJ."

"What are you two fighting about?" Krysta took a seat next to AJ with her usual lunch, a diet Coke and a Slim Fast bar. As if *she* needed to diet; she was skinnier than a toothpick.

AJ turned to Krysta and pointed a finger. She made no attempt to control her loud voice. "Sophie's figured out how to pry into other people's business."

"Would you keep your voice down?" I hissed, "I wanted to help."

"So, how'd you help her?" AJ snapped.

I took a deep breath, preparing for AJ to pounce again. "I don't know how to help her."

AJ slammed her fist on the table. "Just don't try any of that crap on me because I'll know when you're doing it."

I jerked back, surprised by the loud sound and AJ's reaction. "I didn't plan on it, AJ."

"Okay, you two." Krysta jumped in with an angry whisper. She nodded toward a bunch of middle school maggots who had stopped chewing their meat products long enough to gawk at us.

Kids at this school loved fights, especially little seventh graders. "Stop fighting."

"I didn't start it." I pointed to AJ and rolled my eyes for emphasis.

AJ got up and threw away her lunch. She didn't even bother to say goodbye as she stormed out the door.

"What's up with her?" I asked Krysta. After what I'd been through with Grammy and Lara, I really didn't need AJ adding to my stress.

"She had another fight with her mom last night." Krysta said this with little emotion, as if she was used to AJ and her mom fighting.

AJ had me so pissed off with her attitude, my heart was beating like a drum in my chest, and I could feel red hot anger flush into my cheeks. "Well, she doesn't have to take it out on me."

I knew AJ and her mom fought a lot. Which was why she was grounded almost every weekend, although usually just on Fridays. She would drive her mom so crazy by Saturday morning, Mrs. Dawson would give in, just to get AJ off her back.

Krysta smiled weakly and set down her diet soda. "I never got to thank you for what you did for me and Grammy."

"No problem." Although Krysta was a master at changing the subject to avoid conflict, the reminder of her loss brought on a surge of guilt. I was ashamed I was too busy being mad at AJ to remember Krysta had just lost her Grammy. "How are you holding up?"

"Ok, right now. Ask me again in a few minutes." Krysta lowered her voice to a whisper. "So, are you really learning to control it? I thought last night was just a fluke."

I looked up to see a few of the seventh graders still staring.

I growled at them, and they quickly turned, frantically shoveling fries into their faces.

Leaning toward Krysta, I decided to tell her what I'd just told AJ. I knew she'd be more understanding. "I did, too. Now, I don't know. This past week thoughts have been coming more frequently. Last night with Grammy and again this morning, all I had to do was think about it."

"Who were you trying to help?" She nibbled on her diet bar and raised her gaze in anticipation.

"I don't want to say. Someone at school has started rumors about her and now other kids are teasing her." I didn't mention there was only one 'other kid', Jacob Flushman. I still didn't have proof he was that much of a jerk. "Let's just leave it at that."

Krysta took a dainty sip of her diet drink from a straw. "Are you going to help her?"

"I don't know what to do." I breathed out and rested my forehead on my palms. This day hadn't started out well and it wasn't getting any better. "I don't know how to help her, but I've got to think of something."

What could I do to help Lara? Since I had pried into her mind without permission, now was it my responsibility to help her? What could *I* do? Kick Summer's butt? Doubtful. Tell off Jacob? Then he'd never like me. But if I knew he treated my friends like crap, would I want him to like me? My life was way too complicated.

Chapter Six

Pop quiz.

Two of the most dreaded words in a student's vocabulary. Not the sight I was looking forward to when I walked into English class. I much preferred staring at the back of Jacob's cute ears. I couldn't get the dreaded vision of Dallin's scribble out of my mind, especially since those two evil words were glaring at me in bold red marker on the white board.

Our assignment last night had been to read chapter eight. Yeah, I read it, but I didn't expect to recall any of it. My mind was too filled with other stuff right now, not to mention I could barely keep my eyelids open. My caffeine high from that jumbo Dr. Pepper I had at lunch was already starting to wear down.

Mr. Pick-N-Flick made his way to the front of the classroom and opened his mouth as if to speak, but then he began to hack and cough. God, I felt sorry for the kids in the front row. Debris was flying everywhere. Didn't the guy know how to cover his mouth? He grabbed a tissue and finally coughed up whatever was blocking his passage. I couldn't see it behind the tissue, but I could hear it and it sounded slimy. The kids in the front row were turning green. Good thing I didn't eat that hamburger. I already wanted to hurl my soda.

Pick-N-Flick managed to spew out, "Clear your desks," and then he started hacking again. He grabbed another tissue and spit into it. When he tried to toss the tissue into the trashcan, a long trail of rubbery snot trailed from his lower lip to the tissue.

Now I really wanted to barf.

The tissue dangled from his lip for a second before it hit

the floor. Pick-N-Flick picked it up and threw it away, but he managed to slime his hand in the process. I watched him wipe it on his pants before he grabbed the tests off his desk.

"Sophie, would you hand these out for me?" How did I know that was coming? No telling how many boogery germs were on those tests. All eyes in the classroom were on me. Even if I doused myself with an entire bottle of antibacterial lotion, nothing would sanitize the stigma of being labeled the girl who rubbed her hands in Pick-N-Flick snot.

I sank lower in my seat, trying to avoid the teacher's gaze. "I feel really sick right now, Mr. Dallin."

"What's wrong?" He lowered his gaze, smirking. "Girl thing?"

Okay, if that's what you think, Dallin, I'll go for it. I placed my hand on my stomach and leaned forward in pain. "I just don't think I can get up right now."

"Jacob, get up here and hand these out."

I could see the backs of Jacob's ears turning red. He slowly turned, and narrowing his eyes he mouthed, "You owe me."

Poor Jacob. Poor me. I kept striking out with him. I frantically searched through my backpack, hoping he'd forgive me if I let him use my anti- bacterial lotion. Besides, I didn't like the idea of "The Love of My Life" encrusted in boogers.

Using the tips of his fingers, Jacob placed the test on my desk and scowled before moving on. Other girls in class were getting out their lotion and lathering up their hands as they reached for their tests.

Girls always come prepared. Guys never think of this stuff. Frankie leaned over, smiling, and pointed to the lotion I'd placed on my desk. "Hey, can I use some of that?"

"Help yourself. Do you think Jacob is mad at me?"

"Don't worry about him." He winked and handed back the bottle. "He'll get over it."

Jacob took the lotion from me when he returned. Bending over my desk, he whispered, "Don't think this gets you off the hook."

I shivered at the feel of his warm breath in my ear. The feel of him so near was frightening, yet exciting.

I had a hard time concentrating on the test, especially

since I had to recall information while trying not to touch the paper. It was a difficult task. I ended up touching the test several times. By the end of the exam, I was almost out of lotion.

"Time's up. Now pass your test to the perso who sits behind you. If you're in the last row, pass your paper to the front. We're grading these in class."

Aaugghh, does the torture never end? Was I to touch all of Dallin's boogers before the period was through?

As I reached for Jacob's test, he grabbed my hand, pulling me closer. Was this the moment I'd been waiting for? Was Jacob about to declare his love? I could feel the hairs on the back of my neck stand up in anticipation.

"This is a good time to pay me back. I didn't exactly read the book. An A would be nice, but I'd settle for an A minus."

Had I just heard him right? Did Jacob expect me to cheat for him? Before I had time to respond, I was ready to melt, feeling the warm pressure of Jacob's hand in mine. I looked into his big brown eyes, waiting, hoping. Then I felt the hard, slick object he placed in my hand.

"Use my pen if you need to change anything. Try not to write like a girl."

Wait a minute, I hadn't agreed to this. First, he made me throw away his referral, now I had to cheat for him. I wanted Jacob to like me, but I didn't like the sinking feeling in my gut, the feeling of being used.

"So what'd you do?" Krysta batted her eyes at me from over the top of her *Cosmo*. I couldn't see the rest of her face. She was probably using the magazine to conceal a smile.

I looked out the window, not wanting to witness my friends' reactions. "I cheated for him."

"No way!" AJ leaned into me from the seat in front of us. I could hear her ponytail flapping in the breeze from the open window. "Sophie's a baaad girl." She let out a mocking laugh.

"Shut up!" I wanted to grab her ponytail and throw her out the window, but I knew I'd probably regret it later.

"What'd you give him?" Krysta leaned forward, a slight frown knitting her brow, her voice dropping to barely audible.

"An A."

I barely whispered this, but their resounding squeals let me know they'd heard.

AJ jumped up from her seat, almost falling forward and into my lap. "What did he *really* get?"

"He missed every question."

"Sounds like a real winner." AJ sank into her seat again and rolled her eyes. "Lazy in sports, lazy in school."

I focused my gaze on her smug expression. "Just 'cause he sits the bench, doesn't make him lazy. That's the coach's decision."

"Yeah," AJ jabbed, "and the coach decided to sit Jacob because he's lazy."

"You have a serious attitude problem and I am seriously tired of it." I folded my arms across my chest. "I like Jacob, AJ, and I don't like you talking crap about him."

"Sorry, I've been on edge." AJ's shoulders slumped and she hunched over in her seat.

"Yeah," I said. "Just a little."

"You'd be too if you had a mother like mine." AJ had a point, even though she had a bad way of relieving stress.

"Let's get back to the subject, Sophie." Krysta grabbed my elbow. "Did he at least thank you for fixing his test?"

"Yeah, he thanked me."

AJ piped up again. "I think he's using you."

"I'm not stupid," I snapped at AJ. "I know I'm being used."

"Well, what are you going to do about it?" Krysta squeezed my arm again. Her big brown eyes showed genuine concern. "Are you just going to keep cheating for him?"

"No." I threw my head back and heaved a sigh. AJ narrowed her eyes. "You're not going to pry into his mind, are you?"

"No, AJ," I hissed, "I will not use my gift to find out what other people think of me. Truthfully, I really don't want to know what other people are thinking about me, especially you right now."

"So," Krysta butted in, changing the subject. "How will you find out if he's using you?"

I smiled at Krysta. "I had Dallin two years ago as a sub. My sisters had him, too."

Krysta quirked an eyebrow. "What's that got to do with anything?"

"He gives pop quizzes every week," I explained, "and each time we either pass our tests to the front or back."

Krysta's eyes widened. "Ooohhhh yeeeahhhh. I see, now. So, next time Jacob will grade your test."

Although I didn't want Jacob to use me, I would be crushed if I discovered he had no feelings for me. Still, I had no choice but to find out. Love sucks. "I might have to get a few wrong on purpose, just to see if he'll cheat for me. The only problem is I never know which way Dallin will make us pass our tests."

Krysta scratched her head in contemplation. "What are you going to do if Jacob passes his test to you again? Will you change his grade?"

That was an option I didn't want to consider, but Krysta forced it out in the open. The nagging question would haunt me. "I don't know, Krysta. I just don't know."

Things would have been much easier for me if I didn't have a conscience. Unfortunately, when my parents raised me, they taught me honesty. I had to find out if Jacob liked me, and other than reading his mind, I saw this as the only way. The question was, after all this lying and cheating for him, would I still like myself?

Chapter Seven

"I don't get it." Looking at Mrs. Stein's dry-erase board, I rubbed my throbbing temples.

AJ threw down her pen and rolled her eyes. "Why don't you get it?"

"I don't *know* why." I couldn't hide the irritation in my voice. Algebra was to me what AJ's mom was to her, a nagging pain in the butt. "If I *knew* why, I'd probably get it."

"Sophie, let me see your equation." Mrs. Stein walked over, her algebra book clutched closely to her chest.

The way she carried that thing around all the time, I'd swear it was her child.

"I didn't finish it, Mrs. Stein." I hated to disappoint my favorite teacher, but I really felt like an idiot when it came to math.

"What's the matter?" Her soft, kind eyes scanned my face, and then trailed off in the direction of the scribble I'd written on the board.

"I don't get it." It didn't help I couldn't focus in class. But how could I? Lately, Mrs. Stein's moods had been invading my mind, causing me to lose focus on the lesson. Although I couldn't hear what she was thinking, I could sense something wasn't right with my teacher.

Mrs. Stein smiled reassuringly. "You need to find the 'Y'."

"I found it." I pointed to my equation. "It's a letter. It's on the board."

"Duh, Sophie," AJ laughed. "What does it stand for?"

I was beyond frustrated. "Why do we need a 'Y'? Why can't

we just use a number? Letters are for English class."

Mrs. Stein's smile thinned. "If we used a number, then you'd have the answer and there'd be nothing to solve."

I threw down my dry-erase marker and flung myself into Mrs. Stein's padded chair. She was the only teacher who'd let me get away with that. "I don't see why learning this is going to help me, anyway."

"It helps you develop reasoning and logic skills." Mrs. Stein handed me the marker and pointed to the board. "Try again."

I dragged my reluctant feet over to the board. I was tired and my brain hurt. I didn't want to think about algebra anymore. "I don't see any logic in calling letters numbers."

Mrs. Stein took a deep breath and closed her eyes. I could tell she was silently counting to ten. I knew there were days when I tried her patience but I really didn't like algebra. Still, I admired Mrs. Stein for the countless after-school hours she spent tutoring boneheads like me. The fact she never gave up on me was what kept me coming back for more torture.

AJ understood algebra. I didn't know why she hung around, other than to nag me and maybe spend a few more hours each week away from her mother.

I was seven weeks into school and so utterly confused in my algebra class, I felt like I was falling off a cliff in a nightmare, only I couldn't wake up.

"I don't think I'm getting through to you." Mrs. Stein exhaled deeply and sank into her chair. "Maybe you need a peer tutor."

"I can tutor her, Mrs. Stein." AJ tossed her ponytail and smiled.

"No, you two are too close," Mrs. Stein laughed. "No offense, but I don't think you'd get any work done."

She was right. As much time as we spent goofing off in class, I couldn't blame Mrs. Stein for wanting a different tutor. "Who can tutor me, Mrs. Stein? I'm hopeless."

"Just hang on." She patted her book like a baby. "You'll get it."

"No, really, everything was so easy in pre-algebra, but when it comes to algebra, I'm brain dead."

Mrs. Stein jumped up from her chair and shook her finger

in my face. "Don't say that. Don't ever say that." Clutching her book to her chest, she rushed out the door.

"Now you've done it." AJ nodded to the door as it slammed shut.

I stared helplessly at AJ. My favorite teacher, my mentor, just threw a tantrum. Was it something I said or did this have to do with whatever was plaguing her mind during class? I was overwhelmed by guilt. Caught up in my own problems, I hadn't realized Mrs. Stein's situation was worse than I'd imagined. "What'd I say?"

AJ shrugged her shoulders. "I don't know."

Just as quickly as she exited, Mrs. Stein returned, smiling as usual, still clutching her book. My teacher was trying hard to mask her feelings but there was something underneath the happy façade. I sensed her dark inner turmoil. Through her frozen smile and glossy eyes, deep into her soul, she hid a hollow, aching pain and it took every scrap of willpower for her to hold back the flood of tears.

She kept smiling, her knuckles turning white from the firm grasp she had on the algebra book. "I'm sorry, Sophie, it just pains me to hear my students speak that way about themselves."

No, that wasn't the problem. She was lying. But what was it? Then I remembered how mad AJ got at me the last time I pried into someone's mind. I wasn't trying to be nosey. I just wanted to help her. I thought about closing my eyes and tuning in Mrs. Stein's inner thoughts, but AJ was beside me and she'd know what I was doing.

I decided to let the issue rest—for now. There would be a better day to fight my teacher's inner demons. For the present, I decided to focus on fighting my algebra-challenged brain. "Who will you get to tutor me, Mrs. Stein?"

She sat at her desk and faced her computer screen. "He's in Mrs. Hamilton's honors algebra class. He's very gifted."

He...sounded interesting, but *he* couldn't be Jacob. He was in regular algebra, like me.

"Who?"

"Frankie Salas."

Frankie Salas, the hottest guy in school? Not him. Anyone

but him. I didn't want him to know how stupid I was and not just because he was hot. He could tell Jacob I was a moron. "Isn't there anyone else?"

Mrs. Stein stared at me like I'd just grown an arm out of my head. "What's wrong with Frankie? All the girls like him."

Exactly. I didn't want to be added to his flock of drooling dimwits. "Not *all* the girls."

"How about someone from our class?" Mrs. Stein suggested.

I hesitated, conducting a mental inventory of the possible losers I'd get stuck with if I agreed. I couldn't think of anyone too repulsive. "Okay."

"Cody Miller understands algebra pretty well." Mrs. Stein pointed to Cody in the far corner of the room. Unaware we were watching, he tutored some of his nerdy friends, while simultaneously picking a wedgie.

How could I have forgotten Grody Cody Miller? He stunk to high heaven. It was rumored Cody only washed his underwear once a week and I believed it. "Maybe Frankie won't be so bad."

"Great." Mrs. Stein tapped her keyboard. "I'll email his math teacher and set it up before school since Frankie has football practice after school."

"Of course."

I knew this all too well, as Lara and I had been to the field twice to take pictures of practice. Both times Jacob sat the bench, completely oblivious to my presence. Frankie had kept looking at us and twice he made me miss a good shot because he'd distracted me with his penetrating eyes. He'd made some impressive plays, but I think he was just showing off for Lara.

Just the thought of the hottest guy in school as my private tutor caused butterflies to form in my stomach. Even though I liked Jacob, not Frankie, something about that boy made girls melt in his presence. How could I survive such a close encounter with Frankie Salas without making a fool of myself?

"Isn't Rose Marie in the middle of her semester? Why is she coming home?" I sat with my legs crossed on top of my mom's huge bed and snuggled one of her pillows.

I had gone into her room to get advice. Tomorrow morning, I was supposed to meet with Frankie, and for some reason, my stomach was doing flips. I didn't like Frankie. I liked Jacob. Everybody liked Frankie. Why would I want to be like everybody else? Besides, Frankie would never be interested in me.

As usual, my problem wasn't important and the topic strayed to one of my perfect sisters. "She didn't say why she's coming home." My mom chewed nervously on her lip while she paced the floor. "She just said she had something important to tell us."

My sister, Rose Marie, was five years older than me, beautiful and brilliant, everything I wasn't. As the valedictorian of her class and the state debate champ, colleges had lined up at our door for her. Why she chose to go to a public university in Arizona when Dartmouth and Harvard offered her full tuition was beyond me.

My mom suspected Rose Marie's decision had something to do with Chad, Rose Marie's loser boyfriend. The family had hoped she'd dump him after high school. No such luck. He moved to Arizona to work for his uncle's trucking company and Rose Marie had followed.

"I'm so worried about her." A deep line formed in the middle of mom's forehead. She was way tense.

"She'll be fine, Mom. Rose Marie's smart."

"She's good with books, Sophie, not life." Mom pointed to Rose Marie's homecoming picture. "Look at her boyfriend. What did he do with himself after high school?"

I studied the picture. Rose Marie, adorned in her crown and velvet robe, was the model of elegance and beauty. Her escort, on the other hand, was clad in a tuxedo jacket, denim shorts, high-tops with holes in the toes, and a lopsided, unshaven grin. He looked like he lived out of his car. The funny thing was Chad actually was living out of his car when he took that picture. His parents kicked him out of the house after he'd thrown an all-night party when they went away for the weekend.

"He didn't do much with himself *in* high school," I quipped.

Mom sighed and put her hand on her hip. "You're not helping."

"Sorry."

Waving her hands in the air, Mom looked like a woman on the edge. "What does she see in him?" This question has nagged my mother's poor brain ever since Rose Marie came home her senior year of high school with Chad's rock on her engagement finger. My mom cried, my dad made her take it off, but I saw her wearing it when my parents weren't looking.

"Maybe she's coming home to tell us she broke up with him."

"She could do that over the phone." My mom crossed her arms over her chest and chewed on her thumbnail. "She's missing school. She must have dropped out."

"Now, Mom, don't jump to conclusions." I got off the bed and put my arm around her. "You're getting yourself worked up for no reason. Try to stay calm until she can explain herself."

"If Rose Marie only had your common sense. I never have to worry about you, Sophie."

I hadn't heard my mother say anything like that before. I always thought I had been the dorky disappointment, the problem child. I backed away to get a good look at my mom. "Then why'd you put me in private school?"

"It was a precaution. You've proved us wrong, Sweetie. Look at my baby, growing up into a beautiful, mature young lady." She cupped my chin in her hand and stroked my cheek.

Never had I received such warm praise from my mom. Sure, she gave love in abundance, but she's my mom and I'm the baby. This was the first time Mom saw me as someone other than her fat little munchkin. Or maybe just the first time I knew she did.

I smiled at my mom and savored the moment. Lately, I'd been too busy with my friends or school to spend time with her. Rose Marie had been out of the house for over three months. With my oldest sister, Lu Lu, in med school, I was the only child and I needed to soak up some of Mom's affection more often. I made a mental note to do more things with my mom as soon as Rose Marie went back to college. Hopefully, my sister would only be home for a few days.

Our mother-daughter bonding was cut short by the sound of the doorbell. Mom turned, and without a second glance, raced downstairs.

Dad had already let them in, Rose Marie...and Chad. He was holding her suitcase; she was holding his hand with her other hand resting on her stomach.

I did a double take. Was Rose Marie, my perfect sister, getting fat?

My dad swore. My mom wailed like a baby.

I thought, "Hey, parents, chill, it's just the freshman fifteen. Lots of students gain weight their first year in college." Then it hit me.

Chapter Eight

"So now they're living with you?" Eyes wide, AJ leaned over the bus seat, eagerly taking in my family gossip.

I wanted to tell them last night, but by the time my parents were through with their lecture, it was past midnight. I wasn't about to miss my sister getting her butt royally chewed. "Yeah. I have to give up my bedroom."

"That sucks," AJ complained. "You just moved into that room."

"You shouldn't have to move because they're stupid."

Krysta was right, but I had no choice. When I refused to give up my room, Rose Marie cried, making my mom sob all over again.

"It's closest to the bathroom." I rolled my eyes. "Rose Marie goes at least five times a night."

AJ narrowed her eyes. "What is she going to do about college?"

"She wants to be a stay-at-home mom." I said this with bitterness in my voice. I couldn't help it. The idea of my sister and Chad having a baby was totally absurd.

Krysta laughed. "She doesn't even *have* a home."

"My mother would have sent her packing," AJ said.

"That's what my dad wanted to do, but my mom said we must think about the baby."

"Does Chad still have a job?" AJ's question was the first thing my dad asked Chad last night.

"Yeah, thank God. He works for his uncle's trucking company, so he will be gone three weeks, home one." Getting used to living with my sister again, and a baby would be difficult, but the thought of sharing a bathroom with her boyfriend made me sick. "I hope he keeps this job. He lost a lot of jobs in high school because of his stupidity."

"I thought your sister was perfect, Sophie," AJ flipped her ponytail and turned up her nose, "but she really screwed up."

"Remember how we all wanted to be like her?" Krysta shook her head in amazement.

"Not anymore." We all said this simultaneously, looked at each other with knowing grins, and laughed. It was scary how my friends and I thought alike.

"Well, Sophie," Krysta sounded optimistic, "this has got to be good for you."

"How can you say that? I lost my room. I won't be the baby anymore."

AJ straightened. "At least you won't have to compete with your perfect sister."

"Lu Lu is the top student in her medical school," I reminded her. Although Lu Lu rarely called because of her hectic school schedule, our living room walls were plastered with certificates of achievement from my brainy oldest sister.

"That can be you someday," AJ pointed out. "You won't come home from college knocked up by some loser."

"No, I won't." I didn't know why, but my mind drew a picture of Jacob at AJ's loser comment— Jacob sitting the bench, Jacob playing video games in English class, Jacob getting sent to the office.

But it was unfair of me to compare him to Chad, wasn't it? After all, this was just the ninth grade. A guy can change a lot over four years.

He was waiting in Mrs. Stein's classroom— alone. I didn't know why I expected Frankie not to show up, but he was there, casually leaning back in his desk with his hands folded behind his head, smiling.

I slipped my backpack off my shoulder and tried my best to smile back as I sat in a desk facing him. Knowing how close I was to Frankie made my insides quiver. His heady cologne slowly wrapped its coils around my senses. I tried to back away from the temptation, but there was nowhere to go. These desks hadn't been positioned so closely before.

"So." Frankie grabbed a pencil from his binder. "Mrs. Stein said you don't get algebra."

As I stared into those deep, brown eyes, I nodded but said nothing.

He smiled and opened a book. "Let's start with the basics."

"Uh, huh." I couldn't think, didn't know how to act around Frankie Salas. Words trickled from my mouth but I was powerless over what I said. I was behaving like a complete idiot. And over Frankie? I needed to get a grip. I didn't even like the guy.

Frankie picked up his pencil and scribbled something on a piece of paper. "Mrs. Stein told me you get fractions and percentages, but you get stuck on equations."

"Yeah." Why was the sexiest guy in school willing to tutor me? Why was Mrs. Stein nowhere to be found? Was she just going to leave me alone with him?

"Sophie?" Frankie leaned closer.

I was struck with a rush of cool, minty air. Dentyne Ice. The boy was on fire. I jerked up to see Frankie's lopsided grin. He was facing the paper toward me. I looked at his equation.

$S + F = 2$

"Mrs. Stein told me you don't understand why we use letters instead of numbers. So imagine 'S' stands for the initial of a person." Frankie pointed to the equation. "Who do you know whose name begins with an 'S'?"

Somewhere, in the furthest corner of my mind, I suspected the answer he wanted but was too nervous to give it. "Sally?"

"Sally?" He set down the pencil and rubbed his jaw. "I don't know a girl named Sally."

I smiled and bit my lip. "I made her up." "Alright. Give me the name of someone beginning with an 'F'."

His voice was deep for a guy his age, yet so soft, I had to lean closer to hear him. "Fritz."

He quirked an eyebrow. "Fritz?"

I felt the heat rising in my cheeks. I grabbed the pencil and squeezed, as I tried to still my shaking fingers. "You wanted a name."

"You're right." He flashed a teasing grin. "Let's take Sally and Fritz, for example." Frankie reached for the pencil.

I jumped at the contact of his skin on mine. I could feel my face redden even before he had time to react.

"I need the pencil." He waved his fingers. "So I can finish the equation."

"I'm sorry." I clenched the pencil and tried to squeeze all the nervousness out of my body. Frankie Salas was flirting with me and I didn't understand why. I was too nervous to read his mind. Because I was so nervous, I couldn't even focus on my own thoughts.

His deep brown eyes found mine. "Is there something wrong?" I felt my body tingle at the feel of his penetrating gaze.

"No. I just don't like algebra."

A good excuse, but not hardly the truth. Something was wrong with me and I was feeling incredibly foolish for my nervousness. I wasn't in love with Frankie. The rest of the female population was. So why did I have to remind myself of this? Frankie was a player and I wasn't about to be added to his list of love-sick admirers.

He wrapped his fingers around mine and gently pried the pencil out of my hand. I felt heat race through my neck, my cheeks and down my spine.

"Now imagine Fritz asks Sophie, sorry, Sally to go out with him. How many people would that equal?" Frankie winked, not even trying to conceal the mischief brewing in his eyes.

"Two?" I whispered. I couldn't tear my gaze from his face.

"Great. Sally plus Fritz equals two people." Frankie scribbled something on the paper.

I breathed out. "Yes."

"So what number does Sally represent?" "Stupid," I said it without thinking. This was Frankie's fault. He had my brain all mixed up.

Frankie's eyes widened. "What? Stupid's not a number."

"Sorry, I don't know why I said that." I closed my eyes and pretended to think. I knew the answer but I needed some time to settle my nerves. Unfortunately, Frankie was still there when I opened my eyes, still hot, still tempting me with that playful smile. "One."

"That's right, Sally equals one." Frankie reassuringly squeezed my hand.

I thought about pulling free, but something willed me to squeeze back. I was an idiot.

"So how's the lesson coming?" Mrs. Stein's melodic voice broke the spell.

Thank God.

I quickly pulled my hand away and arched back. Now I saw why so many girls had fallen for Frankie Salas. The boy was magic, pure magic.

Frankie's magic worked on me throughout the morning, because I floated through my first and second periods. Not until I reached Mrs. Stein's class, and I sat in the very seat Frankie used, did it hit me. Was Frankie just flirting or did he like me?

Impossible.

He went to Greenwood in the seventh grade. He should have remembered the fat me. I must have been just flirting practice. He was probably warming up for another girl, a cool girl.

That realization was like a punch to my ribcage. But why did I let it bother me? After all, I liked Jacob, not Frankie.

I tried to focus on Mrs. Stein's lesson, but it was difficult with so much on my mind. But, knowing I was going to be even further behind, I forced my mind to go blank.

Why didn't you take me, too? The sound of Mrs. Stein's agonizing plea threw my brain off kilter. I looked into her haunted expression. What was she thinking? Take her where? Who was she speaking to?

Our eyes made contact. I looked away, ashamed for invading her thoughts. She didn't know I knew what she was thinking. Did she?

"Sophie, stay a minute. I want to talk to you."

The entire class oohed and aahed at the seriousness in her voice.

I sank in my seat. She couldn't have known I was invading her thoughts. "Sure, Mrs. Stein."

The bell rang and I watched my classmates file out. Some of them whispered and looked in my direction. Kids were so nosey and annoying. I figured that's how the rest of my peers had to act when they didn't have the power to read minds.

Clutching her book and timidly smiling, Mrs. Stein settled in the desk in front of me. "You never answered my question."

"What question?" Did she ask me to give an answer when I was mentally absent today? When I was reading her mind?

She leaned forward. "How'd the tutoring go?"

"Oh, fine." I sighed in relief. All this worrying about Frankie was turning me into a nervous wreck.

"Oh, really?" Her voice rose several octaves. "You were red as a beet when I walked in. Does he make you feel uncomfortable? I can find a new tutor."

"No!" Somehow, I'd said that way too quickly. Exhaling deeply, I tried to relax my tense shoulders. "What I mean is, that's okay, Mrs. Stein. He was just telling a joke."

"Good." She patted my hand. "You're a smart girl and I want to see you catch up."

Overcome by disbelief, I stared at her. "You think I'm smart?"

"Of course. Why wouldn't I?" Mrs. Stein shrugged her shoulders. "You know your sister struggled in math."

"My sister? Which one?" Impossible. They were both Valedictorians.

"Rose Marie."

My jaw dropped. Up until the marriage and pregnancy, Rose Marie led a flawless life, too smart to be stupid in math. "I think you have her mixed up with someone else. Rose Marie was Valedictorian."

Mrs. Stein sighed and shook her head. "I didn't say she *failed* math. She struggled, but she went to tutoring every day and caught up."

Could my math brain finally grow, too? "You think that could happen to me?"

"You have to believe in yourself, Sophie."

She was beginning to sound like AJ and Krysta. But she was right.

I shrugged. "That's something I'm working on."

"Keep working on it, dear. You've got a lot going for you. Remember, don't let anything or *anyone* make you think any different." Mrs. Stein looked at me from under her eyelids.

For a minute, I thought *she* was reading *my* mind. Could she have heard about the way Jacob expected me to cheat for him or how Summer bullied me? "Thanks, Mrs. Stein."

"Anytime." She stood up and propped open the door. "If you ever need to talk, my room is open."

"Okay, I'll remember." I didn't need to talk; what I needed was to act, starting with the bully who plagued my passing periods.

I had my eyes on my target. I was ready, charged to take command. Summer spoke to her best friend, Marisela, while leaning against my locker door. I knew she wasn't going to move unless I made her.

This was it. I was either going to get my butt royally kicked or I would finally get some respect. No turning back.

"I think Frankie Salas is going to ask me to the Freshmen Formal dance." Summer sighed and ran her fingers through her hair.

I froze. What was wrong with me? Even the mention of his name made my heart skip. I hunched over, pretending to be fumbling something out of my backpack while I listened to their conversation.

"How do you know?" Marisela looked in Summer's mirror while layering on tons of bright red lipstick.

"The boy can't keep his eyes off me. He's so pathetic." Summer laughed and looked straight at me.

Her eyes danced in mock delight which made me want to punch her.

Of all the girls Frankie could have picked at this school, why Summer? Why couldn't he see she was a self-centered and fake, not to mention stupid? Summer flirted with every guy in school just to get attention.

"Are you going to go with him?" Marisela closed Summer's locker door and slipped her purse over her shoulder.

"I don't know. Lady Gaga's new video comes out on

YouTube that weekend and I don't want to be distracted by a stupid dance." She shrugged, examining her fake fingernails. "I'll have to think about it."

They both sauntered off with heads held high, two cosmetic cretins, laughing and saying hello to every guy within twenty yards.

I was stunned, mortified. I shouldn't have cared one bit. I didn't like Frankie. I liked Jacob. I had to remind myself several times throughout the morning, I liked Jacob. His puppy dog eyes, his small ears and masculine thighs. So, why couldn't I get Frankie Salas out of my mind?

I silently walked into the yearbook room and sunk into my chair.

Lara sat beside me and put a hand on my shoulder. "What's wrong?"

I sighed and listlessly tapped my computer mouse. "Frankie Salas is going to ask Summer Powers to the Freshmen Formal dance."

"Yuk," Lara frowned. "He could pick any girl in this school."

"Yeah, I know."

Last Friday at a football game, Lara had finally told me that last year Summer had started the slut rumors. I knew why. Summer was jealous. Lara had this crazy idea Summer was jealous of me, too.

"Why do you care?" She paused, and then frowned. "You like Jacob, right?"

"Yeah," I hesitated, "I like Jacob." I felt a wave of guilt wash over me. Although she never confessed Jacob was the guy on the bus who called her a slut, I noticed she always seemed reluctant to bring up his name.

She flashed me a mischievous smile and leaned closer. "Can you keep a secret?"

I hesitated. If this was about Jacob, she wouldn't be smiling. "Sure, you can tell me anything, Lara."

Lara opened PhotoShop on her computer and went into a folder marked "Lara's Secrets". I had never seen that folder on the network. She must have had it hidden on her computer.

Lara clicked on a file marked 'Dallin's Twin'. The picture that popped up nearly knocked me out of my seat. Summer looking into the girls' bathroom mirror with her finger shoved up her nose had to be some sort of trick, some awesome, hilarious trick.

My mouth fell open. "How did you get that?"

"I was behind a bathroom stall with my iPhone," Lara whispered. "She didn't even see me."

I couldn't believe I was actually looking at a picture of Summer Powers picking her nose. This was no ordinary pick. This was a good, solid half-an-inch pick. A pick that could rival Dallin's digging any day.

"Have you shared this with anyone?" I asked, knowing that Lara could get in serious trouble for sharing a picture like this. We weren't allowed to use our cell phones in the bathrooms. And something like this would most likely get Lara suspended.

"Mrs. Carr would kill me if I used this in the yearbook. I thought about putting it on Facebook, but I'll be busted for sure. I'm saving it for just the right time." She grinned and rubbed her hands together.

"Any idea when that special moment might be?"

I couldn't wait to see Summer exposed.

When Lara unveiled her masterpiece, I wanted a front row seat.

"No, but when the timing's right." She laughed. "I'm using it."

"Earth to Sophie." AJ stared from over the top of the puke-green, fake leather bench in front of me. "What are you smiling about?"

I couldn't help daydreaming on the bus ride home. I imagined Summer crying and gobs of mascara running down her face as the entire student body laughed and pointed at a life-sized poster of her big dig hanging in the school auditorium.

I let a small chuckle escape. "I was just thinking of something funny that happened today."

Krysta slouched next to me with her knees resting on the

back of AJ's seat. She peered from over her *Cosmo*. "Are you going to clue us in?"

"Sorry." I shook my head. "I promised to keep it secret."

"Aaahhh, you suck!" AJ punched the top of her cushioned seat.

AJ and Krysta both sighed and eyed me intently.

I raised my palms and shrugged. "Sorry, guys."

They pleaded with their best Patches' puppy dog impressions, but I wasn't about to give in.

Luckily, the bus driver distracted them. He took a sharp right and we almost slid onto the floor.

Krysta's *Cosmo* flew out of her grasp and landed across the aisle in Cody Miller's lap. He smiled and handed her the magazine. Krysta shuddered as she retrieved her *Cosmo* with the tips of her fingers and then she shook it a few times as we watched imaginary germs fall to the floor.

She put *Cosmo* in her backpack and scooted closer to me. "How's living with your sister and her boyfriend working out?"

Thank God Krysta changed the subject. My promise to keep Lara's secret was important. I needed Lara to know she could trust me with anything. "It's not. Chad quit his job working for his uncle. Imagine that." I rolled my eyes. "He says he can't be a daddy and be gone all the time."

"He can't be a daddy if he doesn't pay the bills, either." Krysta always made perfect sense.

"I don't think he gets it yet," I complained. "Anyway, he says he wants a job here, but I don't see him looking for one. All he does is eat everything in sight and leave messes all over the house."

"Do you pick up after him?" AJ asked.

I glared at AJ. "What do you think? He left his rotten underwear on my bathroom floor this morning. I stepped on them with my bare feet."

"Eeeewww." AJ and Krysta said in unison as they shrunk back in disgust.

I crinkled my nose. "I banged on their door and Rose Marie picked them up. You should see how she babies him." I used to be jealous of Rose Marie, but now it made me sick to see that my perfect sister had sunk so low. She could have been studying medicine at Harvard, but instead she was playing janitor to her dung pile boyfriend.

"Puke." AJ stuck her finger in her mouth and made the universal sign of vomit.

"Yeah," I laughed. "My dad said she won't have time to baby him when the *real* baby comes."

Krysta's brow drew a frown. "I'm surprised your dad hasn't kicked them out yet."

I had been dreaming of seeing their backsides ever since they showed up at our door. "My mom won't let him," I sighed. "Se's starting to really get on my nerves, too."

Krysta's eyes widened. "Why?"

"Ever since Rose Marie came home, it's been Rose Marie this or baby that. You should see the money my mom has spent. She already bought a crib and they're painting dinosaurs all over *my* bedroom. They didn't even ask me."

"I don't think it's *your* bedroom anymore, Sophie," Krysta reminded me.

AJ leaned forward and narrowed her gaze. "You sound jealous, Sophie."

"Jealous?" I snapped, ready to tear off AJ's head. "How could you say that, AJ? Why would you think I'm jealous? They've just thrown their lives down the toilet and you think I'm jealous?"

AJ leaned back and shrugged. "You don't have to get so defensive. It was just an observation."

"I'm not jealous." The pitch in my voice rose. "It just pisses me off that Rose Marie screws up and she gets the royal treatment. Mom wouldn't do that for me."

"Yep." AJ waved her finger at me. "That's jealousy."

"You know, AJ," I folded my arms across my chest. "I'm really getting sick of your negative attitude." I had enough to deal with at home, being pushed aside by my family, forced to give up my room, because Rose Marie screwed up her life. I didn't need crap from my best friend, too.

"What?" Her mouth gaped. AJ actually had the nerve to act surprised.

"A friend comes to you with her problems and all you do is bring her down."

AJ had been on a negative trip lately and I was tired of her PMS.

"Look." AJ waved her head, pretending she was tough. "Don't get all pissy because your family life sucks. Welcome to my world. I deal with this kind of crap all the time."

"Okay, enough." Krysta put out both hands and glared at me before throwing visual daggers at AJ. "This is getting us nowhere." She looked out the window as the bus slowed. "This is your stop. Now you two kiss and make up."

We both rolled our eyes and stubbornly crossed our arms over our chests.

"Remember, we're all best friends." Krysta smiled and punched me playfully on the shoulder. "Sophie, try not to kill your sister's sweetie pie."

I felt like slapping her for that comment, but I stuck out my tongue instead. She had a way of always finding humor in even the worst situations.

Chapter Nine

How was I going to finish my homework with that noise in the next room? I banged on the wall, my third attempt to get Chad to turn down the volume on his video game. I couldn't believe this moron was about to be a dad.

As expected, Chad didn't respond.

I stormed downstairs just as my mom and Rose Marie came through the door. Rose Marie had her arm around Mom's shoulder when they walked into the living room with tons of baby store bags, compliments of my parents' bank account no doubt.

I couldn't deny it. I was annoyed and I had a right to be. Rose Marie was kissing up to Mom, so she and that bum upstairs could keep getting free rent.

Rose Marie whispered something into Mom's ear and they both started laughing.

This nonsense had to stop.

"Would someone tell that jerk upstairs to turn down his video game?"

Rose Marie's smile diminished, replaced by a cold glare. "What's your problem?"

"Some of us have homework to do, Rose Marie. Some of us want to make something of ourselves." An unnecessary jab, but I was beyond irritated.

"What in the hell is that supposed to mean?" Rose Marie threw back her shoulders and stormed up to me.

"Girls, no fighting, please." Mom got in between us and turned to me. "Sophie, you shouldn't speak to Rose Marie in her condition."

"I didn't know *stupid* was a condition."

"That's enough, young lady." Mom's voice hardened. "Show some respect."

"I'll show respect when *he* does." I pointed toward the stairs. "I've been trying to get him to turn down his game for over an hour. How did he afford a video game, anyway? I thought he lost his job."

Rose Marie crossed her arms over her chest. "How we spend our money is none of your business."

"What money?" I snapped. "You don't have any."

"Chad just got his last paycheck." Rose Marie tried to look me in the eyes, but she quickly averted her gaze.

I could tell defending Chad was difficult, even for someone as blind as my sister.

I laughed. "So he buys a Play Station?"

"For your information, the Play Station is for the baby, too." Her shaky voice lowered, sounding less convincing. "It plays DVDs, you know."

"Of course." I threw my hands in the air. "A Play Station will be first on my list when I have a baby. Maybe he should save up for the baby, or here's a concept, maybe he should be out looking for another job."

"He has his applications in." Rose Marie looked at the floor. "He's just waiting for call backs."

"Yeah, right." How did Rose Marie expect me to buy this crap when she didn't even look convinced? Chad didn't want a job—he liked being a bum. He was using this baby as an excuse to stay home and play video games.

"Sophie," my mom pleaded. "They've already heard this from your father. This isn't your concern."

"Not my concern?" I couldn't contain the bitterness in my voice. "I gave up *my* room. She wakes *me* up all night with her bladder. I can't even do my homework in peace! And this is none of *my* concern!"

Mom faced my sister and gently stroked her cheek. "Rose Marie, sweetie, go upstairs and tell Chad to turn it down." Mom turned to me, her frown full of disappointment.

I hated letting my mom down more than anything, which

only aggravated me more. This was all Rose Marie's fault. "Yeah, why don't you do that?" I yelled to my retreating sister. "That will just solve everything. While you're at it, why don't you tell him to go find another job?"

"You sound just like Dad." My sister yelled at me as she climbed the stairs. "I don't need to be nagged by two of you."

I ran to the foot of the stairwell and shouted. "I can't believe two immature idiots are bringing a baby into this world."

Rose Marie quickly backtracked down the steps and raised her open palm. "If Mom wasn't here, I'd slap you."

"Go ahead," I warned. "I'd slap back if I knew it was a cure for stupid. When are you going to wake up? He's a bum, a loser. You and the baby will always have to borrow from Mom and Dad."

Rose Marie's angry expression froze, her widening eyes showed amusement as she revealed a broad smile. "Sounds to me like you're jealous."

"Yeah, right." I looked away. I was annoyed, not jealous. I did *not* want her to misinterpret one for the other.

"You won't be the baby anymore," she mocked. "You're not going to get all the attention."

"Girls, you're giving me a headache. Enough!" Mom placed both hands on her forehead.

I was just getting warmed up. I had a lot more to say to Rose Marie. If it hadn't been for the tears I could see forming in my mom's eyes, I wouldn't have backed down.

My sister turned on her heel and ran into *my* bedroom. I stormed up to my new room and slammed the door while contemplating revenge against the idiots who were ruining my life and driving a wedge between me and my mom. I needed to get my frustration off my chest. I opened my cell and dialed Krysta.

The call went straight to her voice mail. My only other option was AJ. Even though I was mad at her, I had to vent to someone.

I dialed her number.

"What's up?" AJ sounded annoyed. I knew she knew it was me calling because all of the phones in her house had Caller ID.

"Hey," I blurted. "Chad's a butt munch."

"So tell me something I don't know," AJ retorted.

I was so furious, complaints started spewing from my mouth. "He hasn't even bothered to look for a job. He played video games all day while my mom spent money on his baby."

"Pathetic."

AJ's reaction wasn't what I expected. She almost sounded bored. Probably just my imagination.

"Yeah," I sighed in frustration. "What a bum."

"Sounds like another guy I know." AJ's tone was definitely on the rude side.

"Let me guess," I said sarcastically. I knew where she was going with this. "You're talking about Jacob."

"You're as blind as your sister when it comes to guys." AJ paused before groaning. "Just think, this could be you and Jacob in four years."

"That's not funny."

"I'm not trying to be funny," AJ snapped. "Your sister doesn't have taste in guys and neither do you. You're both too stupid to admit it."

"I gotta go." Her PMS had pushed my temper past the limit.

"Fine," She fumed. "Don't listen to a friend."

I yelled into the phone. "Friends don't call each other stupid."

"Whatever." AJ's sarcastic tone was the same way she spoke to her mother. "Throw your life away then."

"I'm not throwing my life away." I could feel my throat tighten as I tried to hold back tears. "I haven't even gotten Jacob to notice me."

"I don't understand." AJ growled, set down the phone, swore loudly and then picked the receiver up again. "You want to be cool so Jacob will like you, Sophie. Cheating for him isn't cool. Try not letting him walk all over you, that's cool."

"Look, I gotta go." An aggravated laugh escaped my lips. "Thanks for cheering me up." I threw my cell across the room, hoping it would make me feel better. It didn't.

How could she say such things about Jacob? Just because he liked video games, just because he wasn't great at sports and didn't like to read, didn't mean he'd end up like Chad. Besides, he *had* to be the one. He was fat once, just like me. He was the only guy who'd understand me. Not like Frankie. That boy was born perfect. He'd never take a former fatty seriously. Even if he really did like me, one day he'd wake up and remember the former me. He'd find my seventh grade yearbook picture and he'd move on to a new groupie.

I fell onto my bed and closed my eyes. Maybe after our novel unit was over, Jacob would pay more attention in class. Maybe if I could prove to him I was cool, he might even forget his video game and pay more attention to me. Because that's what I wanted, right? A nagging little voice in the back of my conscience whispered AJ was right, but I didn't want to listen. I was destined for Jacob, because...well, I just wasn't good enough for Frankie.

Chapter Ten

The Scarlet letter—would the torture ever end? I thought Huck Finn was bad. The only amusing part in reading this new novel was when Cody Miller taped a big fat crimson "B" on Dallin's back.

Dallin didn't even notice. He was too busy picking his nose.

We had finished Huck a few weeks ago and now we were starting chapter four of this interminable book. We'd had a couple of pop quizzes but so far Jacob still hadn't graded a single one of my tests. We'd passed them to the left, to the right, and backward, but never forward. Jacob had lucked out two more times since I'd first graded his test. I didn't like cheating for him, but I had no choice if I was to follow through with my plan.

The ironic thing was this whole plan to see if Jacob cared for me was starting not to matter. I had intentionally missed several questions on the last three tests. After I'd brought home a C on my progress report, I decided enough was enough.

Although I was hesitant to admit it, the disappointed look on my parents' faces wasn't the only reason I chose to ace all future tests. Frankie had graded my tests twice. He must have thought I was stupid at math and in English. Not that his opinion mattered that much.

I had just finished answering the last question on my quiz when Dallin told us to pass our tests to the back.

Jacob handed me his test and his pen, giving me a sly wink. He didn't even say anything. It was like he expected, no demanded, and 'A' from me now. Suddenly, his cute ears weren't so cute anymore. They were too small and starting to annoy me.

I reluctantly took his test and his pen.

I remembered AJ's harsh words from the argument we had on the phone. "Cheating for him isn't cool. Try not letting him walk all over you, that's cool."

I had been thinking about those words all day—while I was ignoring her on the bus ride to school, while she was ignoring me in algebra, while we both ignored each other at lunch. I thought of little else. AJ could be a real pain in the butt sometimes, but she was my best friend. Was I wrong to completely ignore her advice?

Mr. Dallin perched himself on top of a wobbly stool, ready to call out answers.

Without a second to spare, I reacted quickly. "Here, I don't need this." I handed Jacob his pen and took out my own pink pen—bright enough to emphasize any glaring mistakes.

Jacob's eyes widened, and then narrowed, as he snatched his pen from my hand.

I smiled back while keeping my cool. I could hear Frankie's muffled laughter beside me.

By the time grading was over, Jacob had a D minus and I had some of my self-respect back. Jacob was pissed, but to quote Frankie, "He'll get over it."

I left a little note on his test, too. "Jacob, put away the video game and study harder." I thought I saw steam shooting out of his puny ears when he was reading it.

"I hope this game doesn't run into overtime." Lara leaned her chin on the body of her camera, while her knee settled against her monopod. She looked the part of a professional photographer. She even wore a photo vest.

"Why?" I wondered. "It's just getting fun."

We were in the middle of the fourth quarter. Frankie had just scored a touchdown and the crowd was pumped. I got lots of great shots of screaming fans. Lara caught Frankie just as he made the touchdown. I would get Lara to send me a copy of that picture later.

"Yeah," she looked up and frowned. "But we're losing the good light and this camera doesn't take the best night shots." Lara reached into her bag and retrieved some ancient relic that looked like a camera. "My K-1000 won't fail me."

"How do you use it?"

She smiled. "It runs on this weird fuel called film." She grabbed a roll of film out of her bag and started to manually wind the film into the camera. It looked complicated.

"I'll stick with the digital camera." I patted my Digital Rebel, my baby, actually Mrs. Carr's baby. She practically made me sign in blood that I would protect it with my life.

"Stay here while I go to the fifty yard line." Lara gathered up her gear and started to walk away.

"But what if someone makes a touchdown?" I felt uneasy by myself. I was still new at this.

"Then take the shot," she called back.

"What if I mess up?" I squeezed the leather straps on my camera, trying to calm my fears. Lara had never left me alone to take pictures. What if something bad happened?

Lara walked toward me and put her hand on my shoulder. "There will be plenty more touchdowns. You have no confidence in yourself, Sophie. Your pictures have been coming out great. You're a natural."

I hadn't received a compliment like that in a long time. My chest swelled up with pride. "Really? A natural?"

"I don't lie." As Lara headed back to the fifty-yard-line, she called over her shoulder. "Not when it comes to photography. Remember, follow the ball, not the players, if you want the best shot. Believe me, wherever that ball goes, they'll go too."

"Gotcha," I yelled.

I looked through the LCD, poised, focused, ready. I was going to get that picture of Frankie Salas, or whoever, making the touchdown. It was going to be so awesome, Mrs. Carr would want to put it on the cover of the yearbook.

I heard someone yell, "Look out," but I was in the photo zone, too focused to pay attention to anything else but that pigskin.

Hey, where'd it go? I had the ball in focus just a minute ago.

Thunk.

"Sophie, you okay?"

Was this a dream? I opened my eyes to the sight of Frankie standing over me. Although my vision was a bit fuzzy, I could still make out his beautiful tanned skin and I couldn't mistake his deep voice. I tried to sit up, when I was suddenly struck by a dizzying sensation. The room shook and I fell back against soft padding.

"W...what happened?" The entire left side of my face felt like it had been run over by a steamroller.

"Don't try to get up." Frankie sat by my side and put an icepack on my left eye. "You got hit by the ball."

"Did I? I didn't remember. I recalled looking for the ball through my view finder. Oh, God. The camera! Mrs. Carr would have my head on a platter. "Is the camera okay?"

Frankie laughed. "Yeah, it's okay."

"I've got it, Sophie." I heard Lara in the background, but I couldn't see her.

"Where am I?" I touched a hand to my sore cheek and breathed deeply. Wherever I was, the place reeked of musty body odor.

"Lying on a cot at the fieldhouse." Frankie grabbed my hand and placed it over the icepack.

As dizzy as I was, I still felt the electrifying shock of his skin against mine. "Who won?"

"We're in a time-out." He slowly withdrew his hand.

I immediately missed his touch. "I...it's not because of me, is it?"

"Yep." Frankie smiled sympathetically.

I wanted to crawl inside a hole and not come out for at least fifty years. "I feel so stupid. How long have I been out?"

"Only a few minutes." A masculine voice came from the other side of my cot.

I tried to turn my head to make out his figure, but my neck was too stiff.

"Is she going to be okay, Schotts?" Frankie asked.

I recognized that name. Schotts was the team medic. Now

I felt really dumb. He should have been with the team, not me.

"Yeah," Schotts said. "Her mom still needs to get her an x-ray."

Frankie looked down at me, and even through my blurry vision, I could see pity pooling in his huge brown eyes. "Guess that means you'll miss the rest of the game."

My heart felt like it was sinking into a hole, covered by the sludge of humiliation and self-loathing. I didn't want Frankie's pity. Why did this have to happen to me?

The deep sound of a masculine voice clearing his throat reminded me Frankie wasn't the only person in the room sharing in my shame.

"Listen, I have to get back. Robbins twisted his ankle before Sophie was knocked out." Schotts squeezed my shoulder. "You mom's coming to pick you up." He walked toward the door and nodded to the corner of the room. "Are you staying with her until her mom comes?"

"Of course." I heard Lara's clipped voice as she crossed over to my cot.

"Come on, Frankie. You need to get back in the game," Schotts said.

Frankie stood. "See ya later, Sophie."

"Thanks, Frankie." I called, as his blurred figure moved out of vision.

"No problem." His voice was still near. "Frankie?" My dizziness was fading, so I sat up halfway, trying to catch him before he left.

"Yeah?"

Through my one good eye, I could see his dark form standing by the open door. "Good luck tonight." I tried to smile, but my face hurt too much.

He looked at his feet, and then turned his gaze outside. "Thanks."

I sighed as I heard the door shut. Frankie couldn't even look at me. What did he think of me? Probably what everybody else thought. I was never going to live this one down. I would have rather been labeled the fat dork than the village idiot.

"Lara," I sank into the cot. "I feel like such a loser."

She sighed. "I think the whole thing is romantic."

"What are you talking about?" I turned on my side to face her. The girl was crazy.

"Frankie has the hots for you. He was the first one to get to you when you were hit."

The giddy sensation in my head was returning, but I didn't think it was because of the hit. "You're lying."

"No, I'm not," she nudged my ribs. "Coach got mad at him for leaving the field, but he carried you here."

I felt chills rush through my body. Frankie carried me! Why would he want to do that? "Okay, now you're really full of it."

"Think what you want," she shrugged, "but I'm sure you'll hear it around school on Monday."

"Oh, God, I'm going to be the laughing stock of Greenwood. I feel like crap and I bet I look like crap, too."

Lara looked at me and cringed. Her expression confirmed my worst fears.

She carefully removed my icepack. "It's mostly your eye."

"Get me a mirror."

Lara squeezed my hand. "I don't think you want me to do that."

I squeezed back. "Please. I need to know if I look as stupid as I feel."

Lara grabbed a compact out of her purse. She cringed as she slowly handed me the mirror.

The reflection took me by complete surprise.

My right side looked perfectly normal. The left side of my face looked like a reddened, five hundred pound troll.

Lara drew back, biting her lip. "Not bad," I said.

She slowly exhaled. "I'm glad you're taking this well."

"Of course." I tried to smile, although the action hurt my eye which felt like it was caving in on itself. "All I need to do is find another giant pink ogre who thinks this face isn't ugly."

Lara threw back her head and laughed. "I'm sorry, Sophie. I know this isn't funny but I'm glad you can still make jokes."

"At least now Jacob might notice me."

That comment didn't seem to sit well with Lara. She glared and then shook her head. "You shouldn't worry what someone like Jacob Flushman thinks of you."

I leaned on my elbows and sharpened my gaze. "What do you know about him I don't know?"

Lara put down her head and turned from me. "Listen, there's something you should know about Jacob."

"Can you help me? I'm looking for Sophie, Sophie Sinora."

I recognized the sound of my mom's panicked voice.

"I'm here, Mom." I called, and instantly regretted the sound of my own voice as it echoed in my throbbing skull.

"Oh, thank goodness. Are you okay, sweetie?" Mom rushed up to me, then jumped back when she looked at my face. "Oh, my baby!"

"Try to calm down, dear. She'll be okay." My dad stood behind my mom, placing his hands on her shoulders. He shook his head and winked at me.

I understood Dad's message. Mom panicked easily whenever my sisters or I got hurt. Trying to ignore the pain in my face, I put up a front to calm my mom. "It's not as bad as it looks, Mom."

Mom's jaw twitched and she placed her hands on her hips. "We're going to the hospital."

"See you later, Sophie. I've got your camera." Lara waved as she walked out the door.

I hardly noticed she was leaving. Lara and I left some unspoken words. I feared what she was trying to tell me and was somewhat relieved my parents showed up. Was I being selfish not to want to hear it? Lara had proven to be a good friend and mentor. If it weren't for her, I wouldn't have found an interest in photography. With the exception of the one incident tonight, I thought I had actually found something I was good at. Lara taught me how to make yearbook pages, develop pictures, and she listened to me complain about Summer.

What had Jacob ever done for me?

Chapter Eleven

Humiliation was exhausting. I had hoped my parents would drive me home, so I could crawl under my covers and die. Instead, they took me to the emergency room. My dad stayed at the hospital only long enough to convince my mom I wasn't going to fall down with uncontrollable seizures and foam at the mouth. He had a business trip the next morning, so I didn't mind when he called Chad for a ride. My mom and I waited five hours for the doctor to tell us I had a black eye and a bump on my head.

As we walked to the car, I opened my cell phone to check the time. One fifteen a.m. and three texts, plus a missed message, all from AJ. I remembered I had turned off the volume on my phone, so I wouldn't be distracted during the game. A whole lot of good that did.

The texts were from AJ telling me to call her. I played to her message. AJ sounded like she was clearing her throat. After a long pause, she finally spoke. "Hey, it's AJ. Look, I'm sorry I've been such a butthead lately. I've been having a really bad time with my mother and I'm taking it out on everyone else.

"I know you like Jacob. I know you think I hate him, but the truth is I don't want to see you getting hurt. He's not the one for you, Sophie. You don't need to be gifted to see his future is going nowhere. And I think you know it, too."

I could hear AJ take a deep breath before continuing. "There's something else, too. Something I haven't told anyone...I'm not mad at you because you're learning how to control your gift. The truth is I'm getting better at it, too. It scares me, Sophie. I don't want us to get better. I might not want to know what's going to happen next. What if it's bad? What if I'm going to die tomorrow? Or someone I care about?"

"Anyway, call me back when you get this message. I'll be in my room. I'm grounded this weekend, or at least until tomorrow."

My shoulders slumped against the car door as I thought about AJ's confession. I was not alone.

Her gift was increasing, too. What if Krysta's powers were growing stronger? More ghostly visits? I shivered at the thought. At least my life wasn't that bad.

Well, not until Monday anyway, when I'd have to face the entire student body of Greenwood Junior High. Everyone would have heard about the football incident. Even if I wanted to deny it, I couldn't, not with this messed-up face. I tried not to think about the humiliation I'd suffer. My head hurt enough.

What if Frankie thought I was a dork?

"Are you going to get in?"

My mom's voice interrupted my rambling thoughts. She was already inside the car, revving the engine.

I climbed inside and lowered my seat. The pain in my head was throbbing, and the medication the doctor gave me made me sleepy. I wanted to rest my eyes on the way home.

"You're not going to sleep in the car, are you? I'm not dragging you out when we get home." Mom turned on the A/C full blast.

She knew I hated a freezing fan blowing in my face. Reluctantly, I positioned my seat back up, put on my seatbelt, and switched the A/C to low.

"Good." Mom focused on the road and clutched the steering wheel so hard her knuckles turned white. "I want to talk to you anyway."

Sensing a lecture coming on, I rubbed my throbbing temples.

"I know things have been rough this week with your sister and all the drama." Mom emphasized 'drama' and rolled her head.

Was she trying to make me feel like an idiot for fighting with Rose Marie? Afraid to get into an argument with my mom,

I said nothing. It was late, I was tired, and my face hurt.

Mom inhaled deeply, and then slowly breathed out. "I just wanted to say...I'm sorry."

Huh? Why was she sorry? She didn't tell Rose Marie to date a loser and have a baby. My parents were great role models. They taught all of us responsibility. She couldn't help it my sister was stupid and selfish.

"What I mean to say is I'm sorry this has to hit you right now. I know you're right about Chad. I don't think I've ever told you this, but I was married to someone else when I met your dad."

My jaw dropped. Not *my* mom. She was perfect.

"No, no, it's not what you think," she continued. "We were already separated and I had filed for a divorce." Mom moaned and shook her head. "That was the biggest mistake of my life. His name was Brandon. We were married for six months. I didn't listen to my friends when they told me he wasn't the right man. In fact, I lost my best friend over him."

She paused, sounding choked up. Was my mom crying? Mom turned her head, looking out the side window. "Anyway," Mom turned back, the visible lines around her heavy, saddened eyes revealing her pain. "What I'm trying to say is I understand why you are so against Chad. Truth is I can't stand the boy either; however, the more we fight Rose Marie, the more she'll think she has to defend him. I know it sounds stupid, but love is blind sometimes."

No, I didn't think it sounded stupid. I was beginning to understand exactly how blind love was.

Mom tapped on the steering wheel and clenched her jaw. "I know you want the best for your sister. I do, too. It breaks my heart to see her throw her life away over him...and now their poor baby." Mom's voice cracked as a tear slid down her cheek. "But I need you to do something for me, Sophie, and for your sister, too. She'll come around. I know she will. I *hope* she will. You just need to let her make this mistake, and when she's tired of him, we can be there to support her. She won't resent you if you leave the decision to her. If we force them apart, I'm afraid she'll never get the chance to learn on her own."

I thought about what Mom had just said and I knew

exactly where she was coming from. Even scarier, I knew exactly where Rose Marie was coming from. I had been judging Rose Marie for making the same mistake I was making. I wondered if my sister had lost any friends over Chad. Well, I wasn't about to let some slouch with fat thighs get in between me and my friends.

"Mom," I asked, "whatever happened to your best friend?"

"I don't know," she sighed. "We lost touch."

How sad. I couldn't imagine a lifetime without AJ and Krysta.

"Didn't you try to find her after your divorce?"

"No," she smiled bitterly. "I guess there was too much resentment there."

I just couldn't understand it. How could Mom have thrown away her friendship over a guy? "But she was your best friend."

"I know," her voice cracked again, "but things change."

Well, I wasn't about to let things change with my friends. I wanted to call back AJ immediately, but her mom would have been furious if I woke the family and I couldn't IM her because AJ didn't have a computer in her room. What I had to say had to wait until the morning. I silently prayed I'd never lose AJ's friendship.

I woke to the theme song of Dora the Explorer, the latest ringtone download AJ had snuck on my phone. AJ's mom needed to buy her a phone, so she'd leave mine alone. I flipped open the phone— 9:30 a.m., incoming call from AJ.

As soon as I hit 'talk', AJ started rambling.

"Hey. I wanted to call you earlier. I waited as long as I could. I heard about what happened last night." She inhaled quickly. "You okay?"

"Oh, God," I moaned and gently explored the swelling on my sore face, "I'm sure the whole world knows by now."

"Yeah," she said softly.

I shook my head and laughed. "You should have told me this was going to happen."

"Very funny." AJ sighed.

I knew what she was thinking. I didn't even have to read her mind. She felt awkward about the message she left on my phone last night. Emotions were difficult for AJ, which made last night's message so special. It took a lot of guts for her to confess her fears, and even more courage for her to apologize.

I sensed she was waiting for me to start. "I got your message."

"Oh, it was nothing," She murmured quickly.

But I knew better. "Thanks."

"No problem."

An awkward silence followed. I knew it was my turn to apologize. "AJ?"

"Yeah?"

"Sorry I've been an idiot." I rubbed my brow, trying to think of the right words. "He's the wrong guy for me. I knew it all along."

"It's okay. We all make mistakes."

I fell back on my pillow and stared at the ceiling. "I don't want to pay for it like my sister."

"Good," she huffed, "I don't want to see you end up like her."

"Believe me." I shuddered at the thought. "I won't." The only way to ensure I didn't end up like Rose Marie was to stay away from losers. I decided it was time to completely erase Jacob from my memory. The first step would be to change the subject. AJ's powers were increasing and I was dying to know if I'd be a dateless dork forever. "So how good are you at it?"

"Getting better every day."

I hesitated, wondering if I was ready for the answer. "Am I going to find the right guy?"

"You'll find lots of right guys, Sophie." AJ sighed as she spoke. "That's not my gift talking. Don't you think it's too soon for you to find *the one*?"

"Yeah, you're right again. Maybe I should just focus on the near future." I closed my eyes. Frankie Salas' penetrating eyes were the first thing to pop into my mind. After the football incident, he would never ask me out.

"That's a good idea."

I sensed some hope in AJ's voice.

What good could happen after last night? I still had a small flicker of hope. "So I wonder if someone will ask me to Freshmen Formal."

"Frankie Salas."

My eyes shot open. Had I just heard her correctly? She must have been joking. "You're full of it."

"Okay," her pitch rose, "whatever."

I couldn't believe what I was hearing. Frankie Salas and me? Impossible. "Did you *see* this or are you guessing?"

"I *saw* it."

The pain in my face was worsening. I closed my eyes and tried not to focus on the throbbing pressure. "If you're lying, I'm going to kick your butt." All this time he'd been flirting with me, could he have really liked me?

"I'm not lying." AJ sounded serious. "Humph." I wasn't convinced.

"What?" She laughed. "I thought you would be happy. He's the hottest guy in school."

Exactly. So why would he want to ask me out? I shook my head in disbelief. Frankie had to have a reason. Then I remembered, he was supposed to ask Summer to the dance. "I heard Summer saying he was going to ask her."

"Eeewww," AJ shrieked into the phone. "Are you sure?"

"I heard her talking about it. She said she'd probably turn him down for a Gaga video."

"Summer talks a lot of smack."

"Maybe, but hottie or not, do I want to go out with Summer's reject?" I couldn't believe this was me talking. Frankie was no reject, but I knew Summer would rub my face in it if I went with him after she turned him down.

"You'd be stupid not to."

I wanted to change the subject. All this talk about Summer and Frankie made my head hurt worse. "What else have you seen?"

"You really want to know?"

"Yeah." I lied. In some ways, I *really* wanted to know. In other ways, AJ's gift scared me to my toes. But I doubted my future held anything as bad as the football incident.

"No bad stuff yet, thank God. But," she squealed, "I did see you with your new nephews."

"Nephews?" This was bad news. *Really* bad news. "You mean my stupid sister is going to breed with that worthless dungheap again?"

"No. I mean she's having twins."

"Holy crap!" I thought my life was bad. I would have picked a black eye over twins any day.

"Yeah. Your sister's gonna be hatin' life." AJ wasn't kidding.

"How long is Chad in her future?" I couldn't imagine him hanging around with two babies to take care of and I couldn't imagine Rose Marie putting up with *three* babies.

"I give them less than a week."

"Excellent!" I was too happy. "When Mom and I came home last night, Chad was passed out on the living room floor. He ate all the cookie dough ice cream. I didn't even get a taste. He eats more than my pregnant sister."

"Those twins will be terrors, but you're going to be a great aunt."

"You really think so?" I tried to imagine my new nephews. I hoped they had Rose Marie's eyes and ambition.

"I know so," AJ reassured.

I smiled at the thought of two little boys dressed in identical clothes. I'd have to get a job just to make sure they had cool wardrobes.

I nearly jumped from my bed at the knocking on my door. My sore head wasn't ready for any sudden noises. "Listen, someone is at my door. See if your mom will let you off house arrest tonight."

"I'm already off."

"Ooooh, you're good," I purred.

"I know," AJ bragged.

"I gotta go."

"Later."

I closed my phone and heaved my tired body out of bed. If AJ hadn't woken me up, I would've slept the whole day. My feet felt like bricks. I slowly trudged toward the door. The nagging knock continued.

I opened to see my sister, looking not at me but at the left side of my face. She was probably enjoying the view.

"What's up?" I leaned my aching head against the doorframe. I wasn't in the mood to deal with Rose Marie.

She smiled smugly and folded her arms across her chest. "You look like crap."

Enough of her attitude! I tried to slam the door in her face, but she blocked it with her elbow.

"Don't shut the door. I didn't mean it to be rude." Rose Marie pushed her way into my room. "Mom told me what happened last night and I wanted to see if I could offer my services."

"What services?" This was so humiliating. What did she have to offer me other than teasing for the rest of my life?

"I didn't win runner up in Greenwood County Miss Glamour or get Homecoming Queen for nothing." She grabbed my chin and peered closer at my face. "I'm pretty sure I can cover up that bruise."

"Really?" Was Rose Marie here to be nice? Had she called a truce? I hoped so. I was tired of fighting, and besides, I knew my face needed major help. I hadn't looked in the mirror since sitting in the ER last night. I didn't expect to look any better today, especially since the swelling felt worse.

"Sure." Rose Marie walked to my vanity table and unloaded the contents of her cosmetic bag.

"Thanks." I sat in the chair in front of my vanity and when I saw my reflection in the mirror, I screamed.

"Hey," she quipped, "I didn't say this would be easy." She grabbed my knees and turned me around. "Now, I don't want you looking until I am completely finished. An artist must work undisturbed."

After only a few minutes of Rose Marie smearing and brushing cosmetics on my sore face, she was finished.

"Are you ready to look?" She turned me toward the full-length mirror. .

I couldn't believe what I saw. Not only was the bruise concealed, but the way she did my makeup made me look kind of pretty. "I...I can barely notice."

"Not bad, huh?" Rose Marie rested her hand on my shoulder. "You should let me show you how to do your makeup. You've got nice eyes and I know how to bring out your shade of green."

"Really, you'd show me how to look pretty?" Not only would I show up Monday without a bruise, but I'd look better than ever. Rose Marie's artistry wasn't too overdone, like Summer or Marisela, who caked on all the shades of the rainbow. Although Rose Marie picked natural tones for the eye shadow, blush and lipstick, the girl staring back looked more like a movie star than a fat dork.

"Of course," she said. "Like Lu Lu did for me when I was your age."

"Thanks, Rose Marie." Before she could react, I grabbed her in a tight embrace.

"That's what sisters are for." She patted my head before she pulled away and walked toward the bed. Rose Marie sank onto the mattress and covered her bulging stomach with a pillow.

For the first time, I noticed the dark circles under her eyes and her sloppy sweat pants. Rose Marie had always looked perfect. Why didn't she do for herself what she'd done for me? Her brow was creased into a frown and the corners of her lips were turned down.

I couldn't help but feel something was wrong with my sister. "Rose Marie?"

"Yeah." Her head was down now, as she focused on the pillow in her lap.

"I'm sorry we've been fighting."

"Me, too." She looked up and managed a half smile.

I sat beside her and squeezed her hand. "When the babies come, I promise to be a good aunt."

"Babies?" She jerked back, knocking the pillow to the ground. "Hold on, we're only having one." "Oh, I'm sorry." I bit my bottom lip. "I thought you said you were having twins." Nice save. I couldn't exactly explain my psychic best friend had already predicted two kids.

"Do I look that fat?" Rose Marie ran a hand over her stomach and sat up straight.

"No." But the truth was, she did. Lately, she'd been wearing Chad's sweats and T-shirts. I figured it was to cover her belly, but even under bulky clothes, I could see her round stomach. She resumed her slouch, hand resting on her stomach.

"I haven't even been to the doctor yet." "You haven't?"

"No, Mom is taking me on Monday." Smiling, her eyes lingered on her belly. "I get to hear the baby's heartbeat."

"What if there are two babies?" My gaze traveled to her protruding stomach. I looked for a sign but I couldn't tell. I didn't know what I was expecting. Two heads were not about to pop out and say 'hello'. "Will you hear two heartbeats?"

Rose Marie stopped smiling and tilted her head. "You're not very funny."

I grimaced and shrugged. "I was just wondering."

"I guess so, but trust me, twins don't run in either of our families. We're *not* having twins."

Rose Marie sounded more like she was trying to convince herself than me. Did she have doubts? I focused on her thoughts.

She's right, I'm too fat for three months.

Uh-oh, Rose Marie was in for a big shock. "Well, it's always good to be prepared."

"Sophie," Rose Marie sighed and shook her head. "I'm not even prepared for this one."

Chapter Twelve

Even though I had worried all morning about other kids teasing me about the football incident, I couldn't wait to see if Frankie noticed my new look. My hair was shorter, layered and highlighted with gold and auburn accents. I was also sporting new clothes. The swelling on my face had gone down. All that was left was a barely visible black eye, thanks to Rose Marie and her cosmetic skills.

I felt all eyes upon me as I followed AJ onto the bus. My pace slowed as I inwardly grimaced. Were they staring at me because I looked hot or did they just want to get a peek at the football geek? I couldn't help it. I *had* to know. I willed myself to listen to a few thoughts.

Cute hair.

Wow! She's hot.

Confidence restored, my stride increased when I saw Krysta at the back of the bus. She was waiting, saving the usual seats in front of her for AJ and a spot beside her for me. Her eyelids looked heavy, her makeup a little smudged.

"Hey." AJ threw her backpack on her seat and flung herself onto the bench. "What happened to you this weekend? We tried calling you. You didn't answer Sophie's texts."

Krysta rubbed her temples and looked through half open eyes. "I was visiting old friends."

"Live ones?" I whispered.

I could see the veins pop in Krysta's neck.

She looked at me and shook her head. "Nope."

"Fun," AJ teased. "All we did was go to the mall."

I gently squeezed her shoulder. "Want to talk about it?"

"Let's just say." Krysta tipped back her head and sank into her seat. "You're not the only one with increasing powers."

AJ hung over the front seat, coming within inches of our personal space. "I guess it's happening to all of us."

Krysta's eyes bulged. "You, too, AJ?"

"Yeah." AJ shrugged. "But I don't understand why now."

I had a theory, but it still didn't make any sense. "Maybe it has something to do with puberty."

AJ rolled her eyes. "Yeah, like our gifts bloom with our budding breasts." She pointed to Krysta's backpack with a magazine poking out of the top of the bag. "Does your *Cosmo* mention anything about bra size and supernatural powers?"

"I'll have to check on that." Krysta turned to me and smiled. "By the way, how are you feeling?"

I covered my eyes and sank into my seat. "You heard?"

"I saw it."

Just great! I wonder how many other people were watching. "I'm so embarrassed."

"Things happen." Krysta patted my shoulder and squinted her eyes. "But I can't even tell you were hit. You look really pretty today."

"Thanks." I cupped my hands under my chin and batted my eyes. "Rose Marie did my makeup."

"So you two are talking now?" Krysta grabbed my hand and placed it on her neck.

"Yeah. We're better." I took the hint and rubbed the knots on Krysta's neck and back.

"She still with the loser?" Krysta rolled her head back and closed her eyes.

"Yeah." I smirked. "But AJ says not for long."

"Nice," Krysta softly spoke while keeping her eyes closed. "Not to change the subject, but how are things going with Jacob?"

"You didn't change the subject." I rubbed harder then let go. Jacob was still a sore subject with me. Not because I was offended anymore, but because I felt stupid for ever liking him. "Jacob's a loser, just like Chad. I've ditched that crush."

"Excellent." Krysta shook off her limbs and sat up.

"Anyone new on the horizon?"

"Maybe." I tucked my chin into my chest. I didn't want anyone on the bus to overhear gossip about something that hadn't happened yet. Even though I didn't doubt AJ's psychic ability, Frankie still had to ask me to the dance.

AJ leaned even closer and cupped her hands around her mouth. "Frankie Salas is going to ask her to Freshmen Formal."

"Get out!" Krysta punched my arm. "How do you know this?"

AJ cleared her throat. "I saw it coming." She jerked her thumb at me and rolled her eyes. "Sophie still doesn't know if she's going."

Krysta's bottom lip fell. "Are you insane?"

My shoulders sagged. "I heard Summer saying he's going to ask her."

Krysta crossed her legs beneath her, sitting on her heels. She grasped the back of AJ's seat and turned. "You don't believe that, do you?"

"That's what I told her," AJ said.

"It's not just that. Look, every girl likes Frankie. Can you imagine what that dance would be like? I'd be fighting off groupies the whole time." What if Frankie flirted with other girls and ignored me?

AJ turned her gaze down. "Afraid you won't measure up to them?"

Under the scrutiny of my friends, I shifted in my seat. "No, it's not that." When he tutored me in Mrs. Stein's class, I wanted to melt in my seat at his touch, his scent, his nearness. The boy had cast a spell over me and I didn't trust myself not to act like an idiot in his presence.

Krysta squeezed my shoulder. "You're not a fat dork anymore."

"Yeah, Frankie obviously sees something in you," AJ said. "Maybe you should, too."

All this time I'd been trying so hard to prove I was cool. Now that Frankie was interested in me, I was afraid I wouldn't live up to my new image. What if I said something stupid on our date? What if he no longer thought I was cool? Plus, I had another big problem. A problem normal teenagers didn't have to deal with. With Frankie so near me, what if I read something in his mind I didn't want to know?

The bus *had* to be late this morning. Obviously, the substitute bus driver didn't know I had a schedule to keep when he took three wrong turns. I had barely enough time to get to my locker before first period.

But there was just one problem.

"Hey, Sophie, I saw you knocked out on the football field. Actually, the whole school saw it." Summer smirked while she stroked her fake nails with hot pink polish. Her hand was splayed flat against my locker door.

Knowing she had no intention of moving it, I took a deep breath, dropped my book bag to the ground and prepared to do battle. This was a long time coming. I was finally ready to stand up to Summer Powers. Then why were my knees shaking?

"So what's your point?"

The bite of my best friend's angry voice resonated behind me. I turned to see AJ glaring at Summer, chin raised, fists clenched at her sides.

Now *she* was ready to do battle. AJ's powerful energy swept over me; I felt her rage in my bones. AJ at my back made me feel safer; my knees stopped shaking.

"Nothing," Summer stammered. "I was just making an observation." She quickly put the cap on her nail polish and stuffed it into her purse.

"Really?" AJ crossed her arms over her chest. "You were staring at someone other than your own reflection?"

"Yeah." Summer's hands were trembling as she snatched a notebook from her locker and slammed the door.

AJ threw back her head and laughed. "Good for you. Maybe this means you'll be spending less time at your locker mirror, so my best friend won't be late to class."

Summer hurried to the opposite end of the hall, but not before casting me a sideways glare. I read the intention in her eyes and heard what she was thinking.

Just you wait. She won't always be there to protect you.

"AJ." I shook my head. "One of these days I'm going to

have to learn to stand up for myself."

"You will next time." AJ put her hand on my back. "I just wanted to show you how it's done."

"Thanks." I fumbled with the combination on my locker.

AJ looked from side to side before lowering her voice. "Did you get to hear what she was thinking?"

I opened my locker, shielding my face with the door. "She can't wait to get me alone."

AJ pushed next to me, pretending to get books out of my locker. "I'm no bigger than you, Sophie. The only difference is I don't take crap from anyone. Next time you see Summer, give her the stare, and show her you're not afraid."

I paused. "And what if she kicks my butt?"

"She might." AJ stopped fumbling and turned to me. "And *you* might kick *her* butt. The point is, you'll have to deal with girls like Summer all your life. Are you going to keep taking their crap?"

I squared my shoulders. "No."

"Now, next time she starts something, get in her face, and then listen to what she's thinking. I will bet you'll find out she's scared."

"Maybe." I wasn't so sure. Could AJ be right?

There was only one way to find out. I shuddered at the thought of a future confrontation. If I did get my butt kicked by Summer, the whole school would talk about it. I'd never be cool.

We exchanged knowing glances at the sound of the first bell. AJ waved as she headed to class.

I closed my locker and picked up my bag, anxious to get to first period. AJ told me Frankie scored the winning touchdown Friday night. I hoped Lara got the picture. "Hey, Sophie, you okay?"

My spine tingled at the sound of the familiar voice behind me. I clenched both fists then breathed out, trying to ease my tension. I knew when I turned around, those penetrating eyes would have me stammering like an idiot. I slowly faced Frankie. "What? Yeah, I'm fine."

He was leaning one hand against Summer's locker, his other hand holding a binder to his chest and head tilted to the side. His gorgeous pose could have been ripped from an Old

Navy ad.

"Oh, when you didn't show up to tutoring, I thought you had a concussion." Frankie smiled slyly, his eyes twinkling with something thatnlooked like arrogance.

This guy was a player, baiting me with his hot body. Did he think I was going to drop to my knees and beg for forgiveness? "Why? Does a girl have to have a concussion if she doesn't want to be with you?"

Frankie pushed off the locker, his shoulders falling slightly. *Damn. That cut hard. I knew she didn't like me.*

Frankie's thoughts stunned me into silence. Had I actually hurt Frankie Salas? I hadn't thought guys like him could be hurt.

Head cast down, Frankie brushed past me. "That's not what I meant. Never mind."

Instinctively, I reached out for his arm. My fingers tingled as I felt his muscles tighten. "Frankie, I'm sorry. I can't believe I said that."

Frankie turned abruptly, closing only a small distance between us.

I released my grip before his skin melted my fingers and tried to turn down the heat that coursed through me when I looked into his eyes. "We had a new bus driver. We just got to school."

"That's okay." A slight smile tugged at the corner of his mouth. "Maybe tomorrow."

"Yeah." I bit my lip. I didn't want a goofy grin ruining the moment. "Definitely."

His eyes locked with mine as he placed his hand on my shoulder. Thinking he was drawing me closer for a kiss, I leaned in. I could feel my mouth dry up like I'd just swallowed a mouthful of cotton. My hands shook, my heart beat so hard I thought my chest would explode, but I didn't care. Frankie Salas was about to kiss me. I closed my eyes and opened my lips...ready, waiting.

"Which way are you going?"

"Huh?" I watched as Frankie slid my book bag off my arm. He wasn't going to kiss me. He was just taking my bag. I was a moron.

"I said, 'which way are you going?'" He had my book bag

slung over his shoulder, gripping it with one finger.

"Yearbook," I stammered, the dryness in my mouth almost causing me to choke.

"I'll walk you."

We both turned, walking shoulder to shoulder.

I ran my tongue over the roof of my mouth. "Won't you be late?"

"I don't get busted," Frankie teased. "My teachers love me."

We walked the rest of the way in silence. This gave me ample time to reflect on my stupidity. I just couldn't act cool around Frankie. The weird thing was that he didn't seem to care.

The tardy bell rang. I looked at Frankie to gage his reaction, but he didn't even blink. Although Mrs. Carr wouldn't be happy when I came in late, that didn't seem to matter to me at the time.

When we neared the door to the yearbook room, I knew I had to bring up the football incident, as Frankie was nice enough not to mention it. "Frankie, thanks for everything Friday night."

He shrugged, setting down my bag. "It's nothing."

"I heard you still won the game."

"Yeah." He held up a finger. "By one point."

I sighed, sinking against the door. "I wish I could have seen you make that touchdown."

He moved closer. "There's always this Friday."

I inhaled his scent. Fresh, musky, and not a hint of ketchup.

"Maybe I can get a picture of you." I could feel the butterflies fluttering in my stomach. I'd misjudged his last move. I didn't know what to expect now so I wasn't going to make that same mistake again. I tried to focus on his thoughts, but with my nerves and his dark eyes, there was no hope of any mind-reading.

He placed one hand above my shoulder, leaning against the door, his face within inches of mine. "Or the Friday after that."

My mind was racing. Frankie's nearness had me so confused. It took me a few seconds to register what he was saying. He didn't have a game that Friday. That was the night of the Freshmen Formal dance. "I thought you didn't have a game that Friday." I nearly stumbled over my words.

"I don't." He grabbed a wisp of my hair, toying it in his fingers, his breath lowering to a near whisper. "So maybe you and I can get some pictures together."

I tried to swallow, but the dryness in my throat was back with a vengeance. I looked into his penetrating eyes, searching for a sign this wasn't a dream, the hottest guy in school really liked me. "Like, as friends?"

"Not exactly." He leaned closer.

I smelled his minty breath and saw his lips part. I knew Frankie Salas was going to kiss me.

"The bell rang a minute ago," a gruff voice said. "Get to class, you kids, before I write you up."

I jumped at the sight of Tyler, the gender confused rent-a-cop.

Frankie slowly straightened, turning to Tyler with a wide grin. "Oh, hi, Tyler. You look beautiful this morning. New haircut?"

Beautiful? Feminine term. Finally, the riddle was solved. Tyler was a girl.

Tyler blushed and playfully swatted her hand at him. "Frankie, you little rascal, get your butt to class."

"Yes, Ma'am." Frankie was a player. He even knew how to make the beastie girls blush. "I was just making sure Sophie didn't pass out on the way to class. She got a concussion at the game."

"Oh, so you're the one who was hit by the ball." She peered around his shoulder and looked me up and down with a menacing glare.

I tried to duck behind Frankie. "Uh, yeah." Even though I had solved Tyler's gender enigma, two hundred fifty pounds of grudge with a night stick was still scary.

"I saw the whole thing from the sidelines." She grunted and puffed up her chest. "Girls don't belong on the football field, that's what I've always said."

I felt like saying, "So what the heck are *you*? A few seconds ago, Frankie had me convinced *you* were a girl."

A few seconds before that, Frankie was about to kiss me.

But she, he or it, had to ruin the moment.

Mrs. Carr glared from underneath her rimmed glasses as I floated into the yearbook room and melted into the seat next to Lara.

She was adjusting contrast on photos of screaming cheerleaders. "Mrs. Carr is sending the pep rally pages this deadline. Open up the folder on the network and pick your ten favorite pictures."

"Sure."

I opened up the folder, vaguely aware I was looking at pictures of kids with pie on their faces. Then I came to a group of football players throwing water on their coach. Frankie was holding the bucket. He had that mischievous twinkle in his eyes. He would make a fun date, especially to the Freshmen Formal. The thought of us on the dance floor together brought a smile to my face.

"Sophie?" Lara bit her lip and looked at me questioningly, "Jacob put you in a good mood?"

"Oh, God, no!" I sat up and shuttered, making a disgusting face.

Lara smiled and nodded. "Well, that's good to know."

"Jacob's a loser," I huffed.

"I'm glad you see it." She cast me a sideways glance. "Took you long enough."

I felt like a complete idiot. How could Lara have stayed friends with me when I was such a mental case over a loser? Maybe now she'd tell me the whole truth. "Now that I'm through with him, you gonna tell me what he did to you?"

Lara pushed her shoulders back and narrowed her eyes. "You mean you never heard the rumors?"

"No." Did everyone know Jacob was a vomit heap but me? I guess everyone, except AJ, decided to let me learn the truth on my own.

"Remember when I was crying in the darkroom?" Lara whispered.

"Yeah." I wanted to pretend I didn't remember, but that day had been difficult to put from my mind. Even though I didn't want to believe what she was thinking, that was the first day I started having doubts about Jacob.

"Jacob had just told everyone on my bus I had sex with him." Lara rolled her eyes. "I don't even know him."

"What a jerk. Why didn't you tell me?" She did tell me and now I was silently kicking myself in the butt for not wanting to believe her thoughts. Jacob had insulted my friend. I should have ditched that crush on the spot.

"You're my only friend right now. Everyone else thinks I'm a slut thanks to Summer and Jacob." Lara sank in her seat, lines of doubt drawn across her forehead. "I didn't want you to hate me, too."

"Lara." I squeezed her hand. "I wouldn't hate you."

"I don't know." She wagged her finger at my nose. "You were pretty lovesick over Jacob."

"Uugghh, don't remind me." I laid my hand across my forehead. If I could have erased those weeks. Stupid, stupid, stupid.

"So who's the new crush?" Lara playfully punched me on the shoulder, her eyes twinkling with mischief.

What a good friend. How easily she forgave and forgot my bad taste in guys. After all, it was not like I married the guy. Besides, I had better prospects on the horizon. "Frankie Salas. He asked me to Freshmen Formal. He almost kissed me this morning, but The Beast ruined it."

"Frankie Salas?" Lara squeezed her hands between her knees and batted her eyes. "Oh, Sophie, he's a hottie...and so sweet."

I frowned. "So I've heard from every other girl in this school."

"So what? Just think, all those girls like him but he picked you." Lara nearly fell out of her seat in excitement.

"You're right, but..." I bit my thumb, shaking my head. So many girls.

"But?" Lara tilted her head, raising her brows as if waiting for me to finish. "Sophie?"

"I just don't want to be fighting over him all night, that's all." I didn't see myself in his league, and definitely not with so many pretty girls competing for his attention.

Lara turned up her chin. "Frankie's not a jerk like Jacob. If Frankie wants something, he goes for it. If he wants to take you to the dance, you won't be fighting over him. He'll be all yours."

Even though he did have a lot of female followers, there was something about Frankie's character I liked. Like how he worked so hard in football, how he did so well in school, and how he made me feel with the cute way he teased me. But how did Lara know so much about him? I didn't want to add Lara to my list of rivals. "How do *you* know so much about him?"

Lara cast a sideways smile that shot to her eyes. She must have sensed my jealousy. "I've got him in five classes and I've been taking his football pictures for three years. When Frankie focuses on something, it's like nothing else exists. Besides, I saw how worried he was when he carried you off the field Friday night."

An honest, nice guy who liked me? It didn't add up. "I just don't get it." "Don't get what, Sophie?"

"Why me?" Why me when he had hundreds of girls to chose from?

Lara sighed. "Does this have anything to do with that chubby picture of you from the seventh grade?"

"I was a dork, Lara. Didn't you see me?" The memories of my seventh grade year came flooding back, forming a tight knot in my chest. 'So Fat Sinora', 'Eats-A-Pizza Sinora', 'Cellulite Sinora'. I didn't even know what cellulite was until seventh grade when Cody Miller pointed at my thighs in front our entire geography class.

"People change, Sophie." Lara rested her hand on my shoulder. "Frankie sees that, why can't you?"

I put my head down, trying to repress the tears, as my throat tightened. "They called me 'So Fat'."

"Kids are mean. How'd you like to be labeled the school slut? It's a lot easier for *you* to change *your* image than it is for *me* to get some respect." Lara's voice rose a few octaves as she turned her head.

Poor Lara. The hottest guy in school asked me to Freshmen Formal and I thought I was having a bad day. Her life was much worse. "I'd never thought of that. I'm sorry, Lara."

"It's okay." She quickly brushed the corners of her eyes

with the back of her hand. "I'm used to it. Listen, promise me you'll go with him because if you don't, I'm never talking to you again. Just think about it, you're my only friend so I'll be losing a lot, too."

"Okay." Mrs. Stein scanned the room with a subdued smile that didn't quite mask the sadness in her eyes. "Open your books to page seventy-two. I want you to do all the practice equations."

I looked at the equations. Funny, they didn't seem so challenging now. With enough work, and maybe the right tutor, I knew I could pass math. "Sophie." Mrs. Stein kneeled beside my desk and spoke in a low whisper. "Where were you this morning?"

"The bus was late."

She clicked her tongue and shook her head. "Frankie Salas waited all morning for you." Her voice rose just loud enough to be dangerous.

"Really?" I squeezed the pages of my book and beamed. I had the boy hooked.

Students in nearby desks began whispering and looking at me. They must have overheard us.

"Sophie likes Frankie Salas." Cody Miller yelled to no one in particular.

Mrs. Stein rose and glared in his direction. "Hush, Cody, that's none of your business."

Many students quietly laughed and snickered.

Scanning the room, Mrs. Stein threw her hands in the air. "Leave the poor girl alone and get to work. I swear some days you kids have me at wits end."

Grody Cody stuck out his chin, smirking. "But you know you love us, Mrs. Stein."

"Yeah." She sighed and shook her head. "You know I do."

"Mrs. Stein." Cody chewed on the tip of his eraser, lost in thought.

I held my breath. I never knew what was going to come out of that boy's mouth. He was known to say totally off the wall, weird things. Hopefully, he'd forgotten about Frankie Salas and me.

Cody stopped chewing and a light went on in those dim eyes. "Why don't you have your own kids?"

I knew it was a rude question so I wasn't shocked Cody had asked it. Curiosity got the best of me as I waited among the silent audience for the answer.

Oh, God, why didn't I die with them? I just want to die.

As Mrs. Stein's painful thoughts projected into my brain, an overwhelming, numbing pain washed over me, sinking my spirit into a chasm so deep, I felt my soul encompassed in pure, depressing darkness. I knew I was not just listening to her thoughts, I had entered Mrs. Stein's soul. Who died? And now she wanted to die, too? Not my favorite teacher!

She clutched her book so fiercely, I thought she would crush it. Her eyes welled up with tears, but she didn't say a word as she quickly walked out of the room.

The class waited in silence, but she didn't return.

"What'd you open your big mouth for, Cody?" AJ sneered.

Cody cowered and whined, "What? What'd I say?"

"Her family is dead, Cody."

I gasped at the sound of The Beast's harsh voice. I hadn't even heard Tyler enter the room.

Tyler glared at us from the back of the classroom, arms folded across its chest. "You kids shut your mouths and get back to work. I'm watching you while your teacher cools down."

My heart sank into my stomach, as I closed my eyes trying to understand what had just happened. Mrs. Stein was a great teacher who loved us. She didn't deserve this. She was depressed because her family died and I seemed to be the only one who knew the depths of her inner turmoil. She needed help, but I couldn't help her if she didn't willingly tell me. No adult would believe me if I said, "Mrs. Stein's thoughts said she wishes she was dead." They'd get me the shrink, not her.

The incident with Mrs. Stein kind of shadowed my excitement about Frankie. I thought about my favorite teacher all day, even when Frankie flirted with me in English. He probably thought I was playing hard to get. I hoped not. I didn't want him to think I was some annoying little tease.

I needed to get home, so I could have some privacy. I couldn't really think about Mrs. Stein's problems until I was sure no one else's thoughts would pop into my head. In the meantime, I had the bus ride to face. I was sure AJ and Krysta wanted to know if Frankie had asked me to the dance. Krista had already sent me several texts during fifth and sixth periods, which I ignored. I just wasn't in the mood to gush about my life when the life of my favorite teacher was in jeopardy.

They were already waiting for me on the bus. Their wide-eyed expressions said it all. They wanted me to spill the news.

I couldn't suppress a laugh as I scanned their eager faces. "He asked me."

AJ slapped the back of her seat and yelped. "You said 'yes' I hope."

I shook my head. "The Beast interrupted us."

"You'd better say 'yes'," Krysta squealed.

"Okay, I'll go." I sighed and tilted the back of my head against the seat. "I guess I'll have to fight off his groupies all night."

AJ folded her arms across the top of her seat and looked into my eyes. "What's your plan?"

I raised my chin up, keeping my voice firm. "I need to show all Greenwood girls I won't take any crap, starting with Summer Powers."

"Awesome." AJ nodded approval. "You're learning."

"How are you going to do that?" Krysta didn't sound sure of my plan.

I shrugged. "I don't know yet."

AJ balled her fist into her hand. "You need to throw the first punch."

I grimaced. "That's what I'm thinking."

Krysta shook her head. "You'll be suspended, and then Sparks won't allow you at the dance."

Krysta was right. I'd never considered myself much of a fighter, anyway. I needed to catch Summer off guard. But how? Suddenly, I had a revelation and I sprung from my seat. "Wait a minute! First punches don't always have to be physical."

AJ raised her brows. "You gonna clue us in?" My mind was racing. I had a lot to do to prepare for the first punch. All I needed was some tape, some courage, and Lara's cooperation. My plan could work. It *had* to work.

I focused my gaze on my friends, smiling as it all came together in my head. "It's a surprise. Don't you wish *you* were mind readers?"

Chapter Thirteen

Finally, alone. I threw my bag on the floor and flopped onto the bed, rubbing my aching temples. So much to think about. So much to plan. Mrs. Stein, Frankie, Summer—they were all running through my head and I didn't know where to begin.

"Hey." Rose Marie stood in the open doorway. I looked at my sister, annoyed I'd forgotten to shut the door. "Hey."

Rose Marie put her head down, squeezing the door frame. "I kicked him out."

I couldn't believe what I was hearing. My sister had come to her senses. I had thought she was hopeless. "What?"

A single tear slipped down her cheek. "He decided he's not ready to be a father."

For the first time, I felt sorry for her. I had been an idiot over a guy once, too, although I never let my crush go nearly as far. Still, she was my sister and needed my support. "Are you okay?"

"I'm fine." She managed a half-smile. "Never been better."

I crossed my arms over my chest and narrowed my gaze. "You don't sound better."

"Well, you were right." Keeping her head down, she ran a hand over her belly. "I am fat for three months."

"I never said that."

Rose Marie looked up, more tears began to flow. "There were two heartbeats, Sophie."

I didn't know what to say. She obviously wasn't happy, so I couldn't congratulate her.

She wiped her cheeks with the back of her hand. "How am I going to raise two babies?"

I tried to sound reassuring. "You've got us to help you."

She sat on the bed and placed her head in her hands. "What was I thinking, Sophie?"

"Love is blind, I guess." Unfortunately, I knew what I was talking about.

"No, love is stupid." She stood up and paced the room. "I thought I'd be able to finish college after the baby. I had all these crazy ideas. Now I'll be stuck with a minimum wage job, living with my parents, raising two kids with no father." She turned, pointing an accusing finger. "Don't be stupid and screw up your life like I did, Sophie."

"I don't plan on it."

"So." She threw her hands in the air and rolled her eyes. "How was your day?"

I bit my lip. I didn't know if she'd be eager to share my good news. "Frankie Salas, the hottest guy in school, asked me to the Freshmen Formal."

"That's great!" Rose Marie patted my knee. "Look at my little sister, growing up so fast." She glared at me. "This guy had better have ambition."

I shook my head, laughing. "I'm not marrying him, Rose Marie."

"Good, don't marry or have any kids until you finish college." Her face twisted while she looked me over. "So why the long face when you came home?"

"You noticed?" I sighed and laid back, folding my hands behind my head.

"Yeah, even though I seem focused on only my problems lately, I still pay attention when my sister comes home with a frown, dragging her feet."

I rolled over, clutching my pillow. "Do you remember Mrs. Stein?"

Rose Marie smiled. "Mrs. Stein? If it wasn't for her, I don't think I'd have scored a 1500 on my SATs. She was my favorite teacher ever."

I sat up. "Mine, too." Maybe Rose Marie could help me with Mrs. Stein. I didn't have to tell her all the mind reading details.

"How's she doing?" Rose Marie leaned in and lowered her voice, as if she was about to leak top-secret information. "She lost her family, you know."

My shoulders fell. This was the second time I'd heard the bad news and it didn't get any easier. "Yeah, I heard. She's been pretty depressed, Rose Marie. I'm worried about her."

"Really?"

"Yeah. What exactly happened to her family?"

Rose Marie bit her nails. Something she only did when she was in a really serious mood. "Her husband and kids died in a car wreck a few summers ago. It was really bad. I heard her youngest daughter survived for a few weeks, but she was brain dead. They had to pull the plug."

Brain dead? That's why she got so upset when I told her I was brain dead at tutoring. This was bad. This was worse than bad. What a horrible thing to happen to my favorite teacher! "Was she in the car?"

"No, she was at some teachers' retreat up in the mountains. They were going to pick her up when their car went over a cliff."

"That sucks." I slowly exhaled, trying to process this new information. Was this why she was so overprotective of her students? Why she became distraught when Tyler tried to snatch one of her 'babies'? She wasn't in the car to save her babies, so she was intent on saving all of her students. It made sense, in a morbid sort of way.

"She was still teaching eighth grade math. I was in high school when it happened." She grabbed a tissue off my nightstand and blew her nose. "I went to visit her, but they said she took the year off. Some kids said she was in a mental hospital. But you know how kids lie."

"Yeah." I rested my chin on the pillow. "I know."

"Anyway, I never got back to thank her for everything she did for me. I was too wrapped up in that loser." *I can't believe how many people I'd neglected when I was with him.*

Hearing my sister's thoughts, I looked up to see she'd started crying again. She was hunched over, her forehead resting in her hands.

I leaned over and rubbed her back. "It's too late to change

the past, but maybe you can stop by and visit her. I'm sure it would make her feel good to see an old student. She could use a boost."

"You're right." She perked up. "Maybe I'll stop by tomorrow morning. My morning sickness is easing up."

"Great. You can drive me to school. Our bus driver made me late to class today and I missed tutoring with Frankie."

"Ooohhh." She swatted my shoulder. "So I get to see Mrs. Stein *and* the hottest guy in school."

"Yeah." I cringed at the thought of my sister teasing me or Frankie. "But could you do me a favor?"

"What?"

I looked at her through the corner of my eyes. "Don't say anything to make me look stupid."

"Would I do something like that?" Rose Marie gasped and batted her lashes.

Yeah, she would but Rose Marie was the least of my worries. I had worse trouble than an embarrassing big sister. If my plan worked though...my problem would be solved. Tomorrow morning, I planned to throw the first punch.

Chapter Fourteen

"Sophie, what took you so long?" Hands on hips, Rose Marie stood at the front of Mrs. Stein's classroom. "I thought you would just be gone for a minute."

Rose Marie, Mrs. Stein and Frankie were waiting for me in the classroom, although by the looks of it, they weren't missing me too much. I had walked in just as Frankie and Mrs. Stein had burst into laughter. Something my wicked sister had said, no doubt.

"Sorry." I shrugged, trying to shake off my nervousness. "I had to stop off at my locker."

Actually, I did more than stop off. Summer hadn't made it to her locker yet, and the halls were empty, so I had time to carry out my plan. I tried not to look at what I'd done as revenge. Even though it felt good to know that soon Summer would be the laughing stock of the entire school.

"That's okay. We've been keeping Frankie company while you've been gone." Rose Marie laughed. "I've been telling him *lots* of stories about your childhood."

My childhood? Was she telling him about the fat me? I felt like I should have been alarmed but somehow that didn't matter anymore. "Thanks." I rolled my eyes and gave my sister a warning glare. "I'm sorry, Frankie."

"That's okay." He was sitting on top of a desk in a casual pose, looking just as hot as ever.

"Rose Marie, why don't I take you into the staff lounge?" Mrs. Stein said between laughs while pressing her palms against her ribs. "Mr. Dallin is subbing here. He still talks about you. I bet he'd love to see you." Mrs. Stein's eyes lit upon my sister.

They locked arms and headed toward the door. Well, if it made Mrs. Stein happy, it was worth it to see her laughing at my expense.

"Okay, we'll leave you two alone to your...uh...equations." Rose Marie deliberately bumped against my shoulder as she walked past.

"Go away." I made a mental note to clean my toilet with her toothbrush when I got home.

"So." Frankie grabbed the tips of my fingers and gently placed them in his hands. "What's the answer?"

The shock of his touch sent shivers through me, but I was starting to figure out Frankie Salas and having a lot of fun doing it. "Answer to what?" I batted my eyes.

He instantly released my hand. *You bonehead. She doesn't want to go with you. Just drop it.* "Uh, nevermind."

Listening to his insecurities and instantly missing his touch, I reached for his hand. "Do you mean that equation you taught me?"

He gently squeezed and moved closer. "Yeah."

I bit my lip, smiling. "I've been thinking about that equation all night."

"You have?" His chest rose.

"I think I came up with a better one." "What is it?" He whispered.

Afraid to break the spell, I inched closer. "S + F = FF. Now imagine S stands for a girl and F stands for a guy. What dance do you know has the initials FF?"

He laughed, cupping my chin in his hand. "This is why I like you, Sophie."

His soft touch turned me into butter. I wanted to melt into his arms. "Why?"

"Because you're you," he said softly, "that's why."

"Well, in that case." I looked into his eyes, wanting nothing more than a kiss from the hottest guy in school. "We need to get some pictures together next Friday."

He pulled my chin toward his lips and bent down for a kiss. "What was that?" Frankie jerked his head up.

The shrill scream of the meanest teen in the school echoed

through the halls and broke our spell. Of all the rotten luck.

I groaned. "I think it was a girl screaming." Frankie pulled me toward the door. "Maybe we should check it out."

I pulled back, digging my heels into the pasty yellow school tiles. "It's probably nothing." Which was a lie, but I had two very important reasons for staying put. First of all, I didn't want to blow my second chance to get a kiss from Frankie. Secondly, I didn't want to get my butt kicked.

Suddenly, I started to have major doubts. Yeah, I knew Summer would be furious when she went to her locker. I knew by playing this prank, I would be forced to confront her. But after listening to her angry scream, which was still reverberating in my ears and down to my toes, I wondered if throwing the first punch was actually a good idea.

"It doesn't sound like nothing." He opened the door, dragging me behind. "Come on!"

Summer crumpled the infamous booger picture in her hand while stomping her heels on the floor. The corners of the picture were still stuck to her locker, thanks to lots and lots of duct tape.

A crowd of kids stood behind her, all taking photos of her tantrum with their phones. I wondered if any of them had actually snapped pictures of the booger photo before Summer had torn it down.

"Where is Lara?" Summer was scanning the faces of the amused crowd. "I know she did this! I'll kill her!"

I whispered to Frankie that I had something to take care of before pushing my way to the front. The first punch had been thrown. It was time to see if she'd strike back.

Taking a deep breath, I straightened my spine while trying to control my shaking legs. "Lara didn't do it, Summer." I inwardly smiled after the words came out of my mouth. I was terrified, but it felt so good to finally stand up for myself.

Summer's jaw dropped, her eyes bugging out of her head. "You?" she hissed.

"Maybe." Though I refused to deny it, I didn't want to admit it, either. At, least, not out loud. After all, I didn't want to get suspended. But as I fisted my hands at my sides, a defiant gesture AJ had taught me, I knew Summer would realize I was the one who'd taped the picture to her locker. "So what are you going to do about it?" I taunted.

It was like someone else was speaking. I could barely feel my lips moving, as my body had gone numb. As a voice in my head kept repeating, 'Don't back down,' I realized my next move. Willing myself to read Summer's mind, I wasn't about to be unprepared for Summer's attack.

Sophie? No way! Where did she get the nerve?

Summer glared at the gathering crowd. "What are you all laughing at?"

Perfect. Summer was shocked and embarrassed. As my confidence restored, so did the feeling in my limbs. I decided to strike again before she regained her footing. "I think they're laughing at that picture of you with your finger halfway up your nose."

"You stupid little freak!" She threw the picture in my face as her lower lip trembled.

I caught the picture, laughing, and unfolded it. "Pick-N-Flick Powers—sounds like a cool nickname." Once again, I focused on her thoughts.

Why isn't she backing down? She's gone crazy.

"Give that back." Summer lunged for the picture.

I tossed it on the ground. "Sure. What do I want with your crusty picture, anyway?" I was having fun humiliating her, but I had to be cautious. She was a cornered animal; I wasn't sure if she'd strike out. Luckily, her thoughts came easily to me.

Summer picked up the photo, stuffing it in her pocket. Her body quivered as she eyed the crowd. *Everyone's looking. I need to save face.* "I'll get you back for this."

"Yeah, whatever." I folded my arms across my chest and pretended to examine my fingernails. A trick I'd seen her use.

She backed up a few steps, her chest rising and falling with each angry breath. "You'd better watch your back."

"You'd better watch your mouth." Jerking my head up, I pointed an irate finger and followed her retreat. "Quit spreading lies about Lara. And when I need to get into my locker, stay out of my face."

What's wrong with her? I have to get out of here. Summer turned, pushing her way through the crowd just as the first bell rang. "You're lucky the bell rang," she called over her shoulder.

I laughed as she ran to class. I couldn't help adding one more jab. "Maybe I'll see you around after first period. Just remember to use antibacterial lotion before you come near my locker."

"Summer Powers piss you off?"

I turned to see Frankie behind me, holding my bookbag.

Putting Summer down was like a drug for my ego; I still hadn't come off of my high. "I was tired of her crap."

"Yeah." He shrugged. "I've noticed she starts stuff with all the pretty girls."

My chest tightened and I had to remind myself to breathe. Frankie thought I was pretty. The fat little dork had come a long way and hearing him say it made it so much better. My head swelled. I understood how Frankie could get so cocky. Even though he liked me, something still had been bothering me for the past few weeks. "Summer said you were going to ask her to the Freshmen Formal."

"Yeah, right," Frankie laughed. "She's been begging me to take her ever since school started."

He winked and grabbed my hand. "Let's go before we're late to class again."

"Nice job. I didn't even need to cheat for you." Jacob's fingers slid across mine as he handed back my test.

I wanted to gag. What did I ever see in this guy? "It's called studying, Jacob."

Jacob's eyebrows wrinkled, and then he smiled. "I heard what you did to Summer. Cool."

"Cool?" I pushed back my shoulders, trying to sound as sarcastic as possible. "That's nice. Why don't you play your Nintendo?"

Jacob's mouth fell open and he waited before sneering. "What crawled up your butt?"

I laughed, looking him in the eyes. "You did."

"What did I do to you?"

I narrowed my eyes, giving him my best 'you're an idiot' smile. "Lara Sketchum."

"Whatever." He shook his head and turned. *She deserved it. She's a slut.*

Ooohhh, what a jerk. His thought was too rude to leave unanswered. "She's not a slut, Jacob. She's my friend and you spread lies about her. Even if she was a slut, she wouldn't get together with a loser who only plays video games."

Jacob faced me again, his upper lip curled into a fierce snarl. "Are you calling me a loser?"

Unimpressed, I rolled my eyes. "You caught on fast."

Jacob leaned back and forced a laugh, dramatically shrugging his shoulders as if he wasn't bothered. "I thought you were cool, but I take it back."

"I think she's cool." Frankie glared at Jacob with a steely gaze.

Jacob's voice lowered, faltering as he spoke. "Stay out of it, Frankie."

"Too bad. I'm in it." He continued glaring at Jacob.

Jacob turned, huffing as he slammed his video game on his desk, tuning out the rest of the world.

I was so totally proud of Frankie. He told off his friend for me. I'd never thought the guy could get any hotter.

Frankie leaned over as we passed our tests to the front of the room. "I never got your number." I held out my hand. "Give me your phone."

Within seconds, I entered my number into his phone and I resisted the urge to scan his phonebook. If he had other girls' numbers, it wasn't my business. After all, I reminded myself, I wasn't looking to marry the guy.

Deftly slipping Frankie the cell, I fought the urge to jump out of my seat when his electrified fingers glided over mine. I didn't think I could ever get used to his touch.

He slipped the phone into his pocket. "I'll text you next period."

I slid down in my seat, melting. I still couldn't believe I was going to the Freshman Formal with the coolest guy in school. "Okay." The dance was less than two weeks away; Frankie and I needed to make plans. I didn't think, in all my fourteen years, I'd ever wanted anything more than for that night to finally come. If only everyone else in my life could have been this happy.

Chapter Fifteen

Walking home from the bus stop, I spied Rose Marie in the front yard. She was piling clothes into the back of her SUV. That sight worried me. Had Dad kicked her out? Was she going back to Chad?

"Good news, Sophie." Grinning, Rose Marie grabbed a lamp from off the ground and set it on top of the clothes. "You get your room back."

That much I could tell. But what would happen to my sister and my nephews? "Where are you going?"

Rose Marie paused to rub her lower back. "I'm going to finish my core classes at Central Community."

"Central Community? I didn't know they had dorms."

"They don't." She shrugged. "But Mrs. Stein lives a few blocks away."

"You're moving in with Mrs. Stein?" I couldn't believe my ears. When had this happened? Sure, I noticed Rose Marie was spending a lot more time with her after school, but roommates?

"Yeah. She's going to help me get student loans and scholarships. When the babies come, I'll go to school at night while she watches them."

I felt a pang of jealousy. How was Mrs. Stein going to have the time to do all this and be my favorite teacher? "Wow. That's a lot of work for her."

"That's what I said, but she insisted." Rose Marie picked up another lamp, and then turned. "You know, I think she needs me as much as I need her."

"I think you're right." I shouldn't have been jealous. My

plan to cheer Mrs. Stein worked better than I'd hoped. She would have a family again.

"She already found me a job working at her friend's daycare, so I can be with the babies at work. Besides," Rose Marie grinned. "The daycare will be good experience, since I'm going to be a teacher."

My sister was full of surprises. I would have never guessed she wanted to be a teacher. She'd wanted to be a doctor since before college. "You are? Why?" I didn't try to mask the shock in my voice.

"Mom and Dad always expected me to be a doctor like Lu Lu." Rose Marie's head dropped. "After I had Mrs. Stein in eighth grade, I wanted to be a teacher. To help kids the way she helped me."

I felt more than just a sisterly connection with Rose Marie. It was surprising to know we shared the same views, too. "Yeah, Mrs. Stein makes me feel that way."

Her eyes lit and she came over, squeezing my shoulder. "Anyway, she is getting the babies' room ready as we speak. Wait until you see her tomorrow, Sophie. I'll bet you've never seen her so happy."

"I can't wait." For once in my life, everything was coming together. Summer didn't bother me after the pick incident. Jacob was told to shut up. Frankie thought I was pretty. Rose Marie was getting her life back on track. And now, Mrs. Stein would finally have some happiness. The only thing that could top this was a memorable Freshmen Formal.

The night was already going better than hoped, except for that one little incident when Rose Marie drove us to the dance. She complimented Frankie about his gorgeous eyes and flirtatious Frankie actually turned beet red. I couldn't wait till I got my driver's license. Going out would be so much better.

Thank God for those dance lessons Mom made me take in seventh grade. Even though I was the fattest thing in spandex, I still learned a few good moves. Frankie and I danced for at least twenty minutes before he went to get us punch. Not once had he looked at other girls. Lara was right, 'he was all mine.'

I made my way to the bathroom to make sure those crazy curls Rose Marie formed on my head hadn't fallen. Everything was still in place, thanks to almost an entire can of hair spray. My make-up looked great, too. I was starting to appreciate the benefits of a Homecoming Queen sister.

As I looked at my reflection, I couldn't hide a smile at the pretty girl in the shimmering pink dress. Rose Marie helped me pick it out and I had to admit I looked pretty hot. I would have never been caught dead in a tight dress a year ago, but a lot had changed. The thin straps crossed over the low cut back, and the soft, feminine fabric clung until it ended just at the knee. Mom had doubts about the dress. Dad was furious, but Rose Marie got our parents to back down.

Besides, this gown actually concealed a lot more than what other girls were wearing, especially Summer Powers, whose chest was ready to fall out of her sparkly black tube top. I was shocked, not at what she was wearing, at her date—Jacob Flushman. I was still laughing over that.

I spotted AJ and Krysta when I came out of the bathroom. They looked awkward standing next to the two coolest guys at the dance. They'd told me they had surprise dates; I had kind of suspected they would abduct AJ's brother and his best friend.

The Mikes sneered as they scanned the crowd of freshmen. They probably had lots of better things to do on a Friday night than baby-sit two goofy girls. I looked AJ and Krysta over from a distance. AJ was actually in a dress! I wondered what bribery Krysta used to get her into that thing. Whatever the case, AJ looked pretty as a girl.

Krysta's eyes widened as she spotted me coming toward them. "Love the dress. Jennifer Lopez wore one just like it in *Cosmo*."

"Look at you, girl." AJ grabbed my shoulders and turned me around. "You're a little hottie."

"You clean up nice as a fem, AJ," I laughed.

She batted her eyes and flipped her hair, pretending to be a stupid priss.

"Hey," I asked. "How did you get the Mikes?"

"Mom threatened them." AJ rolled her eyes at their dates.

Krysta bounced, nearly jumping out of her heels. "I think,

after tonight, we'll be the most popular girls at school."

I giggled. "The Mikes don't look like they're having much fun."

"Too bad." AJ shook her head in mock sympathy. "They're ours tonight."

"Yeah," Krysta beamed, "and they'll make great pictures. You have to make sure we go in the yearbook with them."

"Ask Lara, she's the one taking pictures tonight." I pointed in Lara's direction after I spotted her out of the corner of my eye.

Lara looked sophisticated. She opted for sleek, low-rise black pants and a modest cut, matching black top. Her long black hair was swept up in a simple, elegant twist. Her black sequined flip-flops made the outfit. And for jewelry, of course, nothing fit better than her camera.

"Yeah, we saw her." AJ tensed. "The Mikes were flirting with her, but she blew them off."

"That's Lara," I said. "She only cares about taking pictures."

Krysta shrugged. "She doesn't act like a slut to me."

I raised my brows, eyeing Krysta and AJ.

"She's not a slut. I already told both of you Summer and Jacob started those rumors."

AJ swung her little beaded purse in a menacing gesture. "If I hear anyone talking smack about Lara, I'll shut them up."

"Cool." I looked over their shoulders. "Frankie's coming back. I need to go."

"Good luck." AJ smacked me on the shoulder.

I winced, but not at AJ. Grody Cody bumped into Frankie, almost causing him to spill the punch. Frankie looked ready to pound him.

"Hey, where you been?" His voice was tense. "I almost spilled these, twice."

"Sorry. Girl thing." I batted my eyes and bit my lip. A technique Rose Marie had just taught me.

Frankie broke into a wide grin as he handed me the punch.

"Don't you two make a nice couple."

I turned to see Mrs. Stein beaming. She wore baby's breath in her hair and cradled a flower clutch to her chest. I didn't quite get the Hawaiian strapless sundress she was wearing but since she was my favorite teacher, I decided to overlook her fashion flaws.

She whispered in my ear, "I knew my plan would work."

My jaw dropped. "You set us up, Mrs. Stein?"

She laughed. "You should be thanking me."

I loved hearing her laugh. She had been doing a lot of that these past few weeks. But best of all, no more depressing thoughts.

"Thanks, Mrs. Stein. But not just for that, for everything." I leaned over and gave her a big hug.

She patted me on the back. "Just doing my job."

"No," I said, "your job is to teach, but you're more than a teacher. By the way..." I tilted my chin. "I finally get equations."

Mrs. Stein squeezed her handbag tighter, the lines of her wide smile were so stretched I thought her face would burst.

"I never had any doubts."

Frankie poked me in the ribs. "Are we gonna dance or what?"

A thrill ran through me at his words. I couldn't believe it. For a moment, I had forgotten the hottest guy in school was at my side.

He tossed our drinks into the garbage and pulled me to the floor for a slow song.

The magical feeling returned as his fingers locked in mine. I wasn't scared or worried, just excited. Tonight I would not embarrass myself. I shared smiles with AJ and Krysta, who had dragged the Mikes onto the dance floor. The blinding light of a camera's flash caught me off guard. I looked up to see Lara.

"If it's ugly," I roared, "I'm deleting it."

She winked from above her viewfinder. "You look beautiful, trust me. No booger picking." She nodded her head toward a cluster of chairs in the back of the gym.

Jacob was sitting with his Nintendo, stretched out with his legs on a nearby chair. Summer looked absolutely bored as she watched her date play his game.

I tapped Frankie's shoulder and pointed in their direction. "Jacob and Summer don't look like they're having much fun."

Frankie shook his head. "That boy needs a reality check."

I shrugged. "I never thought I'd say this, but I kind of feel sorry for Summer."

"Maybe I should ask her to dance." His lips curved into a mischievous grin.

I pulled back my shoulders and glared. "Maybe you should kiss my butt."

"What?" He leaned in, a grin splitting his lips. "Sophie wants a kiss?"

I pushed on his chest. "Not here." Panicking, I could feel the nervousness shoot through my limbs.

He bent his lips toward mine. "Why not?"

"Mrs. Stein and Mr. Sparks are watching." I tried to scan the room, but his penetrating eyes drew me in. "You do the math."

Trapped by his heated gaze, a thousand different fears seared my mind. I grappled with my brain to find some way out of the inevitable. He was going to kiss me in front of all these people.

There was nothing I could do to stop him but, truthfully, I didn't want to stop him.

He leaned in closer, his lips dangerously a breath away. "I'm sick of equations."

Frankie's mouth met mine in one exquisite kiss. His lips were soft, just barely wet from the punch, and oh so nice. Nothing else mattered. Not getting caught by the principal, not the gossip on the dance floor, not even the light from Lara's flash that I knew had captured our kiss. I was Sophie 'So Hot' Sinora, and I was cool.

Don't
Tell Mother

Book Two

This book is dedicated to my mom, who has always loved me unconditionally and who has given me the gift of a crazy imagination.

And for Heidi, for all the weird memories we created as kids.

Chapter One

Don't jump.

My will was not my own. An invisible force pulled me closer toward the edge. Fear kept my limbs at my side, my arteries as lifeless as an empty graveyard. Only my eyes willed themselves to move—down. The earth below was shrouded in white mist, obscuring the distance to the ground, but I sensed the depth. No person could jump and live to tell. So what propelled my foolish feet forward? Was this a dream? Was I already dead? Another step and I knew I would fall.

Suddenly, I felt the ground beneath me give way. The force of the fall sucked my body into a death-grip; the icy wind slapped my face as I raced downward. I could see nothing through the mist, but the bite of the chill wind licked my arms and legs like a thousand burning whips. As the heat increased, the mist dissolved, and to my horror, I saw my final destination—grey, cold and unwelcoming.

I was going to die.

"Bob? You're going out with *Bob*?"

My best friend, Sophie Sinora, stared at me in mock horror, the juices of her cafeteria hamburger dripping freely onto her napkin. I'd revealed my shocking secret as she was mid-bite of her processed meat product. Bob Klinek had asked me out, and

I'd said "yes".

What made this secret so shocking was that Bob was totally different. He was a skater and a punk. I was the basketball team captain, usually scoring half the team points. Even with that, I considered basketball a warm-up season; I lived for the softball mound. My fast pitch was gaining speed, and my curve ball stumped most batters.

"Forget that he's a freak." My other best friend, Krysta Richards, twirled a carrot stick between the tips of her polished fingernails, her olive skin glowing unnaturally beneath too much Glitter Glam. "What kind of name is Bob? It's so last century."

I glared at them. "I like his name."

"Didn't you have a cat named Bob?" Sophie's green eyes sparkled with amusement as she tossed her long, chestnut hair behind her shoulder, totally unaware as ketchup carelessly dripped down her chin.

I exhaled. "Yeah, so?"

I knew telling them was a bad idea, but I was trying to stay calm, especially with Sophie. Her eyes had been red and swollen since her BF, Frankie, had moved away last week. Now that she was solo again, I guess I wasn't allowed to go out with anyone, either.

Krysta leaned over and delicately patted Sophie's chin with her neatly folded napkin. With a stroke of her hand, she smoothed her frizzy locks down before slanting a smile in my direction. "Bob is a pet's name."

"Or a freak's name," Sophie said while spewing meat debris onto the lunch table.

Krysta glared at Sophie while making a grand gesture of sweeping the table with her napkin. "Jocks don't date freaks."

"In case you've forgotten," I hissed, "I'm a freak, too. Just like you two."

Which is how we ended up as friends.

We found out about each other's gifts when we were kids. Even though I was only eight, I knew I was different, and I felt their differences, too.

Around them, I didn't feel strange, and we pledged to keep our gifts secret.

Sophie scanned the cafeteria and then leaned closer. She reeked of the nauseating, sweet- smelling school ketchup substitute. "I didn't *choose* to read minds and you didn't *choose* to have visions."

"And I didn't ask for dead people to wake me up all night, but Bob *chose* to dye his hair like a parrot and get a Mohawk," Krysta sneered. "What's with the duct tape on his wrists? Are you going out with a cutter?"

"No, he's not cutting." Bob might have been weird, but my BF didn't slash his wrists. I wouldn't have gone out with him if he did. As far as his hair was concerned, green is our school color. Nothing wrong with school pride.

Krysta laughed. "Then he's too cheap to wear a real bracelet."

She sounded like a rich snob. No one would know by the way she turned up her nose that she lived in a run-down apartment. Her dad was just as poor, if not poorer, than Bob's family. Krysta refused to accept that fact and the few clothes she owned were all designer labels.

I clenched my jaw, trying my best to refrain from saying something I'd regret later, although it was hard not to lay a verbal smack down on them—very hard.

Maybe if we talked about something else, I'd cool down. "Speaking of our gifts, I had that dream again last night."

Sophie's eyes widened. "The falling dream?"

"Yeah." I shuddered. Maybe bringing up the dream wasn't such a hot idea. I was the type of girl who liked to be in control. Plummeting from the sky toward certain death was not my idea of peaceful slumber.

Krysta bit her bottom lip, hesitating before speaking. "Did you see who it was this time?"

I shook my head in disgust. "I woke up."

Sophie threw down her hamburger. "Why do you keep doing that?"

"Because I was about to crap my pants," I spat. "Do you know how real my dreams feel? If you were racing toward ice, you'd want to wake up, too." I wanted to see who it was more than anyone, but how could I see the person's face, anyway? I was in the body of the falling person. *Wait a minute!* Fear clenched my jaw, and my spine froze. *What if the falling person was me?*

"You never mentioned ice before."

Sophie broke my thoughts. *Thank God.*

"Yeah," I bit back a bitter laugh. "I finally saw the ground this time. It looked shiny and grey, like ice or dirty snow."

Sophie straightened her spine. "I'm staying away from mountains and airplanes until you figure out who it is."

Sophie and Krysta knew my dreams came true. Usually, I have cool dreams. I knew the hottest guy in school would ask Sophie to the Freshman Formal. Last month was the first time I'd ever foretold a death, Krysta's Grammy. I dreamt of her funeral the day before she had a fatal heart attack.

"Now that I am totally spooked..." Krysta tossed me a sideways grin. "Let's change the subject. What were we talking about again?" She tapped her lip a few times, pretending to be serious. "Oh, yeah, tape."

"He likes tape." Keeping my tone even, I tried my best not to let her see I was beyond frustrated. I was ready to drop the subject of Bob. They wanted to judge him before knowing him, so I didn't see any point in getting angry.

Maybe Bob and I didn't look like we fit together. I'd worn my pale blonde hair in the same ponytail ever since I could dribble a ball. I didn't need gobs of makeup or the coolest fashions to look pretty—just jeans and jerseys. Something about the way Bob's green spikes swayed with his stride was kind of mesmerizing. Although I preferred a natural look, Bob's clothes and his hair seemed like an extension of his unique personality. I couldn't imagine him any other way.

"I bet he likes tape," Sophie laughed, "especially when it's ripping the hairs off his arms."

I half-smiled, narrowing my eyes in Sophie's direction, willing her to read the true meaning behind my grin—*shut your face.* "He doesn't have hair there anymore."

"Nice." Krysta threw back her head. "Can I barf now?"

I sighed, pushing away my half-eaten burger and flexing my knuckles. "I'm leaving before I smack one of you."

"We're just looking out for you, AJ."

Krysta's tone was much too adult, like she was my mother,

which made me even less willing to listen.

"Yeah," Sophie said, "like when I liked that loser, Jacob, and you told me to ditch him."

Before she went out with Frankie, Sophie liked this total vomit-heap, Jacob Flushman, but that was way different. Bob had something Jacob didn't—a life.

"Bob's *not* a loser." I closed my eyes and tried to count to ten, something this stupid therapist Mother took me to told me to do. It wasn't working, because I could hear them snickering about his duct tape. Maybe they'd get tired of me ignoring them and leave.

"He's got earrings all over the place, AJ," Krysta nagged. "I never thought you'd go for a freak."

"Yeah," Sophie blurted, "and speaking of freaks. Your mom would freak if she found out about Bob."

I clenched my forehead. Just the thought of my meddling, manipulative mother getting in the way of Bob and me made the aching vein on my temple throb with a vengeance.

I had another reason to keep Bob away from Mother. Nothing I did was ever good enough. If I brought home an A minus, she wondered why it wasn't an A. If I threw an amazing fast pitch, she complained softball wasn't as fun as watching my brother Mike play football.

He got all the attention and all the cool stuff. The only reason I finally got a computer was because Mike gave me his hand-me-down when Mother bought him a new one. I still wasn't allowed a cell phone. I must have been the only girl in ninth grade without one. Things were about to change; I was tired of playing second string to my brother. This was the year I was going to make my mother treat me with respect.

"I heard a boy's voice on the other end of the phone this morning," Mother carefully spread her fat-free margarine across her whole-wheat toast. "Who was he?"

I clutched my Sunday comics to keep from looking up at her. The joints in my fingers felt as if they were encrusted in blocks of ice. I dared not twitch a muscle on my face for fear she'd know what I was thinking.

I'd been so careful. *How did she find out?* I told him not to call me, and I only called him when Mother was in her garden or at the store. This wouldn't have happened if Mother would just let me get a cell phone.

"Bob," I murmured.

"Bob?"

"Yes, Bob." I tried to sound relaxed, unconcerned, but I knew I wasn't convincing. Mother had some kind of a secret, parent radar, that sliced and diced the meaning of every look, expression or thought.

"Well," she purred, "that sounds like a nice, normal name. He must be a pleasant young man."

"Uh." My brow twitched. "Yeah."

"So, is this Bob a boyfriend you haven't told me about?" Her tone transformed from 'I'm a sweet, loving mommy' to 'I want to plague my daughter with guilt for not confiding in me.'

"Well." I shrugged, slowly easing down my paper. "Kind of."

My gaze gradually found hers. If her brows were raised any higher, she could've used them to scrape the ceiling.

"When do I get to meet this Bob?" Her lips twisted into a slight snarl and then she relaxed her face into a sweeter expression while she smoothed perfectly manicured fingers through her elegant long, blonde hair.

My beautiful mother. The image of perfection.

On the outside.

I wasn't fooled. "Meet him?"

"Why don't you invite him to dinner, Mom?"

My older brother, Mike, was smirking from the other end of the table. During my interrogation, I'd forgotten he was there. By the excited expression on his irritating face, he'd been hanging on every word.

Having Bob over for dinner was the last thing I wanted. Forget that he was a freak. What would he think of my family? "I don't think..."

"That sounds like a wonderful idea, Mike." Mother beamed at him, her icy-blue gaze taking on a much warmer hue.

I narrowed my eyes and shot mental daggers at Mike. *Why did I have to have a brother? Why?* Things were supposed to be different now that we were older. Now that he was out of the 'hold my sister down and fart on her face' stage, I thought he was actually maturing.

Guess not.

Mike lowered his eyelids and leered from under his lashes. Oh, yeah, the jerk was having a real fun time putting me on the hot seat. Just last week, he'd been busted stealing a dead cat from the lab room and leaving it on his English teacher's chair.

Even though Mike was in high school, and I was stuck in junior high, gossip traveled fast in our small community. I'd heard all about the cat incident before Mike's principal got a chance to call home, but Mother didn't even put him on house arrest.

Mike was president of the junior class, captain of the tennis team, starting quarterback for varsity, blah, blah, blah. My friends thought Mike was some kind of bronzed, blonde God. Sure, he had muscles; sure he was okay to look at, but underneath...what an irritating, immature creep. According to Mother, Mike could do no wrong.

Meanwhile, none of my accomplishments seemed to matter to her. She hardly ever went to my games. Captain of the girls' basketball team and starting softball pitcher meant nothing to a former head cheerleader. I could score ten points on the court before any of those stupid cheerleaders counted their toes. But as a jock, I wasn't a *normal* girl, or so Mother told me.

"Yeah, I'd like to meet him, too." Mike grinned, smacking a spoonful of cereal like a pig. "I don't remember him from Greenwood. What sports does he play?"

I hoped Mother didn't notice my cheeks were burning. They felt on fire. "Oh, you know, the usual."

"Let's save these questions for Bob," Mother interrupted. "Invite him over this Friday. Is there something wrong, dear?"

She scrutinized my face as I tried not to breathe.

"Don't worry," she smiled. "We'll try not to be too scary."

Chapter Two

"**B**OO!"

Startled, I dropped my gym-bag as I turned. My first instinct was to punch whoever had screamed into my ear, but before I could react, my senses were overwhelmed by...green?

Green everywhere; it was a total green overload. I didn't know if my eyes, or my embarrassment, could handle it. Bob had painted himself head to toe in our school color. Even his Mohawk looked greener than usual. I barely had time to focus on the frosted tips of his spiked hair before my gaze was drawn to his shirtless green chest. Something, other than all that paint, was definitely not normal. Our other school color was silver, just like the silver duct tape that spelled 'Go AJ' across Bob's torso.

One look at my BF's huge, goofy grin, and I found myself taking on the school color of our rivals, red—bright red.

"Bob, what are you doing?" I hissed through a frozen smile.

Bob's grin faded slightly. "I came to support you. What's the problem?"

"Look at what you're wearing." I scanned the school foyer. A throng of people made their way toward the gym entrance, and everyone was staring.

He threw his arms in the air and yelled, "I got school spirit!"

Oh, God, even his armpit hairs were green. I thought I would vomit.

Bob tugged on his hairs once before lowering his arms. "You like the pits? I looked like a monkey in a tree waiting for these to dry."

I grabbed his elbow and pulled him behind a large potted plant, trying not to transfer too much of the gooey, green grease onto my fingers.

I gazed up at him. Up until this point, I'd been proud that my boyfriend was nearly six foot four, but now, his height only drew more attention as he was waving to people from behind the plant. I had to do something about my BF, quickly, before he made a major fool out of both of us. "Go wash off."

"What?" He scrunched his eyes, looking confused.

Didn't he get it? Was I going out with the school's biggest moron? Maybe Krysta and Sophie were right about him. I exhaled, trying to relax my shoulders, while I thought of the best way to explain. "Everyone's going to make fun of you."

He shrugged. "So."

"So?" The vein in my forehead felt like it would burst. I ground my teeth, trying not to lose my cool. "This is just a scrimmage, not state finals."

If I didn't know any better, I would've thought Bob was trying to get a rise out of me. Were all guys like my brother?

"This is who I am, AJ." Bob shook his head and laughed, his gray eyes sparkling with mischief. "I'm just being myself. I thought that's why you liked me."

"That was...it is." I had to chew on that for a moment.

Bob was just being himself? He wasn't trying to annoy me? Looking into his soft gray eyes, I realized he was being sincere. I guess I knew he was weird before I agreed to go out with him. I should've expected this from a guy who had more body piercings than should be humanly possible.

"AJ! Where are you? It's warm-up!"

I turned at the sound of Keysha, our point-guard, screaming for me in the foyer.

"Okay." Bob jabbed my shoulder. "I'll see you after the game. Watch for me. I'll be the loudest, greenest member of the AJ fan club." He ran toward the gym entrance, hands waving, screaming "Go AJ!" and "Greenwood rocks!"

Stepping from behind the plant, I grimaced at the raised eyebrows of parents as Bob flew by them. I listened to the wave of uproar from my peers, and hoped they were laughing with him and not at him.

As I caught the echo of Bob screaming my name throughout the gym, I felt a twinge of guilt. He was here to support me, and I was too embarrassed to be seen with him. I'd always done what I wanted to do, never caring what others thought about me.

Why did I care now?

Spotting Keysha coming toward me, I realized I needed to shift to game mode and put Bob out of my mind.

"Who's that?" she said, rolling her eyes.

I tensed. I didn't need Keysha telling the whole team their captain was seeing the Jolly Green Giant. "Nobody."

I headed toward the locker room with Keysha beside me.

"I've got some bad news." She frowned.

A list of possibilities ran through my mind. Game cancelled? Our center broke her ankle? Coach Carter was going to increase practice from three to four hours? "What?"

"We have a new coach." She shook her head.

No way! How could Carter have ditched us? We were improving, practicing long hours every day without complaint. She was tough, but a good coach. She encouraged us and sometimes screamed at us, but she knew how to set up picks. Even though she was five months pregnant, Carter never missed a practice or a game.

Wait a minute! Could something have happened to her baby? "What happened to Carter?"

Keysha shrugged. "I don't know, but our new coach is already in the locker room. She barely looks old enough to be our big sister."

That didn't sound good. Coach Carter was the best coach I ever had. Replacing her would be impossible, especially with a newbie.

I paused at the locker room entrance. Nauseating girly giggles were erupting from inside. That couldn't be my team in there. Tentatively, I opened the door, following the sound of annoying laughter.

Turning the corner, I saw her, standing on a bench; my traitorous team huddled beneath her. They gazed at...no, worshipped her like she was some statue goddess.

Hands on hips, she tossed her brown ponytail to the side and looked directly at Keysha and me. "Hey, girlies. What's up?"

Please, don't let this be our new coach. She didn't even look old enough to buy beer.

"Girlies?" I stammered.

"Whoa." She pointed. "Are you AJ?"

This was insane. What happened to Carter? I narrowed my eyes, not bothering to hide the annoyance in my voice.

"Yeah, why?"

"Cool. The star player." She threw a few feints into the air, pretending to shoot an invisible ball into an imaginary basket. "Gonna bust some moves out there?"

Is she for real? Arms folded across my chest, I cocked my head to the side. "Yeah, sure."

"Great, let's get our game-plan. I'm Coach Lowe. Coach Carter is having some problems with the pregnancy thing and has to stay in bed the rest of basketball season." She blew her whistle once before jumping on the bench like a cheerleader pumping up the crowd at a pep rally. "But we're going to have a totally wicked season."

We were way too cool to act like ditzy cheerleaders. Or so I thought. I frowned at the sight of my team jumping and clapping. When Coach Lowe came around and gave everybody a high five, I turned my back, pretending to get something out of my gym-bag.

This *girl* was an adult, so shouldn't she act like one? This was a basketball game, not a slumber party. If she tried to be everybody's friend, the team wouldn't take her seriously when she gave orders. And I knew what that led to—chaos on the court and a losing season.

Unacceptable.

I had a hard enough time getting my mother's respect as the captain of a winning team. If this coach didn't measure up soon, she'd have to go.

Half-time and our side had only twenty points on the board. This was pathetic. The girls weren't listening to me. They kept looking at Coach Lowe as she cheered them on. Not once did she criticize the team when they didn't follow through with their picks. She didn't yell at the ref when I was fouled three times by the same big, stupid, Godzilla girl who was breathing fire down my neck.

Lowe had her eyes glued to her cell phone when Joanna and some scrawny redhead got into a wrestling match over the ball. The referee and the other coach were breaking them up before Lowe took notice.

Throughout the rest of the half, I kept waiting for Lowe to call a time-out, but from the looks of it, she was too busy texting. The other coach didn't call a time-out either. He must have guessed Lowe didn't know what she was doing and decided not to interrupt as long as his team was winning.

Paige, our center, never made it to the basket in time. She was too busy smiling and pretending she was playing while Sophie took yearbook pictures. Our rivals only had thirty points, thanks to Keysha, but she was worn out trying to do hers and Paige's job.

When we all huddled for the half-time meeting, I decided to take charge. Lowe had her chance. She obviously didn't know a lay-up from a screw-up. I'd have to coach the team the rest of the season if we wanted to win any games.

I glared at the downcast expressions of my teammates while they pathetically fumbled with their fingers or rocked on their heels. They weren't fooling me. They played well when Carter was our coach, and I knew they hadn't forgotten how to win a game in one day.

I chewed Paige's butt first. "What I want to know is why haven't you been under the basket?"

"I was distracted." She offered a half-hearted, apologetic grin. "I didn't get down there in time."

"That's a lame excuse," I spat.

"Okay, girls, stop fighting." Coach Lowe invaded our circle, shaking her head. "That won't help us win."

Who invited Lowe into the conversation? Was she making an appearance, so the parents watching would think she was a real coach?

This woman was interfering with my team. I leaned forward, jutting my chin up. "Ignoring the problem won't help us win, either."

Lowering her voice, Lowe held out both palms. "Now, let's take a breath and calm down."

"Paige is slow," I growled. "Give me someone who can keep up with the pace."

Lowe's temple creased, and she wagged her finger like I was my little Shitzu, Patches, and I'd just peed on the carpet.

"We're not here to judge the way Paige plays."

I laughed. Is she for real? "Yes we are. I'm the captain. You're the coach. That's our job. Send in Carly," I demanded.

"Give me another chance, Coach," Paige whined.

"Okay, Paige." Lowe smiled and patted Paige on the shoulder. "I know you can do it."

Rage was about to split my head in two. My heart pounded, and not from the exercise. "What? What kind of coach are you?" In my four years of playing basketball, I had never played for such an idiot.

She frowned. "AJ, I think you're the one who needs to sit the bench, and while you're there, think about being nicer to us. We're your teammates."

I heard the shocked intake of breath followed by the low murmurs of my team. I noticed their bulging eyes before they slowly backed away. They knew my temper.

I clenched my fists, trying to keep from exploding. "No, you're not my teammate! You're my coach. How old are you, like twenty? Do you know anything about basketball?" Anger was welling up in me so fast I could feel tears forming at the backs of my eyes.

Her jaw dropped and she put her hand over her chest, looking as if I'd just sent an arrow through her heart. "Look, AJ, I really want to be your friend, but..."

"I don't want you to be my friend!" I screamed, stepping within inches of her face. "I want you to be my coach!"

Who was she fooling, anyway? Pretending like I'd hurt her feelings. Poor Coach Lowe—my butt. I suddenly realized what this was all about. She was trying to make me look like the bad guy and turn my team against me.

Lowe stepped back, mouth agape, before she finally spoke in a heated whisper. "I'm sorry, AJ, but you're out for the rest of the game."

Steam must have been shooting out of my ears, I was so, so MAD. "You can't throw me out. We've only got twenty points on the board and I've scored fifteen of them."

"It's not always about winning." Hands on hips, Lowe flashed a smug smile.

Tears of frustration slipped down my cheeks, which angered me even more. She made me cry in front of my team, in front of the whole school!

"Yes, it is. We're here to win, to bring pride to our school."

"That's right." She nodded. "We are. Being nice to your team is one way of doing that."

"Whatever. You don't know anything about this school or our principal." I wiped my cheeks with the backs of my hands before pointing to the crowd, which had now gone silent. This only raised my humiliation to a new level. "When Mr. Sparks finds out you made the team lose the game because the star player hurt your feelings, you'll be looking for a new coaching job."

Before I gave into my urge to smack that fake hurt expression off Lowe's face, I stormed off. Tears were escaping freely now, but I was too angry to stop them.

As I neared the locker room, a few people shouted, "Bring back AJ!" I smiled inwardly, recognizing the squeals of Sophie and Krysta, which were almost drowned out by the sound of Bob's booming voice.

"Are you going to be in there all night?" Mike was taking forever in the bathroom, and I was sick of waiting. No way was I using the showers in the locker room. I was too upset to stay around and face my friends. Thank God we only lived a few miles away. I was half-way home before Mother picked me up. This was one night I was actually glad Mother didn't go to my game. If she'd seen me getting kicked off the court, I'd never live it down.

All I wanted to do was curl up in my bed with my doggie, Patches, and listen to my iPod—after a hot shower. But Mike was hogging the bathroom again. Sometimes I thought he stayed in there longer than he had to just to get on my nerves.

"Got to look good for the ladies." Mike opened the bathroom door, admiring his muscles in the mirror one last time and reeking of cologne overload.

"Where are you going? It's a school night." I leaned against the doorframe, folding my arms across my chest.

Mike flashed his bleached whites in the mirror before turning out the light. "Krystal James' house to study."

What? Mother shouldn't be letting him go out now. It was past dark. Why did Mike get to do whatever he wanted? It wasn't fair.

As Mike crossed the threshold and stepped into the hallway, the scent of cologne was almost overpowering.

I coughed several times, waving my hand in front of my face. "Studying. Right. What's all the cologne for?"

He smirked, lifting his eyebrows. "We're studying chemistry."

Sure. I knew exactly what chemistry he had in mind. "Is Krystal James Amber James' big sister?"

Mike puffed up his chest like some big stupid ape preparing for a mating ritual. "She's the one."

"I've seen her at your games. Her skirt barely covered her butt cheeks."

On one particular night, she walked up and down the bleachers, giving the guys in the stands a great view of her legs and what was in between. I wanted to grab that slip of fabric she called clothing and yank it down to her toes.

Mike grabbed my shoulder, looking into my eyes with a knowing grin. "Why do you think I made her my study partner?"

"You're a pig." Intending to wipe that cocky smirk off his face, I shot him my best evil glare.

He put his nose by my hair, sniffed once, and then jerked away. "At least I don't smell like one."

Gritting my teeth, I clenched my fists. "I had a game."

"Early night," he laughed. "Get your butts stomped?"

"Go away." I turned away to keep him from seeing the rising heat in my cheeks. If Mike knew what really happened, he'd torment me for months.

I could still feel his annoying presence directly behind my

back along with that awful smell. Didn't he realize there really was such a thing as too much cologne?

"Don't forget to brush your teeth," he sang in a taunting melody.

Shivers of annoyance and dread raced up my arms. Mike was screwing with me. I recognized that tone in his voice from when we were in elementary school and Mike would spit loogies in my orange juice when I wasn't looking.

"What'd you do to my toothbrush?" I turned, narrowing my gaze.

"Nothing." He shrugged his shoulders, pretending innocence. "I just thought you needed a hint."

I leaned against the doorframe, rubbing my aching temples. "I hate you."

Mike shook his head and gave me his best fake smile. "PMS time?"

That was it! I'd had enough!

"Time to shove my fist in your face." I lunged at Mike, clawing and punching at whatever skin I could find.

Unfortunately, my brother was a skilled fighter. He'd had fourteen years of practice holding me down and farting in my face. Before I had time to stop him, he had my arm twisted behind my back and my face pressed into the wall.

"Allison Jenette," Mother screeched as she came flying down the hallway. "That is no way for a lady to behave."

I pushed Mike off of me and faced my mother, rubbing the sore wrist he had squeezed too hard. "What about him?" I yelled.

How did I know this would all be my fault? Didn't she see *I* was the one in the headlock?

Suddenly, Mike's chest deflated and his shoulders dropped. His blue eyes were as wide as saucers, making him look like an innocent schoolboy. "I was coming out of the bathroom and she attacked me."

"Yeah, right," I fumed. "Like you were doing nothing wrong?"

"She called me a pig." He pointed an accusing finger, batting his lashes and turning his lips in a pout.

As if *I* could hurt his feelings! The maggot had no feelings!

"You *are* a pig."

"Young lady, that's enough." Mother's hands were on her hips, her stern glare sending me warning signals. I'd seen that look thousands of times, right before I got my stereo taken away or I was put on social probation.

"Why does he get to stay out late on a school night?" I demanded.

Mother gave Mike a doting smile, right before turning her eye darts back on me. "He has to keep his grades up."

"Yeah." Mike folded his arms across his chest, tilting his chin. "It isn't easy being so successful."

"Are you going to get her to do your homework like all your other girlfriends, or is she doing *other* favors for you?"

Mother stepped back, fingers splayed across her chest, looking like I had just belched at the table. "I can't believe you are talking like that with your mother present."

I hated it when she spoke in third person, and the way she used the word "mother" like she was referring to a queen.

Mike was laughing under his breath and making faces at me from behind her. Such a child. How could girls like him?

Anger returned with a vengeance. "Do me a favor and die, Mike."

"Allison, that's a terrible thing to say." Mother whimpered like a wounded animal. Her bottom lip trembled, and there was a hint of a tear in her right eye. "Don't ever wish death on anyone. What if he died tonight? Wouldn't you feel bad?"

Would I? At the moment, I didn't think so. I'd have the bathroom all to myself. No more zit juice on the mirror or Vaseline smeared all over the toilet seat. Not to mention my life would no longer be a living hell!

I decided to be the mature one in the situation and bow out. "I'm getting in the shower."

"Good," Mother scolded. "Maybe you should wash that mouth out with soap."

I shut the door on her before she finished speaking. I knew that would really make her mad, but I couldn't trust my temper a minute longer. My friends knew I spoke whatever was on my mind and then some.

I swore as I drew back the shower curtain. Mike had left

the shampoo cap off; the bottle had tipped over, leaving a gooey mess dripping down the center of the tub. What a waste. Now, there was barely enough left for me. *Pig.*

No use complaining. Mike would say I did it, and Mother would side with him—like always.

I groaned, thinking of what she must be telling my step-dad, Ted, about me. How I'd attacked my brother, told him to die, and then shut the door in her face. Mother always complains to my step-dad that I don't care about her feelings and that I intentionally act up to make her life hell.

Thank God Ted doesn't always believe her. I don't know what I'd do without his support. He was the only family member I could tolerate.

If Mother knew what I thought sometimes, how really aggravating she could be when she expected me to be someone I wasn't, she'd lock herself in her room and cry for a month. I was hoping this school year Mother and I would actually get along. So far, we were off to a bad start.

And tomorrow was Friday. Bob was coming over for dinner, which meant my relationship with Mother would go from bad to ugly—really ugly.

Chapter Three

"What happened on the court last night?" Krysta stared accusingly at me from over the top of her puke-green vinyl bus seat.

"Yeah," Sophie scolded. "We waited for you after the game."

Krysta and Sophie shared nods of agreement. I suppose they'd rehearsed my butt chewing. Didn't they understand I wanted to be alone?

"We tried to IM you," Krysta said, "but you never came online."

Sighing, I leaned my back against the window as I recalled how they cheered for me last night. Somehow, no matter how bad things got, they were always there for me. Too bad my own family couldn't do that.

"I was too pissed off to talk to anyone." Even though my friends were trying to help last night, I didn't trust myself not to take my anger out on them.

Sophie's eyes widened and then narrowed in a look of understanding. "Your new coach must have really pissed you off."

I couldn't help but laugh. Sophie didn't need to be a mind reader to figure that one out. "Yep."

Krysta smiled, nudging Sophie as if they were in on some private joke.

Even though I had the night to cool down, I wasn't in the mood for any games. "What's that look for, Krysta?"

Folding her arms across the top of my seat, Krysta leaned

toward me. I could tell by the determined look in her eyes, she had some juicy gossip. "I think your coach pissed off Sparks, too."

"Really?" Finally—some good news. Principal Sparks was one guy you didn't want to mess with. The only teacher I'd ever seen stand up to him and live to tell was my math teacher, Mrs. Stein, but she was way cool. Coach Lowe was a major idiot. Maybe she'd lose her job, and Sparks would hire a real coach.

Sophie propped herself next to Krysta. "We waited forever for you to come out of your locker-room, and when all the other players left, we heard Sparks yelling."

"We thought he was yelling at you." Krysta's eyebrows rose behind her bangs, as she placed careful emphasis on each juicy detail. "But then your new coach came out, and we could tell she'd been crying."

Crying? Good. Now she knew how *I* felt. But what did he say to make her cry? Was it about me? "Did you hear what he said?"

"No," Krysta moaned. "We heard screaming, but we couldn't make out what he was saying. We had our ears against the door, the wall, the floor..."

Hmmm. This was getting interesting. "Sparks must have chewed her butt for kicking me off the court."

"Uhhh, yeah," Sophie snickered. "We lost by over fifty points."

"Holy crap!" Sparks hated losing—for any reason. But getting our butts stomped so royally must have really made him mad. No wonder Lowe was crying, but what did she tell him about me? Did she try to say it was all my fault? "Sophie, did you get a chance to read Lowe's mind?"

She shook her head. "I tried, but when she came out of the locker-room, she looked at us and ran."

"Crap." I pounded the bench with my fist. "I wish I knew what she was thinking."

Squinting her eyes, Sophie creased her brow in confusion. "Well, I did get a chance to hear one thing, but it didn't make any sense."

I shot up. Something was better than nothing. "What did she say?"

"Twenty? Ha! Try thirty, stupid." Sophie shrugged. "I told you it didn't make any sense." "Maybe your coach and Sparks were arguing about points," Krysta suggested.

"No," I chewed on my bottom lip, trying to decipher Lowe's thoughts. "That doesn't make any sense." Then a memory from last night hit me. Something I said to Lowe when we were arguing. "Wait a minute. Last night I asked her if she was twenty."

"O-mi-god!" Sophie squealed. "She's thirty!"

"I want to know what moisturizer she uses," Krysta said. "She doesn't look that old."

"Yeah," I huffed. "And she definitely doesn't act that old."

Sophie pointed, grinning. "That means she called you stupid, AJ."

"That's okay," I laughed. "I called her a lot worse all last night."

"I wonder if the rest of your team knows she's thirty," Krysta cooed.

"Probably not." I rolled my eyes, remembering how Lowe giggled and slapped hands with my team. "They treat her like she's one of them." Then again, she acts like she's one of them. "But that nice piece of dirt might be useful later. Thanks, Sophie."

My elation on learning Lowe's real age was short lived. All morning, I'd had a hard knot in my stomach that was threatening to rise into my chest and force me to hurl. Bob was coming over for dinner tonight, and I couldn't escape the feeling my life was a hopeless scrimmage with bad calls and no time outs.

I looked at Sophie, my mind reading buddy and wondered what the experience would be like if I invited her tonight. Would I want to know what Bob thought about my mother, or what my mother thought about him? Actually, I probably didn't need Sophie. Mother had a way of letting us know her feelings with actions. Tonight was going to be scary, very scary.

I kept telling myself things could have been worse as I sat across the table from my scowling Mother. Even though his hair was still green, Bob wore his Mohawk down and only one nose ring. Also, at my request, he'd left off the duct tape. Bob even wore a tie, although I knew my parents disapproved of the way he draped it over a T-shirt and cut off jeans.

"We apologize, Bob." Ted, my step-dad, winked at me while carefully cutting into his venison steak. "We've never had a vegetarian in the house before."

"Mmmm, meat's good, Ted." Mike shoved a piece of meat into his mouth, never taking his eyes of my BF's green hair.

"Thanks." Ted stabbed a piece of meat with his knife. "Killed it myself."

I rolled my eyes. They were trying to scare him away. My family couldn't make it any more obvious. "You already told us that when you showed Bob your gun collection."

Mother cleared her throat as if to speak. The table fell silent. She hadn't spoken a word since Bob walked through the door. "I hope you don't become a vegetarian, too, Allison Jenette."

I cringed at the sound of Mother using my full name. A sure sign she was less than happy in my choice of boyfriend.

"You'll go hungry in this house," Ted said.

"No, I'm not going vegetarian," I growled while pushing my food across the plate.

I looked at Mother's frozen features. Her lips were twisted in a tight knot as she took dainty sips from her water glass. I'd been trying and trying to get Mother to accept me. Maybe if I changed—*really changed*—she would miss the old AJ.
Don't even think it, AJ, that's crazy. Your mother would go nuts.

Then I looked over at my boyfriend. He was wedged in between Mike and Ted. His elbows were bent at awkward angles and he hunched over his salad, toying with his fork. Poor Bob. He was too nervous to eat.

Maybe it was the overwhelming urge to vomit, but for some reason, I wasn't in the mood to eat, either. I sensed this night would be a disaster. Having Bob over for dinner was a bad idea, and I'd tried to talk my mother out of it all week. She refused to listen. Now my stomach was doing back flips. He was the first guy I ever liked who actually liked me back, and my family was going to scare him away.

Ted stabbed a big, juicy piece of meat with his fork and held it under Bob's nose. "Are you sure you don't want some deer, Bob?"

Bob shifted in his seat. "That's okay. This lettuce stuff is really good."

Mike exploded into laughter, nearly choking on his food. "It's called salad, Bob."

I slammed my fork on my plate, causing my mother to jump in her seat. "Shut up, Mike," I hissed.

I didn't need to have Sophie's powers to sense my boyfriend's discomfort. Just because Bob had green hair didn't mean he had no feelings. He was smart, sensitive, and he made me laugh. They weren't giving him a chance.

"Mind your manners at the table," Mother said between clenched teeth.

I cursed under my breath, trying hard not to throw the mashed potatoes in my brother's face. "Why doesn't Mike mind *his* manners?"

Mike set down his fork and flashed a menacing grin. "I'm sorry, would you like a refill on your drink, Bob? I can get you some *green* punch."

I couldn't help but wish I'd never had a brother.

Bob left shortly after dinner. I couldn't blame him for not wanting to be around my family. I couldn't stand being in the same room with them, either. My mother would probably be mad I didn't help with the dishes, but I didn't care. Storming into my bedroom, I slammed the door in frustration. How could they be so mean to him? My first real boyfriend, and it was over. He wouldn't want to be with me now.

I slumped into the chair in front of my computer. No sense calling my friends. My mother would only try to listen in. At least she wasn't good with technology. She read my email once, but I changed my password. Anyway, I just wanted to message Krysta. She told me she was having *visitors* over and would be home. Hopefully, she'd be near her computer. Luckily, she was on Facebook when I signed on.

- Hey, U there?

— Yeah. How'd it go?

- What do U think?

— Rents don't like green hair?

- LOL.

— What did Bob say?

- Nothing, but I bet he dumps me.

— How do U know?

- Family hates him.

— Maybe not if he changes his hair.

- I can't ask that.

— What if you changed something for him?

- Like what?

— Hey, somebody's here. G T G.

- Company?

— Sort of. Later.

- Later.

Krysta didn't have much family, so I didn't know what kind of company she had. I did know she was getting a lot more supernatural visits lately. Crap. I really needed to talk to someone. Sophie was at a game tonight, and I had no family I could go to.

This sucked.

What could I change for Bob? I liked my image, and my mom would skin me alive if I came home with green hair. But what if? Hmmmm. It was only a passing thought at the dinner table, but could I give up eating meat? Maybe if I went vegetarian, he'd tone down his image for my family.

It was worth a try. After all, I wouldn't be losing much. I ate cereal for breakfast. Giving up the processed cardboard at school wouldn't be hard, which meant I would only make the sacrifice at dinner. How would Mother react? Would she cry? Would she say I was doing this to hurt her? And what about Mike? This would just add more fuel to his endless tormenting.

Sighing, I stripped out of my clothes and pulled on my snuggly flannel PJs. I used to fantasize I'd been switched at birth and my real family was looking for me. I knew that couldn't be true. Mother, Mike and I all had the same blonde hair and crystal blue eyes. Forcing a laugh, I recalled my latest fantasy. Mike was abducted by aliens, and I never had to see him again.

Why did it seem his only pleasure in life was to make my life hell? Exhausted from the night's stress, I crawled into bed hoping that tonight the little green men would pay Mike a special visit.

Chapter Four

"Stay away from the ledge before you fall!"
"You can't tell me what to do."
"Don't do it, Mike!"
Aaaaaahhhhhh!
"AJ, wake up. You're dreaming."
The sound of my step-dad's voice startled me. My eyes found Ted's and then trailed toward his fingers, which had my arm in a tight grip. My focus traveled downward, and I found myself looking at my bare toes that were hanging just over the edge of our empty swimming pool. All I had to do was lean forward, and I'd find myself at the bottom of an eight-foot concrete hole.
"How'd I get out here?" I asked, my voice shaking.
"You were sleepwalking."
Sleepwalking?
"Must have been a pretty wicked dream." Mike's voice sounded strangely hollow, like he was speaking from somewhere miles away. I knew he was right behind me, so why did I think he was still in my dream?
The dream!
The images from that nightmare came racing back and the realization sent my head spinning. Mike was the person who was falling.
My brother was going to die!
I felt my legs give way beneath me. I heard my mother scream as I fell into steady hands.
Then darkness.

My life sucks.

Hand across my forehead, I lay motionless on my twin bed, staring up at my Clay Matthews posters. Mother had restricted me to my room all weekend. I didn't want to be around my family anyway. My thoughts were way too troubling. However, being locked away like this, only gave me more time to mull over that wicked dream.

Only one more day until Monday.

I didn't think I'd look forward to school or basketball practice with my annoying coach, but anything was better than being locked away, forced to dwell on my brother falling to his death.

Tap. Tap. Tap.

I jumped at the sound, nearly falling off my bed. Was that a tree branch hitting my window, or did some of Krysta's friends decide to pay me a visit?

Neither.

Staring at two sets of widened eyes, I gently pried open my window, hoping not to make a sound. Either Krysta and Sophie were awesome friends to risk my mother's wrath, or they were idiots who were about to get me in more trouble.

Squinting into the setting sun, I wondered if they'd brought news or if they were looking for gossip. "What are you two doing here?"

"Did you think of something to change?" Krysta's eager eyes barely peaked from above the window sill.

"We've been trying to message you all day," Sophie scolded. "Did they put you on social probation because of Bob?"

I sighed, sinking into my seat. "Kind-of. Mother took away the phone and computer this morning when I refused to eat bacon."

The effects of my restless night of sleep had set in. Afraid of having that dream again, I'd practically slept with one eye open. Now every muscle in my body hurt from tension, exhaustion and depression. When I said I wanted Mike to die, I never really meant it. I rubbed my swollen eyelids. Mother was right. I would feel really bad if he died, and though he wasn't dead yet, I felt as if he'd already been buried.

My brother was as good as gone—forever.

My visions always came true.

"What's wrong with bacon?"

I broke from my thoughts to see Sophie squinting at me like I was some specimen in science class.

I shook my head, trying to clear it of all thoughts of Mike on a cliff, at a morgue, in a coffin. "What?"

Sophie's eyes widened. "You love bacon. Why wouldn't you eat bacon?"

I exhaled slowly. Since I ate lunch with them at school, Sophie and Krysta would have to find out sooner or later. Hopefully, they wouldn't make a big deal out of it like my mother. "I'm going vegge."

Sophie cocked her head. "You're going where?"

I tensed. "Not where—what."

Contorting her face, Sophie scratched her head. I could see her mentally trying to process the conversation. "What...what?"

I tried to stifle a laugh. My whole world was upside down at the moment, yet watching my friend's confused expression was funny. "Vegetarian."

"Why would you do a thing like that?" Krysta squealed.

I put a finger to my lips. Krysta's big mouth was going to get us caught. Dropping my voice to a hiss, I leaned closer. "It was *your* idea."

Angling back, and nearly sitting on my mother's well-trimmed bushes, Krysta splayed her hand across her chest. "*My* idea?"

"You told me to change something for him."

Krysta's eyebrows disappeared beneath her perfectly sculpted bangs. "I didn't think you'd do something like this."

"What else was I to give up? Basketball? I don't think so."

Sophie was still scratching her head, only now she was seriously chewing on her bottom lip. "So does that mean Bob is a vegge person?" "Yeah, he's a vegetarian."

Their appalled faces reminded me of my family the night Bob came over for dinner. I cringed at the image of Bob accidentally dumping the entire bottle of ranch dressing onto his salad. Mike had loosened the spill-proof top right before he handed it to Bob.

"Whoa," Sophie's mouth fell open. "Bob just keeps getting weirder."

"Look," I snapped. "I don't want to talk about it anymore."

"Come on, AJ," Sophie whined.

"Are you still allowed to see him?" Krysta refused to drop the subject.

Throwing my head back in annoyance, I folded my arms across my chest. "I'll do whatever I want."

"How?" Krysta nagged. "Your mom knows everything."

My heart plunged, and I felt a burning emptiness in my chest. "Not everything."

Sophie bit her bottom lip and moving forward, she eyed me intently. "What happened, AJ?"

I could tell by her fixed gaze; her mind had sensed my despair.

"I had the dream again," I whispered. My eyes locked with hers, as I willed myself to let her see what I was too afraid to say out loud.

Understanding flashed in Sophie's eyes, and I knew that she knew. She leaned back, her jaw locked, and I watched her process what my mind had just told her.

Krysta cleared her throat. "Did you see who it was this time?"

My mouth instantly dried up as if it had been stuffed full of cotton. I couldn't speak. I couldn't say his name. It was as if speaking it out loud would make Mike's death real.

"Mike," Sophie breathed.

"O-mi-god!" Krysta practically yelled. Her hand flew to her mouth as her eyes darted from side to side.

Sophie's serious, steady gaze found mine again. "What are you going to do?"

I barely choked out the words. "I don't know what to do."

"Tell your parents," Krysta said sternly.

"Tell them what?" I shook my head. "I had a psychic vision Mike will fall off a cliff." Knowing how I felt about Mike, they'd think I was just fantasizing.

"Well," Krysta's voice was shaky and high- pitched. "You can't let him die."

"Don't you think I know that?" But how would I save my brother? There wasn't a single adult on the planet who I could tell my secret to. Sometime in the future, Mike would be near a cliff. He would fall. He would die.

And there was nothing I could do to prevent it.

Chapter Five

The doorbell had been ringing for nearly ten minutes. Yet, no one got off their lazy butts to answer the door. Room restriction or not, I couldn't stand the noise anymore. Marching down the hallway to the front door, I was determined to tell whoever it was to go away. Probably one of Mike's girl groupies, anyway.

Shoving open the door, I knew my face was fixed with a pissed-off scowl. I didn't really care. Ten minutes was long enough to ring a doorbell.

My jaw dropped as I stared down in stunned silence at the person who was standing in the entryway. I thought no adult could help me save Mike, but my prayers had been answered—Grandma.

"Well," She pointed a jeweled finger up at my nose. "Are you going to just stand there all day? My bones are tired. I need a hot cup of lemon tea and *somebody* is going to rub my feet."

Even though it felt like an eternity since I'd seen Grandma, she was a person who was hard to forget. I knew she hadn't changed much since the last time I saw her. Still forward, still demanding, still strange.

She was a tiny woman, but her forceful presence more than made up for it. I looked down at her long, silver braids. Cascading from beneath her same weathered, green velvet cap, they flowed down her back, nearly reaching her bottom in two neat rows.

"Grandma," I gasped. "What are you doing here?"

Her eyes narrowed in mock anger, but a slight smile

tugged at the corner of her mouth. "That's a fine hello. I'd prefer a hug." She held her arms open.

"I'm sorry." I reached down and was grabbed in a fierce embrace. "I didn't know you were coming."

"Neither does your mother." She pulled away and winked, her eyes dancing with the same mischievous gleam I'd seen in my two-year-old cousin right before he threw my step-dad's iPad in the toilet.

"You're kidding." I couldn't believe my luck. If there was anyone on the planet who was crazy enough to believe in my dreams, it was Grandma, and now she was standing on the front porch.

"I have two bags in the trunk and one in the backseat." She nodded in the direction of her fire red classic convertible. "I'm going to stay for a while." She stepped inside and sneered at her surroundings, like a queen who was tossed into a dung heap.

"I'll get them in a minute, Grandma." Shutting the door, I followed at her heels. "I have to see the look on Mother's face when she sees you."

Shaking her head, Grandma walked a few steps into Mother's sitting room. Her eyes scanned the pale-pink custom window hangings and the Victorian-style sofa and chairs. Paintings of flowers adorned the walls and a fresh bouquet sat atop Mother's antique coffee table. "Is this a house or an art museum? This won't do. How am I going to get comfortable when I can't put my feet up?"

Standing awkwardly behind her on the plush white carpet, I knew what Grandma must have been thinking. From Mother's antique china to her glass egg collections, everything looked breakable.

And it was. I'd found out the hard way more than once. Even when Mike broke things, I somehow got the blame.

"Go fetch me some tea and find that mother of yours."

Grandma tapped my foot with her long walking stick, which was so withered and gnarled, it looked like an angry, possessed tree limb.

Then Grandma did the unthinkable. I gasped in shock, while covering my mouth to hide a smile. She plopped on Mother's brocade sofa, resting both feet on the spotless, polished coffee table as if it was the most natural thing in the world. I wasn't even allowed to sit on the edge of the sofa.

"Mother? What are you doing here?"

I looked behind me to see my mother standing in the hallway, her skin as pale as a ghost. She was leaning against the doorframe, looking as if she would faint from shock.

I was shocked, too, but not by the sight of my mother. The odious tone in her voice when she spoke to Grandma sounded just like the way I addressed *my* mother. For the first time ever, I felt like Mother and I had something in common. For some reason, this wasn't comforting, and not just because, unlike my mother, Grandma was cool. No, there was something more disturbing about our common thread. Watching as my mother's eyes turned to stone and her lips twisted into an icy sneer, I swallowed hard. My mother was acting just like a hateful snot. Even worse, my mother was acting just like...me.

As impossible as this sounds, dinner with my family was even more tense than the night with Bob. Mother sat at the end of the table with Grandma to her right. I didn't think Mother could fit any food through her tight scowl, but she managed to shove nibbles into her mouth while maintaining a glare at Grandma.

Grandma didn't seem to be bothered, as she smiled serenely at me, winking while she filled her wine glass for a second time. I couldn't help but wonder if Mother always treated Grandma like this? Like I treat my mother? Grandma had only been to visit twice in my life, and the last time had been so long ago, I guess I was too young to notice their tension.

Mother cleared her throat loudly. Something she only did when she wanted to command attention. Her sharp gaze focused on Grandma, as she tightly gripped an eating utensil in each hand. "So how long will you be staying, Mother?"

"Haven't decided." Grandma shrugged, not even looking up as she took another sip of wine and shoved in a mouthful of food.

Mother's voice rose several octaves. "What's there to decide?"

"You sound like you're in a hurry to get rid of me, Margaret, and I only just got here." Grandma gulped her wine, a mischievous smile tugging at the corner of her lip.

Mother gripped her silverware so hard, I thought the metal would break. "Well, had I known you were coming, I..."

Setting down her wine glass, Grandma stared directly at Mother. "You would have taken the phone off the hook and barred the door."

A tiny gasp, and my overly dramatic Mother dropped her fork, splaying her hand across her heart. "Mother."

"Don't 'Mother' me. I'll leave when I'm good and ready. I have a lot of catching-up to do with my granddaughter." Grandma leaned over, patting my hand before she shot Mother an accusing glare. "Since you won't send her to me for summer breaks."

Totally shocked, I jerked back. I could have been spending my summers with the coolest grandma ever? Why didn't Mother tell me this?

Trying to repress my anger, I felt the heat rise in my chest. From the endless nagging by my mother, to the relentless teasing by my brother, summers in my house were tortuous. Just think, all that could have been avoided if Mother had let me go.

Mother's lips tightened and she shook her head. "AJ has volleyball camp every summer. She's the star player." Emphasizing the word 'star', mother raised her chin and smiled at me.

"Basketball, Mother." I spat. Mother had a lot of nerve pretending to be proud. She didn't even know what sport I played. Maybe because she never stayed to watch me practice.

"Yes, well, whatever." She waved me off with a flick of her wrist. "She's too busy to go see you."

I clenched my jaw. "Basketball camp is only four weeks." I wasn't about to be dismissed that easily.

"And the rest of the time," Mother cleared her throat before casting me her 'shut-up-or-die' glare, "I need her at home."

Refusing to let Mother use me as a scapegoat, I threw down my silverware, not even trying to hide the anger in my voice. "To do what?"

"Allison Jenette," she whispered between clenched teeth while somehow still managing a smile, "stay out of our conversation."

I threw up my hands. "This conversation is about *me*."

"You know what, you're right." Mother sighed, tossing her napkin in her plate. "Since this is all about *you*, you and Grandma can finish this conversation." She rose, dramatically pressing both palms against her forehead. "I feel one of my headaches coming on. If you'll excuse me, I'll be in my room." Without another word, Mother swept out of the dining room.

If Mother was trying to make me feel bad, I guess her plan worked as I felt the temperature rising on my guilt-o-meter. Why did everything have to be so hard between us? Why couldn't we just get along? I didn't want to end up hating my mother like she hated Grandma. With the way things were going, ten years from now, I'd be screening my calls. I'd be keeping my kids away from their evil Grandma.
Oh, God.

I had the sudden realization my daughter would hate me, too. Were the women in my family doomed to hate one another? No. I couldn't let this opposition continue. So far, my goal at earning Mother's respect wasn't going well.

I needed some way to clear the scoreboard between us. The only way I saw to end strife on the team was by working on the relationship between two fierce rivals, but getting Mother and Grandma in the same room together was difficult enough. How was I going to get them to play fair?

Chapter Six

Even though it meant the start of a tortuous school week, Monday couldn't have come fast enough. Since I had been on phone and computer probation all weekend, I hadn't talked to Bob in two days. Luckily, he sat behind me first period.

The bell hadn't rung yet, but when I looked through the window, I spotted what was either a cactus growing out of a desk or my boyfriend's hair. Dropping my shoulders, I slumped against the door. He beat me to the classroom. Was he there early to be with me or to breakup with me? I choked back a laugh, thinking how a split would be easier than telling my boyfriend he had to change.

My worrying was interrupted by two ditzy cheerleaders who nearly opened the door before realizing I was leaning against it. I stepped aside, and after a torrent of nauseating giggles, they bounced through the doorway, the ringlets in their pony tails springing back and forth like little slinkies.

Their laughter caused the few students in the classroom to turn. I tried to duck before catching sight of the gleam in Bob's gray eyes. Waving me over, he broke into a wide grin.

Just one look at his smile and I knew he wasn't going to break it off. Feeling the tension drain from my body, I was shocked to realize how important Bob was to me.

"Hey." Dropping my book bag at my desk, I slid into my seat. "I'm sorry about Friday."

"I'm cool." He shrugged. "Rents don't like me?"

I tried my best to smile reassuringly. "They just need to get to know you. Are you still coming to my game Thursday?"

"Your first game of the season. I'm there."

Something in the way he looked at me was just so pure, so honest, so real. That's what I liked about him. He didn't play games.

I needed to be honest like Bob. Just come right out and ask him to rip off the tape and tone down the hair. I suspected that under the façade of green spikes, Bob was a guy who would easily get his feelings hurt. I had to use a more cautious approach. "How do you get two people to change for each other?"

Bob's smile faded, his eyes narrowing. "Who are these people?"

His tone was not reassuring.

"My grandma and mother." Well, it wasn't a total lie. They needed to change, too.

Bob threw his head back, laughing. It felt good to hear his deep, throaty voice. He must have known I was asking the impossible.

"I don't know your grandma, but I don't think your mother will change."

I shook my head. "That's what I'm afraid of. I really want them to like each other."

"Why?"

He turned his gray eyes upon mine, and I felt like melting on the spot. Outside of Sophie and Krysta, Bob was the only person I had in my life who actually showed interest in my needs.

"It's complicated," I sighed. "I just want our family to get along."

"Good luck." Bob rolled his eyes. "My mom hates my dad because he drinks. He hates her because she nags."

A dull pain strummed at my chest. I never knew. Bob was always in a good mood, always smiling and just being real. How could a guy like this come from a bad home?

"So why don't they change for each other?"

"Like you said." Fumbling with a frayed corner of duct tape, Bob turned his eyes down. "It's complicated."

I couldn't imagine dealing with the drinking every day. He must feel so alone. "Are there any other kids in your family?"

Breaking into a wide grin, Bob's eyes lit up. "I have five baby sisters."

Five! I'd never get to use the bathroom if I had five brothers. Sounded like Bob lived in hell, and it also explained why he didn't wear nice clothes. "That's a lot of kids. No wonder you're so..." I bit my tongue. I had a reputation for saying whatever was on my mind, but my big mouth might have hurt my BF's feelings.

Leaning his head forward, I couldn't tell if Bob's locked jaw was suppressing a smile or a frown.

"Finish what you were gonna say."

Pressing my lips together, I shook my head.

Bob moved so close, I could inhale his scent.

Peppermint. Poor or not, he had good breath.

He quirked a brow. "No wonder you're so poor?"

"I'm sorry," I breathed. "I didn't mean it."

"It's okay. I know I'm poor. At least you're honest. That's why I like you."

A wave of guilt washed over me, making my heart clench. Bob liked me because I was honest, yet I couldn't be truthful and ask him to change. Looking into his smiling eyes, I didn't know if I could go through with it.

"So what's it like with all those girls?" I asked, intending to shift the subject.

Bob's attention turned toward his duct tape again, the corners of his lips turning up in a playful grin. "I love my sisters."

He couldn't be for real. No brother loves his sister. Brothers were supposed to put ice down their pants and hide cockroaches in their shoes. "You don't torment them?"

Bob looked at me like I'd just missed a free throw. "No."

"That's strange." What a new concept—a brother who was nice to his sister...sisters. This guy was getting more perfect each day. And I wanted to change him.

"Someone's gotta look out for them."

"I didn't know you had it so hard."

Bob just raised his hands, shrugging, as if to say "no biggie."

But it was a big deal to me. His family life was a lot worse than mine, so why didn't he complain?

"Anyway." He smirked. "Maybe you should tell your mom and grandma to back off."

"Ha. Yeah, right. Maybe you should dye your hair back and take off the tape." My hand flew to my mouth. I couldn't believe I had said that. What an idiot.

Bob jerked back, the prickly spikes on his head clanging together almost sounded like they were hissing at me. "What?"

My loose tongue had gotten me in trouble again, and there was no taking it back. "Look, I'm sorry, but Mother went on and on all weekend about your hair."

"This is who I am." Bob threw his arms out, his slacked jaw and widened eyes made him look like he was being crucified.

"Hey." I reached for his hand, only to feel him pull away. "I know that. I love your greenness. It's not me, it's Mother."

"No." His eyes narrowed. "I think it is you. You're too afraid to stand up to her."

Bob had laid a verbal smack-down—big time. Afraid of Mother? I wasn't afraid of anyone. "Excuse me?"

"I'm not changing." He turned his back to me, fumbling through his backpack. Was that it? He was just going to throw a feint and back off.

Time out!

Feeling my pulse quicken, I knew I couldn't lose my temper with my BF, but first he insulted me and then said he wouldn't change?

"I changed for you," I said while clutching the edge of my desk. "I haven't eaten meat in two days."

He dropped his bag, turning with a scowl. "I didn't ask you to change."

"I don't want to change you forever, just when you're around my mother." Bob was being unreasonable. After Friday, he should have seen what kind of woman I was up against.

His eyes took on the hue of coal. "So...you don't want me to be myself around your family?"

Releasing the desk, my shoulders fell. The image of my mother's twisted snarl invaded my mind, and a realization struck me. "No, well, kind-of. My mother is a little crazy."

Was this what Bob was talking about? Was I afraid of

Mother? No, I didn't fear her. All I wanted was her approval.

Chewing on the end of a pencil, Bob looked lost in thought before his eyes finally turned toward mine. "I'll think about it, but you need to eat meat or you'll crash on the court."

First he said I was afraid of Mother and then he dogged my game. Squaring my shoulders, I raised my chin. "Do you know who you are talking to? I was voted MVP two years running. I don't crash."

That is if my idiot coach lets me back in the game.

Heading toward the gym, I felt apprehension sink in my gut like a lead ball. Hopefully, Sparks yelled at Coach Lowe the other night because she kicked me off the court. If he did, would that be enough to get her off my back?

For some reason, I couldn't shake the fear Lowe would try to take my captain's position away, or even worse, get me kicked me off the team.

"Hey, AJ!"

Absorbed in my thoughts, I hadn't noticed the girl standing in front of the locker-room door until I heard her call my name. I had to do a double take, because that girl, wearing K-Swiss tennies, low-rise jeans and a cut-off tank, was actually Coach Lowe.

Shaking my head, I didn't hide my disgust as I examined her from head to toe. Wasn't there some kind of dress code for teachers? Or some kind of poser law for people over thirty?

Lowe motioned me toward the other side of the bleachers. "I wanted to talk to you about the other night."

Arms folded across my chest, I faced my opponent. "Yeah, what?"

Lowe's frozen smile didn't quite reach her eyes. "I wish things could have worked out differently."

This must have been her insincere way of saying sorry. I wasn't buying it.

"You mean you wish you hadn't kicked me out so the team didn't get their butts stomped?"

Truth hurts. I watched Lowe's smile drop for a second before she pasted it on again. "Look, this isn't easy for me."

I couldn't suppress a sneer. Why should it be easy for her? "It wasn't easy for me to get kicked off the court by some newbie coach after I've been practicing my butt off for four years."

"I regret that had to happen."

Lowe didn't even try to mask the fake sincerity in her voice as she pretended to pick dirt out of her fingernails.

"Yeah, I'm sure you do."

"Look." She jutted a hand on her hip, cocking her head to the side. "The point is I don't want it to happen again."

What she meant to say was she couldn't afford for it to happen again, or she'd get canned by Sparks.

Crossing my arms, I moved close enough to invade her personal space. "It won't happen again as long as you act like a coach and not a fourteen- year-old."

"Fine." A twitch jerked the top of Lowe's lip as she backed up a few inches. "And maybe you can focus less on yourself and more on your team."

"Focus on my what?" I moved closer, cornering her against the bleachers.

Her eyelid twitched. "Everything out there shouldn't be about what you want."

"It's not about what I want." I said, keeping my tone firm. "I just happen to be the only one who knows how to play the game."

"Let's just quit with the insults." Lowe crossed one shaky arm over the other, digging into them with her fingers. "Ever think about just having fun?"

"If I want to have fun, I'd be a cheerleader. I want to win. I want this team to win, but ever since you came along..." Jutting my chin, I sent Lowe a heated glare. "They don't care about winning."

"Maybe they'd try harder," she stammered, "if you were nicer to them."

Not this feel-good bull again. When was she going to realize this was basketball, not group therapy?

"What's nice got to do with it?"

"Just think about it." Lowe pointed accusingly. "Ever smile at your teammates when you walk into the locker room? Do you know their cell numbers, Twitter handles? Are you one of their Facebook friends?"

Twitter? Facebook? Why? Krysta and Sophie were all the friends I needed. What did I have to say to my teammates? It's not like my team partied together outside of basketball.

My jaw dropped. Did they?

"I didn't think so." Lowe smugly smiled. "You don't support them as their captain, so they're not supporting you. That's why we don't win."

Turning my back on her, I marched toward the locker room. I saw what happened on the court Thursday. We've never lost so badly before Lowe came along. I didn't hang out with my teammates last year, and that didn't stop us from winning number one in our division.

But why wasn't there a party after the division championship? Weird how the school made such a big deal out of it, and then nothing. Two seconds on the clock, and my three pointer won us that game. But still, if there had been a party, I should've known.

"What's wrong, AJ?" Sophie's brow drew to a frown as she stared from across her processed meat product.

I never thought it could look tempting, but I was beginning to wish I had a Barfy burger smothered in artificial tomato paste.

"Nothing," I said, though I knew it was a lie.

I sank in my seat, picking through the wilted lettuce, crusty carrot slivers and watery ranch dressing substitute in my cafeteria salad. Somehow, I didn't think the salad had made me lose my appetite. I had a difficult time digesting what Lowe had said. I couldn't help but to wonder...*did my team really not like me?*

Sighing, Sophie rested her chin in her palms before batting her eyes. "I can tell something's bothering you."

"Yeah." Krysta chirped between sips of her diet soda. "Tell us or I'll send Sophie after your brain."

Exhaling, I gripped the sides of the table before focusing my gaze on my friends. "Am I nice?"

Sophie paused, mid-bite, her eyes bulging before she relaxed her face. "What?"

"Am I cool to hang out with?" Narrowing my eyes, I waited for Sophie's reaction.

"Yeah." Sophie shrugged before elbowing Krysta.

"I guess," Krysta said while keeping her eyes averted.

In all honesty, I was hoping they'd tell me Lowe was full of crap and I was a cool friend. Their reactions cut hard. Was I really that bad?

"You don't sound too sure," I huffed.

"No, you're cool," Sophie stuttered.

"Why?" Casting a glare from one friend to the next, I prepared for their next lame reaction.

"Because we can be ourselves around you," Krysta blurted.

That wasn't the answer I wanted. Krysta and Sophie were different like me. What about normal teens?

"No." I waved my hands. "Forget that. Pretend we're normal. Wait. Pretend you don't know me very well. Would you ask me to a party?"

"No way." Sophie jerked back.

O-mi-god. This was worse than I thought. Was I some kind of monster? "What? Why?"

Krysta pointed at me. "That look."

My gaze locked with Krysta's. "What look?"

Lifting her brows, Sophie nodded. "That look like you're going to shove your fist through my face."

"What are you talking about?" I wasn't going to punch Sophie, and I didn't *feel* myself giving her a dirty look.

"You're doing it right now," Krysta laughed.

"Doing what?" My fingers traced the contours of my face. It *felt* normal.

The corner of Sophie's mouth tilted up. "You're pretty scary looking, AJ."

"You're wacked." I shook my head. They were both messing with me. I wasn't scary. I was just AJ.

"No, she's right," Krysta agreed. "You always have that pissed-off look."

"Yeah," Sophie snorted. "Like you're ready to kick some butt."

I couldn't believe what I was hearing. And from my two best friends. "Why didn't you tell me this before?" I shot them both accusing glares.

"I thought you wanted to look scary," Krysta shrugged.

"Yeah, you know, kinda goes with the tough jock-girl image," Sophie said.

Heaving a sigh, I rubbed my aching temples. "I want people to respect me, not hide from me."

"So stop giving people that look," Sophie said matter-of-factly, as if she was making a simple request.

"What look?" I demanded. How could I stop doing what I couldn't see?

Leave it to Krysta to have a cosmetic mirror handy. "Here." She held it in front of my face. "See the snarl? The way your brows crease?"

Looking into the mirror, I finally saw what others were seeing. That scowl, that pissed-off expression, made me look like...like...holy crap!

I looked just like my mother!

Lips trembling, my voice lowered to a whisper. "Why are you two friends with me?"

Krysta set down the mirror, squeezing my hand. "We know the real you, AJ."

My throat felt like it was closing shut. Krysta and Sophie were great friends, but they were just two people. "But my team hates me."

Krysta shook her head. "No they don't."

"We don't email or friend each other. I don't know their cell numbers."

"Really?" Sophie blurted before covering her mouth.

"And," I continued, though I felt my throat tighten even more. "I think they have parties without me."

Krysta and Sophie exchanged quick glances. Something in the way Sophie bit her bottom lip confirmed my fears.

My heart leapt into my throat, as I fought the anger welling inside. I felt betrayed, not just by my team but by my best friends. Looking at Sophie, I tried to keep my voice cool. "Why didn't *you* tell me about these parties?"

Sliding in her seat, Sophie looked like she was going to

hide under the table. "I've only been to one. You were on restriction that weekend so I thought that's why you didn't go."

I could feel my pulse quicken, the heat rising up in my cheeks. It didn't matter what my team thought of me. I was their captain! They still should have invited me.

Before I could respond, Krysta's mirror was back in my face.

"There's that look again."

Chapter Seven

"Have a nice day at school, dear?" Grandma was there to greet me when I stormed through the door. I wasn't in the mood to talk to anyone; but just one look at Grandma's smile, and I knew I couldn't refuse her.

"No," I dropped my bookbag on the floor, sinking into Mother's perfectly stitched sofa. I knew if Mother caught me she'd freak, but at the moment I just didn't care.

Besides, I inwardly laughed; Mother would be more pissed-off if she walked in on Grandma sitting in her hand-crafted, floral chair. Grandma's feet were propped on a fresh polished, mahogany piano bench while she chewed on the end of an unlit cigar. Her other hand draped a glass of red wine over the side of the chair. What would Mother say if any wine spilled on her plush white carpet?

Crossing one foot over the other, she sank deeper into the cushion. "Wanna tell Grandma about it?"

I shook my head. "You wouldn't understand."

The corners of Grandma's lips turned in a wicked grin. "I wouldn't understand what it's like when everyone keeps their distance because you're strange?" Grandma took an imaginary puff of her cigar.

I always knew Grandma was weird, but that's why I liked her. I feigned shock. "Kids thought you were strange?"

Eyes narrowing, Grandma pointed at me with her cigar. "I wasn't as adept at hiding my gift as you are, dear."

A jolt of surprise shot through my body. How did she know? "My, my gift?"

"Don't pretend you don't know what I'm talking about." Grandma absently took a sip of wine. "Runs in the family, you know? All the women have it. It's a shame your mother didn't have this talk with you before."

My jaw slacked as I stared at Grandma. I wasn't the only freak in the family? I-I got this from my mother? Struggling to find my voice, I managed to speak in a hoarse whisper. "Having visions runs in the family?"

"So is that your gift?" Grandma tapped her cigar. "I was wondering."

"What do you mean? You said it runs in the family."

Grandma's strong gaze found mine. "Having gifts *does* run in the family, but we all have *different* gifts, dear."

Whoa! Totally weird. My arms and legs felt numb from shock, and a strange chill ran up my neck. "What's your gift?"

Grandma turned her head, her eyes resting on an open bottle of wine sitting on top of the piano. Grandma stretched her palm outward. Though I had a hard time believing what I was seeing, a wine bottle actually floated in mid-air toward my grandma. Hovering above her wine glass, the bottle tipped until the red juices poured. After the glass had been filled, the bottle raised and floated back to the piano.

I looked at the bottle, and then at Grandma's glass, and then back a few times. "Holy crap! I want your gift."

"Be careful what you wish for," she laughed. "Sometimes controlling a gift like mine can be a bit of a trial. Like the time I was craving chocolate and Jimmy Somerday's Hershey bar flew across the cafeteria and into my hands."

I scooted toward the edge of my seat. "You didn't mean to take it?"

"No," she chuckled, "but it was a powerful craving."

No wonder she didn't have many friends. If I hadn't been used to strange happenings between me and my friends, I would've bolted for the door when Grandma lifted that wine bottle. Then a thought struck me. Grandma said this was a family trait.

"What's Mother's gift?"

"That is for her to tell." Grandma sank back in her chair. "She likes to pretend she's normal, so I suspect she'd be pretty angry with me for revealing her gift."

Lost in thought, I chewed on my lip, trying to recall some sign. I really, really wanted to know. "I don't remember seeing her do anything weird."

"No, your mother tries to deny her ability."

"Why?" I asked.

"She likes things to be..." Grandma paused, looking as if she was trying to find the right word, "normal."

No, Mother wanted more than normal. Sometimes I felt she tried too hard to make our family perfect. Was she just doing this to disguise the fact we were freaks?

"Anyway, it's a shame she doesn't use her gift now. I suspect it could come in pretty handy with two teenagers in the house."

What was Mother's gift, and why would she need it with teenagers? Did Mother know I had a gift? She had to. Maybe that was why she always disapproved of me. If she refused to use her gift, did she resent me for using mine?

This would explain why she liked Mike better than me. Grandma said that the women in my family had gifts, so Mike must have been normal. I, on the other hand, reminded her of our family freak gene.

I suddenly realized what I had to do to gain Mother's respect. Before Mother could accept me for me, she had to face the fact she was strange, too. Now all I needed to do was figure out what made her so strange.

Sitting across from Mother at the dinner table, I saw through her for the first time. With each precise, dainty little nibble, she was the image of perfection—on the exterior. Now I knew she struggled to appear normal while knowing she was a freak.

What was her gift? My brain gnawed on that question while my insides were gnawing on each other. I shifted focus to my plate. Rice, carrots and salad. No meat.

Thump. Thump.

My attention was riveted to my brother as he pounded the last of the steak sauce all over his juicy T-bone. "This looks like a delicious steak, Ted." Mike nodded to my step-dad and then sneered at me while sucking the sticky steak sauce off his finger.

What a waste of a good piece of meat. Didn't he realize the flavorful juices, spilling from the perfectly grilled, medium-rare, choice-cut steak, would be overpowered by the sauce?

"That looks like a tasty salad, Sis." Mike shoved a huge, syrupy morsel into his mouth. "Sure you don't want a bite of my steak?"

"Why don't you bite me?" I spat.

"Allison Jenette!" Mother shrieked through the noisy din of silverware hitting her plate.

"Sorry, Mike," I flashed him a forced smile, "but I'm almost full from this salad."

Grrrrr.

"What was that?" Mother's eyes widened.

Ted lifted the tablecloth, his head disappearing under the table. "I don't see Patches under here."

"Sounded like AJ's stomach." Mike laughed.

Mother rolled her eyes. "I knew this diet was a bad idea."

I clenched my silverware. "It's not a diet; it's a lifestyle change."

But as I fought the dizziness creeping into my head, I thought this change wasn't working out. I wasn't a rabbit. I needed real food. Still, I couldn't back out of it now. That would only give Mother one more reason to gloat that she was right.

"I think you're just doing it to piss Mom off."

Mike spoke with his mouth full, making sure I got a good glimpse of his chewed meat.

My upper lip turned in a snarl. Pangs of hunger were replaced by a burning desire to punch Mike in the face. "Kind-of like you always do stuff to piss me off?"

"Enough!" Grandma threw both hands in the air, her booming voice ricocheted in my brain. "Grandma is trying to enjoy dinner." She winked at me before dropping her gaze to her plate.

I sat in stunned silence. I didn't know Grandma had it in her, but the whole table was quiet. The only audible noise in the room was the sound of Patches licking himself.

After what seemed like several minutes, Ted spoke up. "Don't you kids have winter break soon?"

"In two weeks." Mike grinned. "The guys want me to go snowboarding at Hell's Peak."

"Snowboarding?" I nearly choked on my tomato. "Like on mountains?"

"Sounds like fun." Ted puffed up his chest before giving Mike one of those fatherly jabs in the ribcage. "I remember doing that stuff when I was your age."

I knew exactly what kind of 'fun' Mike was in for. As much as my brother annoyed me, I still didn't want him dead.

"That sounds dangerous," I ground out.

Mike stuck out his tongue. "That's why it's fun."

My jaw hardened, along with my determination. "I don't think you should go." Mike wasn't going to die. I wasn't going to *let* him die.

"What?" Mike lurched forward. "Are you my mother?"

"Don't go!" Panic seized my brain.

Mike threw his head back, his eyes widening in shock. "Chill, AJ."

"Allison," Mother gasped, "what's gotten into you?"

Turning pleading eyes to my mother, I had to make her understand the severity of the situation. "Don't let him go, Mother."

"I get it." Mike threw down his silverware. "She's trying to ruin my break."

"No, I'm not." Feeling my throat tighten, I swallowed hard, trying to regain composure. "You could...you could fall or something."

"Wouldn't you like that?" Mike spat.

"This isn't a joke." Tears of frustration threatened at the backs of my eyes, but I couldn't let my family see me cry. They would think I was faking.

"Allison, this isn't your decision." Mother turned up her chin. "Your step-father and I will decide..."

"Don't let him go, Ted." I looked across the table at my step-father. Whenever Mother and I disagreed, he usually came to my rescue. Ted was smart. He had to stop Mike from killing himself.

"My buddies and I spent plenty of winters at Hell's Peak when we were growin' up. You're getting worked up over nothing, AJ."

"No, I'm not." I turned to my Grandma. My last hope. "Grandma, you understand. You know he can't go."

Relief washed through me as Grandma gave me a look of understanding.

She set down her napkin, folding her hands in front of her. "I think you should listen to the girl, Margaret. She has *very* strong intuition."

Mother's eyes looked on fire. She twisted her lips before turning up her nose. "There is no such thing as strong intuition."

I gasped in disbelief. How could Mother ignore my gift when her own son's life was at stake?

Laughing under her breath, Grandma shook her head. "What would you rather I called it?"

"Nothing," Mother spat. "Allison is just a normal kid."

"Mother." I pounded my fists on the table. "Please."

"Mom," Mike whined, "please."

But Mother ignored both of us, as her heated eyes were locked with Grandma's.

"You can go, Mike," she said with frozen features.

"You'll let him die!" I screamed.

Suddenly, Mother jerked away from her stare- down with Grandma. "Go to your room, Allison."

The tears flowed freely, as I threw back my chair and ran to my room. Before I could reach the door, my heart clenched at the sound of my step- dad and Mother casually joking about what just happened.

"Teenage girls these days are so dramatic."

"Tell me about it."

Chapter Eight

Picking up my lunch tray, I made my way toward our usual spot, the last table in the corner of the cafeteria. The one spot in the lunchroom that gave us privacy. Sophie, Krysta and I shared many secrets during lunch. It was our time to unload our psychic burdens on each other. Still, we had to whisper. A large table full of seventh grade maggots was only a few feet away. Too bad we didn't eat in the courtyard. It was much quieter out there—only a handful of freaks.

I had a sudden thought of Bob sitting outside, his green hair blending in nicely with the bushes. We'd been going out for a week and I hadn't sat with him at lunch. Looking down at my veggie salad, I grinned. Wouldn't he be impressed?

Hoping Sophie and Krysta hadn't spotted me, I made a quick right and slipped out the side exit. My heart did a little skip at the site of my BF. Towering in the center of a group of freaks, he looked like one of the courtyard trees. His friends were laughing as Bob showed off his green armpit hairs, which were now braided and tied in little bows. No doubt, the work of one of his sisters.

I smiled. Only Bob could do something like that and still be cool.

Just then, his gaze met mine and I thought I'd melt at the site of his large, goofy grin. What was it about Bob that made me like him so much?

As he waved me over, the freaks parted to let me through. I couldn't help but wonder if they moved aside out of respect for Bob, or if they feared me like my teammates did. Did everybody on campus think I was a bully?

Forcing a smile, I hoped Bob's friends would see I could be cool. The goth girls dropped their heads, concealing their eyes with long, jet-black hair. The dog-collar and chain kids retreated into a corner, huddled around a few Gameboys. The rest dispersed behind trees or benches.

Did they think I had the plague?

The only person to acknowledge me was the kid who claimed to be a reincarnated Egyptian Pharaoh. Placing his hands together in a prayer pose, he bent forward in a deep bow, the gold bands on his neck and wrists reflecting the light from the sun. Without a word, he remained bent over and slowly walked backward into the shadows.

Bob smiled and plopped down on a bench, apparently unfazed by the weirdness of what just happened. "I thought you ate with your friends."

Sitting next to him, I placed my salad next to me on the bench, pretending my best to act like hanging out with the freaks was a totally natural thing to do. "I decided on a change today," I shrugged.

Picking up a fry from his plate, Bob twirled it between two fingers for several seconds. His jaw clenched as his narrowed gaze swept over me.

His silent treatment was annoying. Was I breaking a major rule by eating with my BF?

"Is that all you're eating?" He asked.

Oh, so is that what the dirty look was about? He held a grudge against my salad? "I told you I gave up meat."

"You might as well give up basketball, too," Bob said evenly.

Not this again. Feeling the rising irritation pump through my veins, I exhaled, trying to keep from losing my cool. "We already had this discussion."

Something about the strain in his features told me the smile he flashed was forced. "Are you eating any other protein?"

Great. Just what I needed—another nag in my life. As if my mother wasn't enough? "Can we drop it?"

"What are you two doing here?"

I looked up at the sound of Sophie's accusing voice. She

and Krysta were standing in front of us, but I was so annoyed by Bob's nagging, I hadn't seen them approaching.

Krysta cocked a hip while sipping on a diet soda. "We don't like being ditched."

Just then the Egyptian Pharaoh swooshed past us, making a circle around our group, his long, golden cape bellowing in the breeze. Sophie let out a yelp as he dove toward her before disappearing behind some bushes.

Shifting from one foot to the other, Sophie's gaze trailed the pharaoh before she leveled a glare at me. "I don't feel comfortable eating out here."

"Don't be a chicken." Krysta rolled her eyes before making a gagging sound. "Eeewww, what's that smell?"

"I think that's the smell of too many freaks in one area," Sophie whined.

Krysta fanned her nose. "Don't these beasts shower?"

"Bob," I sighed, "these are my friends."

"Hey." Bob held out a food offering. "French fry?"

Krysta held her nose while shaking her head.

"No, thanks." Sophie said while nodding to the tray in her hands. "I've got a Barfy Burger."

"Cool." Bob smiled before scooting to the end of the bench.

I scooted with him, making room for my friends on the other side of me.

Sophie sat next to me while Krysta sat on the end of the bench, crouching over and making a grand gesture of pretending to be sick by the smell.

I sniffed the air. Yeah, I hadn't noticed it earlier, but it did smell a little. Kind of like rotten eggs, but Krysta was making way too big a deal about it. Not wanting my blood pressure to soar again, I did my best to ignore her.

Peering around me, Bob pointed a fry at Sophie. "You must really like those Barfy Burgers."

"Not really." She shrugged. "But it's the only digestible meat product on the menu."

And without asking, Bob reached over me, picked up Sophie's Barfy burger and took a bite.

My jaw dropped. "I thought you didn't eat meat," I snapped. I wasn't just surprised. I was pissed!

Exposing a mouthful of food, he laughed. "Cafeteria food doesn't classify as meat."

"He's right." Sophie grinned. "I think it falls in the 'other' category."

A tide surged through me and swelled my brain with anger. Feeling every muscle in my body tense, I tried to steady my breathing. "I took a lot of crap from my step-dad because you wouldn't eat his steak, but you'll eat processed vomit?"

"Chill." Bob raised his palms, as if creating an imaginary barrier between his lies and my annoyance. "It's just one bite."

Did he think that stupid excuse would work? "You could've had one bite at my parents' house. *I* went meat free for *you*."

He shook his head, green spikes of hair follicles swaying with his movement. "I didn't ask you to."

Shoving my salad toward him, I stood. "Here. If you're so freakin' hungry, you eat it."

Bob took my salad, setting it on the bench. "What are *you* going to eat?"

"Why do you care?" I spat.

He stood, looking down with a scowl, his eyes darker than thunderclouds. "Because you're my girlfriend. I'm *supposed* to care."

I wasn't intimidated. I'd battled much scarier beasts on the court. "Don't give me that crap. If you really cared, you'd clean up for my mother."

Crossing his arms over his chest, Bob narrowed his gaze. "I'll think about it."

If he could swallow processed, petrified puke, he could tone down his hair and change his clothes—just around my mother.

"Gee, thanks." I turned, needing to get out of the freak pit before I said anything more. Knowing Sophie and Krysta would be at my heels, I stormed through the door and sat at our usual table. Resting my head in my hands, I rubbed my throbbing temples.

How could he eat meat and then just blow it off? How could he commit to a cause one minute and forget about it the next? If he couldn't stick to his lifestyle, how else would he flake?

Would he stay true to me? Or was I just another bowl of salad he'd toss when he got the urge for a Barfy burger?

Burning questions I should be asking my friends. I looked up, expecting to see them, but they weren't there.

Nice.

Even my BFFs thought I was old lettuce. Only one thing left to do. Athletic period was after lunch. Might as well get a head start on the game. Tonight we had a tough match against Quinten Junior High, the team we beat in overtime last year during the first division playoffs. The rest of my team didn't care if they looked like idiots on the court, so it was up to me to bring on the game.

Walking toward the locker room, I thought I heard voices. As I drew near the entrance, I recognized the sound of Paige's high-pitched, girly giggle, her new irritating habit in trying to mimic Lowe.

Was my team practicing at lunch?

No way!

They didn't have the drive. Not now Carter was gone. Whatever they were doing, nobody invited me. Curiosity, and maybe a little bit of annoyance, got the best of me. *What is going on in the locker-room?* A sinking feeling in my gut told me Lowe had something to do with it.

Stopping by the door, I opened it a crack and listened. Yeah, call it spying. I didn't care. The team shouldn't be meeting without the captain, anyway.

"Okay, so here's the deal," Paige squealed. "Coach said she's not buying us beer for the party. She did say she'd have beer in her fridge, and if we took some, she wouldn't notice."

"Cool!" Several voices, who I recognized as my teammates, yelled.

"She could get busted." That was Keysha. Her voice was easy to pick out. She knew how to lay on the attitude.

"No, she can't," Paige whined. "She's not *giving* it to us."

"It doesn't matter," Keysha spat.

"How's she gonna get busted?" Paige said. "No one's gonna tell."

"AJ will tell." Carly bawled.

"AJ doesn't even know about the party."

Who does Paige think she is? She excludes me from the party and then gives orders like she's in charge. She's not the captain—I am! I was so pissed I could feel the heat rise into my chest and swell my brain. I restrained my impulse to storm in there and give Paige the smack-down. I wanted to hear more.

"The captain doesn't know about the team sleepover?" Keysha asked.

Well, at least one teammate was on my side. "Coach doesn't want her there," Paige said. "AJ's not a team player."

Not a team-player, my butt! Besides Keysha, I'm the only one on the team who plays! What Paige meant to say was I'm not a Lowe groupie, butt-kisser.

"AJ's the reason we have a team," Keysha barked.

"Look, Keysha," Paige groaned, "are you in or out?"

"I don't know if my parents will let me go."

I knew Keysha's parents would let her go. Unlike my mother, they were pretty trusting. Keysha didn't want to go. Was it because of me?

At least one good thing came out of this. I knew I had one teammate I could count on.

"Whatever." Paige took on the voice of a ditzy cheerleader. "But don't go ratting on Lowe and ruin our fun."

No, Keysha, don't. That's my job.

The bell sounded, signaling the end of lunch. I raced out of the gym before my team caught me spying.

Let them have their party. Let their supposed-to-be-a-responsible-adult coach get them drunk so they'd think she was cool. So she could pretend to be sixteen again and chill with her buds. So she could turn all of them against me. If this woman refused to grow up, maybe she needed a little help from the authorities. I just had to find out the date of the party.

Lowe was so busted.

Fifth period was English honors, a class I shared with Keysha. She was my best bet for finding the night and time of the party. I didn't know how to get to coach's house, but was pretty sure I could Google her address.

Still not totally sure Keysha was on my side, I had to be cautious when asking her questions. I didn't want her warning the team I was onto them. Lowe needed to get fired, and catching her giving beer to minors was one sure way of doing that.

Keysha was sitting in her desk, reading from her literature textbook when I walked into the classroom. She sat on the opposite side of the room. I had three minutes until the tardy bell, so I had to act fast. Taking a spot in the empty seat beside her, I cleared my throat to get her attention. "Hey, Keysha."

"What's up?" she said with a disinterested tone and keeping eyes glued to the pages of her open book.

What was that all about? The book couldn't have been *that* interesting.

Pretending not to notice, I kept my voice upbeat. "Ready for the game tonight?"

"Yeah," her voice trailed off as she turned a page.

Total blow-off. Grrrr. Her behavior was beyond irritating, making me want to slam my fist on the desk to get her attention. That would only piss her off, and then I'd never get her to tell me about the party.

I tried another approach. Maybe if I bashed our coach, I'd know for sure which side she was on. "I don't know if the team's ready. Lowe doesn't work us hard enough."

She shrugged. "Nope."

Okay, enough was enough. She was obviously trying to get a rise out of me, although I didn't know what I'd done to make her act this way.

"Is there something wrong?" I asked, totally aware my voice was laced with just a hint of attitude.

"No," she replied flatly.

Fine, if that's how she wanted to act. No use messing around with her. Might as well get to the point. "Okay. What are you doing after Friday's game?"

Since we had a game tonight and another on Friday, I was pretty sure the party would be after the next game so they could have Saturday to recover from their hangovers.

"Look, I can't talk right now." Keysha looked up from her

book long enough to roll her eyes at me. "I didn't finish last night's reading assignment."

"Whatever!" I huffed, heaving myself out of the desk and storming back to my seat.

Whatever side she was on before, I knew where her loyalty lay now. One more friend lost to Lowe. One more reason to get her butt canned. This wasn't a popularity contest. This was basketball, but for some reason, my immature coach had found a way to make it personal.

Personal!

A smile came to my face as I thought of a brilliant plan. Lowe wanted to make it personal, so be it. I had just the friend who knew how to get very personal. One little slip into Lowe's mind, and Sophie could tell me exactly when and where to bust the party.

"You want me to do what?" Sophie looked at me like I'd just asked her to French kiss Grody Cody Miller.

I had drug Sophie behind an empty bus, which was parked just outside the gym. As people were piling inside the gym for the game, I knew inside would be too crowded.

Looking over both shoulders, I had to make sure no one was within gossip distance. "Find out about the party," I whispered.

"Okay, I get that part." Sophie cocked a brow. "But how do you expect me to do it?"

Grrr. Why was she acting like this was so complicated? "When you're taking pictures at the game tonight, just pop into Lowe's head."

Sophie smirked. "So you want me to log in to your coach's brain and download the file marked *Don't tell AJ.*"

I exhaled a low, frustrated breath. She still hadn't said sorry for picking Bob over me at lunch today. Now she was baiting me with stupid jokes.

"Very funny."

She rolled her eyes. "I can't just dig around for old thoughts. She has to be *thinking* about the party when I'm in her brain."

"Then pick Paige's brain or any of my teammate's brains." I threw my hands in the air. "Everybody knows about the freakin' party but me."

"Okay." Sophie's gaze narrowed. "Let me get this straight. You want me to forget about my yearbook assignment, which is to take pictures of the game, and keep invading brains so I can find out about a party which you're not invited to."

Why was she making this so difficult? She was my BFF, after all.

Folding my arms across my chest, I leveled a hard stare. "Yep."

Sophie mimicked my posture and returned my stare.

Gawd. Did I really look that mean?

Cursing, I deflated my arms and rubbed my throbbing temple. My day was getting suckier by the minute. To make matters worse, that dizzy nauseated feeling was growing and I had a feeling it was directly related to the hollow in my gut.

"What's the matter, AJ?" Sophie placed her hand on my shoulder.

Just that little show of affection from my best friend and I almost lost it. Turning from her, I choked back the mounting frustration from my crappy day. Taking a deep breath, I slowly exhaled. I wasn't going to cry. Crying was for wusses.

"AJ..." Sophie came up behind me, her voice laced with concern. "What's wrong?"

Forcing the tension from my balled up fists, I faced my friend. Although I was afraid of the answer, I had to know the truth. My entire team hated me. Did Sophie and Krysta feel the same way? "Why did you stay with the freaks at lunch?"

Sophie quirked a brow. "The freaks? You mean Bob?"

"Yeah."

"You seemed pissed." She shrugged. "We thought you wanted to be alone. Besides, Pharoah showed us a cool magic trick. Wanna see?"

A smile sliced through my ebbing tension. Sophie would never hate me. I didn't think she could hate anyone. "Not really," I laughed. "So you're eating with me tomorrow?"

"Duh." Grinning, she rolled her eyes. "Yeah."

"Cool." I nodded while straightening my shoulders. I was

acting like a stupid little whiny girl over nothing. Must have been the hunger pains.

"Is that what's been bothering you?" Sophie asked.

"You know, the usual." Okay, enough talking about my problems. I didn't want to get worked up again. I nodded toward the back entrance of the gym. "I need to get ready for the game." Turning on my heel, I nearly ran head first into Krysta.

"What's up, girlies?" A smile stretched across her face.

I rolled my eyes at her cheesy Coach Lowe attempt. "Ha, ha."

"Good luck tonight." She jabbed me in the ribs. "So I take it you're not going to the team party this Friday."

My jaw dropped, a million questions racing through my mind at once. "Who told you about the party?"

Krysta cocked her head to the side. "Alisha texted me. She got a text from Victoria who heard it from Kurtis, who's going out with Paige."

Information overload. I shook my spinning head. "What did Alisha tell you?"

"They're going to celebrate the game and get wasted."

My insides rumbled, a mixture of hunger and annoyance. "What are they going to celebrate if they suck at the game?"

Krysta shrugged. "Paige told Kurtis you don't need to win to celebrate, as long as you try."

I swore, loudly. "What kind of crap is Lowe feeding them?"

Sophie grinned. "Beer, Friday night."

Who needed meat? I had enough anger to fuel a lifetime. "Not if I can help it."

Prep time before the game was tense. All the girls in the locker room averted their gazes whenever I looked in their direction—kind-of like they had a dirty little secret. They were unusually, quiet, too. Were they afraid of getting their butts stomped by our rivals or by me?

Finding a private corner in the locker room, I stretched my muscles, trying to ignore the gnawing hunger in my belly. Only a few more hours, and what the heck, I was going to the snack bar and eating a big hamburger. Forget what Bob thinks. He didn't care that I'd changed for him. In fact, I was beginning to wonder if he cared for me at all.

Fighting a yawn, I rubbed my eyes. Why was I so tired all of a sudden?

"Okay, girlies, let's go have some fun." Lowe hopped on a bench, hooting and pumping the air with her hands.

Puke.

I barely had the energy to give her a dirty look.

The team jumped up and down, high-fiving each other and giggling. Maybe we should suit up the cheerleaders and have the team do the cheering. Honestly, I didn't think it could get any worse.

I stood quickly, trying to shake the fatigue out of my limbs. That's when a rolling wave of dizziness hit me. Instinctively, I lunged for a locker, using it to steady myself while the room spun around me.

"AJ, you okay?" Keysha said at my back.

"Yeah, I just stood up too fast." I shook my head, allowing a few moments for my body to regain balance. Once again, the room was in focus.

Whew.

I reminded myself not to stand up too fast during the game. Probably just a little dizziness because I didn't finish lunch. Maybe at half-time I'd ask Sophie to go get me a snack.

Heading out the door, I saw the Quinten team was already warming up on the court.

Not good.

Their coach was barking at their heels and they responded with a look of fear in their eyes. Ahead of me, Lowe and the girlies were skipping toward the sidelines.

Oh, God, we were so skunked.

Trailing several yards behind, I hung my head, pretending I was with another team. I almost made it to the sidelines before running into a tall, dorky kid.

Looking up, I was about to tell the idiot to watch where he was going; I was met with a pair of familiar, gray eyes.

Bob?

At least I thought the tall blonde with slicked back hair

and not a single body piercing or strip of duct-tape was my BF.

His smiled weakly. "Good luck, AJ."

He appeared so normal in a simple, green polo shirt. Like someone I could take home to Mother.

Gawd, he looked horrible.

"Why do you look like this?" I asked, unable to mask the disgust in my voice.

He winced, a flash of pain marring his eyes. "Isn't this what you wanted?"

"Yes...no." I slapped my forehead. Nothing was making sense anymore. My mother had psychic powers she refused to use. My coach thought she was back in junior high, and now my vegetarian BF ate meat and dressed like a prep.

"Make up your mind," he groaned.

"You don't look like Bob." Grabbing his hand, I entwined my fingers through his.

Bob arched a brow before looking at our entwined hands.

The confusion I read in his eyes mingled with my own bewilderment. Touching his warm, calloused fingers felt awkward. Why?

O-mi-god! I've never held hands with my BF and we'd been going out for over a week! Then another thought marred my brow. We've never even kissed.

"I'm still the same on the inside." As if reading my mind, Bob did something remarkable. He bent over and brushed a kiss across my lips.

Bob was my first boyfriend, the only guy who'd ever shown interest in me, and now I was experiencing my first kiss in the middle of a crowded gym.

Tension from my miserable day drained with the feel of his lips on mine. The springy sounds of balls hitting the court, screaming fans, annoying girlies, blaring music, all hushed. Bob and his soft, perfect lips were all that mattered, as if the rest of the world was on pause, then slowly fading away.

Chapter Nine

"What happened?" Mumbling the words before the room came into view, my eyes struggled to focus on the shadows above me.

"You passed out." Sophie's voice cut through the confusion.

"Are you serious?" My hand flew to my aching temple as the site of my two best friends became clearer. Inhaling the familiar musky scent, I knew they'd probably carried me to the locker room. Looking down at my side, I recognized the cushy, leather padding on the table our trainer used for physical therapy.

My arm, feeling like it wasn't even attached to my body, fell limp at my side. *Why am I so weak?* I tried to recall the events that led up to my fall. *How did I end up like this? Had I even gotten to play? Was I hit by a ball?*

"That must have been some kiss," Krysta practically sang the words.

"Kiss?" What was she talking about? I struggled to lift my head, finally leaning up on my elbows. The room slowly rocked, as if I was on a gently rolling boat.

"Your BF kissed you and then you fainted," Sophie giggled.

My breath hitched while I waited for Sophie to tell me she was just kidding. Like I didn't just pass out in a gym full of spectators like a stupid, weak female who'd been overwhelmed by the touch of a guy.

A weird silence hung in the air. Were they waiting for me to say something? Finally, a mixed sound of groaning and gagging oozed from my lips. "Oh, gawd, can I die now?"

What was everybody thinking of me now? Team captain, campus kick ass, faints after being overwhelmed by her boyfriend's passionate kiss.

"Kind of romantic the way she fell into his arms," Krysta purred.

"Yeah," Sophie said dreamily, "just like an old romance movie."

Well, at least he didn't let me fall on my butt.

Krysta laughed. "I didn't know AJ could be so *girly*."

"Please," I moaned against the rising tide of bile threatening at the back of my throat. "You're making my head hurt worse."

Not to mention my ego. Acting like some silly cheerleader, I passed out before the game. Gawd, how bad did we get skunked? "Did we lose?" I asked without really wanting to know the answer.

Sophie shook her head. "Game's not over."

Fighting a wave of nausea, I struggled to sit. The rocking room was making it difficult for me to find my balance. "Help me up. I need to get in the game."

"Oh, no, young lady." An icy chill blew into the room at the sound of Mother's shrill voice. "It's straight home to eat some *real* food, and then it's off to bed."

My jaw dropped at the site of her standing in the locker room entrance. Arms folded across her chest, eyes blazing, she looked ready to smother me in a big bottle of guilt gravy.

"Mother," I gasped. "What are you doing here?"

"Never mind. Mike, help AJ to the car." My brother stepped from behind her, and before I knew what was happening, I was hoisted into his meaty arms.

Mike would understand my situation. He was a jock, too. I turned my pleading gaze on him. "My team's gonna lose without me."

An evil grin creased the corners of his mouth. "Your team's gonna get their butts stomped either way."

"Kiss *my* butt, Mike," I spat, although the words didn't have the venom I'd intended. I hated to admit it, but I was just too weak to be pissed. Besides, he could drop me if he wanted, and I really didn't feel like passing out again.

Still, I wasn't giving up without a fight. Turning my head toward Mother, I blinked my eyes until the room stopped spinning. "Mother, I'll just get something at the snack bar. I'll be fine. Honest."

"Mrs. Dawson, I can't allow AJ to play in her condition." Coach Lowe had emerged from the shadows.

Had she been standing there the whole time? Gloating at my moment of weakness? Anger shot through my veins like liquid fire. "What are *you* doing here?" I growled.

"AJ," Mother squealed. "That's no way to talk to your coach."

I shrugged, pretending my head didn't feel as light as a helium balloon. "She's not a real coach."

"That's it!" Mother yelled. "We're going home right now!"

Now I'd done it. Made her crack her honey-coated charm in front of everyone.

Mother closed her eyes and then breathed out a gush of air. Turning toward Lowe, she batted her eyes like an innocent schoolgirl. "I'm sorry, Ms. Lowe."

Lowe frowned. "That's okay," her voice broke off, as if she was trying to repress the urge to cry.

Barf.

I looked in stunned silence from Lowe to Mother, trying to decide who was the biggest fake.

Mother walked up to Lowe, placing a hand on her shoulder. The two shared a look of understanding. I didn't need Sophie's gift to know what they were thinking.

Lowe sighed, "All I wanted was to be her friend, but I'm used to her attitude."

Rolling my eyes, I repressed a gloating smile as I remembered her upcoming all-night beer-fest with my team. Lowe wouldn't have to put up with my attitude for long.

Why was my mother's silent treatment way worse than her nagging? Maybe because I knew she was brainstorming a strategy to make my life a living hell. As we drove home from the game, Mother gripped the steering wheel white-knuckled, her line-drawn eyes focused on the road. Even my big mouth brother had nothing to say. I stared out the front seat passenger window, replaying the day's events, which seemed to escalate from crappy to very crappy.

My BF was willing to eat meat, just not for my family. My BFFs would rather eat lunch in a smelly pit of freaks than with me. My coach had turned my team, including my one remaining friend on the team, against me. I blew the game by making a total fool out of myself and passing out.

But that wasn't the worst of it. Mother's disappointment in me brought my day to a new low. I knew Mother and I rarely got along, but I wanted that to change. After the way I yelled at Lowe, Mother thought I was hateful to everyone. If only she knew how Coach Lowe was ruining my life, maybe she would've understood.

I stole a glance in Mother's direction. Face twisted in a snarl, narrowed eyes blazing with fury.

Never mind. As perfect as she pretended to be, I knew Mother's temper. I had crossed the line, and it would take her a long time to get over it.

A deep sense of hopelessness washed over me. Covering my face with my hands, I groaned as I thought about the state of my life. Oh, well, I should have been used to Mother's anger by now. No matter how well I did in school or on the court, she would always find a way to be mad at me. Mother was the angriest person I knew, except maybe...me.

Oh, crap.

Was this woman who I was forced to endure every evening at home just like the person my teammates had to put up with? If my mother was on my team, I wouldn't like her either, and I definitely wouldn't invite her to parties.

That still didn't excuse Lowe's behavior. The coach's job was to unite, not divide; she definitely was not supposed to get a bunch of freshman girls drunk. I'd work on that problem Friday night.

Tonight, I had another problem to fix. The silent treatment couldn't go on forever. Clearing my throat, I turned toward Mother. "I've decided to eat meat again."

"I told you not to give up meat." She spoke through lips that barely moved. "You should have known this would happen,

Allison."

Her attitude stirred my blood. I was trying to call a truce and all she could do was nag.

"You're right," I said with a laugh. "I don't know why my psychic abilities weren't working tonight."

She shot me a hard glare. "You're not in the least bit funny, Allison Jenette."

Uh-oh, she called me by my full name. Now she was pissed. Was it what I said, or the meaning behind those words? I had a suspicion Mother was angry I'd mentioned my gift.

"Maybe if you'd take me more seriously, I wouldn't have to be funny."

"I really don't like your attitude," she said with an icy air.

My attitude? Did she realize I got my attitude, my anger, from her? Maybe if she'd accept me for who I was, I wouldn't be angry all the time? "You raised me this way." I shrugged, flipping my ponytail behind my shoulder.

"No, I didn't," she spat. "I raised you to be a well-mannered, normal, young lady."

Exactly. She had spent my entire life trying to stuff me into a different mold because she wouldn't accept my gift. "What do you mean by normal?"

"Forget it, Allison." Mother vigorously shook her head, as if purging herself of the stench of weirdness that had permeated the car.

I folded my arms across my chest and blew out a frustrated breath of air. "That's right, let's just avoid talking about my gift. Maybe it will all go away."

Mother shrugged, as if she was in total agreement. "You're eating dinner in your room tonight. Tomorrow, I'm driving you to school and we are going to Ms. Lowe's office, so you can apologize for your behavior."

Folding my arms across my chest, I resolved to stand my ground. "Lowe can kiss my butt. I'm not apologizing."

She shook her head. "Yes, you will, or believe me I will..."

"Will what?" I snapped. "What can you possibly do that will make my life any worse?"

Face contorting, I could see the flames of rage fanning her cheeks. "You will be on restriction from everything for the rest of the school year—friends, computer, sports..."

"You can't take sports from me!"

Mother's bottom lip trembled. "Why should I allow you to play when you shame me with your attitude toward your coach?"

Despite my dizziness from the gnawing hunger in my belly, Mother's rejection gave new life to my anger. "Shame you? This isn't about *your* life. This is about *my* life! Lowe's not even a real coach. She's about to get canned, anyway."

Why did I have to play these games with my mother, the one person who should accept me for who I am, the one person who should understand my differences?

"Oh, really?" Mother smirked. "You know this as a fact, or is this part of your '*intuition*'?"

Grrrr. Rubbing my throbbing temples, I sank into the seat's soft, leather padding. Silently, I counted to ten. I had to keep cool just long enough to get home and retreat to my room. I never thought anything could be worse than house arrest, but sitting in a car with Mother, I'd discovered a new form of torture.

As soon as we got to the house, Mike jumped in his truck and drove off. He didn't ask Mother if he could leave. She didn't scold him for not helping me inside, but I didn't need him, anyway. I'd eaten a bag of peanuts during the rest of the silent trip home, and my strength was returning.

I stormed through the front door, just wanting to go to my room and away from my mother. Maybe she'd make me eat alone tonight and I wouldn't have to deal with her.

Bolting from Mother's brocade sofa, Grandma tossed the frayed end of a cigar to the floor. "AJ, are you okay?" Concern marred her brow.

How I loved her. Even if Mother didn't like me, I knew Grandma cared. Somehow, that softened the edge of my stressful day.

"She's fine." Mother grunted while picking up Grandma's cigar with the tips of her fingers and making a grand show of throwing it in a nearby wastebasket. Her cold eyes turned on me. "Allison, go to your room."

"Is it all right if I look at my granddaughter first?"

Stepping in front of Mother, Grandma grasped me in a strong embrace.

For a small woman, she sure could squeeze hard.

In her arms, I felt the warmth I'd known I'd been missing for a long time. Like my heart was being hugged, too. I wondered how long it had been since Mother held me. I didn't understand why I felt as fragile as an eggshell locked in this tiny woman's grasp. Why tears threatened the backs of my eyes. But I didn't want Grandma to stop holding me.

Keeping her fingers locked on my forearms, she stepped back. The creases on her eyes deepened as her gaze traveled the length of my body.

My heart gave a little lurch, but it was time for her to let go. A moment longer, and my burning eyes threatened to unleash a flood of tears. Swallowing a lump in my throat, I watched Grandma examine me.

After several moments, she released me and her gaze locked with Mother's.

Mother's eyes looked glossy. The deep lines creasing her frown had softened. Was she touched by the moment, too? Did Mother really care for me?

Eyes blinking, her head snapped as if she'd just recovered from a trance. "She's not hurt from the fall. If anything, she's got even more attitude than before."

Guess she didn't care.

My heart felt like it was sinking into a deep hole. For a moment, I thought maybe...

Grandma laughed under her breath and my gaze found her smiling eyes.

Odd how she could look at all this with a sense of humor. Maybe I should try laughing every time Mother threw a fit.

Determined not to let Mother's mood ruin my own, I raised my chin. "I'm going back to eating meat, Grandma."

"Good girl." Grandma patted my back. "I didn't like seeing you pretending to be someone you're not." Her eyes darted toward my mother.

I smiled, understanding her reference. "I know that now."

"You're special in your own way, AJ. You don't need to change for *anyone*." She winked and then her gaze slid more slowly toward Mother.

Mother tapped her foot, her narrowed gaze shooting daggers at Grandma. "You're not helping."

"The only one not helping AJ is you!"

Grandma bellowed.

I jerked back, totally unprepared for my sweet little, Grandma's rage, but she laid the attitude down with a heavy SMACK!

I suddenly realized where Mother and I had inherited our anger streak.

"Mother, please..." With a stern voice, my mother held her palms up.

"No, Margaret." Grandma widened her stance, fisting hands at her sides. "I will not be silenced this time. You have a beautiful, gifted daughter. Don't destroy her with your own fears."

"Why don't we just announce to the world that she's a freak?" Mother's words came out in a choked sob. "So kids at school can torment her like they did to me. Is that what you want for her?"

Why did Mother always think she had to make the decisions about my life? Using my gift should have been *my* choice, not hers.

"Kids at school already hate me!" I yelled, as both of their startled gazes found mine. "How can I expect anyone to like me when my own mother hates me?"

Mother's stifled scream pierced the tension. "I don't hate you, Allison," she rasped.

I couldn't hold back the tears which had threatened to escape earlier. They pooled my eyes and streamed down my cheeks. I didn't care about being too emotional in front of Mother anymore. I'd held in this hurt for too long, allowing it to sour and turn into bitter, hateful anger.

No more.

Time for me to stop allowing her rejection to rule my emotions. To allow kids at school to fear me because of the anger I projected on them.

"Yes, you do," I cried. "You hate me because I'm not normal. I might be different, but I'm not a freak. You're the freak, Mother. You're the only one who is in denial here."

"Listen to the girl, Margaret," Grandma pleaded. "Listen to her before your son is killed."

The angles on Mother's face sharpened, hardened, her icy shield encasing her features. She turned on Grandma with a cold stare. "Mother, I want you to go."

My heart stopped and then the tempo renewed with urgency. "What? You can't send her away!" I couldn't lose her, the only person in my family who cared about me.

"Allison, go to your room." Mother's gaze remained fixed on Grandma as she spoke to me.

I was a fly on the wall. Not even worthy of her dirty look. "No!" I screamed. She wasn't going to brush me off that easily, not when my happiness depended on it.

Mother's narrowed gaze remained locked on Grandma as she held up a silencing hand. "Stay out of this, Allison. This does not involve you."

"Fine. If she goes, I'm going with her."

"No." Mother finally looked at me, her eyes momentarily softening before turning back to Grandma. "You're not going anywhere," she said with a more subdued tone.

Funny, but I expected the same icy shards she'd been shooting at grandma to fly in my direction. Was she being nicer to me because I'd threatened to leave?

Didn't matter. I couldn't live with someone who resented my gift...resented me.

"Grandma, take me with you," I pleaded.

"AJ," Grandma sighed, her shoulders dropped like a wilting flower. "Maybe it's best if I leave for a while."

"But you're the only one who understands me." Grandma was giving up so easily. How was it that Mother always got her way? Didn't Grandma realize that more than my happiness was at stake? My brother's life depended on us.

"Your mother understands you," Grandma said with a weary shrug. "She just doesn't want to admit it."

Despite my urge to throw myself into Grandma's arms and beg for her to stay, my feet felt like they'd been encrusted in concrete blocks. I couldn't bring myself to beg. My dizziness had returned and I was tired. Tired of crying. Tired of Mother. Tired of my life. All I wanted to do now was crawl into bed and cry.

"When will I see you again?" I asked through the shakiness in my voice.

"Dearest, you know that answer better than anyone." Grandma closed the distance between us and stroked my cheek with a tender hand. "Try not to kill your brother before he kills himself."

I choked on a sob. "You're not funny, Grandma."

"I'm being perfectly serious." Her soft eyes clouded, dark, thunderous. "I just hope your mother realizes this before it's too late."

Chapter Ten

"Hey, thanks for going with me." As I crouched behind a car in Lowe's neighbor's driveway, my gaze assessed three pairs of eager eyes, my two best friends and Bob. They'd all risked serious social probation by sneaking out of their houses past curfew to help me bust Lowe.

"That's what friends are for," Krysta grinned.

"And boyfriends," Bob winked.

"What's your plan, AJ?" Sophie asked with a shaky voice.

This bust was toughest for her. Sophie was a good girl, and even though we'd be busting an underage drink fest, I knew she still didn't like sneaking out of her house. Bob and Krysta on the other hand, well, their parents were never home, so it didn't really matter to them.

But if anyone had a right to complain, it was me. My butt still itched from falling into the bushes below my window. I grimaced, knowing Mother would notice if one twig was out of place in her perfectly trimmed shrubbery.

"I don't want to rat on Lowe unless I see they have beer," I whispered.

That's why I'd waited until midnight for the bust. Our game ended at a little past nine tonight. It should have lasted longer, but it didn't take much time for the other team to stomp our butts. I figured by the time my team showered, dressed and headed to Lowe's house, they wouldn't be drinking until at least eleven.

I wanted them to have some alcohol in their system before I called the cops. They might've been able to hide the evidence, but they sure wouldn't pass a breathalyzer test.

"How do we see the beer?" Sophie asked with wide eyes.

I nodded toward the house. "We have to get a view of the window."

Krysta shook her head. "The drapes are closed."

"We have to sneak into the backyard." I pointed toward the six-foot privacy fence, which appeared to have a lock on the gate.

Sophie grimaced. "What if we get caught?"

I muffled a nervous laugh. "Then we make a run for it."

Didn't know why, but I'd never thought of getting caught. I wanted so badly for Lowe to get busted that I'd never considered failure. She'd go to jail for giving minors beer and then she'd be canned from coaching. Something good had to happen in my life.

Then Sophie squealed, Krysta gasped and Bob swore.

Red and blue neon lights reflected off the hood of the car we were using for cover. We all ducked, and I sucked in a huge breath of air before speaking through a hiss. "Who called the cops?"

"I don't know," Sophie squeaked, her voice shaking.

A million questions raced through my brain. Were the cops here for Lowe? If so, who stole my revenge? What if they were here for us? What if someone spotted four suspicious teens hiding behind a parked car? We could get arrested any minute.

Oh, God, Mother would kill me. I'd be grounded for eternity.

If they were coming for us, I had to know. Maybe we could still make a run for it. Since I was the closest to the fender, I hesitantly peered around the edge of the car.

What I saw amazed me.

I could almost hear Sophie's silent scream as she pulled me back.

Looking into my friends' widened eyes, I had to cover my mouth to muffle my laughter.

"What's happening?" Krysta breathed.

I knew they wouldn't believe it. I couldn't hardly believe it. "Paige ratted out Lowe."

All three jaws dropped. "What?" they simultaneously choked.

I peered around the car one more time to make sure my eyes weren't playing tricks on me. "She's at the police car with her mother and the principal," I said while turning back to my friends.

Bob smiled. "Is Lowe cuffed yet?"

At the risk of getting caught, that was one moment I had to witness—the ultimate humiliation of Coach Lowe. After the incident in the locker room this week, Mother had forced me to apologize to Lowe in front of the entire team. Either that or I'd have my computer and phone revoked and no sports for the entire year.

Time for payback.

Peeking around the car again, my vision was obscured by a tall pair of black clad legs.

Stretching my neck upwards, I grimaced as I looked into my principal's thunderous expression.

Once Sparks realized we were there to bust Lowe's beer fest, the cops allowed him to drive us home. Looking out the window at the lights from passing cars, I realized Sparks was very understanding about the whole thing, even letting Bob watch a movie on his portable dvd player. Too bad I couldn't convince Sparks to let us stay and see Lowe come out in cuffs.

We'd been asking him a million questions, but he dodged almost every one. From what we could figure out, right before the party, Paige went crying to her mother that Lowe was going to get them drunk. We couldn't figure out if Paige's mom called the cops or Sparks or both. Didn't matter. Lowe was so busted.

What I didn't understand was why Paige turned on Lowe. I thought they were buds. Guess I'd have to wait to find out. Once Sparks brought me home to Mother, I'd have no communication with the outside world until Monday.

"You realize we probably won't have a team."

"What?" Looking at his hardened gaze reflecting in his rearview mirror, I hadn't realized Sparks was talking to me.

Sparks cleared his throat. "District policy. The girls will be suspended from sports for a year."

"Oh, crap. I hadn't thought of that." They broke the law. They broke their contract. All athletes had to sign one stating that if they were caught consuming alcohol or doing drugs, they'd be suspended from sports for a year.

Shoulders slumped, I heaved an aggravated breath and rubbed my throbbing temple. Maybe I should have warned Sparks before the party. Then he could have stopped it and I'd still have a team.

Or not.

All Lowe and the team had to do was deny it. Make me out to be a jealous troublemaker. I would've ended up losing my cool and then I would've been kicked off the team.

Oh well, what did it matter? Mother would probably take me out of sports once she found out I'd snuck out of the house. I knew she'd do it not caring how badly it would crush me; after all, she took away my Grandma. Too bad Grandma wouldn't be there when Sparks brought me home. That would have made my punishment much more tolerable. Gawd, my life sucked. I just wanted to sink between the cracks in the seat cushions and disappear.

Sparks dropped off Sophie first. He walked her to the front door and I watched as he talked with Sophie's mother. Her mother's squeal sounded much like an older version of Sophie's cry. Instead of scolding Sophie, her mom embraced her, squeezing her so tight I thought Sophie's head would pop off.

Heat suffused my cheeks as I envied their tender moment. Why couldn't Mother love me the way Sophie's mom loved her?

When we drove up to Krysta's apartment, I could see her shifting in the seat in front of me, knowing she was nervous about Sparks knocking on her apartment door. Nobody would answer. Her dad worked nights, leaving her alone.

What would Sparks do? Could he report Krysta's dad to social services?

"My dad's probably sleeping. You don't need to come up," Krysta said to Sparks with a shaky voice.

"Nonsense," Sparks said in a tone that left no room for argument. "He needs to know where you've been."

The butterflies in my stomach multiplied as I feared for

my friend. Turning to me before opening the truck door, she shot me a worried glance.

I flashed her an apologetic grin. "Sorry I got you into this."

"Don't worry about me," she said. "Good luck with your mom."

Watching Krysta and Sparks walk up her apartment stairs, I knew they'd be waiting for a while.

"Hey."

I looked over at Bob as he turned down the volume on the movie. I was so consumed with panic, I'd forgotten he was in the truck.

But how could I have forgotten him? He was sitting right next to me, his green spikes made a gentle grating sound as they scraped the top of the truck's interior. He smelled so good, not like musk, but like fresh soap. Not like the rest of his freaky friends.

And his warmth... I hadn't noticed until now, but just his nearness spilled heat into my bones. Even though the nights were getting cooler, I felt so warm and secure around Bob.

His eyebrows tilted in a frown. "Sorry I ate meat."

"What?" My BF wasn't making any sense.

"Is that why you don't eat lunch with me?"

Remembering the incident with the Barfy burger Tuesday, I realized I hadn't eaten lunch with my BF since then. That wasn't why I'd stopped eating with him. Actually, even though I was really busy with basketball practice, I'd kind of been avoiding him at other times. We hadn't really done much together until tonight. I'd only asked him to go with us because I knew we'd be safer walking the streets if we had a green giant at our backs.

I guess, maybe I was starting to think this relationship thing wasn't working. My family hated him, his friends stunk and gave me the creeps, and I liked meat. Why did I ever think this would work?

"No, that's not why." Running my fingers through my hair, I exhaled a sigh of resignation.

"Do you want to break up?"

Bob's question sent a jolt of electricity through my spine. I knew I couldn't mask the shock in my voice. "Do you?"

He shrugged. "How can we be together if we're never 'together'?"

I didn't know the answer to that question. I liked him. I really did. He was funny, original, and Gawd, he was an awesome kisser. Did I really want to lose him?

I jerked at the abrupt sound of the truck door opening. "One more down," Sparks rumbled. "AJ, you're next."

Well, we couldn't exactly continue the break- up discussion with Sparks in the front seat, so it was off to my house. We only lived a few miles from Krysta, but the minutes ticked away like hours. Bob went back to watching his movie. No comfort from him as I approached my impending enslavement.

As Sparks pulled into the driveway, Mother was standing in front of the garage, arms folded across her chest, her brows drawn together in a continuous line.

I was in deep doo-doo.

How did she know I was coming? Sophie's mom must have called her.

I looked at my future ex-BF one last time before opening the truck door. "Later, Bob."

In the next second, I felt his warmth around me, surprised to find myself locked in a giant bear hug.

I wanted it to last forever. It wasn't like Mother could get any more pissed off. Bob released me much too soon, and my gaze locked with his.

He smiled weakly. "Don't let her get to you, AJ."

"Okay," I choked, afraid if I said any more, I'd launch into a big wimpy cry-fest.

Why was Bob so nice when I'd been avoiding him like the plague? How did I hook up with such a cool BF? And now he wanted to break up.

Cool air hit me as I stepped onto the pavement. Was it the night breeze or the cold wind blowing from Mother's heart?

As I approached my principal and mother, I heard Sparks explaining the night's events. "Don't be too angry with her, Mrs. Dawson. Even though she should have come to me first, I believe she was trying to do the right thing."

Eyes downcast, I stood next to my principal. I wasn't afraid to look at Mother, really. I just didn't feel like dealing with a major guilt trip. "I'll just go to my room now."

Why should she have all the fun of putting me on restriction when I could beat her to it? Stepping in between them, I was determined to lock myself in my room forever. Or at least until Grandma came back to stay. I needed a hug from her right now. She was the only member of my family who I thought really loved me.

Mother's outstretched arm blocked my path.

Exhaling a frustrated breath, I looked at the intrusive object, my gaze traveling the length of her arm and up to her angry glare.

My breath hitched as I looked into her eyes. They didn't look angry. They looked soft and sweet and kind of...motherly.

What had she been smoking?

In the next second, her arms were wrapped around me and she was crying.

Crying? My mother?

Her tears flowed fast as she sobbed into my hair, drenching my neck and squeezing me so hard I thought I'd burst. But I didn't want her to let go.

Not ever.

And without thought, my pent-up emotions broke through the damn, welling in my chest. The tears poured down in sheets as I pressed my face to Mother's neck, and all the pain, anger and rejection washed through me in waves.

From somewhere deep in the hollow of my consciousness, I heard the moans of a girl, realizing that girl was me. I was sobbing in my mother's arms and I didn't care who saw, my principal, my BF, even if my stupid brother was watching.

Mother was hugging me.

She loved me.

Chapter Eleven

What in the heck was wrong with me?

Sitting in a bathroom stall, wiping the remnants of tears from the corners of my eyes, I wondered just when exactly I became such a wussy girl. After my big cry-fest Friday night, Mother didn't put me on restriction, but I didn't ask to go out that weekend, either. Mother and I sat on the couch and watched movies all day Saturday and then we went to the mall after church.

We didn't argue once.

Whatever had happened to make Mother like me, I wasn't about to give it up. Which meant I'd have to make a few major sacrifices.

Starting with Bob.

Fresh tears threatened to burst from my eyes at the thought of breaking up with him, but what else could I do? We really didn't have much of a relationship, anyway, other than talking on the computer and a few sneaky phone calls.

Bob deserved better. Someone whose mother actually liked him. Maybe a girl who also wore duct tape and dyed her hair strange colors. As odd as it sounded, I guess I just wasn't strange enough to be Bob's girlfriend.

The first bell sounded. Only five minutes until class.

Might as well get this over with.

My backpack felt like a lead-weight as I drug my feet toward first period. Today was going to be a very long day. The only thing I had to look forward to was pot roast tonight—Mother was making my favorite.

"Hey, AJ!"

Turning at the sound of Bob's familiar voice, I saw him leaning against a puke-green locker, surrounded by a group of freaks.

They scattered like flies as I approached. Guess it didn't matter anyway if they feared me. I didn't need to worry about my BF's friends anymore.

"Hey." My voice faltered as I tried to paste a smile on my face.

One dark, questioning brow shot up. "House arrest all week?"

"No." I shrugged.

"Then why didn't we talk?"

Because I wanted to break-up with you in person.

I sighed, postponing the inevitable, and dragging out my torture. "I hung out with my mother this weekend."

His voice lowered to a tender caress. "What's up with you?"

Bob didn't even get mad. Any other guy would've been laying on the attitude, but not him. I really didn't deserve a BF like Bob.

"I...I think we should break-up." The words rushed out in a tangled heap of emotions as I choked back the rising tide of tears.

I averted my gaze, focusing on the glaring duct tape patched over the knees of Bob's weathered jeans. I couldn't look into his tender eyes for fear of sobbing like a cheerleader who'd just broken a nail.

Get it together, AJ.

"Was it something I did?" Cupping my chin, he forced me to look into his soft, saddened eyes.

The feel of his fingers on my face was distracting, making me have second thoughts about dumping him. "No," I exhaled, pulling away from his touch. "It's my Mother."

"Oh." His lips turned down in the most adorable pout.

Why couldn't he be a jerk? That would've made the break-up so much easier.

Squaring my shoulders, I was determined to make this a clean break. No second thoughts. After fourteen, long, miserable years, Mother finally liked me. "She's nice to me now, and I don't want to lose that."

He nodded. "I understand."

Swallowing a sob, I looked into Bob's wounded expression. I'd done it. I'd broken off with Bob without making it a major ordeal. So why did I feel like a deflated balloon? "Do you hate me now?"

His lips curved into a slight smile. "I'll never hate you." Dipping his head toward mine, Bob brushed a tender kiss across my lips before turning and walking into the classroom.

A vortex of emotions threatened to swallow me into a bottomless pit. Placing a hand to my tingling mouth, I couldn't help but wonder if I'd made a huge mistake. I hadn't even given our relationship a chance to bloom, and now I was letting this awesome guy go.

All for Mother.

I only hoped she continued to love me.

Heading into third period I'd tried to forget about the breakup, but I just couldn't shake the feel of Bob's kiss from my mind.

At least some good news helped in distracting my thoughts from Bob. Lowe was canned from coaching. Rumor was she'd spent the weekend in jail and only three second-string players were busted for drinking. The rest of the girls flaked on her party.

Maybe my team had finally seen that Lowe was a poser. Maybe they were cooler than I'd thought.

Sparks had already found a replacement coach; Coach Stanley was Coach Carter's sister. Hopefully, she'd be as tough as Carter and we'd get back to a winning season.

Yeah, for once, my life didn't suck.

Kind-of.

Throwing down my bookbag, I poured my weary body into the desk. I couldn't be tired from lack of meat. Mother and I had gigantic hamburgers at the mall yesterday and she made me bacon and eggs for breakfast.

As images of Bob's sad smile clouded my vision, I wondered if I was just suffering from post-break-up stress.

"What's got you?"

I looked over at Sophie. A dark frown marred her brow. It wasn't like my friend to look so upset.

"Nothing. What's got you?"

"Your depression won't stay out of my brain." she whispered through a hiss.

"Oh, sorry." One thing about my friend's power was if someone nearby was extremely depressed or happy, their emotions, or sometimes even thoughts, projected into Sophie's head without warning.

Shoulders slumped, I exhaled the words. "I dumped him."

"Why?" Her eyes softened.

I threw up my hands in surrender. "Mother was nice to me all weekend."

Sophie's jaw dropped and she looked at me like I'd just missed free throw. "She was?"

"Yeah." I shrugged. "I don't want to give her a reason to hate me."

"You think she'll hate you because of Bob?"

"Yeah. He's not normal." But as the words came out, I didn't feel like it was me saying it. I envisioned Mother's scowl from across the dinner table as she eyed Bob with disgust.

Sophie pierced me with a glare. "You're not normal, either."

Looking around the classroom, I noticed the desks were filling with students, but they were too busy copying equations off the board to pay attention to us. "Yeah," I breathed, "but I can hide my weirdness."

"No," Sophie stammered. "You can't."

Squaring my shoulders, I was determined to win this coin toss. My mother liked me now. The breakup was over, so why was she forcing me to relive the pain? "I just won't *see things* around Mother."

Sophie shook her head. "Have you forgotten break starts this weekend?"

"Break?"

"Yeah, your brother's snowboarding trip."

Oh, God, Mike!

How had I forgotten about my brother? I was being too

damn selfish thinking about my own problems, that's how. Mike and his best friend were supposed to go to Hell's Peak this Saturday.

If I didn't convince Mother to make him stay home, my brother would die, but how could I convince her when I knew she'd hate me for acting strange?

Mike hadn't been teasing me as much lately. If I talked Mother out of letting him go, he'd make my life hell for sure.

Clenching my fists in grim determination, I psyched up for the toughest challenge of my life. Only this wasn't a game. The winner loses her family's love, but the loser forfeits his life.

Placing her hands to her head, Sophie moaned. "There go your thoughts again."

My dark thoughts, shifting from Bob, to my mother, and then to Mike, consumed me for the rest of the day. Just this morning, I'd thought my life was getting better. No, I was just smack in the eye of the storm, thinking my troubles had blown over, but the worst was yet to come.

The only end in sight resulted in my mother hating me, which made my break-up with Bob even harder to take. Why the heck did I break-up with him? Besides Krysta and Sophie, he was the only good thing in my life.

Well, maybe basketball could be added to the positives.

I hoped.

I wasn't off to a good start. First day with a new coach and already I was running behind, but my stupid locker wouldn't open. Or maybe I was just too busy absorbed in my problems to remember the code.

Heading through the locker room door with my backpack slung over a shoulder, I breathed the heavy air of rotten sock stench, remembering how that smell was a source of comfort last year. Before my team sucked. Before I found out they partied without me.

"Nice of you to show up on time. You're three minutes late!"

The gruff voice startled me. Looking at the frightened expressions in my teammates' eyes, as they huddled in the rear of the locker room like frightened sheep cornered by a hungry predator, I realized I'd walked in on a major butt chewing.

"Listen up, ladies," Coach Stanley bellowed from the center of the room. "I've been looking at the stats. Don't know what the hell has been going on since my sister went on maternity leave."

Uh-oh. This coach was mean. I liked her already. I decided to quickly take a seat with the team. If I stood behind the coach much longer, I was sure to be singled out.

"What I want to know is how does a championship team go from first to last in district?"

Her fiery glare swept the team, coming to rest on me. Of course...had to happen with my luck.

"You there, before I send you on laps for coming in late, maybe you can tell us why we suck!"

"It's not her fault. She's the only reason we score," a girl squeaked from behind me.

As I turned toward the direction of her voice, my eyes had to do a double-take. Paige was actually defending me.

"I don't remember asking you!" The coach raged.

"I know." Paige's voice cracked. "It's just that AJ's the only good player."

"AJ, huh?" Stanley's narrowed gaze swept me from top to bottom. "Aren't you the captain?"

I shifted uncomfortably. "Yeah."

"Well, then," she smirked. "It is your fault. Why haven't you been leading your team?"

"She has," Keysha stammered from behind me. "The team wouldn't listen."

"It's the captain's job to make the team listen!" Stanley hollered.

"Coach Lowe said we didn't have to listen to her," Paige's skin was ash while she spoke, her entire frame trembling. "She said we just had to have fun."

I thought I saw steam shooting from Stanley's ears. "There's nothing *fun* about getting your butts stomped!"

"We know that now," Paige turned her mouth down as her gaze dropped to the floor.

The rest of the team nodded in agreement before I felt

their gazes on me.

A warm feeling crept into my chest and curled around my insides. Not like an uncomfortable feeling. Kind-of like Mother hugging me the other night. For the first time in a while, I felt like my team respected me.

Maybe even liked me.

They risked a lot by taking my defense. If Coach Stanley was anything like her sister, they'd all be doing laps until they puked.

At the sound of Stanley's ear-shattering whistle, I thought I'd jump out of my skin.

"Forty laps for everyone!" she barked. "AJ, suit up and get your butt on that court, you've got thirty laps!"

I hastily changed into my practice uniform. Although coach had only given me thirty laps, I was determined to do forty. My team and I were in this together.

Despite Lowe's attempts to get the team to hate me, I actually thought I saw respect reflected in their apologetic faces.

Maybe now they understood what it took to be a winning team. I made a mental note not to be so hard on them. This season, they might actually invite me to a party.

One problem down, only a few major issues left.

Chapter Twelve

Thursday night, and I still hadn't gained any ground with my mother. I'd tried everything to convince her not to let Mike go on that trip— everything short of confessing my dream. I'd Googled the statistics on snowboarding related deaths and injuries and showed her the risks. Mother had just asked Ted to go over safety instructions with Mike.

Then I suggested we spend my break on a horrifying family trip instead of letting Mike go to Hell's Peak. Mother and Ted took me up on the offer, promising we'd go camping after Mike came back. If they only realized he'd be dead.

Finally, I bribed Mike that I'd do all of his chores for a year if he didn't go snowboarding. He just laughed and told Mother she needed to take me back to the therapist.

If only Grandma were here. She'd know what to do, which only brought my aggravation to a new level. She knew my dream was real, so why wasn't she helping me? Why'd she just give up and leave her grandson's life to chance?

Frustration mounting at every thwarted attempt to cancel the trip, I'd let my failure consume me. Concern over Mike's imminent death was making me lose focus on my game. And forget concentrating on studying for finals this week. I'd blown my game, my grades, my life.

Only one option left; I had to make Mother realize my gift was real. That I was a psychic, but I was not a freak. She could no longer deny my gift— *or hers.*

As I gnawed on a pencil at the kitchen counter, I looked down at the equations I was studying for algebra. Oh, well, I pretty much knew equations. Hopefully, I'd remember enough to pass the test tomorrow.

"Studying for finals, dear?" Mother came into the kitchen and poured a tall glass of diet lemonade.

I leveled a hard stare in her direction. "Mike's gonna die if you let him go." Since other methods of persuasion failed, I might as well be blunt.

She nearly choked on her drink. "Excuse me?"

"I saw it in a dream. My dreams *always* come true." I fought to keep my voice flat, calm. No need to provoke Mother further. "It's my gift. Just like Grandma has a gift, just like *you* have a gift."

Mother slammed her cup on the counter. "Allison Jenette, the only gift you have is the gift of imagination."

Rising from my chair, I pounded the counter with my fists. "Deny it and you'll be pouring dirt on Mike's grave this Sunday."

"Allison!" she gasped. "How can you speak such horrible things?"

"I speak the truth, Mother." Pointing my finger at her, rage infused my voice. "You know it." Was she so afraid that in accepting my gift she'd ruin her normal life? Well, her perfect little world was about to come crashing down with Mike's death. How would she cope then knowing she could have saved him but she let fear and prejudice cloud her judgment?

"Allison, go to your room." Mother's bottom lip trembled before she cupped her mouth with her hand.

My gaze narrowed as I watched Mother struggle to still her shaking limbs.

Was she hiding her fear from me?

Or herself?

Storming off to my room, I'd decided to give Mother a chance to cool down. Maybe she'd allow her thoughts to settle and she'd see I was right.

If not, what else could I do to save my brother's life? I wished Grandma were here to help me.

Throwing myself onto the bed, the tension from the week washed over me and came out in dry, convulsing sobs. I'd cried too much these past few days and doubted I had any tears left.

As I closed my eyes, dark thoughts consumed me. Fear of

losing my only sibling gripped my heart, squeezing my chest until I thought it would burst. If Mother wouldn't do anything, I had to find another way to save him. But how?

Lost in a spinning vortex of despair, an ominous cloud swirled around my brain, stripping my mind of the power to think. Yawning into the pillow, I remembered I hadn't slept much this week. Maybe I just needed some rest. Then, I could wake and think of a plan. Right now, the only thing separating my brother and a several hundred drop of unforgiving ice was me.

The ear-piercing squeal of skidding brakes and the thunderous sound of crashing metal filled my brain, gripped my soul, as shivers of dread raced down my spine. Sitting up in bed, a profusion of cold sweat dampened my skin. This was a dream. I could tell by the hazy feeling in my head. As I fumbled for the light switch by my bed, I noted how the smooth texture of my blanket, the glare from the overhead light, felt so real.

This was no ordinary dream. This was a powerful vision.

I choked back the rising bile in my throat, realizing that whatever I was meant to see, had something to do with the crash I'd heard outside.

Was I about to see another death? Trying to quell my shaking limbs, I didn't know if I was prepared to see who was next. I slowly slipped on my shoes and then reached for my jacket, not really sure I wanted to go outside. But I had to go. I had to know who was in that accident. I'd never forgive myself if I denied my power to prevent a death.

As I opened my bedroom door and stepped into the darkened hallway, I walked toward the front entrance. Each step seemed to take an eternity. A nauseating feeling of dread settled in the pit of my stomach, and I felt as if I was marching to my own funeral.

By the time I opened the front door, neon red and blue lights already glowed against the night sky. Trying to still my shaking limbs, I breathed deeply. A cold, stale stench permeated my senses, leaving a dull, metallic taste on my tongue. Somehow, I knew that was the taste of death.

Someone died in that car accident.

Now I just had to walk across the street and find out who.

Sounded so easy, but icy fear clenched my muscles, making it difficult to breathe, let alone move.

Go, AJ. You need to see the future so you can save them.

Putting one foot in front of the other, I walked onward, wedging the distance between me and the tangled heap of metal wrapped around a light pole in front of my house.

Then the trickling ice which had seeped into my veins froze solid. Somehow, among the twisted wreckage I recognized the familiar Greenwood High Honor Student bumper sticker. The perfectly polished gold paint of Mother's car was now crumpled and burned, as if a dragon had set it on fire. A large black truck had plowed into the side of Mother's car, and now the two vehicles were an extension of each other, like a twisted tree branch.

There was no way anyone could have survived that.

My gaze shifted from the horrible site, drawn to an eerie glow beside the wreckage; a shimmery- blue dress lay surrounded by a pool of crimson.

A scream tore through my throat at the site of my mother's lifeless body. My step-dad was lying a few feet away. Both were motionless. Their blank stares focused on the starlight.

Turning away, I vomited onto the pavement, retching so hard, I fell to the cold surface. Mindless of the pain that shot through my leg, I closed my eyes before I was swallowed up in a maelstrom of pain and depression.

"AJ, AJ, wake up! What's wrong?"

Opening my eyes to the blinding light, I realized Mother was kneeling beside me, and I was lying on my bedroom floor, gagging on my own vomit.

"Sit up, darling," she soothed while stroking my forehead. "Ted, bring me a glass of water," she said over her shoulder to a shadowy figure standing in my doorway. As I listened to the sound of retreating footsteps, I realized Mother and Ted were still alive—for now.

I wanted to breathe a sigh of relief, but I knew a dream that powerful would come to pass unless I could prevent it.

"Mother," I moaned.

"I'm here, baby." She continued to stroke my hair while wiping the puke off my mouth and neck with a towel.

Her touch felt so good, so soothing. Just like a mother comforting a child. Huh, kind-of hard to believe. As I dropped my spinning head back in her lap, I wanted to soak up all her love before I broke the news. Before she turned me away for being a freak.

"Here's the water." Ted knelt beside us and handed Mother the glass.

"Drink this," she said. "It will make you feel better."

Sitting up, my head spun only slightly before my eyes were able to focus on their concerned expressions. Mother's eyes were large and moist with dark shadows framing her brow. Ted's mouth was set in a grim line. For a moment, they looked as if *I* had been in an accident.

I hesitantly took a sip of water. It was cool and soothing. My throat had felt on fire, probably from choking on vomit.

After finishing the entire glass, I wiped my mouth with the back of my sleeve and handed the glass to Mother.

"Feel better?" she smiled.

"No." I said the word before I had time to think. Maybe tonight wasn't a good time to tell them about the dream, but when was a good night to break the news? I didn't know when the accident was going to happen and I couldn't risk losing them and my brother. The thought of my entire family—dead— overwhelmed my emotions and I broke into a fresh wave of tears.

"What's wrong with her?" Ted asked.

"I don't know," Mother said as she pulled me against her chest. "Maybe we should call a doctor."

"No, I don't need a doctor. I need you to Listen." Pulling away from my mother, I groaned in between sobs, knowing panic had crept into my voice. I felt like an actress in a bad horror flick, but I couldn't help my emotions. I'd just seen the corpses of my parents.

Ted reached over and patted me on the back. "We're

listening, AJ."

Mother tried to wipe my eyes with the towel, but I pushed it away. Our gazes locked, and I saw her fear, saw how she tried not to blink as her eyes widened. She knew I had a vision. "I had a dream you both died in an accident," I said as flatly as possible, trying to reign in my emotions.

"Oh, is that all?" Ted laughed while squeezing my shoulder. "You're awake now, and the dream is over."

"No, it isn't. Don't you get it?" The staccato of my voice climbed higher as my panic increased. "My dreams always come true." What if they refused to believe me?

Ted looked at me with a blank stare before turning his questioning gaze to Mother. "Margaret, what is she talking about?"

"I...I don't know." Her lips trembled as she looked away.

Why couldn't she look me in the eyes?

"Yes, you do!" I shrieked.

Ted shook his head. "Margaret, I don't think she's fully awake. Maybe she's having one of those waking dreams."

"You're right," Mother whispered hoarsely, her voice laced with emotion.

Ted placed his arms around me and lifted me into bed. "Let's get her back to sleep. Then I'll help you clean up this mess." He nodded to the pile of puke on the floor.

Mother mumbled an agreement.

My hair still reeked from the stench of vomit fumes, but I didn't care. I laid there helplessly while I watched them wipe up the carpet. I was too exhausted to fight. Every muscle in my body burned like I'd just run five hundred laps around the court.

Closing my eyes against the glare of the overhead light, I just wanted to pretend tonight really had been a bad dream. My mother and father weren't really going to die.

But I knew the truth.

Despite her refusal to accept my freakish power, I sensed Mother knew the truth, too.

Now she just had to accept it before it was too late.

Chapter Thirteen

School was torture. How could I sit through eight long hours of exams and lectures, knowing my family would soon be gone forever? I knew my exam scores would suck. My science and algebra teachers had scheduled exam day for today, and those were no easy subjects. I had a difficult time focusing with the image of my dead parents haunting my every thought.

Seeing Bob at school didn't help my conflicting emotions. He was greener and cuter than ever, but something was different about him as I watched him walk slowly out of first period, eyes downcast and shoulders slumped. I noticed him several more times throughout the day. His sad face haunted me. Had my breakup really hurt him?

Why?

Bob should've been happy to be rid of me. My mother hated him. Everyone at school thought I was a bully. It's not like I hung out with him that much, anyway.

Sophie and Krysta were no help. They kept nagging me about Mike. What was I going to do to stop him? They'd even accused me of giving up.

I hadn't given up. I'd tried everything. Everything! How could I save him when Mother wouldn't listen?

So I decided not to tell them about the accident dream. The nagging would never cease, and honestly, I'd had enough nagging from Mother to last a lifetime.

Basketball practice was even more excruciating when coach forced us to run thirty laps. Even though I was dreading the break, I was actually looking forward to two weeks off from basketball. My weary body needed a rest.

Walking through the front door, I noticed the house was quiet. My carpool ride had dropped me off late tonight. Paige's mom had to go to the bank and run into the store. Add that to the extra long practice, and it was nearly dark by the time I got home.

So where were my parents? They should've been home from work by now.

"Mother! Ted!" I yelled. A surge of panic gripped my chest as images from the dream raced through my mind. I had to see that they were alive.

"I'm here, dear."

I gasped as Mother stepped into the hallway wearing a stunning royal-blue dress that was tapered at the waist and flared out at the hips. With each step, the dress cascaded down her legs like a tropical waterfall. Her blonde hair was swept up in an elegant twist. Her dazzling pendant necklace and matching earrings complimented her dramatic blue eyes.

She looked beautiful and feminine.

Perfect.

So unlike me.

Just the way my mother wanted everything in her storybook life.

Mother twirled for me a few times, her dress sashaying around her slender hips. "Do you like it? I bought on sale when I was coming home from work today." She giggled. "Ted's taking me out for our ten-year anniversary."

As I gaped at her beauty, a familiar sense of nausea crept over me. The unease of a sinister deja vu coiled around my spine at the site of the iridescent glow reflecting off mother's blue fabric.

Where had I seen that dress before?

Oh, God, the accident! Images I'd been trying to repress all day came flooding back. Mother, lying on the ground, her blue dress surrounded by a pool of crimson.

"Mother, you can't go out tonight!" I pleaded.

She stopped mid-twirl and eyed me suspiciously. "Why not?"

Choking on a sob, I did my best to reign in my emotions,

to quell my shaking limbs. "Don't you remember...the accident?"

Mother planted her hands on hips, leveling a glare. "Wake up, Allison. It was only a dream."

"When are *you* going to wake up?" I cried, unable to mask the panic in my voice any longer.

"When are you going to *grow up* and be a normal girl?" she shouted. "You're trying to ruin your brother's holiday, and now you're ruining my anniversary!"

"Sorry my gift is such a burden to you, Mother," I spat. She believed me. I knew it. Deep down inside, she knew I was right.

"What's going on here?" Ted bellowed as he stepped into the hallway.

I had to do a double-take at my step-dad. His beard was trimmed and his chestnut hair was combed back in soft waves. The only other time I recalled him wearing a suit and tie was for his wedding. He was a handsome match for my mother. Too bad they were both going to die tonight.

My step-dad was usually more understanding than my mother. Up until I'd had that dream about Mike, Ted was the adult I went to when I needed advice. He'd always been there for me; maybe he'd listen to me now.

"Ted," I pleaded. "You can't go out. A big, black truck is going to ram you into the stoplight in front of our house."

He had the nerve to laugh.

"What the heck are you talking about?"

Folding her arms across her chest, Mother groaned. "It's that stupid dream she had last night."

"Oh." He flashed a tender smile. Stepping in between Mother and me, Ted cupped my chin in his hand. "Listen, sweetheart. Last night was only a dream."

"No." Tears gushed out my eyes and flooded my cheeks. "I felt the dream like I was there. Mother was wearing that blue dress, but she just bought it today."

"I'm sure your mother has lots of blue dresses." Pulling his hand away, he grasped me firmly on the shoulders. "Now, listen. Your mother and I want to have an enjoyable evening together."

"But you can't..."

"It's the least you can do after what you've put her through lately."

My heart sunk at the look of disappointment in Ted's eyes. Did he really think I was such a horrible teen that I'd been trying to hurt my mother? Despite how she treated me, despite who she pretended to be, she was my mother and I loved her. I'd always loved her.

And I wasn't about to lose her.

Grim determination hardened my resolve to save them both, no matter how stupid they were acting. Squaring my shoulders, I leveled them both with a heated glare. "Ted, I'm not trying to hurt you, I'm trying to save you. Walk out that door, and you're never coming home."

"All right, that's enough, young lady!" Ted's roar shook me to the core.

I flinched, jerking back as if I'd been struck. Ted had never lost his temper with me before.

"Margaret, go wait in the car," he barked.

Mother rushed to the door, and then her questioning gaze caught mine. I stared at her with a look of intensity, willing her to read the truth in my eyes.

"Maybe we should stay home tonight, Ted," she stammered.

"No," he spoke through a clenched jaw. "It's time we put our foot down." Pools of fire burned beneath his deep brown glare. "AJ," he commanded. "Go to your room!"

His anger only strengthened my resolve.

My parents were not going to die tonight.

I looked out the side-window. The sun had already gone down. The accident was going to happen after dark. Leaving the house was *not* an option.

Folding my arms across my chest, I planted my feet firmly on the ground "No."

Renewed anger flared in Ted's eyes, before he broke into a wide grin. He eyed me suspiciously while rubbing the stubble on his chin. "I see what you're doing. Well, you're not going to win tonight. We're leaving."

Mother slipped on her coat with shaking hands while Ted held open the door.

Without saying a word, Mother stared at me for a long

moment, her eyes pooled with moisture, before she stepped out the door.

Ted's gaze passed over me with a look of contempt. "I expect an apology when we get home." He slammed the door behind him.

I just wanted to sink into a hole. I loved Ted like he was my own father, and now he was acting just like Mother.

But not for long.

Soon, they'd both be dead, and neither would know just how much I loved them.

Not if I could help it.

My legs propelled forward without thought, as if I was racing to save my life. I was; I couldn't live without my parents. I couldn't let them die hating me.

My heart screamed at the site of Ted pulling out of the driveway. I had to reach them—had to save them.

So I did what any normal teenager would do.

I jumped on the hood of their car.

Wincing at the pain that shot up my side, I braced at the screech of Ted's brakes. I bucked against the windshield before rolling off the hood and onto the pavement.

Luckily, I landed on my feet, stumbling backward before falling on my butt.
Ouch.

That's all I could think at the moment, too stunned by what had just happened.

In another moment, Mother's screams brought me back to reality. She was kneeling by my side, holding me and sobbing hysterically into my hair.

"What in the hell is wrong with you?" Ted yelled above us. "You could've been killed!"

His rage was muffled by the din of screeching breaks, followed by the sickening crash of metal slamming into metal. Our heads all jerked at the sound.

Directly in front of us, about one-hundred yards away where the stoplight divided the intersection, the smashed frame of a black truck had wrapped around the light-pole.

A familiar cold, stale stench permeated my senses, leaving a dull, metallic taste on my tongue. Just like in my dream. The taste of death.

      Ted swore. Mother wailed.

      I puked my brains out.

Chapter Fourteen

"**M**ike, this is Mom. I've changed my mind. You're not going on that snowboarding trip tomorrow."

Sitting in Ted's overstuffed chair with an icepack under my butt, I beamed at Mother. She was on the couch next to me, her hand firmly grasping mine. She hadn't let go since the accident, except when she made an ice-pack for my sore fanny.

I had to stifle my laughter when I heard his pathetic whining from the receiver of Mother's cell phone.

Mother's face could have been carved from granite as she spoke firmly into the phone. "Listen, Mike, my decision is final. No snowboarding. I want you home first thing in the morning."

His whining intensified and it sounded like that time the neighbor's cat fell in our pool. Mike's teenage tantrum was cut short as Mother flipped her cell phone shut. I was sure we wouldn't hear the end of it when he got home from his buddy's house in the morning. Mike and his friends were all packed and ready to go.

I wondered why she didn't make him come home tonight. Maybe after the accident she didn't want him on the road. Or maybe she just didn't feel like dealing with his attitude right now. We'd had enough stress for one day.

Flashing me an impish grin, Mother threw back her head and sank into the couch cushions.

But she didn't let go of my hand. If anything, she held it tighter.

I didn't mind the pressure. Soaking up Mother's love felt kinda good.

"Tomorrow we go on a nice family trip." Mother scrunched her face in what looked like a cross between a wince and a smile.

I couldn't recall a time when my family had a 'nice' trip. This was going to be interesting. "Where are we going?" I was almost afraid to ask.

Mother's face reddened and she swallowed hard. "I think we need to go visit your grandma."

"Grandma!" I squealed, bounding off the chair and into my mother's arms.

I winced at the jolt of pain that shot through my bruised butt, but it was worth it. What an awesome way to spend Christmas. Visiting Grandma's ranch seemed a distant memory to me, as I vaguely recalled riding horses and chasing frenzied goats.

Lips turning into a slight frown, Mother's eyes shone with moisture. "I think it's time Grandma and I made up."

I gave her a big squeeze before pulling back and looking into her soft blue gaze. "I think it's time we *all* made up, Mom."

My mom made these weird choking sounds, her eyes pooling with tears as they trailed freely down her cheeks.

Startled, my first instinct was that my mom was having a seizure. Grabbing her shoulders, I gave her a gentle shake. "Mom, what's the matter? Are you okay?"

My attempt to help her didn't work as her convulsions became stronger. After a few tense moments, I realized my mom was crying—hard. Harder than I'd ever seen her cry before. Grabbing the box of tissues off the coffee table, I handed them to her.

She took the box, hastily grabbing several sheets. Sitting next to my mom, I waited for what felt like an eternity.

After her tears had subsided, she found my hand again and squeezed harder than ever. Pulling me into an embrace, she kissed my cheek while hugging me so hard I thought I'd break. "You've never called me 'Mom' before," she breathed.

"What?" I choked out. I'd never called Mother 'Mom'? Mom—I repeated the word in my head. It did seem kind of foreign. Why didn't I ever call this woman in my arms 'Mom'? Maybe until now she hadn't really felt like a mom.

"I'm sorry, I've been such a bad mother," she cried as fresh tears poured down her cheeks.

I'd waited so long to hear those words. To have my mother finally realize how badly her rejection hurt me. Now, I guess it didn't matter anymore. I just wanted her to love me. To accept that I was different. Panic gripped my chest as I wondered how long her love would last. Would she wake up tomorrow, realizing her daughter was a freak and treat me the way she had in the past?

Now that she loved me, I didn't want it to end, but I had to know. Feeling the bile of fear bite the back of my tongue, I struggled to push the words past my tightening throat. "Mom, sometimes I have dreams, visions. They tell me the future. I didn't ask to be different than most kids, but I am." With a trembling lip, I lowered my head, afraid to see my mom's reaction.

Cupping my cheek, Mom raised my gaze to her. In her bright, blue gaze, I saw only the warmth of a mother's love. "I've been a fool for denying your gift this long."

"Why?" My question was spontaneous. As if it had hovered at the back of my mind for years. Why had my mother rejected my gift? Rejected me?

Sighing, my mom fell against the sofa while rubbing her temples. "When I was a child, kids found out about my gift. They feared me. They hated me." Her voice was laced with bitterness as she rolled her eyes to the ceiling.

Although I hadn't experienced what she went through, I felt sorry for my mom. That's exactly why Sophie, Krysta and I had promised to keep our gifts secret. We knew kids at school would hate us, too.

"After Grandma moved me to a new school, I pretended to be normal. I had so many friends. Kids liked me then." She shrugged off a weak smile.

Why did so many people in my life feel they had to change to be liked? To be accepted? Why did Bob take a bite of a hamburger? Did he think I wouldn't like him if he didn't eat meat? Coach Lowe was so worried about the team liking her that she ended up in jail. I was stupid enough to blow my game by becoming a vegetarian.

"But did you like yourself?"

Mom shrugged. "I was so wrapped up in making kids like me, I never thought about that. I didn't want you to experience what I went through. I only wanted you to be normal because I love you."

The dam of tears I'd been holding at bay threatened to break free. "I always thought you hated me."

"Oh, baby," she caressed my cheek, wiping away a tear with her finger. "I'd never hate you."

I choked back a sob, determined not to turn into a big cry baby. My mom loved me now. Time to stop crying and start celebrating. I still had one question left unanswered.

"Mom, what is your gift?"

She smiled, a sparkle of mischief dancing in her eyes. "You mean you don't know?"

"No." I shook my head. How could I know when I'd never seen her use it?

"Hmmm." She tapped her chin, pretending to be lost in thought. "As often as I use it on you, you should have figured it out by now."

Scratching my head in confusion, I tried to understand what she was talking about. "Grandma said you never use your gift."

"I don't," she reddened, "usually, but sometimes I can't help it. I think that's why I'm always barging into your bedroom. I'm trying to fight the urge to use my gift."

"Hey, ladies, how are we doin'?" Ted's gruff voice echoed from the hallway.

Maybe it was all the drama from today, but I was suffering from a major brain fart and my head hurt too much to figure out Mom's gift. Guess I'd have to find out later. I wasn't sure if Mom wanted my step-dad discovering the freak gene ran in the family.

Ted walked into the living room, looking like he'd just been dragged through the gates of hell. As a paramedic, it was his duty to rush to the scene of the accident but he forced us to go inside the house. After my dream last night, I really didn't want to visit the wreckage again, anyway.

Holding a longneck beer in one hand, he sat in his chair. One of the knees on his black, dressy pants was torn. His white shirt was trashed, ripped at the pocket and smudged with filth. As he rubbed a hand through his tousled hair, I noticed lines around his eyes that hadn't been there before.

After taking a long gulp of beer, he finally spoke. "Guy had a suicide note in his pocket."

Mom gasped.

My limbs went numb.

"Is he dead?" Mom asked.

Ted looked at her for a long moment and then finally nodded.

A tremor shook my body with earthquake magnitude as I was vaguely aware of Mom's muffled scream.

Setting his beer on the coffee table, Ted leveled me with a haunting look. "AJ, I don't understand how you..." His voice trailed off as he fisted his hands until his knuckles turned white. "I just wanted to thank you and to apologize for not believing."

Swallowing a lump in my throat, I nodded. "That's okay."

Turning to Mom, Ted leaned over and took her hand in his. "Mike isn't going snowboarding tomorrow."

"Believe me," Mom said, "he knows better than to disobey me."

Chapter Fifteen

Sweat dripping from my damp hair, I nearly fell out of bed while fumbling for my cell phone. I had to know the time.

Six-thirty. I swore.

Mom, Ted and I had stayed up until nearly two in the morning, playing board games and watching movies. I couldn't remember having so much fun with my parents, even though a dark gloom haunted the back of my mind. Mom should've made Mike come home right away, but she and Ted were spooked after the accident and agreed no one was driving until morning.

I'd finally fallen asleep about three in the morning, despite the uneasy feeling that had settled in my stomach. But not long after I'd surrendered to a fitful rest, I'd had the falling dream.

Despite Mom's orders, Mike had gone snowboarding. How did I know he was going to do this?

Besides the fact I'm psychic.

Oh, yeah, Mike was a spoiled brat who was so used to getting his way, he just thought he'd ignore Mom and go on the trip.

Turning on the light switch, I hastily dressed, all the while calling Mike every bad word on the planet.

I had to go wake up my parents. Hopefully, we'd stop him before it was too late. Panic and anger forced my blood to pump overtime. I didn't know just how big this mountain was and I hoped I wouldn't have to climb it to save my stupid brother.

Another question triggered the alarming tempo of my heart. How would we be able to find Mike in time to save him?

Just as I opened my bedroom door, I nearly ran into my Mom standing on the other side of the threshold. She was already dressed in jeans and a thick coat.

"Here." She handed me a coat and gloves. "It's cold up there."

"But how did you..."

"No time to explain," she said. "We've got to get your brother before it's too late."

Ted was in the driveway revving his truck engine.

Climbing into the backseat, I squealed at the site of my grandma sitting next to me. Lunging toward her, I wrapped my arms around her tiny frame.

"Easy, dear," she laughed, "Your grandma's got only one set of lungs."

My mom turned around, smiling at us both through the lines of worry that creased the edges of her mouth. "Thanks for coming, Mom."

Grandma nodded, and for a long moment, their gazes were locked. As the seconds ticked by, I felt the familiar tension between them melting away, like snow thawing in the spring time.

"I'm glad I came, Margaret," Grandma spoke through a weathered smile.

Inhaling deeply, I realized I'd been holding my breath while waiting to see if Mom and Grandma would get along. "How did you know?" I asked Grandma.

"I didn't." She winked, tossing her long ponytail over her shoulder. "I just figured your brother would be going to that stupid mountain, so I came here to slash his tires."

Despite the thick smoke of fear that stifled the air, I laughed. Grandma hadn't abandoned my cause. She had meant to help me save Mike all along, even if it meant vandalizing his truck.

"I caught her skulking around the yard with a butcher knife." Ted said.

Way to go, Grandma!

"I didn't see Mike's truck in the driveway, so I was hoping he parked by Ted's workshop."

Ted had a workshop out back with a large overhang that

my parents and Mike would park their cars under whenever we had bad weather.

Turning onto the highway, Ted stepped on the accelerator. I felt like we'd been thrown into warp speed, as my head jerked back with the truck's movement. My brother might be a complete, immature idiot, but his family was determined to save him.

I prayed we'd find him in time.

After nearly three hours of driving, I'd fallen in and out of a fitful sleep. Mom and Ted encouraged me to rest. My brother wasn't answering his cell phone, so I think my parents wanted me to dream again so I could find out Mike's next move.

But I hadn't slept long enough to dream. Pulling my jacket closer, I tried to warm my bones from the growing chill that had sliced through the barriers of the truck's warm cabin. As we made our ascent up the mountain, the air in the truck thinned, which meant each worried breath was even more difficult to inhale. Every mile or so there was a new turn-off to a different peak or detour.

How would we know which road to take?

I thought about asking, but I knew my parents had enough on their minds. Maybe Mike had already told them where he was going.

Leaning forward, I tried to examine their faces to see if I could read anything from their expressions. Ted's gaze was on the road. Mom had her eyes closed tight, her fingers pressed to her temples.

Weird.

Was she shielding her eyes from the sun?

Mom's eyes flew open, and her blank stare made her look more like a zombie. "Turn left at this next road."

"Are you sure?" Ted asked. "Those jumps are too high. He said they were going to start on beginner hills."

"Do it!" Mom commanded.

Ted had to apply the brakes hard for us to make the turn. I screamed as the truck nearly spun out of control.

Soon we were on the new road, heading up a winding hill

that had me gripping the sides of my seat. Looking over at Grandma, I wondered if she was ready to piss her pants, too.

She flashed me a rueful smile.

What was that all about?

Following Mom's orders, Ted made a few more turns, always taking the more treacherous paths in our spiraling ascent to the land where AJ is eternally wetting her undies.

It suddenly dawned on me that I really didn't like heights. I couldn't believe my brother was stupid enough to go this high.

Why did Mom insist we go this way? I didn't think she'd ever been to Hell's Peak before.

But Mom seemed so certain, almost like she knew exactly where Mike was.

Oh, crap. How could I have been so blind?

She knew about my secret phone calls with Bob. She was there for me when I left the game early. She'd been waiting when Sparks drove me home from Lowe's beer bust.

Widening my eyes, I looked at my mom with a new understanding. She was telling Ted where to turn, but she had closed her eyes again. How did she know how to get there, unless she'd been following Mike's progress?

Unless she was watching him right now with her mind.

"Only a few miles and we'll be at the bottom of the hill." She said with a shaky voice. "He's just started the climb."

O-mi-God.

He was already climbing the hill. Were we too late? How totally weird that my mom was watching my brother, but they were still miles apart.

After a few more tense minutes, we were at the base of...of...what the heck was that thing? That giant tidal wave of white, hard frost was no hill!

Jumping out of the truck, my body was immediately assailed by the frigid air. I rubbed my shivering arms before Mom spun me around and helped me slip into a thick coat. Pulling the hood over my head, I strained my neck to try and see the top of this monster glacier. An enormous hill swept up to the clouds in an almost picture-perfect slope. It was breathtakingly beautiful, until my gaze found the top.

Nothing but a sheer drop on the other side.

Just like in my dream.

Was Mike really that stupid?

Yes, he really was.

"Everyone, stay here!" Ted barked before plowing through the snow toward a group of teens huddled at the bottom of the hill.

As Ted climbed over a leaning fence, I noticed all the 'danger' and 'keep out' signs attached to the posts. My brother and all these other idiots had ignored the warnings. You didn't need to be a psychic to know this hill was a death trap.

Ted's booming voice seemed to echo throughout the mountains as he flashed his badge at the teens and demanded one of them get off his snowmobile. Revving the motor, Ted raced toward the base of the hill.

Even with a motor, would my step-dad reach my brother in time to stop him?

"He's not going to make it! Mike's almost at the top!" Mother wailed.

Bundled in a large wooly jacket and ten too many scarves, Grandma bounded up to me with the energy of a snow bunny. "AJ, is that where he'll fall?" She was pointing to the other side of the slope, to the drop, which had to be several hundred feet.

Visions of the dream assailed my memory.

Icy hard, gray and unwelcoming. "If there's ice below that drop, then yes."

"Then we need to go find out!" Grandma ordered.

Looking at the fluffy soft padding that nearly swallowed the entire bottom portion of my legs, I knew that solid ground was far from here. Then I realized just how cold my feet were getting. And aching, too, kind of like they were numbing and bruising at the same time.

Probably not good, but I didn't have time to think of my pain right now. If I had known I'd be trekking through forbidden glaciers trying to save my brother from breaking open his head, I'd have worn snow gear, not jeans and athletic sneakers.

Ignoring Ted's command to stay put, Mother, Grandma and I stepped over the sideways fence and did our best to race through the thick snow. It was hard, and with each step, my shoes threatened to slip off completely. I knew I'd get total frostbite if I lost them. My toes were numb enough already.

"He's at the top!" Mom screamed. "Hurry!"

She plowed ahead of us, crying as she pushed forward. As we struggled to get to the bottom of the cliff, I could see just up ahead where the snow ended, swallowed up by a sea of ice, gray and solid.

Then Mother stopped and stilled, as if the frigid air had frozen her solid. Closing her eyes, she grasped my arm. Even through the padding of the jacket, I could feel the pressure from her grip.

"Ted made it," she whispered hoarsely. "He's talking to Mike."

But panic, not relief gripped my heart as my brain was flooded with images from my dream.

My step-dad yelling at Mike. "Stay away from the ledge before you fall!"

Mike retreating back from Ted as he argued. "You can't tell me what to do!"

My step-dad lunging toward my brother. "Don't do it, Mike!"

But as Mike tried to dive out of Ted's reach, he stumbled backward, tumbling right over the side.

"He's falling!" Mother and I screamed in unison.

Sucking in a huge breath of air, I braced myself against the image of my brother splattering all over the cold hard surface. Falling into each other's arms, Mom and I gripped each other tightly as a tiny falling shadow came into view.

My jaw dropped but only a silent scream escaped my lips as my brother's death unfolded before me.

There was no way he could survive the fall. Only then did I notice Grandma pushed several paces ahead of us. She was standing on the ice, directly below my falling brother. Her arms were stretched open as her long, gloved fingers reached out toward Mike.

Was she crazy?

In another instant, my screaming brother was hovering just above Grandma's head, suspended in mid-air like he was connected to an invisible bungee cord.

With a wicked giggle, Grandma stepped aside and lowered her arms.

Mike fell to the ground with a thud, cursing and cradling his arm as he curled into a ball on the ground.

A startled cry escaped my throat before it bubbled over into uncontrollable laughter.

Chapter Sixteen

"Krysta," Sophie squealed. "How much of that stuff are you going to use? It's not even Christmas anymore."

Rolling her eyes at Sophie, Krysta flashed me a devious grin while hanging wads of mistletoe over the living room entryway. "This is so cool of your mom to let us have a New Year's party."

"Yeah," I shrugged. "My mom is pretty cool." Even as the words came out, I couldn't keep from smiling—something I'd been doing a lot lately.

Mom had offered to throw a New Year's party at our house. I'd never had a real party before. All of my teammates and even some of my classmates said they were coming. Other kids were having parties, but they chose to come to my house. They must like me now.

Mom and Ted promised to keep to their bedroom while we had the house to ourselves. Mike was on house-arrest for eternity because he went snowboarding without permission. Mother promised to add another eternity of restriction if he ruined my party.

My family had just returned from Christmas at Grandma's ranch. Although there were a few annoying moments when I had to listen to Mike whine at the dinner table because he couldn't cut his meat with a broken arm, or when he pouted because Grandma, Mom and I went horseback riding without him.

Other than that, my life had gone from total crap to totally perfect.

Well, almost perfect.

Every time I looked at the spiky green needles of our table-top Christmas tree, I was reminded of Bob.

Things change, AJ. Time to move on.

So why couldn't I get over him?

Eyeing the tree with more determination, I decided it was time to let go of the past. Pulling down the empty ornament box from the top of the bookcase, I went over to the tree and began tearing it apart.

"AJ, what are you doing?" Krysta demanded. "That's the centerpiece for the party."

"It's not Christmas, anymore, Krysta," I huffed. "Time to move on."

From the corner of my eye, I caught Sophie and Krysta exchanging knowing glances.

Heaving a sigh of frustration, I turned to both of them. "What?"

"Do you miss him?" Krysta asked.

"Who?" Trying to mask my true feelings, I didn't move a facial muscle while pretending not to know what they were talking about.

Sophie cocked a brow. "Don't lie to me, AJ. I can *feel* it."

"Look, can we drop it?" Tonight I just wanted to have fun and not think about what could have been.

Mom liked me now. My house was actually peaceful, well, with the exception of the few reporters who kept calling the house and asking to interview the boy who fell three hundred feet and only broke an arm.

Mom wouldn't allow them an interview as she refused to let Mike enjoy any fame for his stupidity. Besides, if they asked too many questions, they might discover the real reason Mike was alive, and Grandma, Mom and I had pledged to keep our gifts secret.

As I thought of the new bond the women in my family shared, a sense of belonging swelled my chest with happiness. I wasn't going to give Mom a reason to hate me now, no matter how much I missed Bob.

"Wow! Your emotions are all over the place," Sophie exclaimed.

Shaking my head, I just laughed. I definitely had weird friends.

The smell of something yummy assailed my senses. Mom was in the kitchen cooking for me and my friends. She really was cool.

Walking into the kitchen, I put my arm around Mom. Something we'd been doing to each other lately. "What smells so good?"

Mom flashed a sly smile. "It's a new recipe." She pulled a pan out of the oven. "Veggie quiche."

"Can I have a taste?" But before she could answer, I carved out a small bite with a fork. The quiche warmed my tongue and then a combination of spices, cheeses and veggies exploded in my mouth. "Mmmm, this is good," I said before stealing another bite. "You've never made this before."

"Well, I thought some of your guests would appreciate a few meat-free dishes." Turning her gaze down, she focused on arranging a mountain of chocolate chip cookies.

My heart fluttered wildly in my chest.

Bob was the only vegetarian I knew and I hadn't invited him.

Would Mom ask him to my party? Was she really that cool?

The doorbell rang and Krysta raced to get it.

As I eyed my mom suspiciously, she kept her gaze averted. I thought I saw the traces of a slight smile.

I turned as a horde of friends piled into the living room. Paige, Keysha and a few other teammates were removing coats and hats and handing them to Sophie. Several more friends came in after them.

An odd sensation curled in my stomach before slamming my chest with a punch.

I knew no one would bring an extra Christmas tree along.

So that tall, towering pine leaning against the wall had to be Bob. My jaw dropped and I looked at my mom who was grinning sheepishly. I launched into her arms for a big hug before pulling back and rushing into the living room.

Making my way through the crowd, I said 'hi' to all my friends before I spotted him against the back wall.

"Hey." A familiar pair of soft, gray eyes glistened down at

me. Looking kind of out of place, he played with the frayed end of some duct tape on his wrist.

As I struggled for the right words to say to him, I finally gave up and reached for his hand, lacing his fingers in mine. What could I say to this totally perfect guy who'd come back even after I'd tried to change him and then dumped him?

He looked down at our entwined fingers and then his gaze found mine, as a soft smile curved his lips.

Neither of us spoke.

Even as the noise from the crush of teens grew louder, we stood there mute, just holding hands.

Then I was bumped from behind. I turned to see Krysta standing on the stepstool, hovering above us with mistletoe in one hand and a thumbtack in the other. She let out a low whistle as she hung the mistletoe.

Feeling the crimson tide surge in my cheeks, I looked into Bob's beautiful cloudy eyes. In the next second, his lips were on mine.

This time, I wasn't going to faint.

I kissed my green-haired BF in my Mom's living room, surrounded by tons of cheering friends.

Life definitely didn't suck anymore.

Krysta's
Curse

Book Three

This book is dedicated to my awesome peeps at the Eclective.

Prologue

Sophie's house—six years earlier

"Sophie, AJ!" Where are they? Where are they? We have to get out of this house. My legs were shaking so badly, I could barely stand on them. You can't faint, Krysta.

"Boo!"

"Aaaahhhh!" Making a hasty retreat, I tripped over my own legs, landing on my butt. Looking at the puzzled expression of my third-grade classmate, I breathed a sigh of relief.

"What's wrong with you?" Sophie bent over me, offering a chubby hand. "Why didn't you come get me?"

I grabbed her by the wrist, unsteadily pulling myself up. "I...I think I saw a ghost."

Scowling, she crossed her arms. "Just because you couldn't find me, doesn't mean you should make up a ghost."

"I'm not making it up." I cautiously turned my head in both directions, terrified he was still in the house. "I saw him. I really did."

Lifting her rounded chin, Sophie tapped her foot. "Okay, what did he look like?"

How could I forget? I would forever have his image in my head. In the bathtub, in my bed at night, whenever I was alone, I would remember his floating spirit, his pained expression. "He was maybe a little older than us. He had red hair and a red and white striped shirt."

"Corbin!" Sophie's hands flew to her mouth.

"Corbin?" Somehow, putting a name to his spirit only made my experience more real, more frightening.

"My neighbor," Sophie gasped. "He died two weeks ago. He had red hair and always wore that shirt. Did he say anything to you?"

"No." I shook my head.

Sophie swallowed, her eyes nearly popping out of her head. "Where did you see him?"

"The living room," came a raspy voice. Sophie and I both shrieked.

I turned to see AJ standing motionless in front of the living room entryway, her sun-kissed skin was now nearly as white as the ghost. I had forgotten that she still hadn't come out of hiding.

"Did you see him, too?" I asked AJ.

Her mouth opened, but nothing came out. Finally, she just shook her head.

"Then how did you know where he was?" I wondered.

She stuttered a few times before spitting out the words. "I dreamed him."

A strange chill raised the hair on the back of my neck. Fear and awe pushed blood through my veins even faster than when I'd seen the ghost. This couldn't be happening. This was just too freaky to be real. As I shakily moved toward AJ, I looked into her frozen expression, and somehow, I suspected what she meant.

But how?

"What do you mean you dreamed him?" I whispered.

AJ's lips trembled, as she wrapped her arms across her stomach. "I had a dream about this day, us playing, the ghost. I...I didn't think it would really happen."

"What was he doing when you saw him?" Sophie asked.

AJ's eyes and mouth appeared to be encrusted in ice, her arms and feet motionless, like she was rooted to the floor. "He just glided, like he was on skates." Her tone was even, but not calm.

Somewhere on the edge of AJ' voice, suspended in her breath, was the tangible fear that I also felt in my bones. Something weird, something major, was happening.

The act of lifting my arm felt like lifting dead weight, as I pointed toward Sophie's darkened living room. "He kind of glided from one side to the other and disappeared behind a window." Recalling that image sent new shivers down my spine.

Sophie's eyes bulged even more and her mouth fell open. "What window?"

"The window behind the couch," I said. Although the window was huge, it was veiled in heavy drapes, casting an eerie gloom over the area.

I looked at Sophie, who began to sway from side to side. "You're turning green."

She put her hand to her throat. "I was hiding behind the couch."

I grabbed their hands, tugging them in the direction of the front door. "Let's get out of here."

BOOM. "Aaaahhhh!"

I found myself locked in a tight embrace. AJ was pulling on my hair and Sophie's nails had dug into my back. Sophie screamed so loud I thought my eardrums must have burst. Somehow, I summoned the courage to look in the direction of the loud noise.

Sophie's parents stared at us before exchanging confused expressions with each other. A big suitcase, which probably caused the loud noise, was lying at their feet.

Pinching Sophie and AJ, I made them open their eyes. Sophie squealed, running into her mom's arms before pulling back and pointing at AJ and me. "Krysta and AJ saw our dead neighbor."

"What?" Sophie's dad laughed, narrowing his eyes in our direction.

"He was in our living room," she blurted. "He walked right through me!"

"Rose Marie," Sophie's mom looked over my shoulder. "What is this about?"

I turned to see Rose Marie, Sophie's older sister, standing behind us. She was supposed to be our babysitter, but she took off after Sophie's mom went to pick up her dad at the airport. She must have snuck into the house when she saw them pull up.

"They're just pretending, Mom." She laughed, flinging her body onto the couch. The couch that Corbin had walked through just minutes earlier.

"No." Turning to her sister, Sophie stomped her foot. "They really saw him. They described him and everything."

Grabbing the remote, Rose Marie rolled her eyes and turned on the TV.

My heart sank as I heard the faint laughter of Sophie's parents. We really did see a ghost. Why didn't they believe us?

Sophie's head jerked back toward her mother. "We are not being fanciful girls."

Sophie's mom gasped. "I didn't say that you were."

Pointing a shaky finger at her mother, Sophie's eyes began to water. "But you were thinking it."

"How did you?" Her mom shook her head. "Never mind. I don't want to hear any more ghost talk. You girls listen, and listen good. There are no such things as ghosts!"

Chapter One

"Emmy Jane, wake up."

Trying to rub the sleep from my eyes, I propped myself up on wobbly elbows. An old couple hovered above me with determined expressions.

Determined to drive me crazy! "What are you doing in my room?"

The old woman turned a frown. "We need your help."

She could have been anyone's grandma. She could have been my grandma. But I didn't care anymore. I was tired of these intrusions into my sanity.

"Don't you realize I have school tomorrow?" God, why couldn't I have been a normal girl?

The old man shifted in front of the woman. The outline of a long, scraggly beard was still visible despite his translucent form. "It's me, your grandpa, Emmy Jane."

Annoyed, I rolled my eyes. "I don't have a grandpa."

The old woman attempted to nudge him, but her elbow just slipped in his body, like running a knife through Jell-O. "This ain't Emmy Jane, Ed."

Scowling, he shook his head. "Of course she is, Grandma."

"Look, aren't you people supposed to be sleeping...like all the time?" Why did they wake me up just to argue? I was tired and getting more annoyed by the second.

Ignoring me, Grandma proceeded to prove Grandpa wrong. "Emmy Jane was a good head taller."

Great, now even the dead were poking fun of my height.

What would they criticize next? My dull brown eyes or my hair which looked more like an electrified mop on my head?

"Hello, dead people, please leave." Waving my arms at them, I tried to get their attention. "I can't go to school with circles under my eyes."

Grandpa threw up his hands. "Well then, who is she?"

Holy crap! Did people lose their hearing when they died? They were treating me as if I was dead.

"I don't know." Grandma shrugged. "But she sees us and that's all that matters."

The spirits turned toward me.

I instinctively rubbed my arms. I didn't know why dead people always gave me the chills, but they did. Still, I was relieved to finally get their attention, yet weirded out, too. I mean, yeah, I was used to dead people waking me up at night. But I couldn't say I liked it.

I realized by their clothes that they must have lived in the last century. Grandpa's long beard was kind of goofy, but the way his eyes fixed on me creeped me out. Make that one eye. The other eye kept rolling to the back of his head. Although Grandma had a sweet kind of smile, she looked a little too cliché with her knit shawl and hair pinned back in some out-of-style bun.

I hoped I wasn't going to be that uncool when I died. I mean, I knew I couldn't take my cosmetics with me, but I would still insist on a decent hairstyle for my burial. Hopefully, by the time I died, longer lasting anti-frizz products would be on the market.

I sighed, realizing that getting rid of these pests wouldn't be easy. "Do you mind telling me what you're doing in my room?"

"I'm Gertrude." She pulled tightly on her shawl before nodding toward Grandpa. "This here's Ed. We'd be much obliged for a moment of your time."

Feeling my teeth grind together, I had to remind myself to unlock my jaw before I rubbed off all my enamel. "Do I have a choice?"

"No." Ed shook his head. "She's much too sassy to be Emmy Jane."

What nerve! As if he had any right to come into my room without asking, waking me up on a school night. I clenched my fists into balls, only releasing my fingers after realizing my nails were breaking skin. "Excuse me, but I was sleeping."

"So was I." Punching his fist in the air, Ed started yelling. "But them people started poking around my restin' place. They tore down that old oak tree. That tree been there before I was buried."

An involuntary chill raced up my spine as the air around me grew colder.

"Don't mind him." Gertrude rolled her eyes, making another futile poke in his ribcage. "He's been a grumpy old goat for over a hundred years."

Ed wagged his finger at me. "You'd be hotter than a poker stick if they turned your tombstone to rubble."

"Shush now, Ed." Gertrude swatted him, only to have her hand swoosh through his chest. "You're scarin' the girl."

"I'm not scared. I've seen plenty of dead people." I sat up, pulling the threadbare comforter over my midsection and hugging my knees for warmth. I kept my gaze fixed on the unwelcome guests. "Now what do you want?"

Ed's shoulders fell, the bottom portion of his face turning down. "We want our graveyard back."

Unbelievable! What did they expect from me? Go to a graveyard in the middle of the night and fix their tombstones? "What am I supposed to do about it?"

Clasping both hands together, Gertrude's eyes twinkled with an unnatural glow. "We thought you'd never ask."

Closed Facebook Group/Some ungodly hour of the morning

Just call me your average, everyday fashion goddess who knows how to accessorize any outfit or summon a poltergeist.

You heard me correctly.

I don't know why dead people want to talk to me, but they do. It's not like I can help them. Dead people don't know a thing about fashion and they're really not interested in the latest trends. Too bad. That would make my life so much easier.

Why, you ask?

Because a couple of ancients visited my bedroom last night and asked me to do the unthinkable! I mean, they're already dead, so why do they have to ruin my life, too? It's bad enough they're always spooking me when I'm trying to sleep, but now they want me to stop the new mall project and save their sacred burial site. Come on! I'm just fourteen. Why don't they go bother the mayor or something?

I don't have time to fix the lives of the deceased. I've got a lot going on right now. Bryon Thomas, my new lab partner in science, is a total hottie. He's coming over tomorrow night so we can work on a project. What if they show up? He'll freak. And worse, he could tell the whole school. My social life would be, excuse the pun, dead.

Besides, they really don't understand how badly I want that mall. Only five minutes from my apartment. How cool is that?

No, I can't do it. I won't.

The mall is expected to open when I turn sixteen, just when I'm old enough to get a real job. I heard employees get a thirty percent discount at most of the stores. No more traveling to the outlet mall forty-five miles out of town. Besides, don't they realize what stopping this mall would do to my reputation? I mean, I know I'm barely five-feet-two, but I still have time to grow. One day, I'm going to be on the cover of Cosmo. But if these ghosts keep driving me crazy, I'll be the poster child for Weirdo.

Chapter Two

"Hey, Krysta, missed you on the bus." Sophie Sinora, my best friend of six years, sat at the far corner cafeteria table. Her bright green eyes sparkling with amusement, she flipped her smooth chestnut hair over her shoulder before pointing a fry in my direction.

"Slept in. My dad had to drive me to school." I sat down with my usual lunch, diet soda and a side salad.

"Did you get my text?" she asked.

I sighed while shaking my head. "My dad's late paying the phone bill."

No surprise there. My dad was usually late paying every bill. Losing electricity or phone for a few days was something that happened all the time in my household.

"Well, I got the scoop on some fashion news. In fact, I doubt you even know about it." Sophie flashed me a smile before shoving a fry into her mouth.

Impossible. No one heard fashion news before me, especially not Sophie. That girl just lost all her baby fat and I still couldn't get her to try on low-rise jeans.

"What is it?"

"My mom found out from another realtor that the new name of the mall is supposed to be The Crossover."

"Sounds right," I shrugged, "considering where they're building it."

Sophie's eyes widened. "What do you mean?"

"I mean the mall is on an old burial ground." I sighed, trying to brush back a piece of hair frizz that slipped out of my headband, making a mental note to go gel it before lunch ended. "Didn't you read my entry last night?"

Even though I had a huge Facebook account with more friends than anyone I know, I also had a private account, just for Sophie and AJ. Sophie was called Mind Whispers, AJ was Dream Whispers and they called me Ghost Whispers. Instead of pictures of our faces, we use the backs of our heads. That was Sophie's idea, just in case one day Facebook did something weird and made all private groups public. One could never be too careful.

"What time did you post it?" "About two."

"In the morning?" Sophie rolled her eyes. "Some of us actually sleep, Krysta."

"Just tell us already." AJ Dawson, my other best friend, came up behind us, wearing her softball jersey, old jeans and scuffed shoes.

Out of all my friends, AJ really had the worst fashion sense, but there was nothing I could do. She was a stubborn jock. I'd tried putting makeup on her a few times, but she washed it off within minutes. Lucky for AJ, she was a natural beauty, tall with pale blonde hair and flawless, tanned skin.

Some people like me had to work at it, wearing uncomfortable, high heels and spending a small fortune on hair gels.

After tossing her barfy burger on the table, AJ wadded up her wrapper and shot it into a garbage can. "Did you have company last night?"

"More like uninvited pests," I huffed. They ruined my sleep, causing me to use a lot more concealer to cover up the dark circles under my eyes. How could I go on like this? They said they'd be back to see if I had any ideas. I didn't know when, but I knew I wouldn't get much sleep while waiting for them to return.

If it wasn't for my two best friends, I don't know how I would have kept my sanity. They were the only "living" people who knew of my gift, if that's what you'd call it. Most times, my gift felt more like a curse. After the time I saw a ghost in Sophie's house, no one believed me except Sophie and AJ. They knew I was telling the truth. Maybe because they also had freakish gifts. Sometimes, people's thoughts just popped into Sophie's head. And whenever AJ had a dream, it always came true.

"Let me guess," AJ laughed, narrowing her crystal blue eyes, "they're going to crash with you for a while until they find a new cemetery?"

Well, at least someone thought this was funny. AJ acted the tough jock, but I knew her wise cracks were just a way to avoid dealing with real feelings.

"No." I shook my head. "They're still at that cemetery. The mall developers just moved the tombstones and left the bodies."

"Gross. I'm not eating at that food-court." Sophie stuck out her tongue.

I wondered if she knew she had just shown the world her French fry residue.

"What?" AJ jabbed Sophie in the shoulder. "Are you afraid you'll find an old finger in your French fries?"

"Hey, Krysta."

My drink froze midway to my mouth at the sound of that familiar voice. The commanding way he said my name was almost like he was making me take notice, but I didn't need any prodding to notice Bryon Thomas. The boy was gorgeous. He had short blond hair, spiked with the perfect amount of gel. And those clear blue eyes. I just wanted to die every time I looked at him. And he was my new lab partner!

"Hey, Bryon." I casually turned in his direction. He was standing just a few feet behind me munching on a cookie while he selected a coke out of the vending machine.

"How do you know Bryon?" Sophie leaned over and whispered behind a frozen smile.

I shifted in my seat, trying not to act too excited. "He's my new lab partner."

AJ wagged her eyebrows. "He's a hottie."

"We know what kind of chemistry you'll be working on." Sophie snickered.

Hoping Bryon couldn't hear my shameless friends, I knew I must have been turning ten shades of red. Just as I was giving them the "shut up or die" stare, I felt his familiar heat behind me. I turned back around. His gorgeous tanned arms were folded across his chest while he clutched an unopened soda.

"Tonight at seven, right?"

Feeling quite awkward that my face was level with his belt buckle, I craned my neck to look up at him.

A few cookie crumbs were pasted to the right side of his mouth. It took all my willpower not to reach up and wipe them off. I had imagined myself caressing his lips for way too long and I'd make a complete fool of myself if I stared much longer.

"Yeah, about tonight." I shifted again, trying to shake loose the nerves that shot cold heat through my veins whenever Bryon was near. "I was wondering if we could study at your house."

"No. My dad's got some clients coming over and wants me out of his hair."

"I understand." Biting my bottom lip, I had to come up with a plan. What if they showed up when we were studying? "Maybe we could go to a café or something."

Bryon sat next to me and I nearly jumped out of my skin. Unfortunately, only my hair was doing the jumping. That invisible light socket attached to my head zapped a piece of frizz out of place and I tucked it behind my headband with shaky fingers.

"Those places are always too noisy. What's wrong with your house?" Bryon popped the lid on his drink and took a swallow, but not before shooting me a heated glance with his icy eyes.

He was so close to me, I could almost inhale the fizz from his soda. He smelled so sweet, kind of like a fresh batch of cookies. The warmth radiating from his body turned my brain to mush. Every nerve ending in my body was doing back flips and my tongue felt like a dead-weight in my mouth.

"Nothing, it's just..."

"Great, I'll see you tonight." Bryon squeezed my arm before getting up and walking away.

Looking at the fading imprint of Bryon's fingers on my skin, I felt as if I was melting.

I mean, yeah, expecting a hottie like Bryon to like a short, frizzy-haired girl was a long shot, but I had a right to dream. Besides, we had a lot in common. He had good taste in clothes, and I heard he lived with his dad, just like me.

"What if your friends show up while you're studying?"

AJ's question brought me back to reality. What if they did show up? If I told them to go away, Bryon would think I was insane for talking to myself. So what if I told him the truth? He'd think I was insane for having ghost friends. Either way, I was screwed.

Chapter Three

"Holy crap!" Nearly jumping off the toilet, I threw down my Cosmo at the sight of the two dead people hovering above me. "Can't a girl get a little privacy?"

Ed nudged Gertrude before pointing at me. "This one's got a mouth on her."

Gertrude planted hands on her hips, her eyes taking on a supernatural glow. "Nothin' a good bar of lye soap won't fix."

"It's not my fault you scared me." Hastily wiping, I jerked up my pants.

Snickering, Ed shook his head. "You said youz used ta dead folk."

Feeling the heat rising in my cheeks, I flipped my hair behind my shoulder, trying to forget my total embarrassment. "Not when I'm on the toilet."

"Sorry, miss." Ed's smile quickly faded. "But this couldn't wait."

"Yep." Gertrude moaned. "We got some terrible news."

"Look." I blew out a breath, mentally counting to three. How could I put it nicely that I really didn't care? I had my own problems. "Tonight's kind of bad. You see, I've got this hot guy coming over and—"

"A parking lot." Ed's deep voice bellowed, rattling the cosmetics I'd laid out on the sink. Creepy. The action reminded me of how ghosts could make things fly across the room, even though their spirits weren't solid.

An eerie tremor shot through my insides and that familiar chill raced up my spine. "What?" I choked out through a shiver.

"You know." Ed threw up his arms. "Where you pen those motor cars."

How could I be creeped out by this guy? He was too dorky. "Look," I sighed, "I know what a parking lot is."

"Did ya know that's what they're puttin' on us?" He shot his fist in the air. "Right next ta that big tradin' post."

I bit my lip to keep from laughing. "It's called a mall."

"I don't give a damn what you call it." Ed fumed. "They got no right tearin' up my tombstone."

Once again, his voice shook the room. Only this time, my eye shadow shattered on the floor.

"Now, Ed, don't go breakin' all her face paints." Gertrude scolded.

I bent over, scraping up what was left of the makeup that cost me two weeks babysitting money. My turn to get mad! "I'm really sorry, but this isn't my problem," I spat.

"Ain't your problem!" Ed's scream rattled the walls so hard the medicine cabinet on the wall flew open, spilling the contents into the sink.

"I can't stop that mall. I'm only fourteen," I raged. Was this lunatic determined to break everything in my bathroom?

"Hogwash!" Ed thrust a fist into the air.

"I was already married when I was your age." Gertrude laughed.

"Well, things have changed, thank God, so could you please leave? My study partner is coming over and I really don't want him to know I talk to dead people."

Grabbing a grocery bag from under the sink, I quickly scooped in the contents from the medicine cabinet.

Totally absorbed in getting my bathroom clean before Bryon came over, I had momentarily forgotten the annoying dead people behind me.

Then Ed loudly cleared his throat, although what he was clearing I didn't know. After all, he didn't have real lungs anymore.

"S'pose we don't leave." Ed clung to each word slowly, as if he enjoyed the flavor of each syllable.

He couldn't be serious! Turning to the ghosts, I felt my jaw twitch in annoyance at their silly grins. "Excuse me?"

"Seein' how we got booted from our graveyard, I think we'll make ourselves at home right here." Ed made a point of looking around the entire bathroom and resting his good eye on an orderly shelf of lotions. Was he threatening my moisturizers?

Stepping in front of the lotions, I barred Ed's path before he destroyed any more of my stuff. I could feel my heart racing wildly. Bryon would be here any minute and I hadn't even retouched my makeup.

"No, you have to go. Do you want my study partner to think I'm a freak?" I tried to fan them away, like they were clouds of smoke, but they just continued to stare like idiots.

At the familiar sound of a distant chime, my blood froze. "The doorbell!"

Crossing her arms across her chest, Gertrude tapped her foot. "Then promise you'll help us."

"I can't." Turning toward the mirror, I made a hasty attempt to smooth my unruly hair.

"Suit yerself." Ed shrugged.

The deep, muffled sound of a familiar voice assailed my ears.

"Oh-mi-god!" I shrieked. "I hear Bryon. Dad must have let him in."

"Krysta, your friend is here." My dad spoke through the door. "You can study in your room if you leave the door open."

"NO!" I yelled at the door. Facing the ghosts, I turned my lips in to a pout and batted my eyes. "Please leave. What if I find you an old house to haunt?"

"We want our graveyard back," Ed answered evenly.

"Who are you talking to?"

I jumped, dropping the contents from the medicine cabinet on the floor.

Bryon was on the other side of the door.

"Nobody." I tried to sound casual, but I could feel the shakiness in my voice. "Go wait in the living room. I'll be right out." I kneeled, and once again, scooped makeup into the bag.

"Your dad and your sister are watching a movie in the living room," Bryon said.

I rolled my eyes. Dad's newest girlfriend looked like she'd just graduated high school. "She's not my sister."

"Oh. You okay?"

Even through the door, I could feel Bryon's sincerity. Any other guy wouldn't have asked if I was okay, but Bryon was different. That's why I'd been thrilled when Mrs. Jackson made him my study partner. I couldn't tell him why I was still stuck in the bathroom, though; I needed an excuse.

"Yeah, I'm just putting on my ghosts," I blurted. "Your what?"

The old people laughed hysterically.

How childish. Weren't they like 200 by now? When were they going to grow up?

Don't be an idiot, Krysta. Calm down, breathe.

"My clothes. I just took a shower and I'm putting on my clothes."

Nice save.

"Okay, I'll clear off your desk and get started." Listening to the sound of Bryon's retreating footsteps, I breathed a sigh of relief, slumping my back against the door. When Ed and Gertrude floated through me and into my bedroom, my pulse jumped. Not cool. They were going to mess with him.

"Get back here!" I threw open the door, running smack into Bryon's chest.

Stunned, I looked up into the palest blue eyes I'd ever seen. A girl could get lost in the heat of his gaze. Until I remembered them.

Bryon quirked a brow. "I didn't go anywhere." "Oh." Totally embarrassed, I stepped back and felt the flames race up my chest and across my cheeks. He must have thought I was yelling at him.

Hearing Ed's chuckle, I stole a quick glance at the ceiling and spotted them hovering above Bryon's head. I bit my bottom lip.

Please don't do anything I'll regret.

Resting his chin in his hand, Bryon smothered a laugh while looking at my midsection. "You forgot to zip."

"Ho!" My feet made a hasty about-face, while I struggled with the zipper which was caught in my underwear. Grimacing, I recalled my response just a few seconds ago. What does 'ho' mean, anyway? Get it together, Krysta.

Turning around, I brushed my hand through my hair, a lame attempt at looking cool, but Bryon wasn't looking at me. His head jerked from side to side before he turned in circles, reminding me of AJ's dog, Patches, whenever he chased his tail.

Mortified, I watched as Ed and Gertrude spun circles around Bryon so fast their translucent forms had turned to glowing flashes of light.

After what felt like an eternity, a stabbing pain in my chest reminded me that I had stopped breathing. I tried to inhale, but air was only coming in gasps.

A few more rotations and Bryon stopped, looking at me with a glazed-over expression. "Do you feel that?"

"What?" I stammered.

The ghosts were, once again, hovering above my lab partner, holding their stomachs with shouts of laughter.

Clenching my fists, I shot the pair a heated glare, warning them to leave Bryon alone. Although, really, how could I have stopped them?

"I don't know." Bryon scratched his head. "It felt like a breeze, a really cold breeze."

"I think it's the air conditioner." I shrugged, chewing on my lower lip.

"Maybe you should turn it down."

"I can't. It's broken and we're waiting for the apartment manager to fix it." The perfect excuse to get Bryon out of my apartment and away from the ghosts.

"That sucks." Raising his eyebrows, Bryon scanned the room.

For the first time, I worried what Bryon thought about my home. Did he think me uncool because I lived in a run-down apartment? My dad had a crappy job as a graveyard shift security guard. I had heard rumors Bryon's dad was rich. I followed Bryon's gaze as they rested on a stack of crates holding my old laptop computer.

Smiling softly, his gaze found mine.

Was that pity I saw in his eyes? Even without Sophie here, I could figure out what he was thinking. Poor kid can't afford real furniture or keep her pants zipped.

Suddenly, I felt very small, like I was shrinking into the

carpet. If only I could. I knew getting Bryon interested in me could be challenging. Making him feel sorry for me was not the way I wanted to do it.

Bryon pulled on his jacket. "Didn't you say there was a coffee house down the street?"

Thinking he was desperate to escape my ghetto home, I nodded toward the door. "Yeah, maybe we should go study there."

"Sure." He rubbed his arms. "It's too cold here. I don't know how you sleep like this."

"If you only knew." I sighed and followed him to the door, leering at the annoying spirits from the corner of my eye.

Before turning out the lights, I caught Ed's toothless grin and Gertrude's lopsided smile. Would they tag along? Maybe going there wasn't such a hot idea. Oh, the tricks they could play with hot coffee.

Chapter Four

As we entered Mocha Madness, I scanned the area for the ghosts.

All clear—so far.

Would they really come here and ruin my entire evening with Bryon?

Sighing, I rubbed my temples in frustration, a habit I usually saw AJ doing whenever she was pissed. Maybe it would relieve my ever-growing headache. Dropping my book bag on one of the four empty tables, I headed to the counter where Sunny was cleaning coffee pots while swearing.

I don't know who thought to name her Sunny. She was a Goth who never smiled. Her arms were covered in skull tattoos, which I was pretty sure were fake because they seemed to move to new locations each time I saw her.

Looking at Bryon, I could see he already had his eyes on the pastries. He was kneeling in front of the glass case, licking his lips and looking too cute.

Mocha Madness had the best desserts ever, but I rarely ordered any sweets. I had to watch my weight if I wanted to pursue a career in modeling. Besides, their desserts were expensive.

Leaning over Bryon, my gaze followed the direction of his transfixed stare. He was looking at the triple chocolate chunk, peanut butter brownies topped with marshmallow crème. Sounded kind of like too much of a good thing, but they were awesome. They sure had Bryon under a spell. I couldn't help but feel a little jealous. What chance did a short, frizzy-haired girl stand against triple chocolate heaven?

Bryon put his hand on the glass. "Come to Papa," he whispered.

"Do you want one of those brownies?" I asked, unable to refrain from smiling.

Jerking his head up, he flashed me an impish grin. "Heck, yeah!"

I couldn't refrain from laughing out loud. "Anything to drink?"

"Yes." He nodded before turning his gaze back to the chocolate bliss. "A tall double-mocha latte."

"I'll have the usual." Rising, I called to Sunny's back. "Got that, Sunny?"

"Sure," she mumbled without turning around.

I knew she'd heard me, but I still wanted to get a response from her. She liked to play this fantasy game that she was the only person in the room.

Usually, I didn't mind.

Mocha Madness was a small espresso bar. Tucked away in the back of the run-down shopping center down the street from my apartment, it didn't get much business. I liked it that way. I could escape here after school whenever my dad brought home a new 'friend'. Dad and his barely legal girl toy were usually nice to me at first, but I caught on real fast that Dad wanted me out of the picture.

I'd ask for ten bucks to go eat and then I'd disappear to Mocha Madness, drink a diet soda and read my magazines. The system worked to my advantage because I usually pocketed about nine dollars each time. I already had this totally adorable handbag on layaway. With just ten more visits to Mocha Madness, the purse was mine.

Sitting at our little table in the corner, I opened my chemistry book and turned to page seven. We had a test this Friday and chemistry really wasn't my thing. Luckily, it was just the Periodic Table of the Elements. Seemed easy enough, but how would I be able to keep all those letters in my head without getting totally mixed up? So far, the only one I could remember was oxygen.

When Bryon sat next to me, I nearly jumped from my seat.

He sat next to me every day in class, so why was he having this effect on me now? Something about his nearness in this deserted café had my nerves on edge.

Not to mention the ever gnawing threat of Gertrude and Ed floating in and scaring him away for good.

I tried to push it from my mind, but the possibility of my impending embarrassment was always looming.

Inhaling a deep breath, I slowly exhaled, a technique I'd learned in my Yoga-to-Go videos. "I thought we'd just study the elements tonight and worry about the project later."

"Sounds good." He smiled, barely casting me a glance before opening his book.

Barely a look, huh? I bet if I was a brownie, he'd notice me.

Ah, well, what was I expecting? I never thought a guy like Bryon would like a girl like me. So why was I feeling totally disappointed?

My head jerked at the rattle of dishes against the table. Sunny had deposited my diet soda and his coffee and brownie with a sneer before turning her back to us and walking behind the counter.

"What's her problem?" Bryon rolled his eyes in Sunny's direction.

I shrugged. "She doesn't like people much." Bryon's face dropped as he eyed my diet soda. "That's all you're getting?" Then his eyes softened. "I'll pay if you want something else."

I heard the pity in his voice as he flashed me a half-hearted smile.

I didn't need Sophie's mind reading powers to know what he was thinking. Krysta, the poor kid with a crappy apartment, can't even afford a brownie.

"I don't need you to pay for me," I spat with maybe a little too much edge in my voice. "I have money."

"Okay." He held out both hands. "Sorry." I sighed. "It's just that I'm on a diet."

"Why?" His eyes bulged, then trailed up my torso and across my arms. "You don't need to be."

Was he checking me out? For some reason, I got the feeling he didn't like what he saw. Aw, crap!

I blew out a frustrated breath. "That's what everyone says,

but the minute I let my guard down, I know I'll gain like fifty pounds."

"So you're always going to drink diet and skip chocolate?" His gaze scanned me again with raised brows. "Don't you worry you might be a little too skinny?"

Too skinny? Was he dogging my weight?

A wave of heat rippled through my chest and up my neck before the burn spread to my cheeks. "Are we here to study or to talk about what I eat?" I spat.

I didn't know if I was more embarrassed or pissed off by his comment, but it cut—hard.

"Maybe both." He shrugged.

Rolling my eyes, I flipped open my science binder. "Well, let's not." I said tersely. "We have a test this Friday and our project is due in three weeks." Tapping my pencil on my binder, I glared at him while awaiting his response.

So far, my efforts to make Bryon like me weren't going very well.

His gaze dropped to the table and this time his cheeks turned red.

Good, I thought, before a surge of guilt washed through me. Maybe I over-reacted to his 'skinny' comment.

"You two have to leave soon."

My gaze shot up to see Sunny hovering above us. Like a rain cloud on an already crappy day, her aura seemed to cast a gloom on our table.

Why on earth did her parents name her Sunny?

"We just got here," I snapped. Geez, I was majorly on edge. Maybe PMS time was around the corner.

"Yeah." She rolled her eyes in a much more dramatic fashion than I could ever hope to imitate. "My boyfriend wants me to close early." Rolling her sleeves up to her elbows, she turned her gaze to the window entrance while chewing on the ends of her fingernails.

That's when I noticed the bruise.

Not just any bruise, but a welt that swelled across the entire length of her forearm like a red and purple plague.

"That's a huge bruise." Jaw dropping, I couldn't help but gawk. "What happened?"

"None of your business," she hissed, shooting me daggers of venom from her narrowed eye slits.

Beside me, I heard Bryon clearing his throat loudly through a chuckle.

He must have thought he was front row of a boxing match between two rabid cats.

"Sorry for asking," I grumbled, knowing my eye roll wasn't nearly as dramatic as hers.

"Sunny, what gives?"

The bark came from the café entrance. I looked up to see some tall, wiry guy with a shaved head and too many tattoos to count. He was glaring at Sunny with his top lip turned up in a snarl.

The guy was probably in his early to mid- twenties. With his lean, muscular arms and pale green eyes, he could have been hot if he cleaned himself up, but something about him gave me the creeps. He had an angry aura about him, and I just couldn't wait to leave.

Sunny's wide gaze darted from him to me. "You two have to go—now."

Was that panic I read in her eyes?

I looked at Bryon, but he seemed to be locked in a staring contest with the tattooed guy. Did he have some kind of death wish?

"Bryon, let's go," I whispered.

When Bryon turned his gaze on me, I thought I was looking at someone else. Not the totally sweet baby-faced boy who sat next to me in science class. Nostrils flaring, eyes were on fire. He looked like a wild animal ready to attack.

This guy was majorly pissed.

As he stood, I could see his hands were clenched into two tight fists. Grabbing his binder, he looked at Sunny. "Are you gonna be okay if we leave you here?"

"What are you, my babysitter?" she spat through a shaky voice.

Grabbing my things, I stood and pulled on Bryon's sleeve. "Let's go."

My eyes darted to the guy still standing in the doorway. His angry gaze was bearing down on us and I thought I saw steam shooting from his ears. All I needed was a little red flag and I was sure he would charge us.

Clutching Bryon's shirtsleeve like it was my lifeline, I pulled him out the door and past the raging bull. Bryon and the guy exchanged glares and growls, coming within inches of each other's faces, but to my surprise, no one threw a punch.

"Now you know how she got that bruise," he mumbled as we made it to the pavement—still alive.

On the walk back to my apartment, we both decided this study session was a total waste. As we turned the corner, Bryon's dad was waiting in his very expensive, luxury car. Without saying a word, he flashed me a half-hearted smile before walking to his dad's car.

I had the feeling he'd be asking Mrs. Jackson for a new partner come tomorrow.

My limbs still shook and I marveled at how I made it all the way home without wetting my pants. Through all my nocturnal experiences with dead people missing their limbs or eyeballs, entrails hanging out of their stomachs, or knives protruding from their chests, I'd never been more scared in my life than that moment in the café.

My life seemed much less scary when I thought of what Sunny had to endure with her boyfriend. I only wondered how she could live like that.

"Have you seen my dad?" Sighing, I dropped my book bag on the floor. Gertrude and Ed were still there, hovering above me with their goofy expressions.

Well, at least they didn't follow Bryon and me to the café. Not that tonight could have gotten any worse.

"Yeah, he went out with the little lady," Ed replied.

Rolling my eyes, I kneeled on the floor. "She's no lady if she's with my dad."

I exhaled before folding my legs beneath me in a meditative pose. After tonight, I really needed to de- stress.

Breathe in, breathe out.

First, he felt sorry for me because I'm poor.

"What in tarnation is she doing?"

Ignoring Gertrude's comment, I continued my breathing exercises.

Sucking in a deep breath of air, I slowly released, feeling the tension roll through my body and exit through my fingertips.

Then, he said I was too skinny.

"Seems like she's goin' ta sleep Indian style." Grrrr. Dead people can be so annoying. Another deep breath and a slow release.

It was pretty cool how he tried to defend Sunny, even though she's a b—

"Wake up, Emmy Jane!"

"All right, that's it!" I glared at the dead people. "I'm trying to meditate! Do you mind?"

Ed rubbed his translucent, scraggly beard. "Med-a-what?"

"Never mind!" I yelled.

Obviously, they weren't going to give me any peace. Maybe if I talked to one of my friends, I'd calm down. Dad promised he'd paid the cell phone bill today. Hopefully, he'd made good on his promise. Opening my book bag, I reached to pull my cell out of the holder.

Nothing.

Looking inside, I shuffled through papers and pencils, but it wasn't there.

Oh, crap.

Had I left it at Mocha Madness? Swearing, I rubbed my aching temples.

"What's the matter, Emmy?" Ed's hollow voice echoed from above.

"For the last time, I'm not Emmy!" I yelled.

They both jumped, like a shock wave had spiraled through the air, sending their spirits backward. I could tell by their widened eyes and turned down mouths that I had somehow hurt their feelings.

Great.

"Look, I'm sorry, it's just that I think I left my cell at the espresso bar and I'm afraid to go back there."

Clasping both hands together, Gertrude's mouth turned up in a soft smile. "What's there to be afraid of, dear?"

"Cell? Espresso bar?" Ed itched his scalp, his face scrunched in confusion.

"A cell is how we communicate. I punch some numbers and my friend miles away can hear me. An espresso bar is a place where they serve coffee. It's also called a coffee shop."

They both nodded, but I could tell by their drawn brows that they were still confused. Maybe they did need to go back to their graves.

"Look," I groaned. "There's this scary guy there and I don't want to go back." Leaning back against our small living room wall, I felt my limbs ice over at the thought of facing tattoo guy again.

"What if we go with you?" Gertrude asked.

Startled, my gaze scanned their smiling faces. "What are you going to do if he messes with me?"

"We'll mess right back." Ed flashed a huge, lopsided grin. "Don't worry; we can cause quite a poltergeist if we need to."

Ghost bodyguards? Who would've thought?

The lights were still on and through the glass window, I could see Sunny at the rear of the shop, her back to the counter. I didn't see tattoo guy. He was probably somewhere in the back. Exhaling a deep breath, I opened the door and walked inside. From the corner of my eye, I saw Ed and Gertrude slip in through the windows.

I quickly scanned all the empty tables and the little hot pink phone was not there.

My teeth began to chatter. I didn't know if the sudden chill that swept up my spine was due to fear or maybe Sunny had the thermostat way too low. I tried to blame it on her, but despite my personal ghostly bodyguards, I was ready to wet my pants in fear.

"Hey," I called to Sunny's back through the crack in my voice. "I just came to get my phone and then I'll be out of your way. Have you seen it?"

When she turned to me, I gasped at the huge black and blue splotches on her face and across her neck. Her eyes looked bloodshot and grotesque, like they were trying to pop out of her face.

"Oh-mi-god, Sunny," I breathed. "Are you okay?" She looked at me with a glazed over expression. "It was my boyfriend," she spoke with no emotion in her voice. "He did it."

"Is he here?" I asked, feeling my limbs turn to jelly.

Shoulders slumping, she shook her head.

Relief washed through me. "Maybe you should quit going out with him."

Turning her gaze upward, she looked dreamily at the ceiling, right through the bodies of Gertrude and Ed. "I never thought he'd go this far."

Spying my phone on the counter next to the register, I grabbed it and stuffed it in my pocket. Something about this place gave me an even creepier feeling than before. I just wanted to get out. Even though I didn't like Sunny, I couldn't just leave her there. What if he came back?

"Do you want me to call for help or something?" I asked while nervously fidgeting with the phone in my pocket.

"No, it's too late now." Shaking her head, she walked into the back room.

Watching the door slam behind her, I was left with the most nauseating feeling in my gut. Swallowing a large lump in my throat, I looked at the ghosts behind me.

Their expressions were heavy—grim.

Something about this night just didn't feel right. There was a stagnant weight in the air, and though I thought I recognized the familiar feeling, my mind would not allow me to acknowledge it. Turning sharply on my heel, I raced out the door and back home to my apartment.

Facebook rant/Four a.m.

No use going back to sleep now. Dad just came home from work, or maybe a bar.

I don't know and I don't care.

I woke up when I heard a crash in the kitchen. Dad had fallen, shattering the bottle he was holding. Blood and beer everywhere.

He sat on the floor, slumped against the refrigerator door,

swearing while he picked shards of glass from his palm. His hair was a mess, sticking up in all directions like he'd just lost a fight with a rabid cat. He reeked of cheap perfume and rotten alcohol.

Gawd, I just wanted to puke.

I told him we needed to go to the emergency room to remove the glass from his hand, but he swore at me and sent me to my room.

In a way, I'm glad he hurt himself. He had no business getting so drunk. What kind of a father is he, anyway?

This is a time in my life when I need him most. I need someone to talk to, not just about school and normal teenage problems, but my 'other' issues.

After my encounter with Sunny tonight, I should have been able to run to my dad for comfort.

AJ's mom understands her gift because she has psychic abilities, too. At least AJ has an adult she can talk to.

My dad?

He can't take care of himself. How can I expect him to help me?

Chapter Five

Dragging my feet to the bus stop, I was vaguely aware of my actions as I slumped in the puke-green vinyl seat. I barely slept last night. Something to do with the gnawing fear in my gut.

And guilt.

I hadn't done enough for Sunny. I should have followed her to the back room, but I was afraid.

I'd tried calling them from my home phone because my cell phone still hadn't been turned on. No surprise that my dad lied when he said he'd pay the bill.

It took me awhile to remember AJ had a softball game and Sophie was the yearbook photographer assigned to cover it. AJ's coach didn't allow phones in the dugout, and they were playing against Central, our toughest rivals. The game probably lasted late into the night.

So I was alone with no one to listen as I confessed my fears. Well, except for the old people, but they cut out not long after I got back to the apartment. And, of course, my dad was out getting drunk. Wherever he was, he wasn't there when I needed him. I couldn't tell him about my encounter with Sunny.

She seemed odd. Too odd. I didn't like the look of those bruises, especially the ones across her neck. I didn't like the glazed-over expression in her bugged- out eyes.

I thought about walking past the café on my way to the bus stop, but I was too chicken.

And I hated myself for it.

Suddenly, all of my problems seemed insignificant

compared to Sunny's. I just hoped it wasn't as serious as I feared.

The bus came to a halt. This was AJ and Krysta's stop. Maybe they'd be able to comfort me.

"Oh-mi-god, Krysta, we're so glad you're all right!" Sophie squealed as she rushed down the aisle. AJ was right behind her.

Looking into my friends' grim faces, I knew they had bad news.

Swallowing back the rising bile, I cleared my throat. "What's wrong?" I choked.

"We know you go to Mocha Madness, like every night," Sophie blurted while sliding into the seat next to me, her eyes ready to pop out of her head. "We thought maybe you were her."

"Her, who?" But I already knew the answer. I'd felt it in my gut last night.

AJ's expression was as hard as granite as she faced me from the front seat. "A girl was murdered there last night."

The finality of AJ's words sliced through my stomach like a cold, hard blade.

She pointed to Paige who was in the seat across from me, gaze engrossed on the screen of her cell phone. "Paige's sister just texted her the news. Said the girl was strangled."

"Krysta, are you okay?" Sophie asked, but her voice sounded distant, like she was in a dream.

Maybe that's what this was, just a bad dream. I closed my eyes, wishing everything would just return to normal. But in my mind I saw her, face and neck blotched with bruises, staring blankly at the wall behind me. Or was she staring at Ed and Gertrude? She could probably see them since she was dead, too.

"Poor Sunny," I breathed while opening my eyes. "Do you think it was her?" Sophie asked, maybe a little too eagerly.

"Probably," AJ nodded. "She's so rude to the customers; maybe she pissed someone off real bad."

Sophie gasped. "I wonder who did it."

"Her boyfriend," I said through the hollow ache in my chest. Yeah, she was rude, but she didn't deserve to die.

Tilting her head, Sophie looked at me with a quizzical expression. "How do you know?"

Sunny's haunting words came rushing back to me. It was

my boyfriend. He did it.

Leveling each of them a hardened stare, I saw recognition flash in their eyes.

Choking back the emotion in my throat, I spoke through a whisper. "She told me last night."

Bryon was waiting for me when the bus pulled into the school parking lot. I could see through the window that he had the same angry look I'd seen last night.

He knew she was dead.

Chewing on my lower lip, I cast AJ and Sophie a look.

They both nodded.

I rose to exit the bus, feeling like I was marching to my own funeral.

My legs felt like lead weights, dragging me down each step as I exited the bus. I couldn't tear my gaze from him even if I tried. The guy was majorly pissed, clutching his binder in one fist so tight, I could see the white outline of his knuckles. Jaw locked, shoulders squared, I could clearly read the anger in his narrowed eyes.

"Hey." He jerked his head, his facial features as hard as steel. "Did you hear?"

"Yeah." I nodded, unable to say any more. Keeping my face forward, trying really hard to keep it together before I turned into a waterfall of sobs and ruined all my mascara, I walked toward the school building.

I should have done something last night. I shouldn't have left her there. I knew she was dead.

I knew.

I was vaguely aware of Bryon following beside me.

All the other students had walked into the main entrance of the building. Without speaking aloud our mutual decision, we both walked to the secluded entrance to the side. Strange how no one was lurking in the darkened hall. Gossip in my small community traveled like a super-virus, so no doubt everyone was in the main hall or the cafeteria talking about the high school student who was murdered at the coffee house.

A light breeze blew across my face. My hair bobbled like a

dandelion in a windstorm. I picked up my pace and Bryon followed. I caught the scent of peanut butter in the air.

And chocolate?

Why did Bryon always smell like a sweet shoppe?

I looked over at Bryon. His mouth was drawn in a tight line, his eyes expressionless. I could feel vibes of tension radiating off his body.

How strange that he didn't even know Sunny, except for the brief few moments she insulted us. Yet, this guy was taking her death pretty hard. Seeing this sensitive side of Bryon made me like him even more.

Walking ahead, he stopped and faced me, his body barricading the doorway. "Do you think it was her boyfriend?"

Forcing myself to look at him, I gasped at the pained expression in his eyes. "It was him."

"How do you know?" His eyes narrowed, darkened.

Turning away from him, I tried to restrain my tears, but a few slipped down my cheek anyway. Crap. "I just know." I shrugged, unable to say more before I cried even harder.

"We should tell someone." Emotion was audible in his cracked voice. "We might've been the last people to see her alive."

Turning to him, I threw up my hands. "Who do we tell?" Inwardly groaning, I struggled with an even heavier problem.

Who do I tell?

No one would believe me if I told them I'd spoken to dead Sunny and knew the killer was her boyfriend.

"I don't know." Bryon came up beside me and placed a hand on my shoulder. "Let's go to the office. Maybe they'll know what to do."

Looking into his softened eyes, I just wanted to melt. He must have sensed my turmoil. God, what would he say if I told him about dead Sunny? About my ability to speak to ghosts?

"Are you sure that's a good idea?" I asked before nervously chewing on my lower lip. I was scared.

I felt it in my stomach, which was about to drop to my knees, and in my brain, which was ready to explode from the weight of it all.

What if they asked me too many questions? What if I

slipped and told them about my incident with Sunny's spirit?

"We're witnesses, Krysta." Dipping his head, his wintery blue gaze was level with mine. "We can't keep this to ourselves."

Deep in my heart, I knew he was right, but that gnawing fear in my brain told me my life was about to go from complicated to really complicated.

Chapter Six

After we'd spoken to Principal Sparks in private, he called our parents and the cops and we gave the police a statement in Sparks' office. Thankfully, Bryon did most of the talking. He remembered loads of stuff about Sunny's boyfriend, even details about each tattoo. All I really had to do was nod and agree to everything Bryon said.

I should have felt more at ease with Bryon there answering questions for me, but the way one of the officers kept looking at me made me feel uncomfortable.

Not to mention the fact that I had to take shallow breaths to keep from gagging on stale beer fumes radiating off my dad. Even though he was several feet behind us, tilting back in his chair, his stench had somehow drifted across the room.

Hadn't he ever heard of a shower?

I wondered briefly if Bryon could smell my dad, but I already knew the answer to that question.

My life totally sucked.

I shifted focus again to the officer whose gaze was practically glued to my face.

Officer Garza was an older Hispanic guy with a receding hairline and dark eyes. He smiled at me a lot and handed me tissues when I broke down crying, but something in the way he looked at me made me feel uneasy. Kind of like he was looking through me. Like he was waiting for me to say more. But he couldn't have known about my visit with dead Sunny. Maybe I was being paranoid.

Just as we had finished with our statements, Sparks came

into the office and nodded to both of us. "You two have had a trying morning. I think your parents should take you home."

Turning, I noticed my dad was now positioned forward in the chair, knuckles white as he gripped each knee. His graying black hair was a mess, as usual, and the buttons on his stained white shirt weren't even lined-up correctly. Brow furrowed, he stared blankly at his feet. Was he seriously concentrating on something, or was he ready to pass out?

If he wanted to embarrass me, he sure succeeded. I cringed, stealing a sideways glance at Bryon, fearing what he thought about my dad. Krysta's drunk father who just rolled out of bed.

Suddenly, Dad's gaze met mine and his dark eyes bore into me. I couldn't tell if he was concerned or just angry.

My gaze dropped to the floor; my chest felt even tighter than before. Maybe I'd interrupted time with one of his 'girl' friends.

I knew having a teenage daughter wasn't easy for a guy like my dad. He had a hard enough time trying to pay the bills and now his child was a witness in a murder case.

"So you're Andy's little girl?"

Startled, I turned to Officer Garza who stared down at me with a knowing expression.

"Yeah," I mumbled, before looking away from his penetrating stare.

I wondered how he knew my dad. Maybe Officer Garza had been a security guard once, too. I didn't want to start a conversation with him; the way he stared at me made me way too uncomfortable.

I just wanted to get out of the office. Away from the cops. Away from my dad. Bryon, the other cop and a man who looked like an older version of Bryon were talking in front of me, blocking the doorway, and I saw no way of getting through.

I hated being short.

"You look a lot like your mom." The tone of Garza's voice behind my back softened and ended on a raspy note.

"No, I don't," I blurted, looking back at him with narrowed eyes. Even if I wanted to, I knew I looked nothing like the woman who abandoned our family. She was tall and had red hair and pale skin. I looked nothing like my mom.

"Time to go home, Krysta." Dad's strained voice came from behind Garza.

The other men parted as Dad plowed through. "Hey, Richards." Garza nodded. "Feeling okay?"

"Yeah." He flashed Officer Garza a thin smile. "We need to get home." Dad pulled me to him.

Looking into Dad's strained features, I knew he was far from happy. As he led me between the men and out the door, I thought my hand would crush under the strength of his grip.

"Nice seeing you, my friend," Officer Garza called as we retreated.

Remembering I'd left Bryon without saying goodbye, I tried to turn and wave, but Dad jerked me forward.

Dad didn't release my hand until we hit the pavement. "Damn, Krysta, I don't like you being a witness in a murder case." Swearing again, he jerked open the passenger door of our little rust bucket and then erratically waved for me to get inside. "I wish you would've kept quiet."

I knew having me in his life was a major inconvenience, but it wasn't my fault I was born. Like it or not, I was his problem and he'd just have to deal with it. Besides, Sunny's murderer needed to pay, and I wasn't going to stand aside and do nothing. Slamming the door shut, I turned to him. "But her boyfriend should go to prison," I growled.

Dad shook his head, laughing through clenched teeth. "You don't even know he did it."

"Yeah." Exhaling a groan, I rolled my eyes. "I do."

Dad's eyes widened. "Did you see the murder?" "No," I threw up my hands. "But—"

"I'm taking you to AJ's house tonight." Jarring open the door again, he pointed at the torn bucket seat with a determined expression. "I don't want you at the apartment alone."

My shoulders fell at his angry dismissal. Sliding into my seat, I wiped a stray tear with the back of my hand. He didn't even care what I had to say.

The tension between us was thick enough to touch as Dad sat next to me and slammed the door. I knew he'd rather just pawn me off on AJ's parents than deal with me himself.

"Why can't I stay home?" I pleaded.

Dad swore again, this time using words I hadn't heard since he'd tried to give up drinking a few months ago.

"Krysta." He turned to me with a look of irritation clearly written across his creased brow. "Don't you understand? If you were the last person to see this girl alive, her murderer might come after you now."

Tattoo guy come after me? I hadn't thought of that. I didn't even think this guy knew my name or where I lived. Besides, he didn't know I was a witness in this case. Dad was just freaking out over nothing.

Wasn't he?

Chapter Seven

"What are you doing, Emmy?"

Looking up through tear-soaked eyes, I saw Ed and Gertrude hovering above me. "Packing my things," I said on a sigh.

Arms folded across their chests, concerned expressions marred their brows. I guess they weren't going to stop calling me Emmy. Oh, well, it didn't matter anymore. Weird thing was...they were kind of starting to feel like family.

"Where are you going?" Gertrude asked, her voice laced with worry.

"Dad wants me to stay at my friend's house." I shrugged, trying to pretend it didn't matter that he was sending me away. But it did matter. My life had been turned upside-down ever since Sunny's murder, and now my dad wanted me out of his hair. I had always felt plagued by my ability to see ghosts, but never like this. I was in way over my head and had no one to help me.

"For how long?" They asked simultaneously. Weird how they were always doing that. I guess if you spend over a hundred years with the same person, you learn to think alike.

Throwing the last pair of socks into my torn duffel bag, I hung my head. "I don't know."

"Mind if we tag along?"

Looking back up at them, I laughed. "Do I have a choice?"

"Nope." They both nodded.

I threw up my hands, knowing they'd follow just to bug me about their tombstones. "Look, I'm sorry about your graves, but I really don't know how to stop the mall."

"We understand." Placing both hands on her hips, Gertrude nodded. "We've got bigger problems right now, anyway."

"Like what?"

Ed's lip turned in a snarl. "Seein' that fella hang for killin' that girl."

"Really?" A jolt of excitement shot through me. They wanted to help. I didn't know how two dead ancients could help me, but just knowing they were on my side made me feel better. "You want to help Sunny?"

"Sure." Folding her arms across her chest, Gertrude nodded. "We all gotta go sometime, but that ain't no way ta die."

They were right. Then a thought struck me. How was Sunny handling all this? Last night, she seemed in a state of shock. I wondered if she was coming to terms with her death.

"Have you been over there? I mean, have you talked to her to see if she's all right?"

Ed's glowing eyes nearly jumped out of his sockets. "Oh, no. We ain't goin' anywhere near that coffee house."

"Why not? She might need someone to talk to."

"Honey." Brow's raised, Gertrude shook her head. "We spirits ain't all the same."

"You're not?" Scratching my head, I wondered why. I mean, weren't they all in the same ghostly dimension?

Ed held out his palms. "Gertie and me, we died natural-like. We was expectin' ta die."

"That girl, though." Scowling, Gertrude shook her head. "She didn't die like us."

"Why should that matter?" I was majorly confused. It shouldn't have mattered how they died. Ed and Gertrude could still go comfort her.

Looking at each other, they both nodded before turning back to me and answering simultaneously. "Well, I guess you'd have ta be dead ta understand."

Then Ed did something I'd never seen a ghost do. He started pacing, hands clasped behind his back. I felt like a little kid about to get a big fatherly lecture. "Ya see, Emmy, she wasn't ready ta go, so she's not takin' death real well."

Gertrude wagged a finger. "She's in a real dark place and we ain't goin' in there."

"A dark place?" What was this dark place like? Was it cold, lonely, scary? My heart clenched, thinking of Sunny's bleak existence in the afterworld. "How do I get her out?"

The ghosts shared a nervous glance.

Ed shrugged. "The thing is...we don't really know."

Chewing on her lower lip, Gertrude turned to me with grim determination in her iridescent eyes. "Maybe if we punished that boy who kilt' her, that would be a start."

"Hey, how you doing?" Lying supine on her bed, AJ tossed a softball into the air. The ball barely scraped the ceiling with each throw before falling straight in her outstretched palm.

AJ had a gift for making the ball go wherever she wanted. Sometimes I thought she inherited a little of her grandma's gift for teleporting objects. Unlike Sophie and me, all of the women in AJ's family had some kind of gift. Actually, I never knew any women in my family. It's been just Dad and me. My worthless excuse for a mom left us last summer after the money started running low. Her leaving wasn't much of a loss, anyway. She was never really a loving mother. I could count on one hand the number of times she'd hugged me.

But all of that seemed so long ago, so unimportant now that I had much bigger problems.

"Not so good." Slumping into AJ's bean bag chair on the floor, I rubbed my throbbing skull. The pain spread through my shoulders and neck to the back of my head. Every nerve in my body felt like a coiled spring.

I rested my head against the wall. Looking toward the ceiling, I thought AJ had installed some new kind of lighting. I blinked once, before realizing I was looking at two pair of dangling legs. Then I remembered Ed and Gertrude said they were going to tag along. They bent over and waved at me, two huge goofy grins plastered on their faces.

You know, I was really starting to like them.

AJ stopped throwing the ball and sat up.

I gasped, thinking she was seeing ghosts, too.

"Want to talk?" Looking straight through their legs, AJ leveled me a stare that showed concern in her crystal blue eyes.

She wasn't seeing them; she was just concerned for my problems.

"Where do I begin?" I threw up my hands, trying my best to keep my focus on her and not the two dead wall fixtures.

"I tried texting you." The pitch in her voice rose and she sounded like her mother right before an explosive 'nag session'.

"Well, not that it matters since my dad still hasn't paid the phone bill, but he took away my phone." I shrugged. "He doesn't want me talking to the cops if they call."

Her brows dipped into a frown. "Why?"

I exhaled a heavy sigh. "He's mad at me for telling the cops about Sunny's boyfriend."

Although he pretended he was worried about me, I knew the real reason he was angry. It was much harder to ignore me when I was a witness in a murder case. This was cutting into his girlfriend and beer time.

"But you had to come out!" AJ barked, her face draped in her infamous heavy scowl. The kind of face she used whenever a ref made a bad call or an obnoxious cheerleader was bugging her.

"Yeah, I know," I groaned. "It's not like I told them about dead Sunny telling me he did it."

Jaw dropping, she looked ready to piss her pants. "Will you tell them about dead Sunny?" she breathed.

"Are you crazy?" A nervous laugh escaped my throat.

AJ gripped the side of her bed so tight her knuckles turned white. Leaning forward, she spoke in a heavy whisper. "What if they can't prove he did it?"

"I don't know what to do, AJ." I shot a glance at Ed and Gertrude. "Maybe the old people and I will come up with something."

AJ tilted her head in confusion. "The old people?"

"Yeah, they'll be staying with me." I pointed to their hovering spot on the ceiling. "I hope you don't mind." How strange that they like to float. Why can't they hover four feet lower?

AJ's deep golden tan started taking on the ash- white hue of Ed and Gertrude. "Uhhh," she said through a frozen smile.

"Ed, Gertrude, this is AJ." Holding out my hand, I motioned from the ghosts to my friend.

The ghosts waived to AJ with their silly grins, acting as if she could see them.

"They say 'hi'." I waved to AJ for them.

AJ swallowed, eyes bulging, her skin turning even whiter. "You brought ghosts to my house?"

"They've got nowhere else to go." I shrugged. "The mall developers tore up their cemetery."

"Okay, I'm a little freaked out right now." Throwing up both palms, her arms visibly shook.

Why was she acting so weird? She knew I could channel spirits way before this. She should have known this was going to happen one day.

"What's the big deal, AJ?" I groaned. "You can't even see them."

Folding her arms across her chest, she spoke through a squeal. "How am I supposed to sleep knowing there's ghosts in my bedroom?"

I rolled my eyes. "I do it all the time."

I've had to put up with ghosts in my bedroom almost every night of my teenage life, so why couldn't she just deal with it for a few days?

"Yeah, well, you're used to it." With her arms still folded across her chest, AJ raised her shoulders, leveling me with a glare.

"Fine," I spat before turning my gaze upward. "Ed, Gertrude, you have to go." I waved them away. "Sorry."

They didn't budge. Instead, they folded their arms across their chests and mimicked AJ's panic- stricken expression.

For the first time in a while, I laughed out loud. These dead people were hilarious.

AJ's brows rose so high, they could have scraped the ceiling. "They didn't really leave, did they?"

I looked into her direct gaze. Sometimes the living could be such a pain in the butt.

"Look." I shook my head. "It doesn't really matter. I'm

sneaking out tonight and they'll go with me."

"What?" Arms flailing, AJ jumped off her bed. "Are you crazy? My mother will kill us!"

Sighing, I rubbed the back of my head, trying not to let her get me too worked up. Unlocking my jaw, I reminded myself not to grind my teeth. "She's not even going to know, AJ," I said in the calmest voice I could manage.

"Duh, yes, she will." AJ's head roll followed the direction of her eyes. "Have you forgotten that woman can see through walls?"

Crap.

AJ's mom had the power to see people anywhere, anytime. Usually, she used her power on her daughter. Last summer, I turned to alcohol in order to deal with my mom's abandonment. I was having a bad life trip and I took AJ with me. We were busted when we went to the gas station and asked an undercover cop to buy us beer. AJ's mom showed up moments after our arrest. It didn't dawn on me at the time how she found out so fast, but over Christmas break, she revealed her power to AJ. She could watch AJ's softball game without ever leaving the house. Or spy in her bedroom without us knowing. Kind of like Superman, but more nosy.

I had to take the chance though; Sunny had no one to talk to.

"Look, AJ, I'll wait until she's asleep, but I need to go talk to Sunny."

"Can't you send the old people to talk to her?" AJ waved to the ceiling, about two feet from where Ed and Gertrude were hovering.

"No, they can't talk to her." I held up my palm to silence her next question. "Don't ask—long story."

Hand on hip, AJ started the attitude head bob. "Why do you need to talk to her?"

"She's in a dark place and I need to see if I can help."

"Okay, this is getting creepier by the second." AJ paced her plush white carpet while chewing on her fingernails.

I squared my shoulders, hands fisting at my sides. "This is something I have to do."

"You know what?" Stopping mid-stride, she turned to me,

pointing a finger at my chest. "Do whatever you want, but don't blame me if my mom catches you. She might already know your plan."

Chapter Eight

"Sunny, where are you?"

Oh, God, what was I doing here in the darkest, spookiest corner of Pyramid Lake? The old people had led me to this spot through a narrow trail in the woods after I biked over an hour from AJ's house. Bending down, I rubbed a cramp in my leg. I wasn't used to this kind of exercise. With exaggerated movements, I stood up, shooing away bugs that swarmed around my head.

Gross. This place totally sucked.

Why a lake, anyway? I'd thought Sunny would still be hanging out at the café, but I guess she thought a lake was a better place to haunt. It sure was creepy enough. Even Ed and Gertrude looked a little weirded out as their apparitions appeared to be shaking above me.

Thankfully, I managed to break through AJ's hard-coated shell of stubbornness and convince her to sneak me a flashlight out of her dad's garage.

"Sunny, please come out. It's me, Krysta." Shining my little beam into the bleak wall of overgrown trees, I could barely see a few feet into the forest.

A sudden breeze at my back sent shivers racing up my spine.

"I'm here." The voice was hollow and strangely dark.

Gasping, I turned toward the rocky beach behind me.

It was then that I saw her, hovering above the water; an eerie, pale aura reflected off her body and illuminated the lake.

The bruises on her neck were even more noticeable

beneath the pale lantern of her body. Her gaze, though fixed on me, was lifeless and lost.

"Sunny?" I rasped, barely breathing the words through frozen features. Had this been my first ghost, I would have crapped in my pants. Even though I'd seen plenty of dead people in my life, this chick looked pretty scary.

"What do you want?" she asked in a cold, even voice.

Gone was the venomous sarcasm of the Sunny I knew. This shadow was just an empty Sunny, a dark Sunny.

"I want to help you," I stammered, as my veins turned icy cold under the weight of her lifeless eyes.

"You can't help me," she said evenly.

"Sunny, you're in a dark place. We need to get you out."

Her gaze trailed off behind me. "Someone is coming."

"What?" Jerking my head around, I thought I heard a voice in the distance. My flesh crawled with fear.

"You should not come here." Turning her gaze down, she focused on her hands as she folded them in front of her. "This is where he used to take me."

The icy cold terror that swept up my spine was nothing like the fear I had felt before. My limbs were frozen, my brain numb from fear.

Who was coming? Was it him?

Ed and Gertrude floated down beside me and a sudden warmth seeped into my bones. For a moment, my flesh stopped crawling.

Weird.

How were they able to do that?

"We needs ta leave," Ed said gruffly.

"Yeah," I nodded, unable to say any more.

Turning back toward the water, my shoulders fell.

Sunny was gone.

Maybe coming out here wasn't such a hot idea. With brisk movements, I took off and stumbled over a tree root as I desperately searched for the trail. "Do either of you see the way out?"

"I don't think we should go that way. What if we run into him?" Gertrude's bulging eyes made her look like she was afraid she'd die all over again.

Shining my flashlight, I scanned a long length of rocky sand before it disappeared behind a canopy of trees. "If we follow the shoreline, maybe we can find another trail and walk around to my bike."

"We better get a move on." Ed made a shooing motion with his arms. "I think I hear him."

Just as I'd taken my first step, the glare from another flashlight appeared from the darkened forest.

"Let's run," I called as the air rushed from my lungs.

I wasn't a runner. I didn't care for high impact exercise, but I couldn't exactly yoga my way out of there. As fast as I could, with my feet sticking like suction cups to the ground, I darted through the sand. I had to make it around the trees before he found me.

"Krysta!" A familiar female voice called behind me. "Come back here right now, young lady!"

Oh, crap.

With a slow turn of my body, I faced AJ's mom. One hand on a flashlight and the other cocked on her hip, she glared at me through slitted eyes.

I was so busted.

"Mrs. Dawson?"

Go figure, AJ was right. Her mom really did know everything.

Even though I knew I was going to be majorly punished by my dad, I had to stifle a laugh at Mrs. Dawson's pink fuzzy pajamas and matching slippers.

She was usually very pretty and a good dresser—for a mom—but her blonde hair was pinned back, exposing a pale face with no makeup.

I'd never seen AJ's mother look anything less than perfect.

"Oh, my goodness, child." One hand flew to her throat. "What are you doing here?"

Then my heart sank at the expression in her eyes. Could she really care about me? I wasn't used to that sort of concern from motherly figures.

The only other time I thought AJ's mom showed interest in me was a few months ago, when we'd told her about our gifts. AJ said it would be okay, since her mom was gifted, too.

"Sunny is here." I tried to explain while keeping the don't-tell-Dad whine out of my voice. "I needed to talk to her."

A man stepped from behind her and I stifled a scream. When the gold of the police badge strapped to his belt reflected off my glowing flashlight, I breathed a sigh of relief.

"Oh, hi." I nervously fumbled with my fingers. Now the cops were involved in my search; I was definitely busted.

"Hi, Krysta." Flashing a smile, he wrinkled his brow. "Remember me?"

As I closed the distance between us, I recognized Officer Garza, the cop who took my statement today. "Yeah."

"Officer Garza came to our house tonight looking for you." Brow drawn in a heavy frown, Mrs. Dawson used the motherly guilt voice she had perfected on AJ.

"We have a suspect." Garza motioned for me to come closer. "We need you to identify him."

"Sunny's boyfriend?" I gasped, feeling tension from my body ebb away at the thought of Sunny's killer behind bars.

"Yes, Krysta." Garza nodded. "What were you doing out here?" He ended on an accusatory note, like I was up to no good.

How could I tell him the truth? He'd have me committed.

"Nothing." I shrugged, biting my lower lip.

His mouth tilted in the slightest of smirks, and for a moment, I saw a sign of recognition in his eyes, like he didn't believe me. "I thought you told Mrs. Dawson you were talking to Sunny."

"Sunny's dead," I blurted.

Folding his arms across his chest, he leveled me with a hard stare. "I know."

Something in my gut told me Officer Garza knew the truth.

"Look," I spoke through a shaky voice. "I just came out here because I couldn't sleep and it's so beautiful out here." I swept my hand across the dark horizon before swatting a mosquito on my neck.

His smirk turned into an all out accusatory scowl. "This is no place for a young girl to be by herself."

"Yes, sir," I mouthed, unable to stop the uneasiness that settled in my bones.

"You're lucky Mrs. Dawson knew where to find you. Do

you know we arrested Sunny's boyfriend from this spot earlier today?"

My throat went bone dry. He was here. What if I'd come earlier?

His facial features suddenly dropped. "Given what happened to your mom, I'm surprised you'd take such a risk." Garza's voice sounded choked with emotion, as his eyes glossed over with moisture.

"What does my mom have to do with this?" I spat.

Was he suggesting I was trying to run away like she did? This was the second time today he'd mentioned that woman and I was sick of it. I had always been a fly on the wall in my dad's life, but after my mom left us, I felt even more insignificant.

"Krysta, you look cold." Mrs. Dawson spoke in an authoritative tone. "Officer, let's get her in the car."

Mrs. Dawson glared at the officer as I silently trailed behind them through the forest. All the while, I couldn't shake the feeling that something wasn't right. When the three of us arrived at Officer Garza's police car, I remembered.

Where were Ed and Gertrude?

Scanning the tree line, I spied them hovering among the trees. Ed winked at me and I smiled.

All the while, I could feel the weight of Officer Garza's gaze on my back.

"Is this the guy you saw with Sunny last night?"

Officer Garza eyed me with a steady, concerned gaze. "Don't worry." He flashed a warm, but wary smile. "He can't see you."

My throat was too dry to speak, like an internal vacuum had suddenly sucked out all my mouth's moisture at the sight of him.

He didn't look any less scary in the faded orange uniform. His eyes showed no signs of remorse. If anything, he looked even meaner than before, like a confused, rabid dog. Smiling through a snarl, his gaze swept across the one-way mirror. Though I'd seen it in the movies, and I knew he couldn't see me,

I still cringed as his glare passed over where I was sitting.

"Yes, that's him," I breathed.

"Good." Officer Garza squeezed my shoulder once before letting go. "That's all we need from here."

"That's it?" My jaw dropped, a mixed feeling of relief and uncertainty washing through me. "Don't I need to testify or anything?"

"You already gave your statement." Garza peered down at me with that all-knowing gleam in his eyes. "Unless you have something else you want to tell me."

"No." I resolutely shook my head.

"Are you sure?"

I could read the disbelief in his voice.

"Yeah." I nodded vigorously, all the while my insides trembled.

"Ok." He shrugged. "Then you're free to go."

A female officer motioned to me, and I followed her, vaguely aware of my own actions. As I walked out of the room on wobbly legs, I couldn't help but feel this wasn't my last encounter with Officer Garza.

He knew about my powers. I could feel it.

But who told him?

Walking down the corridor of the substation, my legs were so shaky I felt like I would faint. There was also another issue. The huge bottle of water I drank after my bike excursion was wreaking havoc on my bladder.

After the officer pointed out the bathroom, I rushed inside, barely taking notice of the ugly mustard yellow walls before I threw open the stall door.

The last thing I expected to see were two ethereal spirits hovering knee deep in toilet water.

I yelped, a hand flying to my chest, before I had time to process the sight before me. Standing side- by-side, Ed and Gertrude each had one leg in the toilet. They just floated there, staring at me with those goofy grins, like haunting toilets was the most natural thing to do.

"What are you two doing in the toilet?" I asked through a

spurt of anxious laughter.

"We was waitin' for you." Gertrude nodded. "Seein' as you like them mirrors so much, we knew you'd come in here." Tilting his chin, Ed folded his arms across his inflated chest, looking proud of himself that he'd figured out my favorite hangout.

"Well, thanks for hanging around." I ended on an awkward note, not too sure what to say to them while standing inside a cramped urinal and waiting for my bladder to bust open.

"No problem." They answered in unison.

"They caught him." I nodded, trying my hardest to fall into a natural conversation during this incredibly awkward moment.

"Yeah." They grinned. "We knew that."

Not knowing the right gestures to use during dead person toilet talk, I nodded again. "He confessed, so I don't need to tell them about dead Sunny."

"That's good."

"Yeah." Smoothing my frizz down with shaky fingers, I struggled with the right words to say to them. "Listen, I've been thinking."

And I had been thinking, a lot. The only trouble was that my thoughts kept leading me to the same horrible conclusion.

I had to help them stop that mall. Even though I was committing social suicide, it was the least I could do considering how they'd helped me with Sunny.

"Yes, Emmy." Eyes bulging, their expressions were eager—hopeful.

Exhaling a deep breath, I struggled for the words that would end my social status as I knew it, but I figured worse things could happen to a girl, like murder. Besides, after a few years, maybe it would all blow over. Once I moved to Paris to start my modeling career, all of Greenwood would have forgotten about Krysta, the loser who protested the mall.

"I'm only fourteen and I really don't know how to stop a mall. Even though I'll fall several steps down the stairway of popularity if I help you, I'll do it."

Ed and Gertrude exchanged wide grins. "Thank you, Emmy!"

Swallowing hard, I cleared my throat while forcing a smile.

"Now will you please leave before I wet my pants?"

Chapter Nine

"Is that all you're eating?"

Looking up from my plate and across the small breakfast table, AJ's blonde brows were drawn together in a heavy scowl as she sneered at my two toast wedges, lightly dusted with low-cal butter substitute.

Sighing, I smoothed my hands up my shaky arms. My nerves still hadn't settled after last night at the substation and now I had to put up with AJ's attitude. Besides, what had my toast ever done to her?

"Yeah, this is all I'm eating." I met her scowl with a direct gaze.

"My mom made bacon." She motioned to a big pile of greasy, steaming pork in the center of the table.

Gag.

I should have just duct taped them to my thighs and butt, because that's exactly where they'd end up if I swallowed them.

I lightly shrugged, before turning my focus back to my toast wedges, as I did my best to pretend AJ wasn't getting on my nerves.

"I don't feel like eating much today." I washed down a morsel of toast with a gulp of water. AJ didn't have any diet drinks in the house.

"You never feel like eating much."

I rolled my eyes. "Excuse me?" I said with enough sarcasm in my voice to make her understand I wasn't in the mood for her attitude.

AJ seemed determined to turn breakfast into a nag session.

"Look at you, Krysta." Narrowing her gaze, she waved an invisible circle around my body. "You're turning into one of those runway skeletons."

"You mean fashion models." Tossing my toast on the plate, I planted both fists on the table. "They know, like I do, that beauty takes sacrifice." I spoke each syllable with clipped precision, knowing I'd need my full arsenal of attitude to keep up with AJ.

Didn't work.

She had the nerve to laugh, but it sounded more like a super loud, annoying burst of air. "What's so pretty about looking like a flagpole with collagen- induced lips?"

Closing my eyes, I focused on my breathing. In, out, in, out. I should have known better than to try and top AJ's attitude. Maybe a little guilt would work instead.

Opening my eyes, I fixed her with a steady stare. "I don't dog your lifestyle, AJ."

"That's because I eat healthy." AJ's eyes and head rolled in her signature major attitude head- bob.

The heavy sinking in my gut told me this was a losing battle, but I kept up the fight. "Greasy bacon is not healthy."

Face contorted in a mask of anger, she threw her hands in the air. A move I'd seen her use many times when she was yelling at one of her teammates for a stupid play. "It's better than starvation. Remember, I tried eating like a rabbit and I passed out on the court."

"Well, I don't play sports, so I don't need to worry." No longer in the mood for food, I pushed back from the table and started to rise.

AJ rose along with me, pointing a finger at my chest. "Of course you don't play sports. You don't have the energy."

Hands on hips, I tried imitating her head bobble. "I biked all the way to the lake last night."

Folding her arms across her chest, AJ smirked. "Yeah, and I bet it sucked to be you."

The air whooshed from my lungs and I almost stumbled back into my chair. Yeah, it did suck to be me. It really sucked.

My mom left me, my dad ignored me, my crush pitied me. I was just a girl with way more problems than the average teen.

How was I going to stop a mall or bring a dead spirit back to the light? The worst of it was that the only two friends I could really count on at the moment were dead.

Fighting back the tears that threatened to ruin my freshly applied mascara, I decided to go wait for the bus. AJ was acting like a major butthead and I didn't need to take it any longer.

As I turned to leave, a hand reached across the table and held my arm in a strong grip. I looked over my shoulder to see AJ's sharp gaze had softened to a sweet puppy dog expression.

Letting go of my arm, she motioned to my chair as she sat down. "I'm not trying to piss you off, Krysta. All I'm saying is that you need to eat a little more. It's not healthy to be so skinny."

I don't know why I followed her command, but I sat. Maybe it was because my legs were still wobbly from the weight of the world on my back. "Looking good is healthy for my self-esteem." I spoke evenly, although something in the back of my mind questioned my own judgment. Could AJ have been right? Should I eat more?

AJ shook her head. "If you had self-esteem, you wouldn't need to starve yourself." Her voice softened and she flashed just a hint of a smile. "And you'd still look good with a few extra pounds."

"Whatever." I meant to deliver that one word with a silencing punch, but I spoke without conviction. Like my conscience had decided to let her win.

"I'm just trying to look out for you, Krysta. I don't want you to get sick. Besides, guys don't like stick girls."

The image of Bryon scowling at me from across the table at Mocha Madness flashed through my mind. My body tensed as I recalled his words. 'Don't you worry you might be a little too skinny?'

Was AJ right? Guys didn't like skinny girls? Looking down at my one wedge of half-eaten toast, I sighed. Maybe my shaking limbs and the hollow ache in my stomach weren't just due to stress.

Maybe I should eat.

Reaching across the table, I grabbed a few slices of bacon and put them on my plate.

AJ's smile nearly stretched ear to ear.

I forced myself not to smile back. Though she was trying to look out for me, I couldn't shake the sting of her words, comparing me to a skeleton. Sure I was a size one, but I'd always thought skinny looked good on me.

Didn't it?

"Hey."

I saw him coming from several lockers away, his eyes focused on me. My first thought was, 'why?' I mean, after we shared probably the worst study session in history, why would he want to speak to the poor, skinny chick again? I was expecting him to ignore me until we got to chemistry and then to beg Mrs. Jackson to give him a new partner.

"Hey." I half-heartedly grinned and then held in my breath while I waited for his response.

He cocked his head to the side. "You know we still have a test this Friday."

My jaw slackened and my tongue felt like a lead- weight in my mouth as I struggled for something to say. Was he hinting to study with me again? His nearness wasn't helping my brain function. He was wearing an unusual musk today and I could almost feel the heat of it jump off his body and crawl up my flesh. Inhaling deeper, I had to repress a sigh. His smell reminded me of a pastry or a cinnamon cookie.

"Yeah," I swallowed a nervous ball of energy. "Two more days."

One brow arched and his lip tilted in the cutest smile ever. "Wanna study tonight?"

"Yes!" I blurted before biting on my lower lip. I was acting way too eager.

Gawd, he must think I'm a total dork now.

Clearing my throat, I forced my voice to sound much more casual, like I didn't think Bryon Thomas was the hottest guy in school. "I mean, where? I'm not staying at my apartment anymore."

His brows drew together. "Why not?"

"My dad thinks I'll be safer at AJ's." I shrugged, pretending it didn't matter that Dad still refused to allow me back home. This murder worked out to his advantage. Now he could get drunk and have his little playthings come over any time without the annoying teenager in the way.

"But they caught the guy." Bryon's comment sounded way too much like a question.

He'd really think I was a loser if he knew my own dad didn't want me around.

"Yeah, I know." I faked a smile. "But he still wants me at her house until this all blows over."

That wasn't the total truth. After Dad found out about my visit to the lake, he and Mrs. Dawson decided to postpone my coming home indefinitely. Since he worked nights, they were afraid I'd try it again. My apartment wasn't much, but it was still my home and I missed it.

"You can study at my house tonight." Bryon's smile softened and a hint of sadness flashed in his pale blue gaze. "My dad said it's okay."

I couldn't repress the sigh of frustration that escaped my lips. He still pitied me. Just like the other night when he saw my rundown apartment and when I refused to order food. He was probably only keeping me as a partner because he felt sorry for me.

"All right." Unable to look into his pitying eyes, I spoke while playing with the frayed end on the strap of my worn book bag. "I have to do a little research first."

"For another class?"

"No, not really." Keeping my gaze down, I shook my head. "Just for a community service project."

"I've never seen you at Student Council. I didn't know you did community service."

"Neither did I," I groaned, unable to comprehend how I'd gotten stuck with grave recovery.

"So what's the project?"

Looking into his direct gaze, I was relieved to see the pity had washed away and he looked almost interested in what I had to say. With wide eyes, he silently watched me while I stumbled for the right words to say.

"Well, it's kind of hard to explain." How was I supposed to

tell him I was trying to ruin thousands of teenagers' lives by halting their fashion paradise?

All for who?

Oh yeah, the dead people who talk to me in the toilet.

"Do you want to do the research at my house?"

"Uhhh, maybe I'll just use AJ's computer first and then I'll come over." The last thing I needed was Bryon looking over my shoulder, asking questions like 'Why does it matter to you that there are grave sites on the mall property?'

"Okay." He shrugged. "But if you need any help, let me know. I need thirty community service hours this semester for StuCo."

Last time I checked, Student Council wasn't into doing community service for ghosts. The canned food drive this Thanksgiving went to people who were destitute, not dead.

"I'll keep you in mind." I nodded, maybe way too much, like I was trying to convince myself, as well as him, that he could help me.

But he couldn't.

In fact, I didn't see how anyone could help me. I was on my own with this problem, as well as a million others.

AJ was right. It sucked to be me.

"What are you doing here?"

I'd opened AJ's front door to see Sophie clutching a briefcase to her chest, with her large, infectious grin. One look into her smiling green eyes and I couldn't help but smile back.

That girl was way too perky. Something she used to say about me only a few weeks ago.

As I opened the door wider, she practically flew past me on a rush of air.

"Your negative thoughts were rattling my brain all the way home on the bus today." Tossing her briefcase on the polished coffee table with a thud, she threw herself onto Mrs. Dawson's expensive, antique couch.

I cringed.

We couldn't afford to have nice stuff at my place, but I knew AJ's mom would be mad if she saw Sophie scratching her furniture. Good thing AJ was at a softball game and her parents were watching her brother play tennis.

So I was left alone.

Well, with the exception of the butt-licking dog, Patches. All he really did was sit by the front door and munch on old butt mildew while he waited for his favorite family member, Mrs. Dawson, to get home.

Staying here didn't seem much different from my apartment, so I didn't understand why I couldn't have gone back home.

"Yeah, I've been upset lately." Kneeling by the coffee table, I carefully rubbed out a dirt smudge made by Sophie's grimy briefcase.

"As if I couldn't tell." Tossing her head back, she rubbed her temples with dramatic sweeping motions. "My head is throbbing from your negative energy."

"Sorry to be ruining your life, too." I shrugged. "Oh, geez, there go your feelings again." Sliding off the couch, she kneeled beside me. Slanting a soft smile, she swept her long chestnut hair behind one shoulder. "Look, I didn't mean to make you feel bad. I came to help you."

"Help me?"

I was stunned by her offer. I mean, yeah, Sophie was one of my two best friends, but I'd never really relied on her for much help. There was that one time a few months ago when she'd channeled the thoughts of my dead Grammy, but usually, whenever I had a problem, I faced it alone. That was how I was raised to deal with things.

Besides, she and AJ were different and I didn't think they totally understood me. Yeah, we all had freakish gifts, but mine was way different. They had mind powers. I had a curse.

They had something else I didn't have.

A family.

They woke up to breakfast and came home to dinner. They had parents to help them with homework. They went on family vacations and had family gatherings.

Their home life was totally different than mine.

Before, I didn't mind, but, honestly, it was beginning to bother me. Not that I didn't want them to be happy. AJ and

Sophie were great friends, but I couldn't help feeling that our differences were drawing them closer together and pulling me further away.

Maybe they didn't notice as much because their lives were so perfect, but I was beginning to feel more and more like the outsider.

Krysta, the poor kid with the drunk father.

"It would be so easy to pop into your head right now. Your mind is screaming for me to read it."

Gasping, I looked into Sophie's hardened stare. "Don't you dare." I was so absorbed in feeling sorry for myself that I had momentarily forgotten my mind-reader friend was kneeling beside me.

She narrowed her gaze. "Shut your brain off before I go in."

Sophie used to have difficulty turning her mind reading ability on and off, but she was getting much better at it. AJ made her promise she wouldn't jump into our heads without permission, but sometimes our bad moods still projected on Sophie, making her depressed as well.

"I can't help it." I gnawed on my lower lip, eating away the last remnants of shimmery moisturizing lip gloss.

"I can tell." She wagged a finger. "I'm getting a really big sense of self-pity, Krysta."

"Yeah, well, it sucks to be me right now." Without even thinking, I had coined AJ's phrase as my new motto. It fit my life pretty well.

"I brought my laptop." Leaning over the coffee table, she unzipped the big, dirt-stained bag and pulled out her computer. "Do you want me to help you with your research?"

Before Sophie had arrived, I had been staring at the empty Internet browser on AJ's computer for over ten minutes, not really knowing where to begin.

"Do you seriously want to help me stop a mall?"

"Krysta, I'm not into clothes like you are."

Leaning closer, she squeezed my hand, holding me with an earnest gaze. "The real question is...do you want to stop it?"

All at once, the warmth from her touch seeped into my bones, and for the first time in a while, I felt like a living person really cared about me. Looking down at our joined hands, my eyes filled with unshed tears.

The human contact was nice, something I had been missing in my sucky life.

"I have to." I said while pulling away, afraid holding her hand would eventually turn me into a leaky water hose and ruin my mascara. "My friends will lose their graves if I don't."

"Do they really need a place to stay?" Wrinkling her brow, Sophie tilted her head like Patches did whenever he farted and didn't know where the sound was coming from. "I mean...they're dead, aren't they?"

"That's not the point." Fighting the urge to throw my hands in the air, I clenched my fists at my sides. Ed's tantrums were threatening to rub off on me. "We're desecrating their burial site. People don't stop having emotions after they die."

Choking on that last syllable, I turned away from Sophie. The thought of Sunny's hollow, aching eyes seared through my memory. Her boyfriend's betrayal was so painful her soul fell into an empty void, a dark abyss.

"You know what, Krysta?" with barely a whisper at my back, Sophie placed a hand on my shoulder.

"What?" A single tear slipped down my cheek.

"You're a good friend."

"Thanks." I was unable to say more.

For a long moment, we sat there in silence while I swallowed the rising tide of emotion that threatened to burst free.

Tapping me on the shoulder, Sophie cleared her throat. "My mom told me something about the National Historic Preservation Act. She said some cemeteries can be protected."

Startled, I turned.

She was wearing a plastered on smile, the kind friends use when they're trying to cheer each other up.

"Some cemeteries?" A spark of hope kindled in the hollow of my chest.

"Yeah." She nodded while toying with her fingers. "They have to qualify first."

"How do we do that?"

Sophie turned on her computer and plugged in the little

phone receptor. "Mom gave me the website to The National Registry of Historic Places."

"Let's go there," I squealed.

I'd never heard of this registry, but maybe it could help me save my friends' graves.

With a few clicks of her mouse, Sophie began typing. "Okay," she asked while reading though a lengthy checklist on the screen, "did your ghosts die at least fifty years ago?"

Recalling Gertrude's out-of-style bun and shawl, I stifled a laugh. "Oh, yeah. They're so last century."

Keeping her eyes glued to the monitor, Sophie scrolled down. "Are your ghosts famous, like Billy the Kid or something?"

"I don't know." I shrugged. Ed was grumpy enough. Maybe he was some kind of outlaw, but I needed to ask him and their spirits were nowhere in sight.

At that moment, as if Sophie's question had summoned their spirits, Ed and Gertrude floated into the living room.

"Hey!" I called up to them. "Are you guys famous?"

"What?" Falling to her bottom, Sophie scooted back toward the couch. "They're here?" she squeaked while pulling her knees to her chest.

"Please don't pull an AJ on me." I rolled my eyes, holding in my laughter as my friend cowered in the corner like a frightened mouse. "They're not going to possess you or anything."

Ed scratched his beard while speaking through a frown. "I don't reckon we're famous."

Gertrude nudged him in the ribcage. "I won twelve blue ribbons for my peach preserves." Tilting her chin up, Gertrude looked kind of cute for a dead old lady.

Ed nodded. "Gerty had the best jam in three counties."

"I don't think jam counts, Ed," I sighed. "That doesn't make you famous."

Keeping her eyes focused on the ceiling about two feet from where Ed and Gertrude were hovering, Sophie scooted back to the coffee table and ducked behind her laptop. "Is there a historic building on the site?" She scrolled down the screen with a shaky hand.

"Ain't nothin' there but that oak tree," Ed bellowed. "And now that's gone, too. They done tore down our house years ago."

"No," I answered.

"What about a historic battle?" Keeping her eyes glued to the screen, she chewed on her bottom lip.

"No," I responded as they shook their heads.

"Hmmmm." Sophie's lips looked locked in a vice grip.

"What's that flashy thing sayin', Emmy?" Gertrude asked.

I nudged Sophie. "What's wrong?" But I was afraid of her answer. Why did they need a historical battle to protect their sanctuary?

Folding trembling hands in her lap, Sophie looked to the ceiling, then to me with worried eyes. "I don't think their graves are protected under the Preservation Act."

"What about that it's been my home over one hundred years?" Ed pounded the air with both fists.

The pictures on the walls shook with a sudden, violent force, causing one to fall off its hook and shatter on the floor.

"Oh-mi-god, Krysta!" Sophie gasped and then grabbed hold of my arm, nearly breaking skin with her nails.

"Easy, Sophie," I soothed, while pulling my arm free from each claw. I narrowed my eyes at the spirits above. "We'll find a way, Ed. Calm down, you're scaring Sophie."

"I think I wet my pants," Sophie squeaked.

"Don't worry," I spoke while flinching as I pried her fingers from my skin. "He's not mad at you."

Her eyes looked ready to bulge out of their sockets. "Well, that's good to know, I guess." She let out a burst of nervous laughter before slapping her hand over her mouth.

"Did your mom have any other options?" Despite the severity of the situation, I almost lost it myself. I mean, Sophie looked pretty funny when freaked. I wondered if she really did piss her pants a little.

"No, not really." She spoke through a shaky voice while her gaze darted from me to the ceiling. "Lots of people said that old cemetery was haunted. Maybe we can spook the developers away."

"I doubt it." I grimaced at the thought of Ed and Gertrude

haunting away the construction crew. How much could those two do to scare them? Besides, all the developers had to do was throw some concrete over a few graves and they'd be off to build another mall somewhere else.

Sophie gasped, then her eyes bulged.

Oh, crud. I'd seen that look before.

Sophie had an idea. Or what AJ and I liked to call, "A brain fart." Some of her schemes over the years have been pretty crazy.

"What if..." She sucked in a large breath of air before speaking on a rapid exhale. "We get the news involved?"

My limbs froze. "The news?" How did I know she'd go overboard with this?

"We could hold a protest." She jumped to her feet, slapping both hands together.

"Like with picket signs?"

"Yeah!" she squealed.

Above us, Ed and Gertrude hooted and hollered in approval.

As I looked at their beaming faces, the edges of my lips tilted up in a forced smile and I tried to look enthused.

"Super," I spoke through clenched teeth.

Why couldn't I just shrink into the carpet?

The news media meant lots of exposure and that was the last thing I wanted. I was hoping I could just quietly stop this thing. Maybe walk into the developers' office with an official notice and be done with it. I didn't want television cameras and reporters asking questions.

The kids at Greenwood wouldn't just think I was a total weirdo; they'd hate me, too.

I should have known this would happen either way. I mean, my life was doomed to suck.

Chapter Ten

"**B**ryon, the test's in two days. Are you ready?"
"I will be." Turning his pale eyes on me, he smiled faintly before that glazed-over look returned. Slightly rocking from side to side on the tall kitchen barstool, he toyed with his pen while looking somewhere off in the distance.

There he goes again.

My science partner was off in space. After nearly an hour, we'd only gone through the first ten elements. I'd thought having a partner was supposed to make studying easier. He kept staring at the wall or his refrigerator, zoning out by the time we reached neon.

Studying in his house was distracting enough without him adding to it. While we sat in a room as large as my entire apartment, the housekeeper would barge in every five minutes. She swept under the table twice and offered us soda and cookies at least five times.

She was more like a babysitter than a housesitter, spying on the teenagers to make sure we weren't making out on the table.

As if.

He was more turned on by a fly on the wall than by me.

Oh, yeah, and that plate of cookies he'd demolished in about five minutes.

"How are you going to memorize all the elements in two days if you're too busy watching the paint peel?"

He turned his gaze on me again, his cool orbs narrowing. "Why do girls hook up with guys like him?"

"What?" I blurted.

Face hardening, he jutted his chin. "Why did Sunny go out with him?"

"I don't know." I shrugged. "Low self-esteem, I guess."

Talking about Sunny was the last thing I wanted to do now. I only thought about her every other minute. How could I erase her empty, agonized expression from my brain? Bryon was bringing up memories I was trying hard to forget, at least until this science test was over.

Jabbing his finger at me, he raised his voice. "Don't ever do something that stupid." The anger in his eyes was tangible, as if someone had lit a fire in his brain and steam was shooting out of his eye sockets.

What the heck?

Was he adding stupid to my growing list of flaws?

"Are you my parent now?" I snapped.

He jerked back, as if struck by verbal lightning. His eyes shot open and his mouth fell; for the briefest of seconds, he looked...hurt.

Bryon was sending all kinds of signals.

And guys say girls are confusing.

"No." His denial was barely audible.

My heart plunged. I instinctively reached out and squeezed his hand.

With a soft smile, he turned his hand inward and cupped my palm. The feel of his warm skin on mine was electric, like thousands of tiny little buzzing bugs were tickling my palm.

I didn't have much experience with the opposite sex. Keeping up with the latest fashion and celebrity news was practically a full-time job. Who had time for guys? But I had to believe his electrifying touch meant something.

Clearing my throat, I tried to speak through a shaky voice. "This is really bothering you, isn't it?"

"Why wouldn't it?" Dipping his chin, his gaze focused on our joined hands before he tilted his head back up and batted long, pale lashes. "Not all guys are pigs."

He squeezed my hand tighter, a faint smile playing on his lips.

That's when the pain hit my chest. I hadn't felt this before, but I quickly recognized the sensation.

Panic.

For some reason, I didn't like him holding my hand anymore. He was making me way too nervous. First anger, then sadness, and now he was flirting? This guy's emotions were way too mixed up.

"I know you're not a pig," I said while pulling from his grip. "It's just that Sunny wasn't very nice and you didn't know her."

"No, I didn't know her." He spoke through a clenched jaw, his voice rising with each syllable. "I know girls like her. She's not the first woman to be murdered by a crazy boyfriend." He ended on practically a yell.

I jumped back, feeling the force of his words rattle through me. "Bryon." I held out both palms. "You're getting a little too weird."

For the longest moment of my life, he just stared at me with this kind of hurt and angry expression, his face turning an ashen white, kind of like he was holding in his breath.

Holy crap!

He was holding in his breath.

I didn't blink or make any sudden movements, because I honestly was afraid of his next reaction. Finally, his shoulders slackened, as he took a big breath. To say this guy was on edge would have been a major understatement.

"Maybe we should talk about something else, like science," I stammered.

His lips turned into a pout. "Hydrogen is H."

Though he had me totally freaked out a few moments ago, I couldn't help but smile at his cute expression. "That's great," I laughed. "You only have a hundred and two more."

One side of his mouth hinted at a smile as his gaze found mine.

I was lost once again in a pair of radiant blue eyes.

He was so cute.

I was so stupid.

Bryon had issues and I had enough of my own problems without adding a crazy boyfriend to the list.

"How's the study session going kids?"

I jerked at the sound of a man's booming voice from

behind my back.

"Okay," Bryon answered in a cool tone, turning his gaze to his textbook as if he'd suddenly found The Periodic Table of the Elements to be the most fascinating thing on earth.

"Aren't you going to introduce me to the lovely lady?" A man in a perfectly tailored business suit came up beside us. I recognized him from the other morning when the police questioned us in Sparks' office. He was tall, with short, pale blond hair which was graying at the temples. Other than a few lines around his eyes and mouth, he looked exactly like Bryon.

"Krysta." Without looking at either of us, Bryon pointed to me with his pen. "This is my dad," he answered in a monotone, like he was completely bored by our presence.

I wanted to reach across the table and slap him.

"Cliff Thomas." Bryon's dad held out his hand, smiling warmly. "How do you do, Krysta?"

"Fine." My hand was swallowed in his firm grip as he practically shook my arm off.

Was this whole family crazy?

"Would you like a soda or some cookies?" He motioned to the heaping pile of assorted junk food spread out on the counter.

"No, thank you."

Great, even Bryon's dad wanted to fatten me up.

"We're trying to study, Dad." His voice was no longer dull, but laced with attitude, as he kept his gaze firmly glued to his book.

"That's great." Mr. Thomas beamed before clasping Bryon on the shoulder.

Bryon jerked away, acting as if he'd been scalded.

I had to hold in my gasp at the look of hatred in Bryon's narrowed eyes as he locked gazes with his father.

Mr. Thomas pulled back, locking a fist by his side. His expression fell, before he plastered the smile on again. "Listen, I'm going to be using the living room. Some business associates are coming over for cocktails."

"So you want me to stay out of your way?" Bryon growled.

Closing his eyes on an exhale, Mr. Thomas opened them again, looking at Bryon with a soft expression. "I thought we already had this discussion, son."

"We'll just go study by the pool. You won't even know we're here."

"It's breezy outside. I think your friend would be more comfortable in the house."

"Make up your mind," Bryon spoke through gritted teeth.

"Do we have to go through this again? I want you here, Bryon." Mr. Thomas' shoulders slumped, making him look like a deflated balloon. "I've always wanted you."

Bryon rolled his eyes. "As long as I'm invisible."

"No, as long as you don't mouth off to me in front of my clients like you did last time. Now you and your friend are welcome to stay here in the kitchen. Heck, you can even come in and introduce yourself to my guests. Just please, try to act like my son tonight and not some angry, rebellious teenager."

"Okay," Bryon spoke through gritted teeth. "Now that you've totally embarrassed me in front of my friend, I'll be sure to be on my best behavior around yours."

"Bryon, please, these are department store executives." Holding his palms out, Mr. Thomas sounded like a convicted criminal begging for mercy. "They could mean big money to The Crossover Project."

"The Crossover?" I blurted without thinking.

Mr. Thomas's head snapped to me and he plastered on an enormous grin. "I see you've heard of our new mall. Then again, you are a teenage girl."

"Uh," I stammered. "Yeah." But inside I felt like screaming 'No!' As if my life couldn't suck any more, Bryon's dad was connected to the mall project.

Something flashed in Mr. Thomas's eyes as he looked at me like I was a mouse and he was a cat ready to pounce. "Maybe if things go well tonight, I'll have a few mall gift cards for you."

I swallowed a lump of regret in my throat. His proposition was wrong on so many levels. I knew I'd have to refuse his gift cards and not just because he was using me to get to Bryon. This mall was desecrating Ed and Gertrude's gravesites.

Why did this have to happen to me?

I wanted those gift cards. I really wanted them.

"Real smooth," Bryon sneered. "Bribe Krysta because it

won't work on me."

"I was just trying to be nice to your girlfriend." Shrugging, Mr. Thomas winked at me before walking to the fridge and pulling out a bottle of water.

Leaning against the kitchen counter, Mr. Thomas drank slowly while eying both of us. I pretended to study, but I couldn't get anything done with so much running through my brain.

For a long while, none of us said a word, which made the whole situation even weirder. It seemed Bryon argued with his dad about everything, so why didn't he correct him when he called me his girlfriend?

Did Bryon think I was his girlfriend? If so, he'd forgotten to share the news with me.

Finally, Bryon threw down his pen and exhaled slowly. "I won't bother your clients." His voice sounded tired, strained. "Now will you let us study?"

"Okay, then." Mr. Thomas pushed off the counter and threw his bottle in the trash. "You kids have fun." He walked out the door without a glance at either of us.

I sat there for a moment, watching as Bryon continued to stare at the same page in his chemistry book.

What was I supposed to say in a situation like this?

Luckily, I'd had some experience with father/child misunderstandings. "Wow. I thought things were bad with my dad," I blurted.

"I hate him." Bryon spoke in a low, cold voice, his brow marred with several deep creases.

What had his dad done to make Bryon hate him so much? Suddenly, I felt like I really didn't know Bryon—this supposedly cute, sweet guy who sat next to me in science class. Where was the caring guy who'd stood up for Sunny at the café a few nights ago?

"Hate is a pretty strong feeling, Bryon."

He looked up while plastering a passive expression on his face, like everything between him and his dad was okay. Like, suddenly, he didn't have any more issues.

But the guy had lots of issues.

"Are we going to study or what?" He shrugged, feigning a

smile.

"Sure." I nodded, trying my best to act like I wasn't totally freaked out by our study session.

The drive home from Bryon's house was almost as weird as our study session. When Mrs. Dawson came to get me, Mr. Thomas acted like a total jerk and flirted with her, even asking to take her to dinner. Didn't he notice the totally huge rock on her finger?

Mrs. Dawson didn't seem to mind. She just turned her nose up at him before walking me to the car.

I cringed as I heard Bryon in the background yelling at his dad.

"You must have had a delightful evening." Mrs. Dawson slanted me an all-knowing smile.

I shrugged, not wanting to go into the awful details with her. When she didn't press the issue, I wondered if she already knew what went on. If she'd spied on me and Bryon with her powers. Would she really invade my privacy like that? I almost thought I heard AJ's voice in the back of my brain.

Heck, yeah, she would spy. My mother is so nosy. Maybe she thought that was her job. She was responsible for me while I stayed with them. After the lake incident, I guess I lost her trust.

But I still didn't like it. Even Ed and Gertrude were nice enough to give me some alone time tonight.

Sighing, I brushed a frizzy lock behind my ear. I just wanted to go home. I wanted to have my own bathroom to do my makeup and not be forced to share one with AJ, her disgusting brother and his zit juice collection.

Gag. Why didn't anyone clean the bathroom mirror?

Besides, Ed, Gertrude and I could talk freely without worrying about freaking anyone out. Even though the dead were kind of a pain in the butt, they were still easier to get along with than the living.

"We have to pick up AJ at the softball field." Mrs. Dawson flipped her long blonde tresses behind one shoulder. "I brought you some company for the ride."

"Surprise!" Sophie squealed as she jumped out of the back

of Mrs. Dawson's car and pulled me back in with her.

A wave of relief washed over me at seeing my best friend. Someone I could talk to about Bryon and my crazy night with him and his dad. Besides, who better to get to the root of his problems than a mind reader?

"How'd it go?" Sophie's eyes bulged and her voice held a note of fear, like she was expecting me to have a terrible time.

I looked at my friend with suspicion. Had Mrs. Dawson spied on me and Bryon and then told Sophie what she saw?

Mrs. Dawson slid into the seat in front of us and, thankfully, flipped open her phone. I didn't want her invading any more of my personal life.

"There's something wrong with Bryon," I whispered to Sophie.

"Yeah." She nodded all too eagerly. "I wanted to tell you."

I looked at Mrs. Dawson. Her eyes were on the road as she seemed to be into her phone conversation.

I leaned toward Sophie, keeping my voice low. "Have his bad thoughts been popping in your brain lately?"

She rolled her eyes. "Oh, yeah. That's why I worried that tonight would be a disaster."

"Why didn't you tell me?" I bit on my lower lip, almost afraid of Sophie's answer and wondering why she never mentioned anything about this before.

"Because I know you like him." Mouth turning into a pout, she dropped her gaze to her lap, toying with her fingers. "I was going to tell you tonight, I promise." She leaned over and clasped my hands in hers. "I just didn't want to make you mad, like I got when AJ told me to ditch Jacob."

Last semester Sophie liked a total dork named Jacob and got into it with AJ over him. Even though I thought he was a loser, too, I decided to stay out of their fight. I didn't think Sophie needed both of us on her back. Besides, she figured it out on her own, eventually. I guess I couldn't be too mad at Sophie for keeping Bryon's thoughts secret. After tonight, I figured out he had problems.

"He's feeling a great sense of abandonment." Her brows rose and she added the last part with emphasis. "And anger."

Crap. So he wasn't just having a bad day. The guy had

major issues. "I got the anger part. Who abandoned him?" I asked, kind of already suspecting his mom.

"Not to sound selfish." Sophie rolled her eyes. "But I'm more concerned with passing algebra than prying in on Bryon's brain. His depression has been distracting me enough lately."

"Yeah, but I'm worried about him. You should have heard him tonight with his dad. He really hates him."

Sophie narrowed her eyes, her nostrils flaring ever so slightly. "So you're asking me to spy? I promised you and AJ I wouldn't do that anymore."

"I just want to know why he's so on edge," I pleaded. "I don't think it's Sunny's murder. I think it's something worse and I can't help him if I don't know."

"Don't you have enough crap to deal with right now?"

"Yeah," I sighed, then swore as a frizzy curl escaped from my hair band and scraped the roof of the car. "But what's one more problem?"

Chapter Eleven

"Sun-ny? Sun-ny, are you out here?"

The real question was, what the heck was I doing out here? AJ's mom would so bust me if she woke up and used her spying powers, but here I was anyway at two in the morning, channeling a dead spirit like a total idiot.

I couldn't help myself. I'd lain on the cot beside AJ's bed all night, worrying.

Worrying over Bryon's disturbing thoughts.

Worrying about my chemistry test in two days.

Worrying for Sunny's poor lost spirit.

The worst of it was Ed and Gertrude never showed up tonight to console me. Where were they? I'd had a hard enough time getting them to give me any privacy, and suddenly, they just vanished. Were they okay? I mean, I knew they were already dead, but I still worried about them.

My life was totally out of control. I felt so stuck, so helpless. With so many things needing to be fixed, I couldn't just lay there all night. I had to take action.

"Sunny! Come out so we can talk!" I hollered into the crisp night air, scanning the dark, watery horizon for any sign of her spirit. Crap, I should've brought a jacket, but I was in too much of a hurry to sneak out of the house. Rubbing my bare arms for warmth, a shiver raced up my spine. This wasn't the kind of shiver I got from cold weather.

This was something else. More like a blade of ice was slicing my spinal cord.

I was now beginning to recognize the feeling when

Sunny's apparition was suddenly too close.

Turning on my heel, I gasped.

Her pale, bruised face was within inches of mine.

"What do you want?" She asked in a voice almost as cold as her aura.

Backing up a few paces, I swallowed hard, instinctively rubbing my arms again. No matter how much I was used to ghosts, she still gave me goose- flesh. "The police caught your boyfriend."

"Raymond," she breathed and her stone eyes softened.

I nodded.

A crease marred her pale brow. "What are they going to do to him?"

"I don't know yet." I held out my palms. "Maybe put him in jail."

Sunny's eyes widened, her mouth falling open. "He didn't mean to do it."

That strange chill brought on by her presence intensified, like an arctic wind had rushed up my spine.

I shivered through a yelp, backing up more until I felt the soles of my shoes sink into soft mud. With a quick glance behind me, I cursed at the ripples lapping at my heels. Any further and I'd be swimming.

"Sunny, do you understand what happened?" I spoke through a shaky voice while trying to control my trembling limbs.

"He hurt me," she said in a monotone.

Had dying made her that disoriented or was she just in denial?

I shook my head. "You're dead."

"No!" She glared at me through swollen eyelids. "It's not true."

"It's true, Sunny. Listen, you've got to leave this dark place. Find some light and move on."

"I can't leave Raymond. He'll be here for me soon." She nodded at something just beyond my shoulder.

I turned my head, following the direction of her gaze. She was looking at something in the center of the lake. Was mental illness a side-effect of dying? He wasn't going to be meeting her anywhere, unless maybe he got the death penalty.

"Raymond's not coming," I said in a clipped voice, trying to make her understand the reality of my words. "He's the one who killed you."

Without another glance, she turned, floating toward the canopy of trees behind us.

"Sunny, where are you going? Please don't leave!" I screamed, trying to chase after her, but it was hard on wobbly legs. For some reason, all of my energy had suddenly drained and I felt as lifeless as a corpse.

She floated further away until the faint light of her spirit was shrouded in darkness.

Exhaling a deep breath, I sank to my bottom on the nearest small boulder and rested my head in my hands.

That didn't go so well.

I wondered if all dead people in dark places acted this way. When my grammy died last semester, she kind of freaked me out because she wouldn't speak, but I didn't get the feeling of a thousand tiny spiders racing up my spine. Closing my eyes, I briefly remembered her smiling face. She had that same serene expression in death. Sunny's stark glare looked anything but serene.

"Too bad we can't put you on the witness stand. This would be an open and shut case."

A jolt of fear shot up my spine at the sound of the deep male voice. My eyes flew open and I jumped to my feet. Officer Garza stood a few feet in front of me, his flashlight aimed at the ground beneath his feet.

"What are you doing here?" I blurted, my voice shaking with apprehension.

He smiled softly, but not like the smile of a good friend. Kind of like a sorrowful smile that didn't quite reach his eyes. "I knew you'd come back."

I held my breath, afraid to respond. How did he know I'd come back here?

Shaking his head, his gaze shot up to the stars before coming back to me with a hard stare. "You're just like your mother."

I winced, that familiar surge of anger welling inside my

chest. He could have punched me and it would've had the same effect. Just the mention of her name and I wanted to hurl.

She left us.

She left me.

I'd just entered my teen years, right at a time when I needed her most, and she walked out. That was over a year ago and I haven't even gotten an email from her.

Was I that bad of a daughter? I stayed out of her hair when she asked me to—and she asked me to all the time.

And I worshiped her.

She was so beautiful. I did everything in my power to look just like her. She had straight, silky red hair and fair skin. Her eyes were of the brightest green.

I knew I looked more like my dad's side of the family, even though I'd never met them. He told me my aunt had frizzy hair.

That didn't stop me from buying every hair straightener under the sun, from trying to dye my hair red and getting bright orange instead. I dressed stylish, I acted cute.

I wanted to be just like my mom.

Then she left.

"I'm nothing like her." I spoke evenly, with a chest that felt ready to explode.

A deep frown marred his brow and under the pale moonlight, the lines framing his dark, sunken eyes were clearly visible. Not only did the guy need a good moisturizer, he was majorly stressed.

"You dad should have told you." He shook his head. "Your mother deserved better."

"What are you talking about?"

What was my dad hiding from me? Had she tried to call and he wouldn't let her talk to me? Did she have a good reason for leaving?

"Your real mother died when you were a baby."

Bam.

My brain exploded, a pair of lead weights fell to my feet. As I felt my legs give way, I stumbled to sit on the rock behind me.

"W-what?" That was all that came out of my mouth, as I was vaguely aware of my own actions.

"She was murdered." Officer Garza's voice echoed in my ears and he sounded miles away.

That last word wrapped around my brain and threatened to strangle all reasoning from my mind.

Murdered.

Just like Sunny.

My stomach clenched and a sickening feeling shot up my chest.

"This can't be true," I breathed.

Setting the flashlight at his feet, Officer Garza knelt in front of me, his eyes pooling with moisture. "I'm sorry, Krysta."

"Why would Dad lie?"

He sighed, running his fingers through a thinning hairline. "To protect you, I guess." Digging into his back pocket, he pulled out his wallet. "Look, here's a picture of you and her when you were still in diapers."

My jaw dropped as he handed me the picture. An olive-skinned woman with crazy curls held a frizzy-haired baby on her hip. They both had big brown eyes. The same wide smiles.

My dad lied.

A torrent of warm tears slid down my cheeks and I didn't even care about my makeup.

"She looks just like me." I tried to control my quavering lower lip as I spoke.

"She was a beauty." Garza seemed to choke on his last word and took a moment to clear his throat. A single tear slipped down his face before he continued. "Adela had beautiful eyes, beautiful hair."

"Adela?" I didn't understand why, but saying my mother's name out loud brought a chill to my spine.

Shivering, I rubbed my bare arms.

This whole moment felt so surreal. I'd had a different mom. A real mom. Maybe...she even loved me.

"She was my partner. My best friend." His voice broke again and then he plastered on a smile. "She loved you so much."

"She did?"

His gaze drifted off to somewhere beyond my shoulder. "You were her world. You two were so much alike." Garza laughed, before his brow set in a deep frown. "I remember the time she took you to Puerto Rico for your abuelo's funeral."

"My abuelo?"

"Your grandpa. She had just laid you down for a nap when she heard you laughing. She went into your room and she said you and your grandpa were playing peek-a-boo." Garza's cloudy gaze sharpened and he looked at me with smiling eyes. "You were laughing so hard that the whole family came into the room. You and Adela were the only two who saw him."

A tremor of excitement shot to my toes. "She saw him, too?"

Garza nodded. "That's how we solved most of our homicide cases. She spoke to the victims." His voice took on a more eager tone. "Adela was the best detective on the squad." Then his eyes darkened and his features contorted into one massive frown. "Maybe too good."

"What do you mean?" I already sensed his meaning as I swallowed the lump of bile that rose up in my throat.

His gaze dropped to the ground and he picked up a twig, stabbing holes into the dirt. "We were assigned a multiple-homicide. A suspected drug cartel. She knew too much. I think they murdered her."

My poor mom. How could anyone do this to her? To me?

A torrent of feelings ranging from sorrow to hurt to rage infused my skull.

I had never wished anyone dead before but I wanted whoever murdered my mom to pay. "What did you do to them?"

Dropping the stick, he leveled me with blood- shot eyes. "They never caught the guys. I was pulled from the case."

"They killed her and you didn't do anything about it!" Jumping to my feet, I practically screamed. A white hot heat shot through my torso and I clenched my fists, fighting back the urge to strike Garza.

I'd never been so angry in my life. My mom was murdered and what was anyone doing about it? What if she'd gone to a dark place? I shuddered at the thought.

Standing, Garza threw up his hands. "I have a family, too, Krysta. There was nothing me or your dad could do."

"My dad?"

"He was a detective." Garza nodded. "He had to quit to keep you safe."

"Oh-mi-god," I breathed.

Wrapping my arms around my torso, I slid back down to the rock. My entire world was spinning.

No wonder he worked as a security guard all night and drank all day. My dad went from being a homicide detective to a minimum-wage rent-a-cop—all to keep me safe.

He must have really resented me.

That would explain why he had countless women at the apartment but paid no attention to me. That person he'd called my 'mom', she was just a surrogate to fill a void for my real mother.

Still frowning, Garza folded his arms across his chest. "I'm sorry I had to be the one to tell you all this."

I had no response. Life as I knew it would never be the same. The woman who could have brought love and comfort to my life was dead, my dad was a bitter drunk, and the drug lords who murdered my mom were free.

Butt numbing, I sulked on that sandy rock by the beach, barely noticing the cop who had sat down beside me. My tear-soaked eyes had adjusted to the darkness. It could have been daylight outside for all I cared. Nothing really mattered at this point.

My life sucked.

"Krysta, I need a favor."

The pleading in Garza's voice drew me out of my trance.

Looking at him, I saw the deep lines etched around his eyes looked darker than before.

"What?" I asked, not trying to mask the annoyance in my voice.

He needed a favor. The man who did nothing after my mom was murdered.

"You and Bryon are the only witnesses in Sunny's case." Standing, he shook the sand from his jeans. "Her boyfriend is trying to back out of his confession, but you know he did it."

"Yeah, he did it. Sunny told me."

"Raymond was wearing gloves when he murdered her.

Where did he hide them?"

"I don't know." I shrugged while struggling to my knees.

My legs felt so wobbly, but I had to get out of here and back home before Mrs. Dawson caught me. Besides, I'd had enough reality for one night.

"Could you ask Sunny?" Garza held out his hand.

I looked at his outstretched fingers. Was this some kind of peace offering? An apology for not doing all he could for my mother? Or was he just being nice so I'd make solving his case easier?

"She's not talking much."

I took his hand, but only because my body had weakened so much over the past few minutes. I didn't understand this sudden fatigue. Maybe it was stress, but I just wanted to crawl into bed and cry myself to sleep.

"Could you please try?" he asked softly while leveling me with a direct gaze. "We need to make this murder stick. I don't want to see him walk."

I didn't either. Not Raymond. Not any murderer. "Okay," I sighed. "I'll ask her."

"Krysta!" A familiar shrill cry echoed from behind me. "Are you trying to turn all my hair gray?" "I'm sorry." My shoulders fell as I turned to face Mrs. Dawson.

"Officer Garza. What are you doing here?" Mrs. Dawson hissed and her feral glare reminded me of a wild animal protecting her offspring.

Garza threw up his hands. "Just looking for clues."

"Clues?" Her eyes narrowed to slits, before she turned her suspicious gaze on me. "Krysta, what's going on?"

I exhaled slowly. This was going to be a long night. "He wants me to talk to Sunny for him."

She gasped, both hands flying to her mouth. "You told him?"

"No." I shook my head. "He knew my mom. I guess she spoke to ghosts, too."

"Officer!" She nodded toward me, but her fiery gaze was locked on him. "Are you really going to drag this child through a murder case?"

"Just one clue." He held both palms out in a sign of mock

surrender. "That's all I need."

She groaned, then swore—a word I'd never thought Mrs. Dawson would ever use. She marched toward me until we were separated by only a few inches. Pointing a finger in my face, she groaned again. "You know, I'm going to have to speak to your father about this."

"Please don't tell my dad," I whined.

He didn't need one more reason to resent me.

"I'm sorry." Her face hardened. "I can't keep this secret."

I closed my eyes, hoping to chase away another torrent of tears, but it was no use as they slipped from beneath my eyelids.

Opening my eyes again, I wiped my face with the backs of my hands. I tried to give her my most heartfelt, pleading, puppy-dog expression. "He's got enough on his mind."

"I know he does, Krysta," her voice softened and she pulled me into a tight hug.

That hug was just enough to send me over the top and I melted into a pile of heaping sobs in her arms.

It felt good to be hugged, and for a moment, I pretended Mrs. Dawson was Adela.

My real mom who loved me.

Pulling me from her, Mrs. Dawson ended the embrace all too soon and stared down at me with glossy blue eyes. "I'm sorry, dear. If you're going to be looking for clues in a murder case, your father has a right to know."

Chapter Twelve

"You are not to speak to the police again. Understood?"

Uggghhh.

I had been dreading this conversation the entire trip back from the lake, but I didn't think it would happen so soon. I thought Dad would show up tomorrow or the next day, in between work and visits from his girlfriends, which was why I could hardly believe he was waiting for me in Mrs. Dawson's driveway.

That he actually took off work to come here. Like my dad really cared what I did.

Now we were arguing in his rust-bucket car because he refused to go into AJ's house.

"Don't you want to see Sunny's killer go to jail?" I spat while folding my arms across my chest. I was in no mood to argue. I was tired and a spring in my dad's crappy car seat was poking my butt.

"I don't give a damn about her," he growled while clenching the steering wheel. Then his voice dropped to barely a whisper. "I only care about you."

"Yeah, right," I laughed while rolling my eyes.

He was acting way out of character and I didn't like it. Where was the drunk who only wanted me out of his hair? This new dad was weirding me out.

"Krysta." He grimaced, squeezing the steering wheel so tight that veins popped out of his neck. "Don't start with me on that." Letting go of the steering wheel, he pointed a finger at me. "And another thing, if I ever hear about you biking to the lake in the middle of the night again, you'll be grounded for life."

"How would you do that?" I shrugged. "You're never around to ground me."

"That's enough. Buckle up!" He pounded the steering wheel with both fists.

I jumped at his sudden show of force, but I wasn't deterred. Dad had never hit me, but maybe that was because he was too busy ignoring me. "So I get to come home now?"

"Yes." He spoke through a clenched jaw while starting the ignition.

"I still have to get my stuff from AJ's bedroom."

"Well, hurry up," he snapped.

Reluctantly, I fumbled for the handle on the door. I didn't want to go into AJ's house and have him drive off. Some part of me didn't trust my dad to wait around and I still had questions for him.

"We're not done." I let go of the handle while forcing my gaze level with his. A slight tremor was rattling my insides. I wasn't afraid of him. I just wasn't used to talking—really talking with him.

But this issue had been weighing on my mind all the way home from the lake and was too important to dismiss.

His brow furrowed, as he rubbed the stubble on his chin. "What?"

"Why didn't you tell me about my mom?" I spoke through a voice fraught with emotion. Even the mention of Adela and I turned into a big pile of self-pitying goo.

Dad slouched in his seat, moaning into his palms. "Garza told you?"

"Yeah." I nodded, unable to say more.

Sitting upright, he pulled his hands from his face. The lines around Dad's eyes appeared deeper as he turned to me with a stern glare. "Now's not the time for this."

I threw up my hands, determined not to let him brush me off. "When is a good time, Dad? When am I not a major inconvenience to your life?"

"You're not an inconvenience to me, Krysta. I just never planned for our lives to go this way." He lifted his gaze to the ceiling. "You have no idea how hard it is for a single father to raise a teenage girl."

By the way he emphasized the word 'single', I knew what he was implying. He hadn't expected Mom to die and leave him with all the work. One thing he failed to realize was that he wasn't doing all the work. His neglect had forced me to be a self- sufficient teenager. "You're not raising me, Dad. I've been raising myself."

"I'm sorry." He sighed while running a hand through his messy, coarse hair. "I haven't been the best father."

I rolled my eyes while laughing under my breath. "Major understatement."

"You're not going to make this easy, are you?" Dad smiled, though his eyes appeared glossy.

He didn't smell like alcohol tonight. Either he was trying to play the not-drunk-father and had disguised his breath or he was actually ready to cry.

My heart ached a little, but my brain refused to show him any pity. Why should I when he was never around when I needed him?

"I don't do drugs. I don't sneak out with guys. I get good grades—none of it thanks to you," I growled, angry with him for his neglect in the past and pissed at him for waiting until now to show me any fatherly feelings.

"I know." He nodded, his voice sounding choked, before he turned from me and stared out the side window.

So this was my big confrontation with my dad? Him agreeing that he's been a major butthead?

I kind of felt deflated, and for a moment, I had forgotten why we were arguing in the first place.

Adela.

"Why didn't you tell me I had a different mom?" I spoke through clenched teeth. "One who spoke to the dead."

All these years I grew up thinking I was a freak. If I had known I had a mom who was just like me, I would have felt so much better.

Dad jerked, turning to me with glare. "Why was Garza telling you this?"

Dad knew I had the gift, too. I felt it in his panicked voice. I could read it in the way he looked at me—through me.

"Why do you think, Dad?" I raged. He knew about her psychic ability. He knew I spoke to the dead, too, but all this time he ignored it—ignored me!

"Garza is not pulling you into a murder case!" He slammed his fists against the steering wheel again, this time rattling the dashboard. "I knew this would happen!"

My stomach jerked at his reaction. Rage was not a trait I'd been used to seeing in my dad. In fact, I'd never seen Dad show much of any emotion before.

Until now, he'd always been my drunk, complacent dad. A minimum-wage rent-a-cop whose sole purpose was to drink beer and pick up trailer trash. Dad wasn't supposed to have feelings.

In a sudden shift of mood, Dad's hands fell to his sides. His chest caved inward while he dropped his gaze to his lap. "I hear you talking to them," he whispered.

"You do?" It was more of a statement than a question. I guess maybe I couldn't believe he was acknowledging my curse.

"Yeah." He sighed, while slouching in his seat. "Especially at night. That's when they used to visit your mom."

My throat went dry and then choked with emotion. She was like me in so many ways. I knew I'd have a better understanding of myself if she was here with me now.

Why isn't she here with me now?

My mother was dead, but she didn't have to be dead to me.

Unless she was in a dark place like Sunny.

Neither of us spoke for several moments. Too many thoughts were running through my brain and I didn't know what to say next. I did realize that talking about my mom was too much for me right now. Too much raw, unchecked emotion. I needed to adjust to the fact that Adela was my mom. That she died, and for some reason, she wasn't visiting me.

When I looked over at Dad, my jaw dropped.

Silent tears streamed down his face as he stared blankly into his palms. What was he feeling? Did he miss her, too? I suddenly understood better why he drank. It didn't make it right, but it explained a lot.

Maybe that's why he ignored me. What if I reminded him too much of her? Or maybe he was just too depressed to take care of me.

Either way, it didn't matter now. A killer could go free if I didn't help Officer Garza.

Clearing my throat, I summoned the courage to speak. "All I want to do is put a killer behind bars. If I could just ask Sunny where he put the gloves."

Dad's eyes lit up again, a raging fire burning beneath two wide orbs. "He could go after you if he finds out you're involved!" he yelled.

"He's in jail, Dad." I forced a shrill laugh, trying to make it seem as if he was making a big deal out of nothing. "Let me help with this one case. Let me help Sunny."

He shook his head. "Just one murder case. That's how your mom got started. Soon Garza will be knocking on our door every week."

"This is different," I pleaded. "I knew Sunny when she was alive. I have to help her."

Leaning his head against the driver's window, Dad heaved a sigh. Closing his eyes, he spoke with a voice thick with pain. "God, you're so much like your mother."

Folding my arms across my chest, I was resolved to win this battle. "If you drive me back to the lake tonight, we can get this over with."

His eyes flew open and he turned to me with a strange expression—half scowl, half smile. "Are you serious?"

"Fine." I shrugged, turning my gaze to a chipped fingernail, pretending I didn't need his help. "I'll just wait 'till you're at work and go by myself."

"No!" Dad swallowed, his chest heaved with a deep breath and then he squeezed his kneecaps with shaky hands. "If I take you tonight, you've got to promise me this will be the last time."

He was going to take me! My dad was actually involved in my life.

My chest warmed, a huge smile spreading across my face. "I promise."

"And no more talking to Garza," he commanded in a stern voice. "You can tell me where the gloves are and I'll contact him."

Just getting Dad to agree to take me to the lake was a huge

accomplishment and I wasn't about to blow it by demanding I talk to Garza. "Okay."

Groaning, he rolled his head back, slumping against the seat in a sign of defeat. "I can't believe I'm agreeing to this."

I couldn't either, but I was grateful, very grateful for his involvement in my life. For once, he actually showed he cared.

"Thanks, Dad." Leaning over, I kissed his cheek. He kind of looked like he needed it. Besides, I wanted him to understand how important his involvement was to me.

I was almost afraid to get my stuff from AJ's house now. I feared he'd change his mind and bolt, but I pushed aside my worries and ran into AJ's house, packing within a matter of minutes.

To my relief, he was still in the car when I ran out the door. Looking through the windshield, I almost forgot that the man in the driver's seat was my dad.

He wore a grim expression, but I read tenderness in his soft gaze.

Did he really care about me?

"Sunny?" Though dawn was breaking, the lake felt colder, more desolate. Even with my dad standing only a few feet behind me, I'd never had such a feeling of emptiness. Like a giant tornado had sucked my soul from my chest. I recognized this feeling whenever I was near Sunny's spirit, but with each visit, it was getting worse. Was her world growing darker? Was I feeling her emptiness?

"Sunny?" I cried again. I knew by the darkness inside my heart, she was nearby. So why wasn't she answering?

"Who's he?" The voice echoed inside my head, around me, then it resonated behind me.

She was standing next to my dad, looking at him with a sideways glare.

I didn't like it.

A powerful urge swept through me.

Get Dad away from here.

I held out both palms. "He's my dad."

She continued to leer at him through pale features.

Dad looked at me wide-eyed, standing perfectly still.

He must have felt her presence, too.

"He won't hurt you." I spoke each word with care. Instinct told me she needed to know he came in peace.

Her gaze dropped from him before she turned cold eyes on me. "Why are you here?"

"I don't want to bother you." I swallowed, preparing for the next question. I didn't want to stay here any longer than I had to, so I decided to get to the point. "I just want to know where Raymond's gloves are."

"His gloves?" She spoke with no feeling, but her eyes narrowed to slits.

The mention of his gloves angered her.

"Yeah," I stuttered. "He, he was wearing them when he..."

Tilting her chin, she glared at me with defiance in her translucent eyes. "When he hurt me?"

"Yeah." The mouse inside me squeaked.

"In our special place." Her heated stare was still on me, growing more ominous by the second.

"What special place?" I asked through a shaky voice, not realizing until this moment how much my entire frame was shaking.

Why did this particular ghost rattle my nerves so much when none before her had this effect on me? Would it always be this way with souls who were murdered?

"Why do you want to know about our cave?"

Her hiss sliced through me, sending more chills up my spine.

"Cave?" So that was their special place. The tension in my neck and back coiled even more. I really wanted to ditch this place, but the information I needed was almost in my grasp. "If we find the cave, we can use the gloves to put him in jail."

"He didn't mean to hurt me!" Her shrill, hollow scream, shattered the cool air.

And my nerves.

My legs felt like they would buckle, but I had to finish this thing. Squeezing the tension from my body into two tight fists, I squared my shoulders, hardly believing I was actually defying her. "Yes, he did, Sunny. What he did was wrong."

"No!" She screamed.

Branches from the nearby trees shook.

My dad swore, his eyes looking ready to pop out of his head.

I forced myself to be still, hardening my face and narrowing my eyes. Neither of them could see I was scared. I wouldn't let Sunny use her ghoulish force to bully me and Dad didn't need an excuse to make me leave.

"Sunny, you are dead." I spoke with strength and determination in my voice. "And it's not a good dead. You're in a dark place because you were murdered."

"No." Sunny jerked back, then shook her head. "I can't be talking to you if I'm dead." Her response floated on a whisper.

Her lip turned down in a pout while her translucent limbs shook. She'd instantly transformed from frightening to frightened.

I swallowed hard, then slowly began to breathe deeper. I didn't want to look too confident, but I inwardly smiled. My show of strength was working.

"Sunny, I can talk to spirits."

"If I wait here, he'll come for me. He'll take me to our cave." She looked beyond me, her gaze lost somewhere on the water.

"No!" I barked, summoning all the strength I could muster. This was my last shot to make her accept death. "He's not coming. He's in jail for killing you."

Her hands flew to her mouth, muffling a scream that not only shook the trees but rattled the stagnant air. "You're lying!"

Her spirit vanished into the trees, sucked into some unseen hole until she was no larger than a pin of light.

Then nothing.

I gasped, too stunned to speak for an interminable second. "Sunny, please come back! I don't know what to do." I called into the darkness, knowing my efforts were wasted.

I'd never seen a ghost disappear like that. She had left me disoriented and confused. Where did she go? What was that hole she'd slipped into?

"There's nothing you can do."

Dad's voice brought me back to reality. As I looked up at

his somber expression, I noted all the sharp, severe angles of his face before his image blurred. The flood of tears that filled my eyes made it difficult to see clearly.

Pulling me into his arms, he kissed my forehead and spoke against my ear. "She needs to come to terms with this on her own."

A new wave of tears gushed down my face and I sobbed out loud into his shirt.

How could this have happened? I was only trying to help. Where did she go? Was this an even darker place than before? Was this why Adela never spoke to me? Was my mom in that hole, too?

But that wasn't the only reason I was crying. My dad was finally here for me.

Hugging me.

I sank deeper into his embrace, not caring if I messed up my makeup. Besides, I'd already ruined it earlier tonight.

Slowly, Dad pulled away from me.

Inwardly, I sighed, missing his affection, but I wouldn't tell him I needed another hug.

I suspected he'd had enough of my drama for one night.

"Your mom had cases like this." He spoke while pulling a wadded up napkin from his pocket and handing it to me. "What did Sunny tell you?"

I looked at the napkin and an involuntary groan escaped my lips. He expected me to use this on my face. I wanted to laugh, but didn't. Despite everything that happened tonight, Dad was still Dad.

"She's waiting here for him to take her to a cave." I said while using a corner of the napkin to dab my eye. "I don't get it. Where is there a cave on the lake?"

"Look there across the water." He pointed beyond my shoulder. "They probably took a boat."

Turning, I followed the direction of his extended finger. The blinding orange glow of dawn's first light made it difficult to see anything. I could vaguely see a faint outline of something, maybe an island. "Yeah, maybe."

"Krysta, let it go." Dad turned me back to face him. The lines around his eyes were set deeper, making him look like he'd aged ten years in the past hour. "I'll tell Garza about the cave."

Looking at the man I called my father, I saw more than just a washed-up cop, a failed parent. Somewhere beneath his dark eye-circles, I saw the remnants of a strong man. My chest welled up with hope. Maybe he could be that man again.

I knew my mom's death had a lot to do with who he'd become.

But maybe...

A crazy thought crossed my mind. What if I brought her back in spirit? He might not be able to see her, but I would speak to him through her. Together, Adela and I could bring back my old dad and I could have the mom I'd always wanted.

Kind of.

First, though, I'd need to find Adela.

A lump formed in my chest at the thought of her lost to me. At the thought of her in a dark place.

"Dad?" "Yeah."

"How come Mom never visits me?" He seemed to know about the ghosts who visited her. Maybe she'd told him how to find missing spirits.

"I don't know." He spoke quickly before turning away, his back rigid.

He does know.

He stomped off to the forest trail which led to our car. I had to walk quickly to keep up with his pace.

Fresh tears threatened at the backs of my eyes. I had to use all of my strength to keep from crying again. "Is she in a dark place, too?"

"No." He spoke in a strained voice.

He was keeping something from me. I knew it. Why wouldn't he tell me?

I nearly stumbled over a tree root. After catching up to his backside, I drew a deep breath. "How do you know?"

"I just do." His answer came on a growl. "She used to visit you when you were a baby."

She did?

It didn't make any sense that she'd visit me when I was an infant and not during my teenage years when my power was strengthening and I needed her more than ever. "Why doesn't she visit me now?"

The clearing to our car had come into view. Dad stopped so suddenly that I nearly ran into him.

I gasped when he faced me.

Tears flooded his reddened face. "Krysta," he spoke on an exhale. "I can't talk about your mom anymore."

Private Facebook Rant/ Too tired to care what time it is

Adela, where did you go?

Why can I communicate with people over a hundred years old and rude waitresses but I can't even talk to my own mom?

I've been holed up in my bedroom, crying for what seems like hours. My chest hurts so bad that it feels like it's going to crush my heart.

I need you now, more than I've needed anyone. Where are you? In a dark place like Sunny? Every time I think about you lost and alone and cold, I cry harder.

Garza said you loved me.

If you still do, then please...please come back.

Chapter Thirteen

I couldn't believe I'd agreed to another study session. My brain was so muddled from lack of sleep the night before, I hardly realized I was accepting his text invitation before it was too late. After Dad had finally paid the bill and allowed me to use my phone again, I had so many messages to answer, I hardly remembered which ones I'd replied to, let alone what I'd written.

I had way too much to do instead of wasting my time at Bryon's house, like really studying for this test tomorrow or organizing the protest at the mall site this weekend. Okay, so maybe there wasn't that much to organize. A few text messages to AJ and Sophie and the 'so called protest' was scheduled for Saturday morning.

The protest was another reason I shouldn't have accepted his invite tonight. This was the house of the enemy, even though Bryon probably viewed his dad as more of an enemy than I did. How would he feel if he knew I was protesting his dad's career? I was afraid to know the answer.

And now here I was, sitting across from the cutest and most complex guy in the school, having the most nauseating feeling of déjà vu.

The maid tried to force-feed me soda and cookies. Bryon and his dad had yet another fight at the table. Now, he was pouting instead of studying and we were getting nowhere with a test tomorrow.

I should have been mad at Bryon for wasting my time, for making me feel totally uncomfortable while he argued with his dad. But Sophie's words echoed through my brain.

He's feeling a great sense of abandonment. And anger.

I sensed the anger part, but who abandoned him? Did his father have something to do with it? Was that why he was so angry?

Despite the way he treated his dad, he was always nice to me and I couldn't forget the way he stood up for Sunny that night at the café. I thought about the friendly way he spoke to Mrs. Jackson and the other kids in class, even to Grody Cody Miller, the kid who'd crapped his pants on the bus. Bryon was a nice guy, a sweetheart. There had to be a reason why he hated his dad so much.

One thing I did know, we weren't going to get any studying done when he was so busy fuming over his dad—with all this tension hanging between us. Maybe if I got him to open up about his problems, he'd release some of his pent up anger.

I swallowed hard, thinking how best to approach the subject. "Can I ask you something?"

"What?" He mumbled, too lost in his own thoughts to glance in my direction.

I decided the best option was to be blunt. "Why do you hate your dad?"

He jerked, dropping the pencil as his wide gaze darted to me.

My heart melted.

At first I thought I'd angered him, but I read only hurt in his glossy eyes.

"He cheated on my mom." He spoke through a shaky lip before turning his gaze downward.

The whole abandonment thing suddenly made sense to me. His mom walked out on the family just as my fake mom did and he blamed his dad.

Bryon coughed once into his hand and then picked up his pencil, scribbling something on his notebook.

He wasn't fooling me. I knew his mom leaving was hard to talk about. I also knew, from a very personal experience, he couldn't go on with all this hate in his heart.

For his own good, I had to make him talk about it. "Is that why she left you?"

His eyes shot up again, narrowing. This time he clutched the pencil so tightly his knuckles turned white. "She didn't leave me," he spat. "She divorced him and took me."

"I'm sorry," I murmured, feeling like a complete idiot.

"It's not your fault." He smiled weakly, but the slight turn of his mouth wasn't enough to mask the pain in his eyes. "My step-dad abused her."

"Oh." I didn't know what else to say. Bryon's issues were way deeper than I'd imagined.

Bryon shrugged, his arms and shoulders looking kind of limp with the effort. "And then one night he..."

His voice cracked and he said no more. Wiping his eyes with the backs of his hands, he stood and walked to the kitchen counter. Grabbing a cookie, he stuffed the whole thing in his mouth, chewing while staring blankly at the wall.

Bryon didn't need to say any more. I knew his step-dad killed his mom. Now I understood why he was so protective of Sunny that night. Why he'd gotten so emotional over her death when he hardly knew her. I also knew why he hated his dad. If Mr. Thomas hadn't cheated on Bryon's mom, they might still be married and she'd be alive.

It was easy to see Bryon's hatred for his dad was consuming him, cutting into his study time and his social life. He couldn't ever be happy with so much rage in his heart.

I needed to make him understand. "Do you think it's good for you to hate your dad so much?"

Bryon swallowed his cookie, looking me over with a sneer. "You don't know what I feel. Your mom wasn't murdered."

"Actually..." I tilted my chin, meeting his angry gaze "...she was killed by drug lords."

His shoulders fell, his entire frame turning inward. "Sorry. I didn't mean to be an ass."

"That's okay." I shrugged. "You didn't know." How did he go from enraged teen to pitiful puppy in a split second? I suspected he didn't know how to deal with his emotions after his mom's death. I wondered if his dad had been there to comfort him or if he just wanted him out of the way.

Bryon absently popped another cookie in his mouth while staring at the wall behind me.

Leaning forward, I splayed both hands on the table, clearing my throat until he caught my gaze. "My dad and I have issues, but I don't hate him. He's the only parent I've got left."

Bryon shrugged, reaching for yet another cookie. "Not me and my dad."

I shook my head, realizing his issues were way worse than mine. "Maybe you two should go to therapy or something."

"He doesn't want to do therapy." He rolled his eyes while throwing both hands in the air. "He's too busy with this stupid mall project."

"Yeah," I cringed, "about that mall."

Bryon laughed. "I can get you the gift cards. He's got a drawer full."

"I don't want any gift cards." I vigorously shook my head, hardly believing those words came from my mouth. "My friends and I are protesting the mall this weekend."

His mouth fell open, cookie crumbles dropping to the floor. "What?"

"They're building it on an old cemetery."

His features sharpened, a hint of anger flashing in his eyes. "They are?"

"Yeah." I swallowed a lump in my throat. "They should respect the dead."

His lips contorted, making him look like he was either frowning or masking a smile. "My dad's gonna be pissed."

My mouth had suddenly gone dry, my whole body feeling as if it would crack in two. I really didn't want Bryon to hate me for this. Even if he didn't like his dad, I was sure he liked the money that came with his dad's job. "Sorry."

"Don't be." He broke into a grin that nearly stretched from ear to ear. "What time's the protest? I want to go."

Chapter Fourteen

Tossing my book bag on the floor, I sank onto my lumpy mattress and mindlessly stared at the stain-splattered ceiling.

I was tired and disoriented, probably from too little sleep and too much stress. Groaning into my palms, I tried not to think about my chemistry exam score.

Mrs. Jackson had my exam graded in a matter of seconds. Fifty elements correct out of 103. My teacher must have thought I was a total waste, more interested in make-up than in school. Luckily, she'd agreed to let me redo the test next week. I was determined to pass, and that meant plenty of study time—alone.

No Bryon, no drama, no ghosts. Well, the ghosts weren't so much the problem anymore and I was wondering, even a little worried about where they went.

A light breeze blew against my skin, hardly worth noticing unless you were someone like me. I recognized the slightly tingly sensation, like fairy dust was falling on me from above.

Looking up, I smiled at their hovering forms. "Hey, you two; where've you been?" I squinted, having to do a double-take as I looked into the pale faces of Ed and Gertrude. I didn't know if it was possible, but their apparitions looked even more translucent.

Ed's entire face was a mask of stone, even his crazy eye stilled. "We're slippin', Emmy."

"What?" I choked, as a rush of fear shot straight to my heart. I sat up, leaning my tired bones against the headboard.

Gertrude splayed both her hands wide, pointing at the

floor with her fingers. "We're losing the only thing tyin' us to this earth."

"What does that mean?" I asked through a shaky voice, already afraid I knew the answer.

"We're fading, Emmy." Ed shrugged, his eyes reflecting a resigned sense of despair. "After they finish diggin' next week, we'll be gone."

"No!" I shouted, my limbs shaking with rage.

How could the developers do this to two harmless souls? Didn't they know that by desecrating their graves, they were destroying their spirits?

"We didn't want ta have to tell you this." Gertrude smiled, her lips trembling with the movement. "That's why we've been keepin' away. We know it's not your fault."

My back rigid, I came up on my knees, leveling them both with a determined stare. "My friends and I are protesting the mall tomorrow. Just try to hold on."

"You're a real good girl, Emmy Jane." Ed floated down to my level, his lower body disappearing beneath my bed. "We want you to know that...just in case we don't make it." He made a gesture of squeezing my shoulder.

Looking into his weird, but tender gaze, my resolve was hardened even more. "You will make it. I'm going to fight for you."

Oh-mi-god.

I'd never been so scared in all my life. No ghost or ghoul or bump in the night even came close to the terror I felt while staring into the lens of the television camera.

This was no way to begin my career in fashion. Models had to smile for cameras all the time.

Thank God Sophie and AJ were with me. They stood at my back while Mindy Mays from Seven News applied her lipstick. I should have felt comforted with my two BFFs behind me, but I was so nervous, my ankles wobbled in my mid-calf boots.

Breathe, Krysta, Breathe.

I didn't want to dwell on the fact that all of Greenwood would soon know I was trying to sabotage the mall. Looking around me, I tried to remember this place as a cemetery. We were standing on the top of a gentle grassy slope, so the people on the road could get a good view of the protest. I imagined the giant oak tree was once on this slope and Ed and Gertrude were buried beneath me. At the bottom of the slope, closer to the road, was a makeshift, gravelly parking lot. Probably where the developers parked their luxury cars.

The reporter, with big buggy eyes that looked drawn in with permanent marker, turned her penetrating gaze to me. "Ready kid?"

My mind went blank. "I...I..."

Without waiting for me to answer, she turned to the lens. "Mindy Mays here at the future site of Greenwood's first mall, The Crossover. I'm talking to a ninth grader from Greenwood Junior High, Krysta Richards, who is protesting the mall development. So tell me Krysta, what made you decide to protest?"

Her wide gaze focused on me and I wanted to squirm out of my skin. I tried to swallow a lump in my throat that would not go down, making me feel like I had a banana in my windpipe.

After averting my gaze from the reporter, somehow I found the courage to look sideways into the lens. "They're building it over a graveyard." My voice sounded strange, like it came from some small child.

"Yes, but it's centuries old." She motioned to the old crumbled tombstones behind us with a flick of the wrist. "No one in Greenwood has claimed ancestry here."

Her casual attitude was annoying. I knew who was buried there, but I couldn't tell her that. Still, that shouldn't have mattered. "That doesn't mean we should disrespect the dead," I huffed, summoning courage to raise my voice.

She flashed a wide smile with what looked like miles of white teeth. Then the reporter laughed while leering at me through lowered eyelids. "What makes a fourteen-year-old girl take such an interest in the city's history?"

This woman had me unhinged. Not only was she condescending, she was just plain annoying.

And I was so angry, I couldn't think to speak. "I- I just..."

"She just believes in doing what's right!"

The unmistakable tenor of Bryon's booming voice echoed from somewhere behind me.

I gasped when I turned and saw him standing on top of a parked tractor. Wearing a tombstone shaped 'Stop the Desecration' sign around his neck, Bryon was dressed in a black and white skeleton leotard.

My stomach did a little flip at the sight, compelled by a strange mixture of nausea and pride.

Thank God he didn't paint his face, too. That would have been creepy overload.

Mindy Mays gawked at Bryon and then turned back to me. For an eternal second, she was speechless.

Looking into the camera lens, she wore a grim expression. "Well you heard it here first on TV Seven at Five. Local girl puts morals before the mall."

A deafening roar erupted from behind the camera man.

Mindy yelped.

I shuddered at the sight of Bryon's dad charging toward us like an enraged bull.

"Wait!" Mindy waved at the camera man to turn to Bryon's dad. "I think that's Cliff Thomas coming this way. Mr. Thomas just announced his candidacy for mayor and is also the leading developer for The Crossover."

Stomping up to Bryon, he grabbed him by the arm and jerked him off the tractor.

Bryon shoved his dad, but Mr. Thomas held his ground, then leaned over and grumbled something into Bryon's ear.

Even though I couldn't hear what he was saying, I got the feeling it wasn't good.

Pulling Bryon by the elbow, Mr. Thomas marched him down the slope, making a wide circle around the camera crew.

Mindy chased after them; like an idiot, I chased after her.

Waving her arms, Mindy's heeled feet bent awkwardly as she tried to maneuver the grassy terrain. She looked like a deranged chicken.

"Mr. Thomas, may we have a word with you?"

"No," he barked. "Not today."

She was undaunted. "Will this protest effect construction

of The Crossover?"

"This is not a protest!" He screamed, his pale face taking on the color of an overripe apple. "It's just a kid's prank gone too far." His angry gaze shot straight to me, his cold eyes narrowing before he turned back to the reporter. "If you will excuse me, I have a personal matter to attend."

The anger in his eyes shocked and scared me. I looked at Bryon for some reassurance.

He only stared at his feet, mouth turned in a pout as he allowed his dad to lead him away by the elbow.

Mindy Mays chased them again as they headed toward the parking lot. "Mr. Thomas, is this protester your son?"

"Turn the camera off!" Anyone within a ten mile radius could have heard Mr. Thomas yelling at the reporter as he shoved Bryon into the passenger seat of his car.

Bryon slouched in his seat, covering his face with his hands.

I just wanted to sink into the dirt and disappear. This protest was a total disaster and now I'd caused an even bigger rift between Bryon and his dad.

Mindy Mays straightened her shoulders and looked at the camera, her eyes animated with excitement. "Well, you saw it first on Seven. A very angry Cliff Thomas, mayoral candidate and mall developer, has just hauled a young man, who is protesting the mall development, into his car. I'm assuming the boy is a relation, possibly even his son. Tune in while we keep you posted on this developing story."

I groaned as I wondered just how this story would develop.

"Home." I breathed the word while propping my knee on the paint peeled doorframe, fumbling in my purse for the key.

Even if it was a dingy apartment, it was my apartment and was far away from cemeteries, television crews and irate dads. All I wanted to do was sink into my lumpy mattress and pretend this day never happened.

Flinging open the door, I was startled by the site of my dad's latest flavor of the month, April, sprawled out on the living room floor. The small gray sofa with rips in the cushions and Dad's recliner with the broken handle, which made the chair permanently recline, were pushed against the side wall. Our coffee table with the super-glued leg was weighing down the cushions of the sofa, looking ready to crash to the floor. April had completely rearranged the furniture in our living room, all so she could watch my Yoga DVD and use my Yoga mat.

This new girlfriend was probably no older than twenty-five. I'd asked my dad her age more than once, but he claimed not to know. I had a feeling he didn't care how old she was, as long as she was legal.

I tried to push back the rising tide of irritation that twisted a knot in my gut. I shouldn't have been annoyed by her presence. So far, this flavor of the month had been nice to me. Besides, she wasn't hurting my mat. Although, she might sweat all over it.

Gross.

Then I noticed her over-bleached, dried out hair was pulled back with one of my headbands.

I suppressed a growl.

"Hi, Krysta," she half-squealed in that high- pitched whine of hers.

I cringed. Her voice affected my nerves like nails on a chalkboard.

"Aren't you going to say 'hi'?" Mouth twisted in a pout, she looked at me from between her legs in a very awkward 'down dog' position.

I didn't want to be the one to tell her that her butt was sticking up way too far. "Hi." I shrugged my purse to the floor, looking around the room. "Where's my dad?"

"He's in the bedroom getting ready for work." She moved to a meditative pose, grinding her butt into my mat.

I only hoped her sweats were clean.

My eyes bulged at the top she was wearing with the sweatpants. The shirt was way too stylish for Yoga and the whole ensemble looked weird.

Judging by the fine trim on the sleeves and collar, I knew the shirt was expensive.

"Nice shirt." The words froze mid-air as they slipped off

my tongue. A little pulse in my neck jumped as I glared at the square cut bottom with a tapered waist.

"Thanks." She shrugged with a flick of the wrist. As if the shirt was nothing special.

As if.

Folding my arms across my chest, I narrowed my gaze. "I have one just like it."

She matched my glare with one of her own, a smug smile plastered across her face. "I know."

"Is that my shirt?" Pressure built at the back of my eyeballs and I felt ready to explode.

Her smile widened and she batted painted eyelids. "I hope you don't mind."

"I saved up for a month to buy it," I growled, feeling steaming jets of rage pummeling my brain.

Laughing, she rolled her eyes. "I won't ruin it."

"You could have asked," I hissed through clenched teeth. I wasn't buying her act. She was pretending that stealing my stuff was no big deal, but it was to me.

"And you could be nicer." She jumped to her feet, rolling her head like she had some major attitude. "I'm the one who is stuck babysitting you at nights."

"What?" I nearly choked. "I don't need you to babysit me!"

My mind raced, my heart plummeted. Had my dad gone demented? Fourteen years of neglect, and now he turns me over to some brainless trailer trash?

April gave me the head-to-toe once over, twisted her lips into a scowl and then hollered over her shoulder. "Andy! The kid's starting with me already!"

Just then, my dad came out of his bedroom door, adjusting the collar on his security guard uniform.

"What's going on here?" he grumbled.

Without looking at my dad, April pointed at me with an obnoxious smile. "She walked in the house with a chip on her shoulder."

Gawd, was she my babysitter or my new big sister? She couldn't have acted any more immature. What was my dad thinking? I was so angry. I felt like crying, but I didn't want to give April that satisfaction. "I don't need a babysitter. I'm fourteen!"

"Krysta." Dad nodded to April while he straightened his tie. "You need someone to look after you." His tone sounded way too stern, like he was suddenly a father in control.

My jaw dropped, my vision tunneling on this guy who was wearing my dad's clothes. His hair was cut and combed and his face was smooth. No nicks and clumps of shaving cream stuck to his neck.

Who was this guy? Did he think I was dumb enough to fall for his sudden transformation? If he was going to act the part of the responsible parent, he'd have to find me a better role model than some girl he dragged home from the bar.

I blew out an irritated breath. "And you think April is mature enough to be my babysitter? She's like twenty."

"For your information, I'm twenty-four and you're not going to sneak out to the lake on my watch." She turned up her chin, a triumphant smile stretched across her annoying face.

I just wanted to slap her—and my dad. "You told her?" My heart plummeted and I felt terribly betrayed. Had he told April I spoke to the dead? I'd thought that was our secret. Not all of the years of his neglect could even compare to the pain I was feeling.

"Of course, he told me." Her voice took on an even more grating tone as she waggled her head like one of those bobble-head dolls. "Sneaking off to the lake to meet your friends. I don't know what you kids do at the lake at two a.m., probably drugs." She made this weird snorting sound, like her nose was choking on boogers.

My anger abated slightly as short sigh of relief wheezed through my clenched teeth. So Dad hadn't told her what I was doing at the lake. I'd rather she think I was a user than know the truth.

"April." Dad sighed, glaring at her from the corners of his eyes. "I told you my daughter doesn't do drugs."

She walked up to him, jabbing a finger in his chest. "Andy, you have to stop being so trusting."

Trusting? What was so 'trusting' about taking clothes without permission?

"She didn't even ask if she could wear my shirt." I cringed

at the whining sound that had slipped into my own voice. This was pathetic. I felt like I was stuck in a really bad reality show.

"Krysta," Dad groaned, throwing both hands into the air. "Can April wear your shirt?"

"No." Folding my arms across my chest, I tried to keep my voice even, controlled. Let Dad see who is mature and who is not. "That's my most expensive shirt."

Looking from me to his girlfriend, Dad took a deep breath, bringing his hands to his sides. "April, take off the shirt."

She gasped, her lips turning in a pout. "Andy, whose side are you on?"

Dad's face showed no emotion as he casually shook his head. "I know what's best for my daughter. I'm not listening to you anymore."

"Fine." Stomping her foot, she made a very dramatic sweep to Dad's bedroom, slamming the door behind her.

Dad turned to me with a soft smile, fatigue clearly showing in the deep lines around his eyes. "Sorry. You okay?"

I shrugged one shoulder while jutting a hand on my hip. "As soon as I get my shirt back."

Dad had the nerve to laugh.

I didn't know why his laughter annoyed me, but it did. I guess I had grown comfortable with him ignoring me, not taking my side in an argument and then asking if I was okay.

Weird.

His new attitude would take some getting used to. Luckily, I had planned to camp out somewhere else tonight. "Can I spend the night at AJ's?"

His smile dropped before he plastered on another one. "Yeah, what do you girls have planned?" Dad looked down at his shirt, adjusting cuffs that were already in place.

What was going on with him?

"We're making bigger protest signs. They're building The Crossover Mall over a cemetery and we're protesting again tomorrow."

His jaw slackened, eyes widening. "Have you gone crazy? You love shopping."

Yeah, I did love shopping, but I didn't think my dad ever paid attention to my passion. Up until recently, I hadn't thought he'd paid attention to me at all.

I couldn't refrain from smiling. "I think I am crazy."

He cocked a brow. "Let me guess, a couple of ghosts convinced you to do it."

"Something like that." I half shrugged and turned away, not wanting him to see how his attention was affecting me.

I felt so strange. Kind of bubbly inside. All because my dad was interested in my life. I used to wonder if he'd miss me if I never came home. How long would it take him to notice if I ran away? I'd always felt like a fly on the wall in his world and now he was finally acting like a parent.

"What time's the protest?" Dad's voice sounded strained. Then he made a strange rumble like he had something stuck in his throat.

"At two." Keeping my eyes focused on the puke green fridge in our compact kitchen, I answered without turning to look at him.

"Do you need a ride?"

"No." I shrugged, focusing my attention on a speck of dirt under my nail. "Mrs. Dawson..."

"Yeah, I should have guessed," Dad groaned. "Other people are always looking after my kid."

"I thought you liked it that way." I spoke, barely a whisper, as my throat tightened with emotion.

I heard something fall behind me. Turning on my heel, I saw Dad on his knees, fighting with the broken leg on the coffee table. The splintered wood would not go back into the slot. Swearing, he threw the leg across the room.

What was up with my Dad? He looked ready to cry.

Just then, April stormed out of the bedroom and threw my shirt at Dad. Jerking open the front door, she flung herself through the doorway like a true drama queen and slammed the door behind her.

The poor rusty hinges practically screamed in protest.

Dad looked at me with a huge goofy grin.

I couldn't help but laugh out loud.

Dad stood up and tossed the shirt to me. "I've got to get to work. Come on. I'll give you a ride to AJ's."

After I grabbed my overnight bag, I hurried to meet Dad in

the apartment parking lot. I had no idea what was going on with him, or why he was suddenly this new person. Even though this afternoon was totally awkward, I still hoped my new dad would stick around for a while.

But I wasn't holding my breath.

Too many years of neglect had taught me not to hope for anything.

Chapter Fifteen

Once again, I felt like I was stuck in the middle of a really bad dream. My friends and I had been touting protest signs for over an hour.

Sunday traffic wasn't heavy, but those who did drive by didn't seem to notice us. I didn't know why I had this crazy idea onlookers would sympathize with my noble cause and join the protest.

The air was hot and humid, making my hair frizz even more than usual. Dark clouds overhead threatened rain. I silently prayed some of the wet stuff would fall on my head and weigh down my dandelion-do.

The flimsy sign I held over my head was feeling like a dead-weight. AJ and I had slept in this morning, but for some reason, I was still bone-tired.

That's when I saw the Channel Seven van pull into the gravelly parking lot.

Great. They had to wait until the weather zapped my hair into a ginormous, magnetic frizz- ball.

Mindy walked across the gravelly road in her heels and business suit. Hadn't she learned anything after last time?

AJ snorted out loud and Sophie squealed into her hands when Mindy fell over. Her whole body tumbled down like a crumbling tower of wooden blocks.

Her camera man rushed to pick her up and she managed to make it to the grass by holding onto his arm.

You don't have to be a fashion diva to know grass and stilettos don't mix, like sinking toothpicks through quicksand.

With each step, Mindy made this little high pitched squeaking sound, as she inched her way toward me.

When she finally arrived at our protest sight, I could tell she wasn't amused by AJ's gloating grin.

I shot AJ a warning look. I needed this woman on my side if I wanted to win my cause.

After Mindy glared at AJ, she applied fresh lipstick and then the camera was rolling.

"Mindy Mays reporting for Seven News where we're live at Greenwood's future site of The Crossover Mall for day two of a protest initiated by junior high student, Krysta Richards. Until recently, many Greenwood residents weren't aware that The Crossover is also the site of an early pioneer burial ground. No one from Greenwood claims ancestry to the residents of this decrepit graveyard, but that hasn't stopped Krysta Richards, who says the dead must be respected."

I inwardly groaned at the tone the news reporter used when quoting me, as if this was all some big joke.

"Joining me now are Krysta and her friends, other Greenwood Junior High students."

The camera briefly turned on AJ and Sophie. They smiled and waved their signs. Sophie squealed like a mouse. AJ was hooting and hollering like she was trying to distract the rival pitcher in a softball game.

Mindy waved her hand at them, like she was shooing away a cat. I guess she wanted them to be quiet.

They both took the hint, but only after AJ stuck her tongue out at the camera.

I wanted my own stilettos, so I could sink into the ground and hide.

"Krysta, have you gotten any response from the mall developers?"

The camera was back on me and I wondered if all my hair fit in the picture.

"No," I sighed. "Not really."

"Why should we respect these gravesites?" She swept her hand across the expanse of grass behind us. "No one even knows who's buried here."

Okay, now I was angry. "Why should that make a

difference? We've all got family members who've died. We wouldn't want anyone disrespecting their graves."

Just then, I heard some commotion behind me. I turned to see Bryon high-fiving AJ and Sophie. My heart swelled. How did he get here? After he didn't answer my texts last night, I was sure he was grounded.

Mindy rushed over to him with her wobbly- legged chicken walk. "I see another protester has joined the group. Could you tell us your name, young man?"

Bryon grinned at me and then looked directly into the camera. "Bryon Thomas."

Mindy licked her lips, her eyes taking on a feral glare. "Are you related to mayoral candidate and mall developer, Cliff Thomas?"

"Yeah." He shrugged.

Poor Bryon was Mindy's lamb on the slaughter. I knew she was only interested in Bryon because his dad was running for mayor. Suddenly, I realized why she'd come back to my pathetic little protest—it wasn't to dig up dirt on the cemetery. No, she was after a bigger story.

Heat filled my chest and flamed my face. I had the most awful feeling of being used.

"In what way are you related to Mr. Thomas?" Mindy had shoved the microphone so far into his face, Bryon was close to choking on it.

"He's my dad." Bryon grimaced, pushing away the mike.

Her eyes were alert. Her features sharpened. If she were a wolf, she would've been howling. "How does your dad feel about you protesting the mall?"

I could tell by the deep mar in his forehead and his twisted scowl, Bryon was unhappy with her questions. "You should ask him."

She was unfazed. "Why are you out here, Bryon?"

For a moment, he looked like he'd walk away from the camera. So many emotions crossed his face at once that I couldn't gauge his mood. His eyes glossed over and I knew he was on the verge of crying.

"My mom is dead. I wouldn't want anyone tearing up her grave."

"I see." Mindy's voice dropped, her mouth turning in a heavy pout. After what sounded like a forced sigh, she paused long enough to appear sorry for Bryon's loss. "And here comes Cliff Thomas right now. Zoom in on this. I can tell by the look on his face, he is not pleased with this protest."

I looked beyond the camera and past the gravelly parking lot. A luxury car had come to a screeching halt. Mr. Thomas bounded out, and in a few long strides, came storming up to us.

"Mr. Thomas!" Mindy crowed.

"Not now," he growled, turning his back on the camera. "I'm just here to collect my son." He scowled at Bryon and with a rigid arm, pointed toward the car.

Bryon wasn't looking at his dad.

His pale puppy dog gaze was focused on me.

I wanted to melt at the look of anguish in his eyes. He was such a nice guy for doing this and I felt so bad for him. I couldn't imagine having Mr. Thomas for a dad. What it must be like for Bryon to live with him. For once in my life, I actually felt grateful for my father.

Tossing up his hands in an apologetic gesture, Bryon slanted a crooked smile in my direction before he turned and shuffled his feet toward the car.

His dad stormed off behind him.

Mindy followed.

Rolling my eyes, I swore under my breath as my feet propelled me forward.

Here we go again.

"How do you feel about your son protesting your development?" Mindy called.

Mr. Thomas swung around, almost going nose-to-nose with the reporter. "I said, not now!"

She jerked her head back and I could see her limbs visible shaking. Then she chased them again. "Will this have any effect on your run for mayor?"

This woman was nuts.

Bryon had already taken a seat inside the car. He slouched down while he fumbled with the buttons on the stereo.

"Turn off the camera," Mr. Thomas growled as he swung open his car door. "Please respect my privacy."

"Like you're respecting these gravesites?"

A strangely familiar, deep male voice rumbled behind me.

I swung around, half-believing who I saw.

"Zoom in on the cop," Mindy squealed.

Dad, still in his security guard uniform, walked down the grassy hill toward us holding up AJ's 'Respect the Dead! Preserve their Past!' picket sign. He threw the sign to the ground, pointing to the gravely drive. "These people deserve a proper resting place. Not crushed tombstones and a parking lot."

Bryon's dad actually slammed his car door and walked up to my dad.

My heart thumped so loudly in my chest, it threatened to explode my eardrums.

"They're dead!" He yelled. "What do they care?"

Dad bridged the distance between them until they were within punching distance.

I was about to crap my pants.

Puffing up his chest, Dad looked Mr. Thomas square in the eyes. "So let's just build over all the tombstones in Greenwood, even your late wife's."

Mr. Thomas took a step backward, wiping perspiration off his brow. "I don't know who you are." He spoke through a shaky voice. "You've got no business talking about my son's mother that way."

Dad folded his arms across his chest, his face a mask of stone. "And you've got no business desecrating a cemetery. There are mothers and fathers here, too."

Without another word, Mr. Thomas turned and marched back to his car. Barely getting the door shut, he punched the gas and tore out of the parking lot with squealing tires.

Mouth agape, I stood there staring at the retreating dust cloud and then to my dad.

My dad.

This guy in uniform who actually appeared sober and in control of a situation.

From the corner of my eye, I spied Mindy standing in front of the billowing cloud of dust made by Mr. Thomas's car. It made quite a dramatic backdrop.

She was grinning ear to ear before the camera lens turned on her. Then, she plastered on a grim expression, as if she was about to report World War III.

"Well, there you have it. Mall developer, Cliff Thomas, is in the hot seat today as he faces protesters accusing him of desecrating a burial ground. One of those protesters is his own son."

The dust cloud inched toward her and she waved her hand in front of her face while choking on fumes. "So much discord in his personal life amid his bid for mayor," she sighed. "How will this affect his future in politics? Will this stop construction of The Crossover Mall? We'll keep you posted only here on Seven News, Greenwood's information connection."

My heart sank.

Was Mindy right? Had this protest really caused this much trouble for Bryon and his dad? If this interfered with his run for mayor, would he resent Bryon?

Would Bryon resent me?

Sitting in my dad's car, I toyed with a crease in the corner of my 'Respect the Dead' poster. I still had a hard time believing I was in my dad's car, that he'd come to support me and then offered me a ride home. "I didn't think you'd come."

My dad's face had been difficult to read since I first saw him at the protest. He kept his stony gaze on the cracked windshield, both hands on the wheel. "This is important to you."

"Thanks," I murmured, not really sure what to say next.

Dad's response was to squeeze the steering wheel until his knuckles whitened. "You don't need to thank me. I'm your dad. I should be doing this."

The muscles in my neck and back tensed. Was I his charity case now? I didn't want a dad who only did stuff for me because he 'should'. I wanted a dad who really cared. "You don't have to do things with me just because you're my dad."

"I want to, Krysta. I want to be a better father." Dad stopped at a red light and turned to me, his eyes had softened.

"Okay." I shrugged, feeling kind of choked up inside.

"You know..." He coughed into his hand and looked at me with searching eyes, like he was trying to find the right words to say. "I don't think I'll ever be comfortable with your other friends."

"You mean spirits?" I laughed.

"Yeah. Adela used to do this kind of stuff and look what happened to her." He sounded like he had to struggle to get out those last words.

The light turned green and he focused on the road.

I could tell talking about this was hard for him.

"I'll be careful." I tried to reassure him.

"That's what she said." He squeezed the steering wheel so hard that it looked like his fingers would snap.

"I can't just ignore my powers." I spoke with determination in my voice. If he really wanted to be my father, he'd have to accept me for who I was.

"No." He shrugged. "I guess you can't." His voice trailed off as he kept his gaze firmly on the road.

I knew he was lost in thought somewhere, but at the moment, I didn't want to know what he was thinking.

"I spoke with Garza," Dad blurted.

I didn't know if his change in subject was a good thing.

"What'd you talk about?" I asked, wondering if I really wanted to know the answer.

"He found the gloves. It's all over for the boyfriend."

"That's good." I exhaled, not realizing until that moment I'd been holding my breath.

I'd been kind of regretting that promise I'd made to my dad not to go back to the lake. Not a day had passed that I didn't wonder what happened to Sunny. Would she be forever stuck in darkness or would her boyfriend's arrest force her to accept her death and move on to a better place?

"He's not contacting you again or he'll have to deal with one pissed-off dad."

"He was nice." I tried to shrug off the dull pain that settled in my chest.

"I don't care, Krysta. He'll involve you with more cases— dangerous cases. Once was enough."

"All right," I murmured. Setting the poster at my feet, I

slumped in my seat, feeling kind of deflated. Even though the thought of working another murder case frightened me, I wanted to see Garza again. He was my mom's partner and I wanted him to tell me more about her.

We came to a stop at an intersection. I could see the pothole filled side street up ahead that lead to our apartment complex.

"I spoke with his supervisor." Dad's voice was barely audible.

I jerked, the dull pain in my chest deepened. "Did you get him in trouble?"

"No," he groaned. Letting go of the wheel, he raked his hair with both hands. "I was asking about a job."

My heart did a little flip. "You're going to be a cop again?" I squealed.

"Maybe." Dad rolled his eyes and flashed a lopsided grin. "I don't know. It beats the hell out of the pay I'm getting now." He grabbed the wheel again and accelerated down the road.

"Yeah," I sighed.

My eyes bulged as we passed Mocha Madness. The lights were out inside. A faded 'closed' sign was hanging in the doorway. My heart ached and I wondered if my little escape would ever re-open. I chewed on my bottom lip, hoping I'd never need to get away from my apartment again.

"A teen girl needs a house, not a rundown apartment and she shouldn't have to starve herself to afford nice clothes." Dad sounded overwhelmed with emotion.

I had to do a double-take. His eyes were glossy with unshed tears.

"I don't mind my apartment and I don't starve myself." What was up with him? Fine if he wanted to be a better parent, but he didn't have to accuse me of being too skinny. I got enough of that from my friends.

Pulling into the complex parking lot, he turned off the ignition and faced me.

I didn't like the look on his face. Kind of like AJ's mom looked at her whenever she'd done something wrong.

"I know what you do with your allowance. I might be a lousy dad, but I'm not stupid."

My arms and legs numbed and this car suddenly felt way too small. "I eat every day," I spoke through a shaky voice.

Why was he doing this? Why wouldn't people leave my weight alone?

"You don't eat enough, Krysta." He shook his head, his voice sounding heavy. "I need to be a better provider."

"It's my choice to diet. One day, I'm going to be a model." But even as the words came out, I spoke them with less conviction.

Leaning over Dad cupped my chin, tears freely streaming down his face. "You grow more and more beautiful each day. God, you look so much like your mother. But, you're not going to be a model, sweetheart. You and I both know that's not your calling."

Turning from my dad, I flung open the door and rushed to the apartment. I wrapped my arms around my midsection as silent tears streamed down my face.

Modeling had been my dream since before I could remember. Why did he have to burst my bubble? I could be a model and talk to spirits. He'd already said he didn't want me involved in murder cases, so what other calling could I have? I hadn't spent the last three years studying every fashion magazine, practicing every cosmetic trick, and starving myself, so I could give up on it now.

I was going to be a model. Wasn't I?

Wasn't that my dream?

My heart sunk to my feet as I wiped tear- stained cheeks with the backs of my hands, silently sniffling as I struggled with the jammed door handle and rushed inside the apartment. I could hear my dad's footsteps behind me, but I didn't want to face him at the moment.

Running into my room, I locked the door behind me. I fell face-forward onto the bed, tears soaking my worn comforter. For the first time ever, I was having doubts about my modeling future.

Chapter Sixteen

I'd been dreading coming to school all last night and this morning after I'd received a few angry Facebook posts and text messages. Some kids had already given me ugly stares on the bus, but nobody yelled at me about the mall protest. Probably because AJ rode the bus with me and, for some reason, practically everybody at Greenwood was terrified of my best friend.

But AJ had to go talk to her softball coach this morning and Sophie was working on a yearbook deadline leaving me to face Greenwood alone.

Right before I dropped her off at the yearbook room, Sophie had reassured me she wasn't getting any bad vibes from people in the hallway. That was because only super-geeks hung out in the halls this early in the morning. Everybody who was anybody was still in the cafeteria.

Until now.

"Hey, Krysta!"

Oh, God, not her.

Cindee Sparks, head cheerleader and daughter of the school principal, was very popular, very pretty and very stuck-up.

I despised her, as did most of Greenwood, but for the sake of my social status, I always smiled when she flashed her bleached whites at me.

Now she wasn't smiling as she stomped in my direction, the entire cheerleading squad at her back. The group collectively marched as a whole, looking like a line of bowling pins with pom poms. By the look of their pinched little noses and twisted mouths, they were determined to knock me down.

"Hey, Cindee." I spoke through a frozen smile, trying to summon the courage to face down an entire throng of perky pests. "What's up?"

"What's the deal with you protesting the mall?" She jerked her head to the side, the springs in her curled blonde ponytail rattled against her hair ribbons, making her sound like a hybrid cheerleader/rattlesnake.

I only hoped the rest of her wasn't venomous.

A diss from the captain of the cheerleading squad could cause a girl's social status to go downhill real fast.

I looked her squarely in the eyes. "They're building it over a graveyard."

"Are you for real?" She groaned, jutting both hands on her hips.

The rest of the squad mimicked her actions.

I looked from them to her and swallowed. "Yeah."

"Do you really like driving two hours out of town to the outlet store?" She rolled her eyes.

The other cheerleaders rolled their eyes, too.

I wondered if they thought as one being, kind of like those schools of fish that swim in the same pattern at the drop of a dime.

Despite my nerves, which had twisted a knot in my gut, I couldn't help but smile. "It's not two hours."

"Whatever." She tossed her hands in the air.

I looked behind her, waiting for the others to follow suit. Sure enough, their hands went airborne.

I had to repress a laugh.

"Listen, stick chick, I want that mall!"

My attention was drawn back to Cindee's beet- red face. I stared at her in dumb silence.

What did she just call me?

"Everyone at Greenwood wants that mall!" She waggled a finger in my face. "So drop this phony protest."

My vision tunneled. I didn't focus on the growing crowd of laughing students. I blocked out their fight chants and obnoxious sneers. I only saw her—the stupid little ditz who called me a stick chick.

I said nothing as I glared at her. I was too choked up with rage to speak.

Cindee's gaze faltered before she turned her stare on me again. Her eyes were losing their intensity. She cleared her throat, fumbling with a dangling earring.

"Hey, Krysta, what's going on?"

AJ's voice boomed behind me. In the next second, her hand was on my shoulder.

"Nothing," I growled.

"Cindee, did you get into a fight yesterday?" AJ was loud enough for everyone in the neighboring hallway to hear.

I inwardly smiled, recognizing the bite of sarcasm in AJ's voice.

"N-no," Cindee stuttered.

Folding both arms across her chest, AJ straightened her shoulders. "I don't know what looks worse, that big hickey on your neck or your botched concealer job."

My hands flew to my mouth and I inhaled sharply. Why hadn't I noticed the red and purple splotch before?

Cindee's palm flew to the bruise and she acted like she was massaging her neck.

"You know," AJ snorted. "You don't need to hide it. Ken Hituro already posted on his Facebook page that you let him sneak through your bedroom window last night."

Cindee's eyes bulged.

"Oh-mi-god!" she shrieked.

"Yeah, I think you've got bigger things to worry about than the mall," AJ bellowed.

A storm of whispers broke out around us. In a matter of seconds, the gossip was spreading, sounding like a swarm of hornets had descended on Greenwood.

AJ cocked her head to the side, her blue eyes dancing with amusement. "Oh, by the way, your dad's looking for you. He mentioned something about 'grounded for life'. You might want to find out what that's all about."

Cindee's hands flew to her mouth and she ran in the opposite direction, crying. Her groupies followed after her without giving me a second look.

"Thanks," I spoke to AJ over my shoulder as I tried to navigate through the buzzing crowd. "She called me 'stick chick'."

AJ's eyes danced with laughter. She casually walked through the crowd as students stumbled to get out of her way. "I guess that's better than being the school bully."

I ducked under a raised arm and practically leaped at an opening in the crowd. We'd finally navigated into a nearly empty breezeway.

I gasped for air. "Yeah, but it sure helps when the school bully is your best friend."

AJ's smile thinned and her gaze softened. Clasping her algebra book to her chest, she leaned toward me and dropped her voice. "So what do you think about being called a 'stick chick'?"

Grrrr.

Was anybody going to give me a break today? Was my life ever not going to suck?

"I'm fashionably thin, AJ. I don't get dizzy or faint like you did when you gave up meat. We've already gone over this." I spoke through a hiss, regretting the attitude in my voice. I knew I should've been more grateful to my BFF after she saved my butt, but I was sick and tired of people dogging my weight.

The first bell rang.

I couldn't have asked for better timing.

AJ flipped her sporty ponytail over her shoulder, flashing me a sideways grin, acting like nothing was wrong. Like she wasn't about to lecture me about my weight. "You're right." The tone of her voice was way too agreeable. "I've got to get to class."

She turned without saying goodbye and walked down the hall.

"Bye!" I yelled to her retreating back.

She answered by tossing her hand in the air, in what was the laziest wave I'd ever seen.

I was a little relieved and surprised AJ didn't argue with me. It wasn't like her to pass up a good fight.

I had the feeling she would come back to this argument later. What I didn't understand was why Cindee would call me a 'stick chick'. She was head cheerleader, had a great figure, and was always fashionably dressed. She, of all people at this school, should've understood my modeling aspirations.

Was I really too skinny? As I passed by the girls' bathroom, I stopped to examine my reflection in the mirror. I didn't think I was too skinny. Other than my too frizzy hair and the ever-growing dark circles under my eyes, I thought I looked good. As for the frizz, well, I was still learning how to control it, but the receding black holes were another issue. I knew the cause was stress brought on by mall stuff, Bryon's issues, my dad's drinking and dead people waking me up in the middle of the night.

Well, nix the dead people.

Ed and Gertrude hadn't woken me up in almost a week.

That worried me, which was yet another reason my eyes were growing darker.

Chapter Seventeen

Walking out of the science lab, my heart did a little flip. Bryon was leaning against the lockers across from the classroom door, almost looking as if he was waiting for me.

I was a little relieved to see he was still alive after the scene his dad made Sunday. When he didn't show up to school yesterday, all kinds of crazy ideas ran through my head.

His dad murdered him. His dad sent him to a boarding school. He ran away from home.

I'd sent him four text messages, but he didn't answer.

"Hey." He spoke through a weak smile.

"Hey." I waved at him, my hand doing this floppy thing like it was made of Jell-O. "How are things with you and your dad?" The words kind of slipped out and I just wanted to slap myself.

Why would I ask such a stupid question?

Things had to be bad, really bad, with Bryon and his dad.

His eyes flashed with something that looked like pain before he turned down his gaze. "We're starting therapy next week." He focused on his shoe as he scraped his heel back and forth.

"Really?" I couldn't contain my excitement. "That's great." I apprehensively inched closer to him, knowing I should've kept my distance.

His gaze slowly lifted to mine and his lips turned up in a sly smile. "My dad and I have issues, but he's the only parent I've got left."

I burst out laughing, remembering I'd used those same

words on him at our last study session.

Bryon pushed off the locker and closed the distance between us, until we were only a breath apart. He smelled like cinnamon cookies. Even though I was no longer dieting, I had to remind myself Bryon was not on the menu.

He bit his bottom lip, batting pale lashes. "You're a good friend, Krysta. Thanks."

Why did my foolish heart react to him this way? I just wanted to reach up and give him a big smack on the lips.

He was just too cute and I was just too stupid.

I swallowed down the urge to act on my impulses and fling myself into his arms. "I hope it works out for you." I tried to keep my tone even.

"Me, too." His voice was soft, mesmerizing. And then he turned those sad puppy dog eyes on me.

I almost melted into the floor.

"I've got some good news."

"What?" The staccato of my heart was suddenly so loud it rattled my eardrums. Were they stopping the mall? Had the protest worked?

Bryon broke into a huge grin. "Dad is moving the parking lot."

"Really!" I shrieked. "That's great!" I was so excited I jumped into his arms and gave him a big squeeze.

He squeezed back, so tight he made my ribs ache.

I had to pull out of his embrace. His gaze darted to the side before he looked at me again.

I could tell he was on the verge of saying something important.

Clearing his throat, he spoke in a whisper. "Do you think maybe we could..."

"I asked Mrs. Jackson for a new partner," I blurted.

His jaw dropped and he backed away. "What?"

"I don't want to cause problems between you and your dad."

Bryon grimaced as his shoulders fell. "He has to buy ten more acres on the other side of the mall for the parking lot. Either that or risk losing the election." He laughed through a thin smile. "He's not liking you right now."

"Sorry." Leaning toward him, I grabbed his hand and squeezed.

Big mistake.

His skin felt so warm, sending tingles up my arm and down my spine.

He stepped closer until we were standing toe to toe. "I still like you."

"I like you, too." The traitorous words rushed out of my mouth before I could stop them.

Gawd, I was such an idiot!

I pressed my lips together, determined not to say any more. I was bad news for Bryon. We both had so many issues to deal with right now. Besides, I knew his dad would never like me. And then there was that little habit I had of speaking to dead people.

How would Bryon and I ever work out?

With my grip still entwined in his, Bryon cupped my chin with his other hand.

His eyes clouded a smoky gray, his jaw was set, his features determined. "I've been wanting to do something for a long time." His soft voice carried a raspy edge.

I didn't need Sophie's mind-reading powers to know he was about to kiss me.

I shouldn't let him kiss me. This will never work out.

But my mind and body were beating to two different drums. Closing my eyes, I leaned closer to his warmth, lips parted.

His mouth barely brushed over mine, soft and slightly moistened. Inhaling his warm scent, I reached for his shirt collar, but his hand fell away from my face and he pulled back. It was over as soon as it began. The faint scent of cinnamon lingered on my lips.

What kind of a kiss was that!

Blinking hard, I searched his clouded features, trying to understand the meaning behind his peck.

A slight smile broke through his haze. "I know we can't get serious now, but I won't let my dad ruin our friendship."

My throat tightened at the sincerity in his big puppy dog

eyes. At the feel of his warm palm still pressed against mine. I knew he was right. We couldn't get serious now, but in time things could change. Did I really want to throw away my chance with Bryon?

I searched his eyes, not knowing what to say.

Slowly releasing my fingers, he took a step back. "Would you give me some time to work things out with my dad in therapy?" A pleading smile tugged at the corners of his mouth.

"Yeah." I breathed a huge sigh of relief, knowing I wouldn't have to break things off with Bryon forever. Knowing I could still have him as a friend. "I've got some issues I need to work on, too."

"We can still talk at school and on the phone. Sorry I didn't answer your texts." He held out his palms in an apologetic gesture. "My phone was dead."

"That's okay. Call me whenever you need to talk." Stepping forward, I leaned up and planted a kiss on his smooth cheek.

Turning on my heel, I somehow managed to walk away from Bryon without glancing back, which was one of the hardest things I'd ever done. Although, because of my supernatural 'gift', something told me my life would be full of difficult choices.

"How you been, Emmy Jane?"

I didn't even jump this time. The cool breeze I'd felt on the back of my neck warned me they were coming.

Looking up at the rotting ceiling above my small kitchen table, I was met by the smiling faces of Ed and Gertrude.

I couldn't help but smile back. "It's about time." I tried to imitate using my best Ed voice.

They hadn't contacted me in over a week, and despite the fact that Mr. Thomas had agreed to relocate the parking lot to the other side of the mall, I was still worried about them.

Ed looked at me with a quizzical grin. "What you eatin'?"

"A cheeseburger and a side salad." I pointed to the half-eaten, juicy burger on my plate. Dad made it before he went to work. Until recently, I honestly didn't know he could cook.

Ed licked his lips. "I wish I could taste."

Clasping her hands in front of her chest, Gertrude's eyes twinkled with more than just the usual ghoulish glow. "You look better, Emmy. Not so much like a skeleton."

I cringed at that comment. You know you're too skinny when a dead person says you look like a skeleton. But that was all behind me now. In the past week, I'd already gained two pounds. "I've decided to try eating again." I nodded in their direction. "You look good, too."

They did look good—for dead people. Their glow was back, shiny and stronger than ever. They weren't as translucent. In fact, they almost looked like real people.

Gertrude smiled warmly. "We came to thank you for what you've done. They even put our tombstones back."

"The oak tree's still missin'." Ed punched his fist into the air, his weird eye going in all directions.

I had to repress a laugh. Not just at them, but at myself. Who else could talk to a crazy-eyed spirit and not crap her pants?

Gertrude patted his shoulder. "They can't put back an oak, Ed."

"Yeah." He shrugged, his lips turning in a pout. "I know."

"My friends and I can always plant a new tree." I said before I took another bite of my burger.

Ed looked down at me with a grin that stretched ear to ear. For a moment, that eye even managed to stay still. "That would be real nice of you, Emmy Jane."

Gertrude splayed her hands, pointing toward the ground. "We're goin' back ta rest now, sweetheart."

I swallowed hard, thinking how much I'd miss them, no matter how annoying their interruptions had been.

"You're a good girl." Ed winked his good eye. "One day, you'll make some young man a very lucky fellow."

"Thanks," I sighed. "I hope so."

They floated through my kitchen wall and I was left alone. Which was not a good thing, because Ed's comment left me missing Bryon.

Facebook rant/Nine p.m.

I can't believe it's only been a few weeks since Bryon and I were studying together at Mocha Madness.

It feels like years have passed.

Although we don't see each other after school anymore, I'm glad he and his dad are going to work on things. He needs to settle his issues with his dad before he can have a relationship with me.

Sometimes, when I close my eyes, I remember the excited expression on his face when he saw that brownie at Mocha Madness. He was so cute and sweet. Then, other times, he was angry and confused. At times, his extreme emotions worried me.

Although, keeping feelings locked away isn't good, either.

I tried to control everything about myself. My emotions, my appearance, even my diet. Not until I saw Bryon stuffing his face with cookies did I begin to understand I was suffering from emotional eating problems, too.

Only I held everything in.

Maybe I just didn't know how to deal with my grief, so I kept it all inside. Maybe I thought if I looked and acted perfect, my dad would pay more attention to me.

After that cheerleader called me a 'stick chick,' I had to do a double-take in the mirror. I was kind of thin and my under-eye circles were getting darker. I'd always thought that was because the dead liked to wake me up at all hours of the night. But I'd been getting less and less visits lately and my eyes were looking worse.

I wasn't sick and faint like AJ got, but I did get some extreme headaches. Funny, but after a week of eating low carb wraps and hamburgers with my side-salads, I haven't had any more headaches.

I guess I don't have to be a size one. A three or a five would be nice, too. Sophie is a seven and she looks great.

The funny thing is, at this point in my life, appearance doesn't mean as much anymore. What would mean more than anything in the world would be a visit from my mom—Adela.

I wonder if I'll ever get that chance or has she gone into some dark void like Sunny? Or maybe she's gone on to heaven. Maybe she's an angel. I still don't know enough about the afterworld to understand what happens to spirits when they pass on. I only hope my mom is happy and that I'll get a chance to speak with her at least once in my lifetime.

That's my new priority in life—and reconnecting with my dad. I don't have time for a Bryon at the moment. No matter how many times a day I think of his cute smile.

After the lights had been turned out, and she could hear her child's slow, labored breathing, Adela quietly floated into the room. Bending over, she planted a kiss on her daughter's forehead, just as she'd done every night for the past fourteen years.

"Goodnight, my angel," she whispered as she gazed lovingly at her child's sleeping form.

And just as she'd done every night since her passing, Adela reached out a hesitant hand, only to pull away. She had so much she wanted to say, but she didn't dare risk waking her child.

Her daughter would ask questions—dangerous questions. And Adela couldn't risk leading Krysta down the same dark path that had led to her own death.

A word about the author...

A former Texas high school teacher, Tara enjoyed coaching her writing team and even the hectic deadlines that came with running the school publications. After taking a break to raise her baby girl, Tara now works from home as a cover artist.

In her spare time, Tara loves to read, exercise and spend time with her family and friends. She contributes the cover art for her own novels and has designed covers for over 500 other books. She'd love for you to visit her at www.tarawest.com where you can check out her Whispers series and sample her artwork.

Made in the USA
San Bernardino, CA
12 April 2015